Songs in Ursa Major

EMMA BRODIE has worked in book publishing for a decade, most recently as an executive editor at Little, Brown's Voracious imprint. She graduated from the Johns Hopkins University's Writing Seminars programme, and is a longtime contributor to *HuffPost* and a faculty member at Catapult. She lives in Brooklyn, New York, with her husband and their dog, Freddie Mercury.

Songs in Ursa Major is her debut novel.

Songs in Ursa Major

emma brodie

HarperCollins*Publishers*

HarperCollins*Publishers*
1 London Bridge Street
London SE1 9GF

www.harpercollins.co.uk

HarperCollins*Publishers*
1st Floor, Watermarque Building, Ringsend Road
Dublin 4, Ireland

First published in the USA by Knopf, Borzoi Books, an imprint of Penguin Random House LLC 2021

First published in Great Britain by HarperCollins*Publishers* 2021

1

A catalogue record for this book is available from the British Library

ISBN:
HB: 978-0-00-843526-4
Export TPB: 978-0-00-843527-1

This novel is entirely a work of fiction.
The names, characters and incidents portrayed in it are
the work of the author's imagination. Any resemblance to
actual persons, living or dead, events or localities is
entirely coincidental.

Set in Adobe Caslo Pro by Palimpsest Book Production Limited, Falkirk, Stirlingshire

Printed and bound in the UK using 100% Renewable Electricity at CPI Group (UK) Ltd

MIX
Paper from
responsible sources
FSC™ C007454
FSC
www.fsc.org

This book is produced from independently certified FSC™ paper
to ensure responsible forest management.

For more information visit: www.harpercollins.co.uk/green

For the amazing women in my family –
especially my grandmothers,
Anne-Marie and Esther,
and my aunt,
Rosemary

AUTHOR'S NOTE

This book was inspired by the records produced at A&M Studios and Sunset Sound in the late 1960s to early 1970s, under labels such as Reprise Records, Ode Records, and Warner Bros. Records.

1

Island Folk Fest

Saturday, July 26, 1969

As a stagehand cleared the dismantled pieces of Flower Moon's drum set, the last shred of daylight formed a golden curve around the cymbal. It winked at the crowd; then the red sun slipped into the sea. In the gathering dusk, the platform shimmered like an enamel shell, reverberating with the audience's anticipation.

Any minute now, Jesse Reid would go on.

Curtis Wilks stood about thirty feet from the platform with the rest of the press. There was *Billboard*'s Zeke Felton, sharing a joint with a Flower Moon groupie in a beaded kaftan; Ted Munz from *NME*, reading over his notes under the nearest floodlight; Lee Harmon of *Creem*, trading stories with *Time*'s Jim Faust.

The Flower Moon groupie approached Curtis with the joint between her lips, eyeing the pass around his neck. It showed a picture of Curtis's face – which Keith Moon had once compared to 'a homeless man's Paddington Bear' – printed above his name and the words *Rolling Stone*. The groupie offered Curtis the joint. He accepted it.

His exhale became a brushstroke inside an Impressionist painting; swirls of smoke rose in the salty air, tanned limbs and youthful faces interweaving like daisy chains across the meadow. He handed the joint back to the girl and watched her skip into a ring of hippies. Someone had a conga; thrift-store nymphs began dancing to an asynchronous rhythm.

Curtis had cut his teeth as a correspondent on the festival circuit. Berkeley, Philly, Big Sur, Newport – none of them could touch Bayleen Island for atmosphere: the hike up the red clay cliffs, the wildflower meadow, the view of the Atlantic Ocean. There was something magical about having to take a ferry to get to a show.

As he watched the girls dance, Curtis felt a wave of premature nostalgia. There was a sense in the industry that folk was on its way out; the Vietnam War had been dragging on so long, the protest songs that had made Dylan and Baez what they were now felt empty and tired.

Curtis had come to see what they'd all come to see: Jesse Reid ushering in a new epoch for the dying genre. As if on cue, the dancing girls began to sing Reid's breakout single, their voices tremulous with excitement.

> *'My girl's got beads of red and yellow,*
> *Her eyes are starry bright.'*

Their feverish giggles recalled Curtis to the time a young Elvis Presley had played his high school in Gladewater, Texas, back in '55. Eighteen-year-old Buddy Holly–obsessed Curtis had watched girls he'd known since kindergarten openly weep, swept away by the fantasy that Elvis might choose them. The full *Bye Bye Birdie*. That was the power of a true rock star.

Soft-spoken Jesse Reid's persona couldn't have been more different from Elvis's, but Reid seemed to inspire the same devotion in his fans. He had the cowboy baritone of Kris Kristofferson (but Reid's sounded effortless), and the lyrical guitar skills of Paul Simon – plus, he was taller than both, with blue eyes that, according to Curtis's guilty pleasure *Snitch Magazine*, were 'the color of medium stonewash Levi's.'

> 'She makes me feel so sweet and mellow,
> She makes me feel all right.'

'Sweet and Mellow' was a Snickers bar of a song; to hear it was to crave it. Hands down the hit of the summer, it had been holding in *Billboard*'s top ten for eighteen weeks. Curtis had been tracking Reid since he opened for Fair Play at Wembley Stadium the previous year – but this single from Reid's self-titled album had turned him from fringe hero to mainstream sensation overnight.

And tonight, Reid would take his place as the heir apparent to folk rock.

The crowd broke into applause as a bald man with a gray beard shuffled onstage – Joe Maynard, the Festival Committee chair. The longer the audience clapped, the more pained Maynard looked. Curtis's news radar bristled.

'Yes, hello, my beautiful friends,' he said. Maynard quieted the cheering with his hands.

3

'Well, there's no easy way to say this, so I'm just going to say it,' he said. 'I'm afraid Jesse Reid won't be performing tonight.'

Curtis felt a stab of disappointment as his mental list of feature headlines turned to ash. A visceral shock wave passed through the crowd. One by one, dreamy expressions began to wilt, a field of dandelions turning white with anger, ready to blow.

And then they did. Cries of outrage rang the twilight like a bell. The girls who had been singing and dancing a moment before collapsed into sobs. Maynard shrank behind the mic.

'But we've got a great act for you up next – it'll just be a few minutes now,' he said, sweat gleaming at his temples. A second roar from the crowd buffeted him into the wings.

Curtis edged toward the platform. Something must have just happened – he'd seen Reid's A&R man backstage after Curtis had interviewed Flower Moon. Maybe Reid had gotten too drunk to go on. Maybe he'd lost it backstage. The festival tonight was performance number thirty-six in a sixty-arena global tour. Sometimes artists just cracked; Curtis had seen it before.

He spied Mark Edison passing from the backstage area into the audience and caught his eye. Edison was a reporter for *The Island Gazette,* a local independent daily. Most of the Fest's press corps found his snide antics insufferable, but he had always been useful to Curtis.

The audience's initial dismay had given way to movement. Amidst cries from the most stalwart Reid fanatics, lines had begun to form through the crowd, pushing toward the exits.

Edison reached Curtis. He offered Curtis his flask – warm gin. They both drank deeply.

4

'What's happening back there?' said Curtis. 'Where's Reid?'

Edison shook his head. They stepped aside as two girls thundered by, ripping up the PEACE LOVE JESSE sign they carried like a banner. Curtis did not envy the band about to perform to this mob.

'Who's going on?' said Curtis. 'Someone from tomorrow's lineup?' Mark shook his head.

'It's a local band – the Breakers,' said Mark.

'I don't know them,' said Curtis. 'What's their label?'

'Label?' said Mark. 'They don't have one. They're just a bunch of kids. They were scheduled to play at the amateur stage down the hill, and the committee just scooped them up. The biggest show they've ever played is forty, fifty people.'

'Holy shit,' said Curtis. This was going to be a train wreck.

As he spoke, three young men began to set up onstage. They couldn't have been more than twenty. The drummer looked the most filled out, with a chiseled jaw, shoulder-length black hair, and almond-toned skin. He and the bassist were clearly related; the bassist looked younger, hair shorn around his chin, a red bandanna tied across his brow. The guitarist was paler, with boyish features and a somber manner. His sandy hair flopped in front of his eyes as he tuned.

'We want Jesse!' a girl shrieked from over Curtis's shoulder.

Curtis began to wonder if it wasn't better just to head back to town. The Elektra producers had rented a yacht and were hosting an after-party for industry folk. Bayleen Island was only five miles from international waters, which meant good drugs; he could be flying within the hour.

'Jesse Reid, Jesse Reid,' a chant rose up in the crowd among the faithful.

As the boys checked their equipment, Curtis noticed a figure plugging in to the amplifier behind the drum set. As she straightened up, the spotlight caught her yellow hair, which hung down to her waist like a bolt of golden silk. Her clothing was simple: jean cutoffs and a white peasant shirt, an acoustic guitar strapped across her back. Her tanned legs looked girlish as she strode center stage, but she had a woman's features: full lips, hollow cheekbones.

She glowed.

'Who is that?' said Curtis.

'Jane Quinn,' said Mark. 'Lead vocals and guitar.'

As she got into position, the boys instinctively inched toward her. Their feet pawed the ground, like horses anxious at the starting gate.

'We want Jesse!' a hysterical girl cried out.

Jane Quinn stepped up to the mic. Curtis saw then that her feet were bare.

'Wow,' she said, flushed with excitement. 'Quite a view from up here.'

The crowd ignored her. Those headed toward the exits continued walking, as if she wasn't there. A small contingent of Reid fans chanted his name like a descant over the din.

'Jesse Reid, Jesse Reid.'

Jane Quinn tried again.

'Hi, everyone,' said Jane. 'We're the Breakers.'

This had no impact; the crowd continued to chatter as though they were in a parking lot rather than at a concert. Onstage, the boys fidgeted in place. Jane exchanged a look with the guitarist.

'Get off the stage,' a shrill voice cried above the chaos.

Jane glanced toward the drummer as though about to count off. She faltered. Curtis felt a wave of pity. How was this slip of a girl supposed to compete with one of the world's biggest stars?

'Jesse Reid, Jesse Reid.'

Then Jane Quinn turned toward the crowd, squaring her shoulders. Her movements were slow and deliberate. She took a deep breath and placed a hand on the mic stand, closing her eyes. She stood perfectly still, listening. The crowd quieted half a decibel.

When she opened her eyes, there was flint in her stare. She leaned toward the mic.

'My girl's got beads of red and yellow.'

Curtis's heart skipped a beat as the chorus from 'Sweet and Mellow' arched over the meadow like a silver comet. Jane's bandmates exchanged mystified looks. The crowd gasped.

Had she really just done that?

'Her eyes are starry bright.'

Jane Quinn surveyed the audience with self-assurance, as though to say, *I know you think you want Jesse Reid, but I'm about to show you something so much better.* It was like watching someone hold a lighter up to a monsoon. The girl was bold as fuck.

'She makes me feel so sweet and mellow.'

What a range – a soprano, in the school of Joan Baez and Judy Collins, though not nearly as patrician-sounding as Collins, or

7

as embattled as Baez. There was an untrained edge in her voice, an almost Appalachian coarseness, that raised the hair on Curtis's neck. Just gorgeous.

'She makes me feel all right.'

Jane glanced at her guitarist. He gave her a nod – she had taken a leap, and they were right behind her. The root chords of the song were a simple A-major progression any practiced group could pick up. The drummer counted them in, and the Breakers began to play.

Time slowed.

'My girl makes every day a hello.'

When Jesse Reid sang 'Sweet and Mellow,' his voice intoned the melody: no ornamentation, just his pure baritone and his guitar. As Jane Quinn sang, she cast off any memory of Reid's rendition, adding runs and grace notes as she went, as though composing the song in real time. Curtis was astounded. She made choices no other musician would have – or could have – made.

'Her eyes light up the night.'

The crowd couldn't help themselves – they began to sing along. They had all come to witness a legend being born, and now they were: it just wasn't Jesse Reid.

'She makes me feel so sweet and mellow.'

Curtis had been at Newport when Bob Dylan had walked onstage with his electric Fender Stratocaster. He'd been in Monterey two years later when Jimi Hendrix had lit his guitar on fire during 'Wild Thing.' Neither compared to this. An unknown taking over the headlining spot – a girl. They'd be talking about Island Folk Fest '69 forever.

'She makes me feel all right.'

Those who had been walking away turned back. Those who had been crying smiled. They whooped and cheered and kissed and hugged. When the song finished, they lost their minds.

'Janie Q!' shouted Edison, applauding beside Curtis.

Janie Q.

'It really is a beautiful night,' said Jane, as though continuing a conversation from earlier.

With that, she counted the Breakers into their next song – an up-tempo original called 'Indigo' that brought to mind 'White Rabbit.' Curtis couldn't catch the words, but the music was hot. The Breakers had a great sound – a mix of art and psychedelic rock, all twisting notes and braying chords.

Even so, Jane's voice stole the show. Her loveliness felt personal – it was impossible to look at her and not take flight in some small part of you. As she sang, Curtis felt that true rock-star feeling – he wanted her to see him. She gave her shoulders a small shimmy, light refracting off the silken strands of her hair. Then it happened. Jane Quinn grinned right at him. He just knew it.

Hours later, as Curtis floated on the Elektra party yacht snorting lines off the Flower Moon groupie's abdomen, Mark Edison received word from a source at the Island's hospital. Thirty minutes after that, *The Island Gazette* went to press with the headline: FOLK FEST'S BREAKOUT JESSE REID NARROWLY MISSES DEATH IN MOTORCYCLE CRASH AND CANCELS REMAINDER OF TOUR.

2

Jane lay in bed, listening to the wind chimes knock against the front porch. Daylight warmed her eyelids, but she kept them closed. She wasn't ready to let go of last night.

A series of images replayed through her mind: kicking her sandals at Kyle as he tuned his bass behind the amateur stage; Greg agape as he placed his snare drum into the back of a beat-up army jeep; the crowd roaring as a Fest staffer dropped them behind the Main Stage; the heat of the spotlights on her own cheeks as she walked on and realized she'd left her shoes behind; Rich's knuckles turning white against his frets when the crowd refused to quiet.

In three years of performing at the Fest, Jane had never imagined she might appear on the Main Stage. It was as much a part of her world as a tri-deck yacht docked in Regent's Cove: sure, she could see it, but it belonged to the sphere of wealth and power. Jane hadn't been scared to walk onstage last night because it hadn't felt real.

Then she'd seen Rich about to lose his nerve, and her instincts had taken over: if they wanted 'Sweet and Mellow,' she'd give them 'Sweet and Mellow.' She could still hear the sound of her own voice crackling over the loudspeakers.

The irony was that Jane had never even heard Jesse Reid's album – she knew 'Sweet and Mellow' because it had been playing nonstop at her grandmother's hair salon all summer, but the album had been so overhyped (namely, by Kyle) that she'd resisted listening to it. She'd had to improvise the hell out of the verses, but in the end it hadn't mattered; she could still hear the crush of applause after she'd sung.

Knuckles rapped against her door. Jane kept her eyes closed.

'Janie.' Grace walked in. 'I waited as long as I could, but we have to be up-Island by eleven.' Her aunt drew back the curtains, illuminating Jane's cluttered floor.

'My shift doesn't start until noon,' said Jane, rolling over.

'Sorry, I know. But I have an interview at eleven-thirty – outpatient care.' Grace pried open Jane's closet and tossed a starched blue uniform at her head. Jane groaned.

'Come on. Today's going to be a *big day*,' said Grace. Jane sat up. She felt a twinge of dread as the uniform slid into her lap.

Downstairs, Jane found her cousin Maggie propped up at the kitchen table, chair pulled out to accommodate her swollen belly. Their grandmother, Elsie, looked up from the stove.

'Morning,' said Elsie. The kitchen smelled like lemons and burned butter.

'Good morning,' said Jane, piling her hair into a bun with a comb. Maggie glared at her, then turned back to *The Island Gazette*'s front page.

'And hello,' said Jane. Maggie said nothing. She was twenty to Jane's nineteen, and in golden hair, long limbs, and sun-browned skin they could have been sisters. That's where their similarities ended.

Elsie gave Jane a wink, then went back to scraping hash browns around the frying pan. She was in her early fifties, and Jane had inherited her angular features and gray eyes – though Elsie's gaze seemed otherworldly, exaggerated by her silvery hair. It had been that color for ten years, since the night Jane's mother hadn't come home.

Jane walked over to the stove and reached her fingers into the pan.

'By all means, help yourself,' said Maggie, without looking up. Jane popped a hash brown into her mouth and felt the oil sizzle on her tongue. She walked to the table and read the headline over Maggie's shoulder.

'Whoa – Jesse Reid was in an accident?'

'Ugh, Jane, your breath,' said Maggie, elbowing Jane into her own chair. Elsie slid a plate of hash browns, bacon, and eggs in front of each of her granddaughters. She picked up the paper just as Grace swept in from the yard.

'Good, you're up, Janie,' said Grace, replacing a watering can under the sink. She walked over to the pan and plucked out a hash brown, just as Jane had done.

'And that's where Jane gets her manners,' said Maggie.

'Relax, officer, it's the last one,' said Grace. She and Maggie shared a strong mother-daughter resemblance, though Grace's brown eyes creased around the corners and her hair had dimmed from time spent indoors.

Elsie let out a hoot. She folded over *The Island Gazette* and began to read aloud.

'While Jesse Reid was having arguably the worst night of his life, Bayleen Island favorites the Breakers had one of their best: indeed,

Reid's absence paved the way for the Breakers to become a main act, and lead singer Jane Quinn was more than ready to take center stage.'

'Mark Edison wrote that?' said Jane. In six years, he'd never given the Breakers a favorable review.

'He goes on to call the Breakers a "slowly evolving but serviceable garage quartet,"' said Maggie.

'There it is,' said Jane. Elsie placed the paper on the table.

'What was it like up there?' she said.

Jane could still feel the music thrumming from her heels to her sternum, the crowd's energy washing over her in waves.

'Like an ocean,' she said. Elsie's eyes twinkled, as though sharing in the memory. Grace gave Jane a weary smile.

'We should head out in a minute,' she said.

A clomping noise shook the stairs as the Breakers' drummer, Greg, descended from Maggie's bedroom. In Jane's mind, Gray Gables was a grand old house; but any time she saw a man framed in one of its Victorian doorways, she was reminded that it was just a cottage.

'Morning, all,' Greg said. He wore his clothes from the night before, caked with dry sweat, his hair sticking up at odd angles. After the show, they'd stayed out drinking until last call.

'Janie Q!' he said, giving Jane a high five. 'Last night was epic. Breakers for life!'

'The Breakers are derivative and trite,' said Maggie.

'Mags, my chickadee,' said Greg. 'I know you're uncomfortable, but there's no need—'

'I told you, you can't stay here until after the baby comes, and last night you just showed up and passed out. You snored for five hours, Greg.'

'You should have moved me.'

'I tried. I could not. You're like a giant drunk porpoise,' Maggie said. She turned to Jane. 'And you brought him here.'

'It's not Jane's fault,' said Greg stoutly. 'I'm sorry, it was thoughtless of me.' He picked a hash brown off Maggie's plate. Maggie looked murderous.

'Time to go,' said Jane.

'Are you heading to the Center?' said Greg. 'Can you drop me at the rez?'

'You're not staying?' said Maggie.

'Can't,' said Greg. 'I need a shower. I need clothes. My feet are swollen – I need to rest.'

'You've got to be fucking jok—' Maggie gave a little gasp. At once, the room was at attention. She was only two weeks from her due date.

'Relax,' Maggie said, shifting slightly in her chair. 'It's just a kick.'

Greg sighed. 'Wouldn't it just be easier to get married and move in?' he said.

'Not for me,' said Maggie.

The Quinn women smiled. The last of their kin to marry had been Charlotte Quinn, traded as a fifteen-year-old bride to the captain of a Portuguese whaling vessel in 1846. When the whaler had landed on Bayleen Island to drop its cargo, Charlotte had stolen off inside a kerosene crate. The seven generations of Quinns who had lived on the Island since had been called many names – harlot, witch, grandma – but never wife.

They left the house in the Quinns' ancient wood-paneled station wagon at quarter to eleven. Jane adjusted the FM dial until she came across 'Yellow Submarine.' She rolled down the window

15

and let the salty air wash over her as they drove from the white cottages of Regent's Cove into the wooded roads of Mauncheake. She hummed along to the radio with tender vocal cords.

A stone's throw off the coast of Massachusetts, Bayleen Island's terrain spanned sandy beaches, wildflower meadows, farmland, and forests across its six towns: the three year-round towns – Perry's Landing, Lightship Bay, and Regent's Cove – and the sprawling 'up-Island' towns – Caverswall and Mauncheake, which abutted the Wampanoag reservation.

The local population was of mixed descent, with Wampanoag, Portuguese, British, and Barbadian bloodlines as inextricably tangled as a fisherman's nets. The Island's diverse community was as intrinsic to its identity as its clay cliffs and beach plums, contributing to its broad appeal as a vacation destination.

Tourism was the Island's main industry, and each summer its population swelled to ten times its normal size. Vacationing families generally stayed in Regent's Cove and Lightship Bay, with their large public beaches, while the rich resort-goers flocked to the yacht club in Perry's Landing. The stratospherically wealthy, including several former first families, oil magnates, and the East Coast bluebloods, lived in thousand-acre Mauncheake and Caverswall estates. The locals and the vacationers interacted on a primarily customer-service basis.

As the Quinns' station wagon approached the rez's south entrance, Grace slowed to let Greg out.

'Thanks for the lift,' said Greg. Grace smiled, shifting the car into reverse.

'Janie Q,' Greg called, 'you working the Carousel later?'

'You know it,' Jane called. He waved as the station wagon pulled back onto the road.

'You can take the car back after your shift,' said Grace. 'I'm on for a double – I'll grab the bus.'

'You sure?' said Jane. Grace nodded.

Five minutes later, they pulled into a long, paved driveway that Jane knew almost as well as her own. She watched a blue-clad caregiver help a patient across the recreation lawn and felt herself go numb. Grace rolled down her window and waved to the guard at the gate.

'The Mighty Quinns,' said Lewis, ushering them inside.

Housed in the palatial home of a nineteenth-century whaling magnate, the Cedar Crescent Hospital and Rehabilitation Center was an upscale private facility known among the wealthy for its state-of-the-art care and its discretion.

Grace had worked there for over a decade, and Jane had become a certified nursing assistant once she graduated from high school. She had intended to work at the Center full-time, but found that she couldn't bear to face its sterile halls every day. Bartending had turned out to be just as lucrative; but with Maggie's baby coming, they needed every extra cent, so Jane had taken a few center shifts.

Grace pulled into the parking lot. She switched off the motor but didn't get out of the car.

Jane turned to face her aunt. In profile, Grace looked almost exactly like Jane's mother.

'What is it?' said Jane.

Grace shrugged. 'I guess I didn't imagine myself a grand-mother at thirty-nine,' she said.

'Gran must have been about that age when she became a grandmother.'

Grace shook her head. 'Maggie just does whatever she wants.'

'I personally can't wait to watch her have to change diapers,' said Jane.

Grace laughed. 'She doesn't understand. She'll never get a day off. And we're all going to be scraping by for the next couple months. Hospital bills add up.'

'She wants a home birth,' said Jane, but Grace wasn't listening. It wasn't just the bills, Jane knew. Commerce ground to a halt during the winter months, leaving Island locals to squirrel away as much as they could during the tourist season. With Maggie out of commission at the height of summer, the Quinns' budget would be tight for the entire year.

'I'll feel better if I can lock in this long-term gig,' said Grace, steadying herself. On occasion, the Center would match-make patients with their staff nurses if a patient needed protracted care or physical therapy. If Grace got the job, her take-home pay would more than double for the time being. 'You will,' said Jane. 'And even if you don't – Gran and I have Mag's clients covered at the salon. And I'll be here a few times a week, plus tips from the Carousel. We'll be fine. More than fine.'

Grace nodded, but still didn't move to get out of the car.

'Is there something else?' said Jane. Grace looked at her own reflection in the rearview mirror.

'I have this uneasy feeling,' she said.

'Because of the baby?'

Grace shook her head. 'No . . . I think it's more to do with the Fest,' she said.

Sugar rushed through Jane's veins at the memory, already growing dim amidst these familiar surroundings. 'It was no big deal,' she said. 'Just one great night.'

'This is how it starts,' said Grace, getting out of the car. 'One great night; then the sharks start showing up and making promises.'

Jane laughed, stepping onto the pavement. 'It's not going to be like that,' she said. 'You heard Maggie. We're derivative and trite.'

'We both know that's not true,' said Grace.

They crossed from the parking lot onto the recreation lawn, waving to a tall blue-clad orderly playing croquet with a patient.

'Hey, Charlie,' said Jane. 'See you in a sec.'

The orderly nodded as they passed.

'Just be careful, whatever happens,' said Grace, taking the flagstone path to the staff entrance.

'Nothing's going to happen,' said Jane.

The possibility that it might both terrified and thrilled her. Music wasn't real life – it was just for fun, a way to blow off steam. If it became more than that, she ran the risk of having her heart broken, or worse. Grace was right to be cautious: their family knew too well how disappointed dreams could lead to tragedy.

And yet part of Jane felt as though she'd met herself onstage last night. It had been so natural for her to sing to all those people – as if she'd been born to do it. Once you knew you could feel like that about something, was it even possible for life to continue as it had before?

'Nothing's going to happen,' she repeated, more to herself than to Grace.

Grace gave her a small smile, but Jane could still trace a curve of unease around her mouth as they entered the hospital.

3

Burrowed under the Regent's Cove Hotel, the Carousel was best known as the pub where the national media camped out during the Folk Fest. The rest of the year, it served as a divey watering hole for locals who wanted to reminisce and get drunk to live music.

Jane surveyed the room from behind the bar. It was a little after 10:00 p.m., and the rush was about to begin. Within the hour, elbows would be circling her like dorsal fins. For now, the wooden booths were filled with regulars, drinking quietly beneath crisscrossed strands of colored lights.

The alley door opened, and her manager, Al, entered, carrying a bucket of ice. Jane kicked open the freezer with her knee, bending to help him dump the ice into the cold chamber.

'Thanks, Janie,' said Al. A cool cloud rose, pressing against the tiers of liquor bottles behind Jane like a kiss.

'How we doing over here?' Al asked, nodding toward the taps.

'We're low on Narragansett,' said Jane. Al nodded, and was heaving himself toward the cellar when Mark Edison slid into his customary seat in the corner.

'Looking lovely this evening,' said Mark.

Jane rolled her eyes and grabbed the Tanqueray off the shelf behind her. She was dressed head to toe in black, a dishrag slung over her shoulder, hair still stacked atop her head from that morning.

'I wanted to say, it really was a great show last night,' he said. Jane placed a coaster in front of him and set the gin-and-tonic on top of it.

'For a "serviceable garage quartet,"' said Jane, pouring herself a shot.

'It's quaint that you care what's printed in *The Island Gazette*,' said Mark.

'We should have had the headline,' said Jane.

'"*Janie Q Conquers World*,"' said Mark.

'"*Local Heroes Become Legend*,"' countered Jane.

Mark raised an eyebrow. 'Not to quibble, but Jesse Reid is local,' he said. 'Actually, I just got a tip he's convalescing here. Family has an estate out in Caverswall – been summering there since he was a child.'

'Not the same,' said Jane. Mainlanders owned summer homes; locals cleaned them.

Mark lifted his tumbler. 'To you,' he said.

'To the Breakers,' said Jane. She drank.

Al reappeared, panting. 'Give it a try,' he said.

Jane let the tap run into a stein until it filled with foam.

The door opened, and a gaggle of college coeds wafted in. Jane could tell by their embroidered clothing and minimal jewelry that they belonged to the Perry's Landing set.

'What kind of bourbon do you have?' asked a tall, tan young woman with hair like penny-colored feathers.

Sometimes Jane felt like a pharmacist guarding a large supply of tinctures. She recited the names on the peeling labels behind her, and poured the girl an eight-dollar glass of bourbon over ice, then proceeded to do the same for each of her friends.

'You can leave it open,' said the girl, handing Jane a credit card with the name Victor Vidal on it – presumably her father. Jane filed the card in the box beside the register as the group headed to a table near the back.

'High roller.'

Jane looked up. The comment had come from a man she didn't recognize, seated a few stools down from Mark Edison. He wore a loud plaid polo and a pair of aviator sunglasses, and looked to be in his early thirties. Jane could tell he was from a city; his shaggy brown helmet of hair had been expensively cut.

Jane watched two green reflections of herself say, 'What can I get you?'

'What do you recommend?' he asked.

They were interrupted by a group of preppy boys in their early twenties – the plus-ones for the group Jane had just served. Sun-kissed forearms rested on the bar, crisp dollars gripped in uncallused fists.

'Two pitchers of Miller,' said the shortest one. 'I'm buying.'

'DIGGSY,' shouted his friend. A chorus of 'Diggs' rang out as Jane topped off the pitcher.

'That'll be nine dollars,' she said.

'Keep the change,' said Diggs, placing a stack of bills on the bar. Jane scooped them up, swift as a blackjack dealer, tucking the gratuity into her bra.

'Now,' said Jane, turning back to the stranger, 'what would you like?' He considered her for a moment, then took off his aviators, revealing a pair of shrewd brown eyes.

'I'd like to talk to Jane Quinn,' he said. Jane raised her eyebrows.

'Who's asking?' said Jane.

'Willy Lambert,' he said. 'I do A&R for Pegasus Records. I heard your show last night – I've been looking for you all day.' Jane glanced over at Mark Edison; she could tell by his posture that he was listening to their conversation.

'Let me guess,' said Jane. She grabbed a highball glass and kicked open the freezer. 'You saw the show, and you're wondering if I'm free after my shift tonight to "discuss my future."'

'Something like that,' said Willy, looking uncomfortable. Jane picked up the Casa Noble tequila and a bottle of orange juice and began to pour both into the glass.

'This may shock you, but you're actually not the first guy who's tried that,' said Jane. She unscrewed a bottle of grenadine and drizzled the syrup into the glass over the back of a spoon.

'What?' said Willy. 'No. I don't mean it like that. I'm married.' He held up his left hand and showed Jane a gold ring. 'Here,' he said, reaching into his pocket to retrieve a business card with his name and title as well as a crumpled piece of newsprint Jane recognized as Mark Edison's story on Jesse Reid.

'Mark, look – someone read your work and didn't immediately throw it away,' said Jane, garnishing the rim of the glass with an orange slice and a maraschino cherry.

'Cheers,' said Mark, lifting his glass. Jane placed the concoction in front of Willy Lambert.

'What's this?' he said.

'A tequila sunrise,' said Jane. 'To go with your glasses.' Willy smiled along but didn't laugh. Jane refilled Mark's drink, expecting Willy to be gone by the time she got back. When she returned, he was still there.

'I told you,' he said. 'I've been asking around all day, I'm not giving up in two minutes.'

'How did you find me?' asked Jane.

'The woman at Beach Tracks took pity on me when I told her I rep Jesse Reid and sent me over to Widow's Peak. And the woman at Widow's Peak said I'd find you here.'

'That was my grandmother,' said Jane, absorbing this information.

'No kidding,' said Willy. 'Oh yeah, I can see the resemblance. Well, if she sent me this way, I can't be that bad, can I?'

'I guess we'll see,' said Jane, privately agreeing. 'Hey, if Jesse Reid's upset about "Sweet and Mellow"—'

Willy shook his head. 'Jesse's living minute-to-minute right now. I'm actually heading over to see him shortly,' he said. 'So . . . I'll get right to the point: are you under contract anywhere?'

All the noise in the room receded, except for the sound of Jane's pulse in her ears.

'No,' said Jane. 'Are you offering?'

Willy smiled. 'I want to,' he said. 'I've never seen anything like last night. Your vibe is totally original. Your style, your voice – I'm still not sure how you hit those notes. Is that your music?'

Jane nodded.

Willy's eyes gleamed. 'With the right setup, you could really take off,' he said.

'The right setup?' said Jane.

'You should have keys, for one thing. Maybe more of a rhythm section.'

'In addition to my band?' said Jane.

Willy shrugged. 'Or instead of them,' he said. 'Have you ever considered going solo?'

Jane's eyes widened. They'd been a band since junior high. She'd never performed without them.

'Nothing against the band,' Willy added quickly. 'I just think you're on a different level. Like, household-name level. Singer-songwriters are about to have a moment, and I think you could be part of that in a big way. What do you say?'

Jane envisioned herself illuminated on a large, empty stage. She wore a black dress, silver chains around her neck, a silver guitar in her arms. She could sense the crowd's attention – that wide ocean feeling. She played and sang, a silver moon pulling on the tide.

The Carousel door opened, and Greg walked through, laughing at something Rich had just said. When they saw Jane talking to Willy at the bar, Greg's eyes narrowed protectively. Rich took his arm and guided him toward the jukebox. Noise flooded back into Jane's ears.

'I'm not a singer-songwriter,' she said. 'I don't do lyrics.'

This wasn't strictly true; Jane had written the lyrics for one of the Breakers' songs, 'Spark,' then announced she would never do it again. When her band asked why, she had refused to give a reason, insisting that the Breakers already had a lyricist: Rich.

Willy's expression seemed to brighten at this.

'We'd set you up with a ghostwriter,' said Willy. 'You'd kill with more personal material – like "Sweet and Mellow."'

'Rich's lyrics are good,' said Jane. Despite Rich's own doubts on this score, his verses had always provided Jane the structure she needed to focus on the music. She couldn't imagine writing songs another way.

'I agree,' said Willy. 'But I'm telling you, you can do better than good.'

Jane glanced up to make sure Rich and Greg hadn't heard him. She leaned toward Willy.

'You seem like a nice guy,' she said in a low voice. 'But I don't trust the music industry. I've seen how they treat people – when they want something, they just take it. We're not even working together, and you're remaking me in your label's image. Why would I want that?'

Willy stared at her. 'More nights like last night, for a start,' he said. 'A record, fans, fame, money . . . I usually don't need to enumerate the benefits of being a rock star.'

Rock star. The words glistened in the air like dewdrops.

Willy considered her. 'How did you guys meet?' he asked.

'Greg and Kyle are brothers,' said Jane. 'Rich was Greg's year in grade school, I was Kyle's.'

'And remind me, who's who again?'

'Rich is on guitar,' said Jane.

Willy nodded. 'All American-looking. He's cute – girls like that. And?'

Jane smiled a little – Rich was painfully shy, especially around girls. 'Kyle's on bass.' Willy sat back a little. 'He plays fretless, right? He is good,' he said.

Jane nodded. 'And Greg is on drums,' she said.

Willy Lambert rubbed his jaw. 'I'm not really looking for a band at the moment,' he said.

'Why?' said Jane.

'Bands are drama,' said Willy. Jane noticed a queue of customers vying for her attention.

'One sec,' she said. She filled the orders, forcing herself to take her time. When she returned, Willy still hadn't touched his cocktail.

'Is there a drink you actually want?' said Jane, nodding to the untouched tequila sunrise. He shook his head.

'I'm driving,' he said. He tapped his business card against the bar. 'Forgive me for saying this, but for someone so young, you have a pretty jaded view of the record business.'

Jane wasn't sure what prompted her to respond. Maybe it was that Elsie had sent him; maybe it was that she doubted she'd ever see him again. 'My mom was a songwriter,' she said.

Willy's eyebrows lifted. 'Who is she?' he asked.

Jane cleared her throat. 'Charlotte Quinn,' she said. 'You haven't heard of her.'

'No, I haven't,' said Willy.

'She wrote a few songs for Lacey Dormon,' said Jane. '"I Will Rise" and "You Don't Know."'

Willy's eyes shone in recognition. 'I know Lacey from L.A.,' he said. 'Those songs made her career.'

Jane took a breath. 'Do you know "*Lilac Waltz*"?'

Willy's eyebrows flicked up. 'The Tommy Patton song? That song was huge.'

Jane nodded. 'That was her song, too. She wrote it, and he stole it.'

Willy shook his head, his face grim. 'That song must have been covered by dozens of artists, been in movies, television programs, commercials. . . .' His voice trailed off.

'She never saw a penny,' said Jane.

'That's terrible,' said Willy. 'I wish it wasn't the first time I'd heard something like that.'

Jane shook her head in disgust.

Willy passed a hand over his face. 'It's an amazing song,' he said. 'I'd love to meet the woman who wrote it.'

'I wish you could,' said Jane. 'No one's seen her in a decade.'

'Oh,' said Willy. 'I'm very sorry to hear that. I . . . I understand why you feel so strongly. And I get the family stuff. My dad is in the business, and so are both of my older brothers. They all made their names on big-band productions, then rock and roll. When I told them soft rock was next, they all thought I was fucking insane. But I had heard Jesse, and I knew I was right, and now . . . he's about to be the biggest star in the world. I trust myself to know something great when I hear it.'

He cleared his throat. 'What you said earlier, about the industry taking what it wants, that can be true – but that's not how I operate,' he said. 'I'm in it for my artists. The suggestions I made earlier . . . I'm just trying to help you get off the ground. But I can also see how that would come off as presumptuous.'

Jane peered at him, unsure of what to say.

Willy continued. 'Jesse's injuries are going to push his album to early next year, and I need to fill the slot in the fall.'

'This fall?' said Jane. Willy nodded.

'We need to be ready to record by October. Could the Breakers be ready by October?' Jane smiled in spite of herself at the name of her band in his mouth. 'We've got songs,' she said.

He stood from his seat. 'I'd like to hear them,' he said. 'I think you're the real deal – so I will consider the whole band.' He placed his business card on the counter. Jane stared at it, shimmering white against the sticky varnish of the bar.

'If we do this, we would need complete artistic control,' said Jane. 'I don't want to hear anything else about a rhythm section or a ghostwriter.'

'*If* I take you on, you would have it,' said Willy. He took down her information and promised to telephone in the morning.

'Until tomorrow,' he said, putting his aviators back on.

As soon as he was gone, Rich and Greg made a beeline for the bar.

'Who was that?' said Greg, elbowing past a group of hippies in town for the Fest. Jane looked from the white card on the bar to her bandmates, and her face broke into a grin.

Her shift ended at 2:00 a.m., and it took until about 2:30 a.m. to close up. As she trudged up the hill to Gray Gables, she could barely see straight. She had a bra-full of cash, but all she could think about was the white card tucked inside her pocket. When she arrived home, she was surprised to find her aunt Grace seated on the porch, a glass of Elsie's homemade lilac wine in hand.

'You're up,' said Jane, flopping down beside her. Grace handed her the glass, and Jane took a sip of the sweet, fiery liquid.

'Couldn't sleep,' said Grace. 'You're never going to guess what happened to me today.'

'You're never going to guess what happened to me tonight,' said Jane.

'You go first,' said Grace, taking back the wine.

'You called it – I got approached by a record label. By Jesse Reid's A&R man.'

'No kidding,' said Grace, eyebrows lifting.

'Yes,' said Jane. 'And I know what you're thinking, but we had a long conversation, and so far he seems like an okay guy.'

'That's not what I'm thinking,' said Grace. 'At least, not yet.'

'Then what?' said Jane.

Grace turned to face Jane with an ironic, dimpled smile. 'You know that long-term-care gig? I got it,' she said. 'And the patient is Jesse Reid.'

4

Willy folded his arms, seated on a crate of L'Oréal dye in the back room of Elsie's hair salon, Widow's Peak. The concrete walls soaked in the final chord of 'Dirty Bastard.' Jane felt Kyle bouncing beside her. Willy had called that morning and asked to hear everything they had; the Breakers had just finished taking him through their entire repertoire.

'Great,' said Willy. He paused. 'So . . . I'd say you have eight songs.'

Jane and Rich traded looks. 'We just played ten,' said Rich.

'Right, right,' said Willy. He glanced at his watch. 'The anthem you just did—'

'"Dirty Bastard"?' said Greg.

Willy nodded. 'It's too similar to the other one – "Rebel Road,"' he said. 'You should swap one out for a ballad. And you need a true pop single.'

Rich's face flushed.

'Not "Indigo"?' said Jane.

Willy shook his head. 'Too trippy for the mainstream,' he said.

'What about "Spark"?' said Rich. Jane's mouth went dry, awaiting the verdict on her song.

'"Spark" is very good,' said Willy. 'Great hook. But it's still four minutes. To get on the radio, you need a song that's quick and catchy – a real earworm. "Spark" could be your second single.'

'So – all we need is two songs?' said Kyle, before anyone could argue. 'Otherwise, it's a deal?'

'Absolutely,' said Willy.

'What do you think?' said Rich.

Jane hesitated. Kyle picked a foam curler off the floor and rolled it over the neck of his bass; the strings pressed dark-pink lines into the sponge.

'I don't want to get pigeonholed doing Petula Clark songs,' she said.

Willy laughed. 'You won't,' he said. 'This is just how everyone starts out – once you get on the radio and build your fan base, they'll follow you wherever you go.'

Jane frowned.

'We'll make it jive,' said Rich.

'Come on, Janie,' said Kyle, tossing the curler at her. It silently bounced off the body of her guitar onto the floor. 'Don't you want to be on the radio?'

Jane smiled. 'Yeah,' she said. 'I do.'

'So – we have a deal?' said Willy.

'Yes,' said Jane. Willy clapped his hands together.

'Excellent,' he said. 'I'll get the contract routing as soon as I'm back to L.A.'

They said their goodbyes and Jane escorted Willy from the salon. As she watched his wiry frame retreat down Main Street, Elsie stepped out beside her for a Pall Mall. She offered one to Jane.

'What do you think?' said Jane, accepting the cigarette. She trusted Elsie's ability to read people above anyone else's.

'He's a real doer,' said Elsie. 'I like him.'

Jane and Elsie had begun the process of absorbing Maggie's clients at the salon, so as Maggie's due date drew near, band practice had to be snatched in fifteen-minute sessions between perms and dyes. The day Maggie went into labor, the air was so thick with ammonium thioglycolate, the Breakers had been forced to drill 'Don't Fret,' whose simple chorus could be sung in a single breath.

> *'Don't fret,*
> *You can't fight life,*
> *Don't sweat,*
> *No blues,*
> *No strife.'*

As Kyle cruised into his long free-form bass solo, Elsie opened the door a crack. The Breakers stopped playing.

'It's time,' she said. Jane looked at the clock; it was just before 3:00 p.m., four hours before Grace's shift ended.

Greg clambered to his feet. 'Can I—' his voice broke. Rich tensed.

'You can give me a ride back to the house,' said Elsie. 'Jane, Mrs. Clemens needs to cook for about ten more minutes; then just cancel the afternoon and go relieve Grace.'

'Wait,' said Kyle. 'You're taking over Grace's shift with Jesse Reid?'

'Looks that way,' said Jane. Elsie gave her a sympathetic smile.

'Won't that be . . . awkward?' said Kyle.

'Why?' said Rich sarcastically. 'It's not like she benefited from his accident in any way.'

Jane recalled what Willy had said: *Jesse's living minute-to-minute right now.*

'I doubt he's even aware of us,' said Jane. 'You guys should get over to Maggie.'

It went against Jane's every instinct not to follow, but this was how it had to be. The Center had stringent policies about continuity of care; a nurse couldn't leave mid-shift unless relieved by another certified caregiver. On such short notice, this would have to be Jane. Maggie needed her mother, and they all needed Grace's paycheck. So Jane dried Mrs. Clemens's hair, locked up, and drove to Caverswall.

Jane knew the way to the Reid house from dropping Grace off at her shifts, but she had never been past the entrance. As she approached the gate, she recognized the Reids' private security guard as Ross Seager, a Carousel regular she'd slept with once, a few summers before.

'Oh, hey, Ross,' she said, startled. 'You look . . . well.' Jane hadn't seen Ross since he'd gone into rehab the previous year – the last time he'd come to the bar, he'd been skeletal.

'Thanks, Janie,' said Ross. 'I don't need to tell you, the Center's no joke. Been clean now for going on eight months. Not bad for a junkie.'

'Not bad at all,' said Jane. She didn't mind most drugs and had tried her fair share with Ross, but she drew the line at smack. That stuff could kill you.

'You played great at the Fest, by the way,' he added.

'Thanks,' said Jane. 'Maggie's having her baby. Mind if I get in?'

'Nice,' said Ross. 'Bet she's still foxy.'

The iron gate swung open, and Jane proceeded down a gravel drive. As a sprawling estate came into view, Grace ran outside to meet her. She got in the front seat, and the two of them undressed; Jane pulled on Grace's uniform, and Grace donned Jane's A-line cambric dress.

'He's upstairs with his friend Morgan,' said Grace as Jane got out. 'You can just wait in the living room and read a magazine – he'll call if he needs anything. I told him another nurse was coming. Phone and notes are in the kitchen. Thank you, Janie.'

'Be safe,' said Jane. Grace nodded and sped back toward the gate.

Jane felt weightless as she approached the mansion. The angular wooden façade had begun turning silver from the salt air; the ocean glistened at the edge of the property beyond. Jane knew from Grace that the Reids privately referred to their home as 'the Shack,' which struck her as even more obnoxious now that she beheld its size. She let herself in the front door.

The house smelled like a museum – professionally cleaned, then left untouched. The entryway was as stately and elegant as a tomb. Jane drifted inside, feeling like an intruder. She twisted her hair up into a bun to mimic the style Grace always used for work.

She found the phone Grace had mentioned in the kitchen, and called the Center to log her arrival. Then she leafed through Grace's shift notes. Jesse Reid had broken his fall with the right side of his body, cracking three ribs and fracturing his ulna, radius, and several metatarsals. He had a smattering of cosmetic wounds, one of which had become infected; Jane would need to give him an injection of gentamicin. Apart from that, this would be a quiet night.

She passed a geometric staircase leading to the second floor and entered a large, circular living room. Skylights illuminated ceiling-high bookshelves and white modern furniture. The chamber's focal point was a grand piano, black and shining like a brand-new pair of patent-leather shoes. Jane gasped when she saw it.

The keys were enclosed in a polished shell, but the lid had been propped up to reveal a horizontal spectrum of metallic cords. She had flirted with the pitchy upright in her high-school music classroom, but she had never actually seen the inside of a piano before.

Jane had a way with stringed instruments the same as some people had a way with animals: she hadn't found one she couldn't tame. It wasn't something she could fully explain, except to say that, with certain instruments, Jane could hear where the notes were just by looking at them. As she stood there, it occurred to her that a piano was no more than an eighty-eight-stringed guitar.

At the sight, Jane felt an energetic presence stir deep within her, as though she were glimpsing the night sky. She felt an overwhelming urge to sit down and sink her fingers into the enamel.

She shouldn't. It was odd enough that she was even here. She looked around the room, wondering how far the sound would carry. There were no photographs on the shelves, just an oil painting of a woman, a man, and a young boy above a white stone mantle.

Jane's eyes traveled back to the piano, and she was again struck by a magnetic compulsion to touch it. As she reached out a hand, Jesse Reid entered the room.

Even standing with his shoulders folded forward to protect his broken bones, his presence was striking. He was tall – Jane guessed about six foot three. Their eyes met, and Jane felt a jolt; his were the color of a jet of blue flame.

Before either of them could speak, a woman walked in behind him; Jane recognized her as the copper-haired coed from the Carousel. She had naturally bronzed skin and long, dark lashes that made her eyes seem golden. This must be Morgan. Morgan Vidal – Jane recalled her last name from her father's credit card. Seeing her in this space confirmed Jane's impression that she was used to being around money; she looked totally at ease in this room where Jane felt like an alien.

'Oh, hello,' she said to Jane, whose heart began to pound. The two of them were like a pair of beautiful jungle cats prowling around an exotic habitat. Jane was suddenly aware of her uniform, and how it made her invisible.

'I'm filling in for Grace,' she said. 'I'm Jane.'

'Jane Quinn,' said Jesse, a spark of recognition in his eye. Jane straightened up. So – not totally unaware, then.

'Nice to meet you,' said Morgan, who had already moved on. 'I was thinking I would make us something for dinner. Keep it simple – I learned a nice ragout recipe in France last year.'

'Sounds fine,' said Jesse. 'But I think all we have in the house are frozen dinners.'

'Let's go get some groceries – I passed at least two farm stands on the way from my parents'.'

Jesse nodded, and Jane's body went stiff. It was one thing for her to be missing Maggie's labor to fill in for Grace. It was another thing to be sitting alone in a strange house while the patient was out shopping for ragout supplies.

'I don't know,' said Jesse, looking at Jane. 'I think I might need a shot, right?' Jane rarely heard patients volunteer for injections; it struck her that Morgan's visit hadn't been expected.

'Can you do that?' said Morgan.

'I can,' said Jane.

'Great, I'll be here when you're done,' Morgan said. She seated herself at the piano and began to play without hesitation. Jane felt a twinge of envy as a classical piece filled the room.

'I think Grace keeps the stuff in here,' said Jesse. He stalked toward the kitchen. Jane followed.

'I'm Jesse, by the way,' he said, stealing a quick glance at her.

'Nice to meet you,' said Jane, helping him off with his sling. Should she say something more? Apologize? Thank him?

She began to unbutton his shirt – almost his whole torso was bandaged, bruises peeking out like a sunset through vertical blinds.

'Your wounds are coming along,' Jane said, at last.

'That's good to hear,' said Jesse. He didn't sound convinced.

'It's my own fault,' he said, taking a seat at the counter. 'Hit a skid up by Middle Road – totaled my bike. Broke twelve bones. Missed the Fest. But, then, you already knew that.'

Jane felt her cheeks redden as she rummaged in Grace's supplies for the gentamicin.

'According to the *Gazette,* you gave me a run for my money,' said Jesse.

Jane met his gaze. 'Seems like you still have plenty of money,' she said.

Jesse's eyes widened. 'I just meant it sounded like a great set,' he said, gently.

Jane pulled on a pair of rubber gloves, glad to have somewhere else to look.

'Grace talks about you and Maggie all the time,' said Jesse. 'How is Maggie doing?'

'She went into labor around three,' said Jane, beginning to test for a vein in his upper arm. 'Grace should be getting there any minute.'

'To Gray Gables,' he said.

Jane took a syringe from its sanitary wrappings and inserted it into a bottle of gentamicin, filling the barrel. 'That's right,' she said. Having to speak about it was making her realize how anxious she felt.

Jesse seemed to pick up on this. 'Honestly, you should just take off,' he said. 'I'm sure this is the last thing you want to be doing right now.'

Jane didn't have it in her to explain that there was no way for her to 'just take off,' that the Center monitored the switch-board to ensure that shift calls actually came from their patients' homes, and that her family needed the Center too badly to risk it.

'Do you want to look away?' she said.

Jesse shook his head. 'I don't mind,' he said.

When they returned to the living room, Morgan stood abruptly from the piano, notes scattering midair, jagged as icicles.

'Ready?' she said, closing the lid. Jane took a step backward as Jesse allowed himself to be led toward the entryway.

'This'll be good for you,' Morgan said to Jesse, threading her arm through his. She looked over her shoulder at Jane. 'You said your name was Jane, right?'

'That's right.'

'We should be back before seven, but if we aren't, do you mind just sticking around a little longer to check on him before heading out?'

'Morgan—' said Jesse.

'Jane doesn't mind,' said Morgan, flashing her a dazzling smile. 'Do you, Jane?' It was a move Jane had seen Maggie pull hundreds of times on her followers in high school.

'I'm sure you'll be back before then,' said Jane directly to Jesse. Morgan's expression hardened.

'We will,' said Jesse. Jane nodded, and then they were gone. She waited until their headlights curved through the entryway. Then she walked back to the piano and flipped open the fallboard, revealing a row of keys white as bones. Jane touched them cautiously, as though making first contact with a wild creature. She began to play.

Jane had a sense of the night sky for a second time; only now it surrounded her.

5

Barbara 'Bea' Quinn was born in the upstairs bathroom at Gray Gables shortly after midnight on August 1, 1969. Jane and Elsie stood in the doorway as Grace eased the baby from the bathwater and laid her on Maggie's chest.

'She doesn't know she's been born,' said Elsie. Maggie let out a disbelieving laugh as Bea sniffed the air, then emitted a piercing cry.

'Jane, she has your voice,' said Maggie. Jane was too overcome to speak; she flashed Maggie their signal from girlhood, a modified coyote hand sign. Maggie smiled, and signaled back.

Outlaws don't ask questions.

They cut the cord, and Elsie wiped and swaddled Bea. She placed the sleeping bundle in the crux of Jane's elbow and shooed her out so she and Grace could tend to Maggie.

Jane made her way down the creaky stairs as though she were carrying water in a scarf; she could feel herself sweating with the concentration it took not to jostle the baby. It was strange how a being so tiny could make a person feel like a stranger in her own home. As she came into view, Greg, Rich, and Kyle sprang to their feet, jostling to get a peek.

'She's sleeping,' said Jane. 'Look.'

The boys' eyes were saucers as Jane brought the baby toward them.

'Baby Bea,' she said.

'Oh, she's perfect,' said Greg, his eyes brimming. 'How's Maggie? That sounded . . . awful.'

'I've never seen anything like it,' said Jane.

Kyle was cooing. 'I'm an uncle!' he said.

'Can I . . . ?' asked Greg, reaching out. Gingerly, Jane placed the baby in his arms, showing him how to secure her head. Jane looked over at Rich, who was staring at Greg with a soft expression on his face. Jane squeezed his biceps.

'Uncle Rich,' she said. Rich looked away.

'Wow,' said Greg. 'Wow.'

By the time they were called upstairs, Maggie's hair had been washed, and she was propped up in her four-poster bed, tucked into a white woven bedspread and clean sheets. The boys flat-tened themselves against the wall to let Jane through. Bea continued to sleep as she was passed into her mother's arms.

Greg stepped forward. 'How you doing, Mags?' he asked. Maggie smiled.

As Greg began to sing a Wampanoag rock-a-baby song, Jane took a step back from this loving diorama into the dark blue of the hall. She looked at Maggie holding her little daughter, and it occurred to Jane that her own mother must have held her like this, protecting her as she slept.

Jane's memories of Charlotte were like photos tainted by water damage – so many of her happy recollections had been spoiled by the horrifying ones. Jane found it easier to block all of it out than to isolate the sunny scraps. But Charlotte always crept in through her dreams.

Her recurring nightmares all began the same way: with Charlotte getting ready for a date. That night, as Jane slept, she saw her mother in a lilac dress, checking her reflection in the hallway mirror. The floral wallpaper was crisp and new. Red lipstick was the final touch.

As the color met her lips, Charlotte arched her back and let out a little squeal, as though she had been stung. 'Put it down!' Jane shouted, but her mother wouldn't listen. She just kept applying the lipstick, kept wincing as though it were a poker.

Jane awoke drenched in sweat. She tried to calm herself, but the image of her mother in the hall flared behind her eyelids as soon as she closed them. Instead she forced herself to envision Charlotte walking along a moonlit beach, her breaths quieting as a line of arched footprints formed in the sand.

The next morning, Jane was surprised to find that, even with Bea's birth, all she could think about was the piano in Jesse Reid's house. She tried to ignore it; she needed to write a pop tune. But Jane didn't feel pop-y. She was working three jobs, and her brain was too busy counting dollars to count beats.

With the new baby, it was hard to find the space to think – someone always needed help. When Willy's L.A. secretary, Trudy, called later that week to inform Jane that their contracts were en route, Jane still hadn't composed a note.

That afternoon, she and Rich put their heads together in the back room of Widow's Peak. Jane's arm dangled over her guitar as she watched Rich scribble on a pad. This was how they wrote most of their songs – they'd discuss an idea, Rich would pen the lyrics, and Jane would do the rest.

Rich scrawled the words 'Spring Fling' across the top of the paper.

'Try this,' he said, tapping the sheet.

> *Strong,*
> *Yeah,*
> *You bring me along,*
> *When everything's wrong,*
> *This is your song.*

Jane grasped the neck of her instrument, letting the pads of her fingers run over the ridges of her low E string. The lyrics were pop perfection – singsongy, irrepressible, an adult nursery rhyme. Jane's nature sought more complexity: these weren't lines she would ever choose for herself.

'I know it's not your thing,' said Rich.

Jane smiled. They'd been doing this together a long time. 'This is a good pop song,' she said. As she spoke, Willy's words echoed in her ear:

I'm telling you, you can do better than good.

Jane began to experiment, but her apathy toward the lines turned them to rubber; none of her chords would stick. Jane's music was an extension of her mood: when she wasn't feeling it, the music didn't come. She tried to think back to another version of herself, one with less responsibility, but her mind kept reciting her schedule instead: pick up Grace, dinner, Carousel. After an hour, Rich had dashed off the rest of the verses, and Jane still had nothing.

'Maybe it's the lyrics,' he said. 'Do you want to take a crack at it?'

'The lyrics are perfect,' said Jane. 'It's me. I'm just distracted. Oh shit, is that the time?'

Jane grabbed the car keys and raced to the Shack to pick up Grace. She arrived ten minutes late, and expected Grace to be waiting outside the gate when she pulled up. But Grace wasn't there. Jane waved down the night guard and drove to the house.

'Hello?' she called, pushing in the front door. The sun was low, hitting the stark edges of the hall in purple rectangles. No answer. Jane walked into the kitchen, then into the living room. The piano gleamed.

'Hello?' she called again. No answer. Jane listened; all she could hear was her own dry swallow. She knew she should go look for Grace, but the temptation to try the piano again was overpowering. She pulled out the bench and took a seat.

The keys were weighted, satisfying to the touch, but the sound – what a release. Thoughts of 'Spring Fling' burst like a dam as a torrent of notes flowed out of her – anxious, intricate, turbulent. As she played, wisps of hair fell across her eyes, golden in the setting sun. Jane didn't know what this was, but it sure as hell wasn't pop.

With a creak, a set of French doors opened, and Grace entered the living room from the back deck. Jane jumped, hands snapping off the keys. Jesse stepped inside, his blue stare fixed on her.

'I didn't know where you were,' said Jane.

'We went out on the back lawn for some physical therapy,' said Grace. Jane could sense the familiar combination of pride and sorrow Grace had in her music, forever a reminder of Charlotte. Jesse was still watching her.

'I'm just going to phone the Center,' said Grace, walking into the kitchen. Jane looked at her feet.

Jesse cleared his throat. 'You were really in it,' he said.

Jane felt breathless, as though she'd been interrupted in the middle of a kiss. She gave herself a little shake. 'How are you feeling?' she asked.

'Weak,' said Jesse, flexing the hand on his good arm. 'Grace is helping, though.'

Jane could see their reflections floating in the darkened windowpanes. She wouldn't like to be alone at night in this house.

'All set,' said Grace, coming back. 'Nice work today,' she said to Jesse.

'See you tomorrow,' he said. They waved goodbye, and Grace put an arm around Jane's shoulder as they left the living room.

'What's for dinner? I'm starving,' said Grace as they walked toward the front door.

'Lasagna à la Kyle,' said Jane.

'My yearly portion of garlic in one meal,' said Grace. Jane's laugh echoed. The house was so quiet, she knew that Jesse could still hear them. She stopped walking. Grace gave her a questioning look. Before Grace could say anything, Jane went back into the living room. Jesse stood at the piano.

'Do you want to come over for dinner?' Jane asked. 'My band will be there. Fair warning – you will be extremely thirsty after.'

For a moment, she thought he hadn't heard her. But when he looked up, his eyes shone with gratitude.

6

The sun had set by the time the station wagon returned to Gray Gables, and the Victorian cottage glowed like a lantern. Jane could see Kyle and Rich moving around the kitchen; Greg and Maggie sat on the porch with Bea. Grace helped Jesse out of the car.

'Did you take the scenic route?' said Maggie as they climbed the steps. Her eyes flicked to Jesse. 'Who's this?'

'This is Jesse,' said Grace. 'He'll be joining us for dinner.' Maggie held Grace's gaze an extra second as Greg gasped beside her.

'Pleased to meet you,' said Jesse. 'I hear congratulations are in order.' He nodded to Bea.

'Jesse Reid – holy shit, man!' said Greg, a grin spreading across his features as he stepped in front of Maggie to vigorously shake Jesse's left hand. Jesse smiled shyly.

'Man, it's good to meet you. I'm Greg – I play drums with Janie. This is Maggie, my love.'

He scooped Bea out of Maggie's arms and brought her over to Jesse. 'And this is Bea, our daughter,' he said.

'She's beautiful,' said Jesse.

Kyle stepped out through the screen door, wearing a floral

apron. 'Dinner's ready,' he said, then caught sight of Jesse and let out a groan.

'Aw, man, Jesse Reid's here? You should have told me – I would have let Rich cook.' Kyle shook his head and put an arm around Jesse, steering him inside. 'Sorry in advance, man. Let me get you a beer. I'm Kyle, by the way.'

Greg followed with Bea. Maggie slowly got to her feet.

'What the hell?' she said.

'Jane invited him,' said Grace.

'Ohh,' said Maggie. 'I see.'

'I'm going in,' said Jane.

'Don't be shy,' said Maggie. 'We get it. He's tall and famous.'

'I can't hear you,' said Jane as she opened the screen door with a creak.

Kyle had installed Jesse at the head of the table and was in the process of adding another place setting, while Greg settled Bea into her bassinet and Rich filled up water glasses from a green pitcher. Elsie appeared at Jane's elbow. Catching sight of Jesse, she gave Jane a wink and took her seat.

After everyone was introduced, they settled in for lasagna à la Kyle. The salty offering seemed to burn away everyone's self-consciousness, and pretty soon they were all laughing and joking – except for Maggie, who seemed determined to let Jesse know he wasn't special. While the rest of them made a point to include him, Maggie forged ahead as if he weren't there.

'How'd it go with Mrs. Robson today?' she asked Elsie. 'Did she end up renewing the feathering or going back to the flip?'

'Back to the flip,' said Elsie.

Maggie rolled her eyes. 'I knew it,' she said. 'When will

people learn that keeping the hairstyle they had when they were young actually makes them look older?'

'Mags, I don't think Jesse wants to hear about Mrs. Robson's hair,' said Greg.

'Well, then, he shouldn't have come – no offense,' said Maggie.

'I thought the flip was over, no?' said Jesse. Everyone laughed. As the conversation resumed, Jane stole a glance at Jesse and found his brilliant blue eyes already watching her.

After dinner, Elsie and Grace insisted on cleaning up, and Maggie went upstairs to feed Bea, leaving Jesse alone with the Breakers in the living room. As they switched from beer to Elsie's lilac wine, the conversation turned to music.

'Do you have any advice?' Rich ventured hesitantly, peering at Jesse through his long, sandy bangs. 'For our first album, I mean.'

Jesse's brow creased. 'Trust me, you don't want my advice,' he said. Instead, he told them about recording in London, how he'd been down the hall from the British invasion band Fair Play, and how he'd gotten to sit in on some of the sessions for their latest album, *High Strung*.

'I can't believe you were recording in the same studio as Hannibal Fang,' said Kyle, stars in his eyes. 'That guy is a living legend.'

'I honestly don't remember that much of it,' said Jesse. 'I was pretty out of it. But, yeah – dude's a hell of a bass player.'

'You said it,' said Kyle, holding up an air bass and imitating Hannibal Fang's notorious pelvic gyrations with his bony hips. They all laughed.

'So – are you going to help Jane?' asked Kyle. Jane glared at him. Kyle was the most outgoing member of their group; it never occurred to him that not everyone shared his openness.

'With what?' said Jesse.

'She needs to write a pop tune,' said Kyle. 'For our album. A single.'

'What about that song you were playing on the piano?' he asked.

'Jane doesn't play the piano,' said Rich.

Jesse laughed. 'Sure, she does,' he said.

Kyle, Rich, and Greg all groaned.

'Is there anything you can't play?' said Greg.

'I don't get it,' said Jesse.

'Jane's a genius,' said Kyle. 'She can teach herself any instrument. First it was guitar, then the violin . . .'

'The mandolin,' said Rich.

'The dulcimer,' said Greg.

'The ukulele,' said Kyle. 'And now she's the *piano tamer.*'

'The *piano tamer,*' chorused Rich and Greg.

'That's incredible,' said Jesse.

Jane averted her eyes. 'Kyle's right,' she said. 'We just need something quick and dirty for the radio. Rich nailed the lyrics. . . . I just need to focus.'

'What's your process, man?' asked Greg, turning to Jesse. 'You write the catchiest songs I've ever heard.'

'I don't know,' said Jesse, looking at his hands. 'I honestly feel like I'm finding the songs more than I'm making them.'

'Jesse Reid,' said Kyle, 'you are too modest.'

As the conversation carried on, Jesse turned to Jane and, in a low voice, said, 'When all else fails, just go with a major seventh chord.'

Jane looked up, surprised. 'Thanks,' she said, making a mental note to confirm what that was.

49

He nodded to her, then turned back to the conversation.

Around 11:00 p.m., Greg started snoring loudly in his chair, and they decided to call it a night.

'I can drop you off,' said Kyle, clapping Jesse on his good shoulder. 'Really glad you came, man.'

'This was so nice,' said Jesse. He looked at Jane. 'Truly.'

'You should come hear us play,' said Greg through a yawn. 'We're on at the Carousel most weekends.'

Jesse nodded. He turned to Jane. 'And you should feel free to come use the piano whenever you want.'

'I'd like that,' said Jane, her stomach flipping as his eyes lingered on her face an extra moment.

Jesse followed Kyle out the door. Rich walked by and mouthed, 'I'd like that,' batting his eyes. Jane punched him in the arm, and he ran after Kyle as Greg headed upstairs.

Jane felt wide awake. Once in her room, she grabbed the notepaper containing the verses for 'Spring Fling.' Suddenly the lines made sense in a way they hadn't before. They were meant for nights like tonight: for feeling young, carefree, as if anything might happen.

> *Strong,*
> *Yeah,*
> *You bring me along,*
> *When everything's wrong,*
> *This is your song.*

Jane grabbed her guitar and the tattered book of tabs Kyle had given her for Christmas their senior year and began to hash out the chords, plucking quietly so as not to wake the baby.

Jesse was right – adding the seventh to a major-C chord made it click. By the time she had finished, her marks outnumbered Rich's on the page. She sat back to admire her work.

Jane heard a knock at her door and knew it was her aunt before she entered.

'Hey!' said Jane.

'Hey,' said Grace. 'Sorry to interrupt – I won't be long.'

Jane closed her notebook as Grace sat at the foot of her bed.

'Tonight was fun,' Grace said. She kneaded her hands. Jane felt dread prickle through her satisfaction. She waited for Grace to continue.

'I didn't realize you were interested in being social with Jesse,' she said.

Jane swallowed. 'I'm not, I just felt bad leaving him there alone.'

Grace nodded. 'He's a sweet person,' she said. 'But he's also a patient.'

Jane shifted uncomfortably. 'And?' she said.

'And . . . people with his history aren't known for being trustworthy.' Grace cut herself off; she wasn't supposed to discuss privileged medical information, even with junior staff.

Jane felt the pool of dread deepen inside her. 'So . . . what are you saying?' Their eyes met.

'I'm saying, don't get too attached,' said Grace. 'And be careful what you tell him.'

These words spoke directly to Jane's ten-year-old self – the one Grace had rescued from a nearly fatal attempt to run away during Hurricane Donna. Throughout their adolescence, Maggie had tested Grace, taking for granted that she had a mother to test. But not Jane. Jane would rather have died than disappoint the woman who had found her lost and terrified in that storm.

'Of course,' said Jane, giving her a quick smile. 'I know the drill. Honestly, I don't even like him in that way. He's just good to know – for the band.'

Grace nodded. 'Okay,' she said. They hugged, and Grace went to bed.

After she left, Jane glanced down at the 'Spring Fling' lyrics; they'd turned back into the stale hieroglyphics they'd been that afternoon.

Jane replaced her guitar in its case and changed into an overlarge *Carousel, Summer 1967* tee shirt. She went downstairs to grab a drink, and found Elsie rereading *Jamaica Inn* at the kitchen table. The green pitcher was still half full from dinner; Elsie watched Jane pour water into a fresh glass. When Jane didn't leave right away, she lowered her book. 'I love my daughter,' said Elsie. 'But sometimes she can be a bit of a killjoy.'

Jane scanned her grandmother's face. 'What do you think of Jesse?' she asked.

Elsie shrugged. 'He's a rock star,' she said. 'His struggles will go hand in hand with his fame. Hardly the first to fit that description. The real question is, what do you think of him?'

'I like him,' Jane admitted. 'But this record is my priority right now. I'd be happy just to learn what he knows.'

Elsie smiled mischievously. 'For now,' she said.

Jane rolled her eyes and kissed her grandmother good night.

7

In mid-August, Maggie announced that she was ready to take on a few select clients at the salon. To ease her return, Greg made Bea a tiny nursery in the back room of Widow's Peak. He scoured a crib he found at the Goodwill in Perry's Landing and installed it beneath a mobile of tin moons. Maggie took one look and laughed. Greg's smile faltered. Jane's heart sank.

'You can't actually think I'd put her in that,' said Maggie. She took Bea and walked back into the salon. Greg looked as though he'd been bitten by a viper. Rich stepped forward as Greg's shoulders began to stoop, and Jane followed after Maggie.

'Who do you think you are?' she hissed at Maggie over the front counter.

'I'm her mother,' said Maggie as the shop door opened. 'Jane, move, we have a customer.'

Jane drove to the Shack early that afternoon, still roiling with anger. She found Grace and Jesse playing bocce in the driveway. His eyes followed Jane as she stepped from the car.

'Jane, it's only six,' said Grace, sounding surprised. She probably didn't think Jane should be there.

Jane didn't care. 'I know,' she said. 'Jesse, can I use the piano?'

Jesse nodded. As Jane walked inside, it occurred to her that Jesse might not have actually expected her to take him up on his offer to come over. She felt a momentary pang of regret that was immediately overcome by the sight of the piano.

Her fingers tingled as she lifted up the fallboard. She let them brush across the keys, head bending forward as though bowing to the instrument. *Help me,* she thought. She was so sick of Maggie. Maggie took all of it for granted – all of them working extra to cover for her, Greg and his kindness. She never said thank you. She was never even nice. Jane could not get over the look on Greg's face when Maggie had dismissed his crib.

As her fingers sank into the keys, a jumble of phrases and runs billowed into the room. Jane recognized them for what they were: a set of components that, once untangled, would constitute a verse, a chorus, and a bridge. As she worked, she sang to herself.

> 'Viper twisted in your nest,
> Wearing wallets for your skin,
> Apple green as original sin,
> How much like a girl you are,
> Lounging breezy in your denim,
> Killing love with words of venom.'

These lines were like a metronome, droning in the back of Jane's mind. To her, they were no more than trail markers as she waded into a fen of melody and harmony. By the time Grace's shift had ended, she had worked out the chorus and the verse for the second song they needed to complete the Breakers album: the ballad.

'You could come back to finish it,' said Jesse as Jane thanked him on the way out. Jane smiled.

'Tomorrow,' said Jesse.

Jane heard Grace start the car. 'Tomorrow,' she said.

The next day, she played Rich what she had so far.

When Rich liked a song, his head tilted ever so slightly to the right. As Jane sang him the chorus, using her makeshift lyrics, she felt a tremor of pride as his skull tipped on its axis.

'I love it, Janie,' he said. 'Lounging in denim, words of venom . . . that's Maggie, all right.'

Jane frowned. 'Those words are like Paul McCartney and "Scrambled Eggs,"' she said, referencing McCartney's place-holder lines for 'Yesterday.'

'Why?' said Rich. 'I really like them.'

Jane was adamant. She handed him his notebook. 'Well, I don't. Do your thing,' she insisted, prompting him with the opening chord. This was not the first time they'd had this conversation, and Jane didn't have the bandwidth to rehash it now.

Sighing, Rich opened the pad to a new page and scribbled a single word at the top: 'Run.'

Jane had been hoping to get back to the Shack early to work on the bridge, but by the time she checked the clock, there was only an hour left in Grace's shift. As Jane ran out the door, she heard Elsie yelling to her that Grace had called.

'I'm heading there now, will talk to her in a few,' Jane shouted back, not wanting to miss another minute with the piano.

The moment she stepped into the Shack, she could sense that something was off. A big-band album was blasting through the first floor, transforming the flat modern surfaces into a marble echo chamber. A voice inside Jane told her to turn around, but she was too set on finishing her song to heed it.

In the living room, she found Jesse slumped over as though trying to make himself invisible. Standing at the center of the room was a man Jane knew immediately to be Jesse's father. He had Jesse's height but none of his gentleness, an imposing figure with eyes like ice.

'If she could see you, she'd be appalled,' he was saying, arm resting on the piano as though it were a piece of furniture. Grace was nowhere to be seen. Jane started to back out of the room.

'Well, who have we here?' said Jesse's father, a strong South Carolina accent coming through. Jane felt underdressed in her worn shift.

'This is Jane,' said Jesse, drawing himself up. He seemed buoyed by her presence. 'She's a recording artist with Pegasus as well. Jane, this is my father, Dr. Aldon Reid.'

'Pleased to meet you, Dr. Reid,' said Jane. Then, to Jesse, 'Where's Grace?'

'I've sent Grace on an errand to take some refreshments down to the dock,' said Dr. Reid.

'I told him that's not her job,' said Jesse, mortified.

'She didn't seem to mind,' said Dr. Reid. 'She's a smart woman. Understands I'm paying her salary. That means something to some people, son.'

'I should go see if she needs some help,' said Jane, taking a step back.

'Hold on just a minute, young lady,' said Dr. Reid, unaccustomed to having people leave before he dismissed them. The phonograph switched keys, and 'Lilac Waltz' began to play over the stereo. Jane's mouth went dry.

'Have a seat. As Jesse's fellow *recording artist,* you can't leave before you've heard this song. Tommy Patton – now, that's a performer. Turn it up, Jesse, will you?'

Jesse roused himself to oblige, even though Dr. Reid was standing closer to the control panel. The beautiful, sad melody of 'Lilac Waltz' began to pulse through the room with forty trumpets blasting past its nuances, the shmaltzy voice of Tommy Patton crooning out the lyrics.

'Sometimes I think about,
The nights we used to dance,
Among the lilac trees.
Summer breeze,
Filled the air,
With sweet perfume,
And promises.'

Jane sat immobilized, listening for a particular turn of phrase in the second verse:

'The moon hangs low,
White as a pearl,
I'm the guy in your arms.'

Jane could still hear her mother ranting about it. 'It doesn't even rhyme!' she'd say. This wasn't the elegant woman from her dreams, but a desperate ghost whose brainchild had been ripped from her. 'The words are so obviously meant to be "I'm the *girl* in your arms." "Girl" rhymes with pearl. *"Girl"* rhymes with *"pearl."'*

Jane hadn't fully understood at the time. *Just write another!* she'd wanted to say. It wasn't until now, on the verge of her own chance, that she could start to comprehend what it must have been like – trapped on this island with no recourse, this song playing over and over on the radio.

'Sure, guitar music is fine,' Dr. Reid was saying. 'Quaint. Like a sampler. But if you really want to be great, you'll take a note from this guy.'

'Or whoever he took the notes from.' After a beat, Jane realized the comment had come from Jesse.

'What was that, son?' said Dr. Reid, taking a swig from his tumbler.

'Just that I don't think Tommy Patton is a person I want to emulate,' said Jesse. His tone was as polite as ever, but Jane could detect the anger in his words. Dr. Reid could as well.

'That's the problem with your generation. None of you think you have anything to learn,' said Dr. Reid. He rounded on Jane. 'You seem like a nice girl. Do you listen to your father?'

'I don't know my father,' said Jane. Dr. Reid stared at Jane, coldly evaluating her; Jane sat there being evaluated.

'You're right, Jesse,' said Dr. Reid after a moment. 'You really do meet the most interesting people through your music.'

Jesse crossed the room and touched Jane's arm as Dr. Reid finished his drink.

'Come on,' he said. 'I bet we can still catch Grace.'

'Watch your step, son,' said Dr. Reid, helping himself to more whiskey. 'I'd rather not pay for another month of supervised care.'

Jesse let Jane out the French doors onto the back porch. They walked together through a tree-lined yard; Jane could see the water glistening in the distance.

'I apologize for that,' Jesse said. 'We tried to call before you came. He showed up last night completely unannounced and . . . well, it's his house.'

'It's my fault,' said Jane. 'I shouldn't have come in.' She stopped and looked up at him. 'Why were you saying that before – about Tommy Patton?'

Jesse ran a hand through his hair. 'Willy told me about what happened with your mom,' he said.

'How did that come up?' asked Jane, surprised.

Jesse blushed. 'So . . . she wrote that song,' said Jesse, avoiding her question.

Jane nodded.

'I don't understand how he got away with it,' said Jesse. 'Wouldn't people have heard her sing it? Wouldn't she have had . . . I don't know, witnesses?'

'She wasn't much of a performer,' said Jane. 'The only place she ever sang it was the amateur stage at the Fest. That's where Tommy Patton heard it. When it first came on the radio, she tried to petition local media, but no one would cover it – the Island needs the Fest too much to risk alienating the big record labels. After we lost her, my grandmother decided to drop the whole thing.'

Jesse shook his head. 'Can I ask – what happened to her?'

Be careful what you tell him.

Jane looked deeply into his eyes; to her surprise, she did feel compelled to tell him. But she couldn't ignore Grace's words. She deliberated.

'When I was young, my mother was . . . different,' she said after a moment. 'She was sunny. She had this great job at the library. We'd spend hours poring over these crusty anthologies

59

– reading Greek myths – until the other librarians shushed us. She'd say when I was old enough we'd go ourselves – to Crete, home of the Minotaur.'

Jane looked at the ocean, sparkling white beyond the trees.

'God, she was obsessed with that story. She loved Theseus, escaping the monster's lair with just a thread. That's what music was for my mom – a thread tethering her to the light.'

'Girl' rhymes with 'pearl.'

Jane paused to steady herself. 'After Tommy Patton released "Lilac Waltz," her personality changed,' she said at last. 'It was like the thread had snapped. She quit her job and stayed home all week watching reruns. She'd go days without speaking to any of us; then she and Grace would go at it for hours.'

Jesse's eyes shone with interest, urging her to continue.

Jane took a breath. 'Toward the end, she really started acting up. She did a few things that weren't strictly . . . legal. Then, one night, she went out and never came back.' Jesse stood very still.

'Where did she go?' he asked.

'I don't know,' said Jane. She felt a chill. 'We never heard from her again.'

Jesse was incredulous. 'You must have looked for her,' he said.

'Of course,' said Jane. She'd already said more than she'd intended.

'And?' said Jesse. His irises had no rings around them – just blue marble right up to the whites.

'And . . . nothing,' said Jane. 'She could be anywhere. She could be dead.'

Jesse's eyes widened. Jane realized she had raised her voice. 'I'm sorry, Jane,' he said.

'My money's on Crete,' said Jane quietly, picturing a trail of footprints on a moonlit beach.

'How old were you when this happened?' said Jesse.

'Nine,' said Jane.

Jesse exhaled. 'That's not right,' he said. He looked genuinely sorry.

'It's sad,' said Jane. 'But I've been lucky. Grace is basically a second mother, and I've got Elsie and Maggie. You know.'

Jesse's eyes looked far away. 'I do know,' he said. 'My mom died unexpectedly three years ago. Pancreatic cancer. We had no idea she was even sick. One day she was fine, and then, three weeks later, she was gone.'

'Jesse, I'm sorry,' said Jane.

Jesse nodded. 'My dad took it pretty hard,' he said. 'I think he blames himself, being a doctor and all. I know he seems gruff, but I haven't been . . . easy. I'm all he has, and after what happened this summer – and before – I think he's just scared of losing me, too.'

'What happened before?' asked Jane.

Jesse considered her. 'I spent some time in an institution,' he said.

Jane stood very still. Was this what Grace had been warning her about?

'At the Center?' she asked. She felt cold picturing Jesse in one of the white patient uniforms, a caregiver leading him into isolation.

Jesse shook his head. 'I wish,' he said. 'I was at McLean, outside Boston. Only the best for Aldon Reid's boy.'

'What was that like?' she asked.

'The Zoo?' Jesse tilted his head back, and Jane watched his

Adam's apple rise and lower. 'Clean. Organized. Like living inside a filing cabinet. Everything is so routine, time just slips by. Go in in June, it's December before you know it. Can't beat the food, though.'

Jane snorted. 'Why "the Zoo"?'

'Bars on all the windows,' said Jesse.

Jane looked into his eyes. 'I couldn't bring myself to work inside a place like that,' she said. 'I hated seeing what it was like for the patients – day in, day out, with no sense of the world outside.'

'That's not always a bad thing,' said Jesse quietly. 'I was very depressed after my mom died. Completely out of it – I couldn't cope. It was all I could do to get through the day. I needed help accepting that—'

'Reality was reality,' said Jane.

Jesse nodded. 'I feel ashamed admitting that, considering I had twice as much time as you,' he said.

'No one expects you to cope when you're nine,' said Jane.

He looked at his feet.

'How are you coping now?' she asked.

Jesse swayed in place. 'It's been three years,' he said. He looked up at her. 'Now things are . . . different.'

They stood together for a moment. Then Jane began to walk toward the dock. She felt a small tug in her sternum as Jesse fell into step beside her.

8

On Wednesdays, Jane helped load Elsie's oils, tinctures, soaps, and candles into the station wagon, and the two of them drove to the flea market in Mauncheake. Elsie usually managed to sell a few candles, but her real objective was to debrief with her friend Sid, who always brought a trunkful of antiques and an earful of gossip from his shop in Perry's Landing.

'The ladies Quinn, radiant as ever,' said Sid, looking up as he tried to get reception on a lime-green 'collector's edition' transistor radio. The radio was only seven years old, but that hadn't stopped Sid from putting a price sticker on it – just in case.

'Lila Charlotte, you'll never guess who's just filed for divorce number three!' he said gleefully to Elsie, reaching for a thermos he'd stashed inside a Victorian wicker pram.

'No!' said Elsie. 'Does this mean that C.C.'s back?'

'Don't even get me started,' said Sid, handing Jane and Elsie each a coupe glass filled with pink liquid. Jane sniffed hers and raised her eyebrows.

'It's mostly grapefruit, Jane,' said Sid. 'By the way, how's it going with the brooding musician boy?'

'I think he's quite taken with Jane,' said Elsie, sipping her drink.

'It's not like that,' said Jane. She had barely seen Jesse in the week since their encounter with Dr. Reid, and they'd only spoken in passing. The distance gave Jane relief – she hadn't meant to say so much and couldn't understand why she had.

'Of course it's not,' said Sid pityingly. 'Speaking of diffident ne'er-do-wells, you'll never guess who sauntered into my shop the other day to give me a lecture about how I parked my car.'

Elsie's eyes narrowed. 'Mayhew,' she said.

As Sid and Elsie fell into vicious patter over Elsie's nemesis, Drexel Mayhew, Jane heard a familiar song on the transistor radio. Jane reached over to turn up the chorus.

'Nothing's wrong when Sylvie smiles,
Yeah, nothing can go wrong when Sylvie smiles.'

It was Jesse. His voice cut through the music like a silver bullet, a sound so pure and sweet it made Jane feel . . . glad. Her heart began to pound as she realized that she'd never actually heard the song before – she'd mistaken liking it for recognition. She sat back, entranced.

At band practice, Jane was still thinking about it.

'Have you heard that song "Sylvie Smiles"?' she asked Kyle.

'"*She's got a funny way of showing it . . .*"' sang Kyle. 'Janie, you're living in the past. That song's been out for months.'

'It's so good,' said Jane.

Kyle nodded fervently. 'If you like that one, you *gotta* hear "My Lady."'

After rehearsal, they crossed the street to Beach Tracks, Bayleen Island's music emporium, where the co-owner, Dana, let them shut themselves in a practice room with the album *Jesse Reid*. Jane didn't love the recording: the London rock influence was over the top. Harpsichord intros had been welded onto songs that went on to be entirely guitar, brass quartets implanted in others like rhinestones in leather. It all seemed unnecessary to Jane, because Jesse was a crackerjack guitar player. Even with the clutter, his voice was astounding, his tone clear and rich and so perfectly in tune it sliced through the overwrought arrangements like a laser. As she sat, consuming track after track after track, Jane had to admit it: she was a Jesse Reid fan.

That night, Willy called to let Jane know he'd arrived on Bayleen Island.

'I'd like to come by tomorrow to hear the new songs – maybe confirm the track order,' he said.

'Sure,' said Jane.

'Great, I'll let Jesse know. Figure he can come, too – give you guys some technical feedback.'

Jane had never felt musically self-conscious around Jesse, but that had been before she'd allowed herself to admit how talented he was. She took a beat too long to respond.

'Or I don't have to if you'd rather—' said Willy.

'It's fine,' said Jane. 'Bring him if he wants.'

The next day, Willy came to the salon with Jesse in tow. The clients watched them pass through the shop from their chairs, eyes following in the mirrors like those of portraits in a gallery. Willy stared back through beetle-eyed lenses, as Jesse hunched behind him like a heron.

'Willy!' said Kyle, giving him a bear hug. 'So glad you're here. And Jesse! This is the best!'

He grabbed a couple of empty crates and flipped them over as seats for their guests. Light streamed in through a strip of clerestory windows, showcasing the industrial supply shelves behind Willy and Jesse. Jane suddenly became aware of the snot-colored carpeting, and how strange Bea's changing table must look in the corner. Maybe Maggie had been right – maybe this wasn't a good place for a baby.

'How's Rebecca?' Kyle asked Willy.

Willy looked up in surprise. 'She's well,' he said, touching his wedding band. 'On a juice cleanse.' Of course, Kyle thought to inquire about Willy's wife; Jane couldn't even remember Willy telling them her name.

Jesse nodded to Jane, who was tuning with Rich. Jesse's face had a little bit of color in it, and his eyes gleamed – if Jane didn't know better, she'd say he was excited. She felt her stomach flip; having him in this space was surreal.

Willy helped Jesse onto a crate and then took his seat. 'Okay, Janie Q,' he said. 'What's the plan?'

Jane cleared her throat. She couldn't recall feeling nervous in quite this way since her early days performing in middle school.

'I figure we can just go through the full set,' she said. 'We're looking for feedback on possible order, but if you have any specific notes, that's fine, too.'

'Interesting,' said Kyle. He looked at Jesse and whispered loudly. 'Jane hates notes.'

'Knowing Jane, there won't be any,' said Willy.

The track list kicked off with 'Dirty Bastard,' an ode to Kyle and Greg's father, who showed up once a year expecting to be treated like the man of the house. Fortunately for Jane, there was no way to sing 'Dirty Bastard' with anything other than full frontal moxie.

After that, Jesse and Willy blended into the room. It was just Jane, Rich, Kyle, Greg, and the music, and they were in it; 'No More Demands,' 'Don't Fret,' and 'Sweet Maiden Mine' went off without a hitch.

Then it was time for 'Spring Fling'; Jane rolled her eyes at Willy's clear excitement during the intro, but once she was in the verse, she gave in to the song's flirtatiousness and dug into the fry tones of her voice. Jesse nodded at the key change into the chorus.

'Hey! We should be a movie,
We should be a show,
Yeah, hey!
You make me feel groovy,
Light it up and go, yeah,
Light me up and go.'

After the number, Willy stood and clapped.

'Okay, okay,' said Jane. She stole a glance at Jesse, and he gave her a wink.

Now Jane found it impossible not to look at Jesse. She had gone into the heightened state of performance, senses alert, inhibitions down.

The album's B side began with 'Indigo,' then 'Caught,' then 'Be Gone,' then 'Run.' As the Breakers finished with 'Spark,' Jane's eyes locked into Jesse's.

'She goes down easy after it's done,
Gale force winds and blistering sun,
She starts at a hundred, ends back at one,

A lightning storm at the touch of a thumb.
Shock comes quick, a wave in the dark,
This will make it better, this little spark.'

When they finished playing, everyone was breathless.

'Yes,' Willy said.

Kyle and Greg slapped five; Rich and Jane grinned at each other.

'"Spring Fling" is *perfect*,' said Willy. 'I'm gonna have that shit in my head for the rest of the week. And "Run"? Goddamn, if that's not about my college girlfriend. You guys nailed it. Jesse – what'd you think?'

Jesse's eyes shone. 'That's gonna be a hell of an album,' he said, his voice deep and gravelly. He looked at Kyle. 'I've never seen anyone play bass like that before,' Jesse said. 'Without the frets – that's amazing. You're like a gymnast, man.'

'Thanks, man,' said Kyle, blushing ear to ear.

'Greg, holding it down – seriously, man, rock on.' He turned to Jane and Rich.

'You two sound like you're a single guitar sometimes. Seriously, the expressiveness is dynamite. And, Janie Q . . .' he said, trying out the nickname for the first time. Jane smiled. He shook his head but didn't say anything further. Jane sensed Willy watching and looked away.

From there, Jesse took them through their set list, number by number.

'I was wondering how that one was going to translate from the piano,' Jesse was saying about 'Run.' 'Kyle, brother – it's you.'

Jesse's biggest overall suggestion was to reorder 'Sweet Maiden Mine' and 'Spring Fling.'

'You can use the break as a compositional tool in its own right,' he said. 'It's better to end the side with something heavy, because your listeners will have to pause after, to flip the record.'

The boys looked at Jane, expecting her to argue, but she just nodded. 'I hadn't thought of that,' she said.

Jesse rubbed his arm in the sling. 'That's gonna be something,' he said. 'When are you recording?'

'Beginning of October,' said Willy. 'We've got three weeks booked at Pegasus's New York studio.'

'Who's producing?' asked Jesse.

'Vincent Ray,' said Willy.

Jesse let out a low whistle.

'Who's Vincent Ray?' asked Rich.

'Visionary producer,' said Jesse. 'Shane's Rebellion, The Deals, Bulletin, Sunrise Eclipse . . .'

Willy looked gratified.

'So do we call him Vincent Ray, or is Ray his last name?' said Kyle.

Maggie walked in before Willy could answer.

'Mom is outside, double-parked, with lunch,' she said. 'Will you go help her unload?' Greg almost leapt over his drum set, and Rich, Kyle, and Willy followed, leaving Jesse and Jane alone. Jesse began to heave himself to his feet, and Jane reached down to help him. As his fingers touched her arm, a jolt ran through her entire body. Jesse cleared his throat.

'I think my leg's asleep,' he said, letting go of her and resting on the wall beside Bea's crib.

'Jane – that music. You really have a gift.'

Jane looked down, unsure of what to say.

He reached out to tap the tin moon on Bea's mobile. '"Spark,"' he said in a casual tone. 'That one seems . . . different.'

Jane looked up. 'I wrote the lyrics on that one,' she said.

Jesse gave her an appreciative look. 'What inspired it?'

Jane paused. The truth was, 'Spark' had come through in a flash after a grueling day at the Center: one minute Jane had been sitting in her room, the next she'd had a song. She had no idea where it had come from, but there it was, words and all. Jane had never experienced anything like it, and the loss of control had left her disturbed. This was something that would have happened to her mother. Jane had given the song to her band in an attempt to dispel its effect on her, and this had mostly worked; still, she had refused to write lyrics ever since.

Now Jesse stood wondering beside her, calm as a lake.

Jane reacted on instinct. 'Sex,' she said. Splash.

Those blazing blue eyes flew to hers in surprise. He laughed. 'And here I was thinking you were going to say shock therapy.'

Jane's eyebrows shot up. 'Are you speaking from personal experience?' she said.

Color rose in his cheeks. 'Are you?' he countered. The way he looked at her made the space between them seem incidental. He was so close, and he smelled so good. It would be nothing to reach for him.

The door to the back room swung open. It was Willy.

'You two coming?' he said, aviators back in place. When he saw them standing together, his face filled with glee.

9

After the session at Widow's Peak, Jane picked up an extra day shift at the Center and worked a double at the Carousel. She rationalized that she was going to be away for three weeks and would need the money. The truth was that she needed to get Jesse out of her head; when she was around him, she said things she didn't mean to say, felt things she didn't mean to feel. On the third day, Jesse telephoned Gray Gables. Elsie handed Jane the receiver with a knowing look.

'Can you come by?' he said. 'There's something I could use your help with.'

'I don't know, I'm pretty busy right now,' said Jane, heart pounding.

'Please, Jane,' he said.

She looked up at the ceiling. 'All right.'

Jane arrived at the Shack around 5:00 p.m. that day and found Jesse and Grace in the living room. Grace went into the kitchen, but Jane felt calmer knowing she was there; she trusted herself not to do anything impulsive with her aunt in the next room.

Jesse looked good; he'd shaved, and his eyes were bright as he offered her a chair.

'I'm due to start recording in December,' he said. 'And I

haven't been able to physically write down a single thing. I still have a month until the cast comes off – I need to start.'

'Do you have any of the music?' Jane asked.

Jesse pointed to his head. 'It's all up here,' he said. 'I was hoping you could help me transcribe, try things out – be my hands.'

Jane's cheeks colored. 'Jesse, I have to tell you, I don't know how to read music.'

To her surprise, Jesse's face lit up. 'I'll teach you,' he said. 'It can be an exchange for you helping me take down my album.'

That first day, Jesse just talked her through basic annotation. He showed her some of his notes from his first album, tracked with five-talon scratches and little musical suggestions to himself, explaining the technical terms as he went. When Jane flipped to the entry for 'Sylvie Smiles,' she paused, memorizing the page.

'Who would have thought a song about Sylvia Plath would be so popular,' said Jesse.

Jane reread the lyrics right where they'd been written:

> *She'll be Venus if you'll be Mars,*
> *Catch her in a glass bell jar,*
> *But nothing can go wrong when Sylvie smiles.*

'Holy shit,' said Jane.

Jesse laughed. 'A fellow McLean patient.'

Jane loved looking at his writing and discovering how these symbols translated into actual songs. Transcribing was a different story. She mainly relied on her memory when composing, jotting down tabs while keeping the rhythm and melody locked in her head. Using staff notation felt as restrictive as the measure bars themselves.

Jesse was patient. 'It's like any form of literacy,' he said. 'Give it time, it will click.'

He was right. At first, their sessions inched by, measure by measure. But as they settled into a routine, Jane continued to improve; by mid-September, she could keep up as Jesse fed her running notes, chord progressions, and time signatures. As she watched him work, she began to realize that the composition of an album was itself an art form. Listening to Jesse talk about themes made Jane feel her own ignorance and unsophistication.

'Our album's just the songs we had in the order they sounded best,' she said, chagrined.

'You're in a great position,' said Jesse. 'First albums are just meant to spread your name around. If you get a song on the radio, you will have done well.'

Jesse's own debut had had two top ten singles, so the expectations for his second album were enormous.

The cornerstone of the album was to be a soulful song he'd written about losing his mother called 'Strangest Thing.' Jane didn't have Jesse's proficiency with the guitar, but even hearing him sing over the chords, she knew the song was special.

'Oh, I know shadow follows light,
I know clouds are only water in the sky,
I know everybody has to say goodbye,
I just didn't know this was your time.'

The first time he sang it, Jane felt as though she was watching him receive a transmission. They were not alike in this way. For Jane, songwriting was a practice of control, a methodical process in which she fashioned scraps of feeling and melody into a shape of her choosing. For Jesse, it was a process of surrender; he seemed to channel from another realm, compositions flowing through him whole-cloth. It was like what had happened to Jane when she wrote the music and lyrics for 'Spark,' only Jesse could open and close the frequency voluntarily.

Unfortunately, the songs that came through didn't always jibe with his directives from Pegasus. 'They'd be happy with ten more exactly like "Sweet and Mellow,"' he told Jane.

Whereas 'Strangest Thing' still had a pop feel, its twin, 'Chapel on a Hill,' sounded more like a canticle. The song was earnest, eerie, and beautiful – not at all in line with Jesse's disaffected image. He had resigned himself to discarding it, but Jane refused to let him.

'Who cares what the label says?' she said. 'It's your album. If it's good, people will buy it.'

'Just wait, Jane,' he said. 'It'll be the same for you when "Spring Fling" hits.'

'What do you mean?' said Jane.

He gave her a wry smile. 'Once you do something that works, they're going to have you keep doing it until it stops working.'

'That song is ridiculous,' said Jane.

Jesse laughed.

'Seriously, I wanted "Indigo." I'm only singing "Spring Fling" because Willy leaned on us to write something catchy.'

'You know that most artists would kill to be able to write a catchy tune, right?' he said, amused.

'That song's not me at all.'

'No,' said Jesse. 'But it's what you look like – and that's what sells albums. Willy knows what he's doing.'

Jane grimaced. 'Are you saying you'd be satisfied just to keep doing versions of the same song over and over for your whole career? Just to satisfy some arbitrary image?'

Jesse's stare hardened. 'All of it is arbitrary,' he said. 'Failure. Success. Who lives. Who dies . . . There's no rhyme or reason to any of it, Jane. So, yeah, I'll play my part in this absurd spectacle, and hopefully I'll make enough to cash in before they kick me to the curb.'

Jane gaped at him. 'Your songs matter to people,' she said. 'Like, really matter. When you didn't show up to the Fest, they were lost. That's what I want – to make music that matters. I'm fine doing crap like "Spring Fling" to get my name out there, but, ultimately, I'm going to decide what I sing and when.'

'We'll see what Pegasus has to say about that,' said Jesse.

'They're just making the recording,' said Jane. 'Why should they have any say at all?' Jesse gave her a knowing look that inflamed her.

'Just making an album doesn't guarantee it will be a success,' he said. 'For every one you hear about, there are dozens you don't. The label determines who gets what – marketing, publicity, tours. Trust me when I say it's in your best interest to keep them on your side.'

'I don't need any of that,' said Jane. 'People will come to the record.'

'They won't if they've never heard of it,' said Jesse.

'They'll hear of it,' said Jane.

'How?' said Jesse.

'You've never seen me in front of a crowd,' said Jane.

Jesse's eyes softened.

'"Spring Fling" is a perfectly respectable song,' he said after a moment. 'For what it's worth, I actually think "Indigo" could come up a level with a fiddle part on the bridge. The studio might be able to hook you up with someone.'

Jane regarded him. 'I can play the fiddle,' she said. 'What did you have in mind?'

As September drew to a close, Jane's anticipation about recording began to keep her up at night. She'd lie awake trying to insert herself inside scenes of the New York she'd seen in television shows and films: eating a croissant outside a department store, or hailing a Yellow Cab. The last week in September, Jane received a call from Willy's New York assistant, Linda.

'You'll be staying at the Plaza – will four rooms suffice?' Linda had said, gum smacking into the receiver. Jane wondered if bands ever demanded more rooms than they had members – probably. The plan was to record for three weeks, after which their producer would mix the tracks into a finished album.

Jane and Jesse had begun working on the sixth song for his record, a tune called 'Morning Star.' They'd tackled the music first, Jesse standing behind Jane as she played chords on his guitar. Jane felt as though she was in a race against her own resistance. She tried to tell herself that their friendship could be enough, but as her departure date drew near, it became easier to admit that having him stand so close to her for hours was torture.

Jesse was fussier about her annotations on this composition than he had been about the rest – ever polite, but insistent that she correct errors he previously would have ignored. It wasn't until her third time rewriting the chorus that it occurred to Jane that she hadn't heard the actual song.

'Maybe it would be helpful if you sang it for me?' she suggested.

Jesse's cheeks flushed, his eyes scanning her face. Jane suddenly found it hard to breathe. He shrugged his assent, and she struck up the opening chords.

> *'Morning Star, and your guitar,*
> *Wherever you are, near or far,*
> *I think of you.'*

As he sang, Jane had a sense of the floor dissolving where she stood. This song was about her.

> *'Morning Star, when clouds roll by,*
> *Through my blue sky, I close my eyes,*
> *I think of you.'*

Jane was no longer aware of what her hands were doing, but somehow they kept playing. The song filled the room like water, suspending them, weightless, as they watched each other. Jane knew the moment the music ended, gravity would return. But the notes lingered, and Jesse was still looking at her even after he stopped singing.

'Jesse,' whispered Jane. 'That was beautiful.' He took a step toward her.

The phone began to ring. Grace answered it in the kitchen.

'Jesse, it's your father,' she called a moment later.

'Of course it is,' said Jesse. Jane came crashing down.

On Jane's last night before New York, Jesse came to Gray Gables for dinner. Maggie and Greg had gone out, leaving everyone else in charge of Bea. They ate with Grace and Elsie, though neither Jesse nor Jane had much appetite. After they cleaned up, Elsie prepared to go down to the cellar.

'Jane, do you mind taking the baby?' she said.

'I can take her,' said Grace.

'No, Grace,' said Elsie. 'I need a hand with the laundry.'

Grace held Elsie's gaze as Jesse and Jane took the baby onto the porch. They sat together, watching the stars come out.

'You ready?' Jesse asked.

'I think so,' said Jane. She couldn't wait to see New York, to make their album. She also couldn't believe she wouldn't see him tomorrow. 'Any last words of wisdom?'

Jesse laughed. 'Woman, you don't need my advice,' he said. 'You know your own head.'

Jane smiled.

'It'll be quiet around here,' he said. He stretched his good arm. 'By the time you get back, this cast will be off,' he added casually.

Bea began to squawk.

'End of an era,' said Jane. She got to her feet, rocking Bea gently in her arms.

Jesse roused himself and stood beside her, leaning his good arm on one of the porch columns. 'You know,' he said, his voice low, 'there's a lot I'm looking forward to when this cast comes off.'

Jane searched his face. 'Like what?' she asked.

He swallowed. 'Well, playing the guitar, for one thing.'

'Wait, you play guitar?' said Jane, feeling herself pull toward him.

He smiled. 'I do. And I'd like to go for a swim,' he said.

Jane nodded. She felt Bea drifting off against her shoulder.

'I'd like to . . .' He stood a little closer to her, and she could see his eyes gleaming in the moonlight. There was such beauty in his face, Jane couldn't help but love to look at him.

His pupils turned to pinpricks as headlights swept the driveway. Jesse stood back, blinking. Jane forced a smile.

'Hey, kids,' said Greg, getting out of the driver's seat. 'Is that my little lion? ROAR!' He bounded up to the porch and scooped Bea out of Jane's arms. Her hands fell to her sides; without the warmth of the baby, she felt a chill in the air.

'Jesse,' said Maggie, 'glad you were here to keep an eye on Jane.'

'My pleasure,' said Jesse. Jane felt her cheeks grow hot as Bea awoke with a sob.

'You're okay,' said Maggie, taking Bea and heading into the house.

Jesse cleared his throat. 'What'd you think, should we get going?' It was usual for Jane to drive him home, but Jane knew with sudden clarity that if she took him home tonight she would do something she couldn't take back. She couldn't risk it; she needed to focus on New York.

'I . . . think I've had too much to drink,' said Jane. Jesse looked at his feet.

'I can give you a lift,' said Greg. His tone was nonchalant, but the way he placed his hands on his hips was almost paternal. 'I need to drop something off at the rez anyway.' He gave Jesse a pat on the arm and headed back to his car. Jane felt frozen. Jesse shifted in place.

'I guess this is it,' he said. He looked at Jane and she felt her breath catch in her chest. She felt physically sore as he ran his good hand through his hair. 'You're gonna knock 'em dead.'

'Thanks,' said Jane, soaking in the color of his stare. He smiled at her shyly, then turned and walked to Greg's car.

10

Simon Spector walked out of the elevator into the glass-and-marble entryway of Pegasus Records. He nodded to the two headset-crowned receptionists and rounded past carrels of cubicles into an industrial hallway, carpeted from floor to ceiling. Using his master key, he let himself into Studio A and switched on the lights in the control room. As he set up for the session, his slight frame and dark hair reflected back at him from the window that looked into the studio.

Simon was curious to meet the Breakers. He'd listened to their demos and had been surprised to learn that the lead singer was a woman. He'd worked on over a hundred albums for Vincent Ray – including seven Grammy nominees and three winners – and not a single one of them had featured a female lead. Simon had a hunch that the only reason Vincent Ray was producing this one was because the A&R man was the youngest son of music titan Jack Lambert – owner of the massively successful Golden Fleece Media Conglomerate.

The band arrived at 9:30 a.m. Willy Lambert waved to Simon as he entered the studio, ushering the band in behind him. Simon adjusted his round glasses as the Breakers looked over the amps and chairs, music stands, and textile-covered surfaces. He stepped from the control booth into the main room.

'Simon Spector – sound engineer,' he said, shaking hands with all of them. Jane Quinn wore a paisley dress, her yellow hair loose down to her waist. She was objectively beautiful, although not Simon's type (his type was more the shy boy playing guitar). Perhaps that was why Simon was most struck by Jane's seriousness. As her bandmates set up their instruments, Jane listened, alert.

'What is it?' said Willy.

'Do you hear that?' she said. She hummed the tone, a B flat.

'It's the overhead lights,' said Simon, who recognized the note because he could hear it, too. He was known for his sensitive ears, but he couldn't recall another artist ever mentioning it.

'Will that be in the recording?' Jane asked. Simon shook his head.

'I've got some lamps in the back,' said Simon. 'We can swap them in before we start.' Jane gave him an appreciative smile.

As far as the band was concerned, today's goal was to adjust the sound levels in preparation for taking down basic tracks. In actuality, today was one last chance for Simon, Willy, and Vincent Ray to assess the band. Vincent Ray never came to work before 11:00 a.m., so the Breakers had a little time to warm up.

Simon cued them from the booth, and they began to play: 'Dirty Bastard,' then 'No More Demands,' then 'Don't Fret,' then 'Spring Fling.'

The two brothers were mismatched: Kyle, the bassist, hid incredible talent behind a playful demeanor, probably afraid of outshining the drummer, Greg, who seemed to have two settings: on and off. Simon noted that this would be a focal point in the mixing. Rich, the cute guitarist, was also a good guitarist.

So, for that matter, was Jane Quinn, though it was her voice that was truly remarkable. She had the versatility of Linda Ronstadt, but her tone was entirely her own. Hearing her sing was thrilling; Simon had rarely worked with a vocalist capable of such nuance. He could tell that every take would be an experiment.

As the band tuned for 'Sweet Maiden Mine,' the door to the studio opened, and Vincent Ray's silhouette darkened the frame. He reached over and flipped on the overhead lights. The Breakers shrank back and squinted. Vincent Ray walked forward, teeth bared, a gray wolf in slim-cut trappings and a crew cut.

'Here he is,' said Willy. He was a little too familiar as he greeted Vincent Ray. Simon had the sense that Willy thought he had proved himself because of Jesse Reid, while everyone else still saw him as ancillary to his father.

'Breakers, it gives me great pleasure to introduce you to your producer, Vincent Ray.' Vincent Ray surveyed them through watery eyes.

Jane stepped forward. 'Nice to meet you. I'm Jane Quinn,' she said, offering him her hand. Vincent Ray seemed confused. He took her hand and shook it limply, looking past her to Kyle, who followed tentatively.

'Hi, I'm Kyle.'

Vincent Ray pumped Kyle's arm a few times, smirking from him, to Rich, to Greg.

'Finally – the Breakers,' he said in a quiet, scratchy voice. 'You guys have a great thing going. Excited to see you in action.'

Simon realized then that Vincent Ray must not have listened to the demo tapes Willy had circulated. He didn't know Jane was the lead singer. He probably thought she was a groupie.

'We were able to steal him away from Bulletin for a couple weeks,' Willy said. Kyle and Greg made noises of appreciation. Jane stared blankly at Willy.

'Aren't they based in London?' asked Rich.

'I'll be going back and forth – call me the *QE2*,' said Vincent Ray. Kyle laughed politely. Vincent Ray glanced at Willy for the first time.

'All right,' he said. 'Pretend like I'm not here.' He and Willy joined Simon in the booth.

'Simon, how're the best ears in the business?' said Vincent Ray.

Simon gave him a nod. He and Vincent Ray got along because Vincent Ray knew nothing about him.

'Simon's been killing it,' said Willy.

'How are they?' asked Vincent Ray, ignoring Willy.

'Good, pretty tight,' said Simon. He and Willy were both in their early thirties, both Jews. But Willy was from Bel Air and Simon was from Lithuania; one was there because of his family and the other because of his talent. Simon would never take a Caribbean cruise with Vincent Ray, something Willy had already done twice as part of his father's entourage. However, Simon had what Willy seemed to crave: Vincent Ray's respect.

'What's next, "Spring Fling"?' said Willy, lightly. He also seemed to have grasped that this would be Vincent Ray's introduction to the Breakers and was having them replay their single.

Simon pressed the com mic. 'Tune for "Spring Fling,"' he said.

Jane's eyebrows flicked up, but she and Rich began to retune without comment. Simon turned off the com. Jane walked over to switch off the overhead lights.

'What is she doing?' said Vincent Ray.

'New technique,' said Simon, cuing up the tape. 'It's big in L.A.'

Vincent Ray looked at Willy. 'Didn't realize this was a girl band,' he said.

'It's a . . . hybrid,' said Willy. 'Jane and Rich write the songs together.'

Vincent Ray frowned. 'Something about this feels off,' he said. 'Is that the only singer?'

'Jane's got it,' said Willy. 'Trust me, this will be just like it was with Jesse. As a matter of fact, they're friends – Jesse himself thinks she's fantastic.'

'Oh, well, then,' said Vincent Ray.

Over the years, Simon had pieced together that Vincent Ray had been raised on a series of army bases by a father who knew nothing but authority and discipline. His origins in music remained something of a mystery; the most credible-sounding rumor Simon had heard was that, after his own stint in the service, Vincent Ray had reinvented himself as a prizefighter, then used his winnings to buy into the record business. Musicians had liked him because he seemed street-smart, and he'd risen quickly at the labels because he was. In his twenty-year career, he had cultivated a cutthroat reputation.

Simon hit the com mic and cued the Breakers in. The band was warm from the morning and laid down a decent take; Simon found himself rooting for them as Jane belted out the last verse.

Vincent Ray said nothing when 'Spring Fling' finished, but he must have thought it was worthwhile, because he stayed. He sat stone-faced through the rest of the session. The Breakers played the remainder of their songs, and Simon took the levels. Willy pretended to watch Simon while really watching Vincent Ray.

When the Breakers finished the last song, Vincent Ray cleared his throat. 'Is that all?' he said.

'That's the list,' said Willy. 'What'd you think?'

'Cute,' said Vincent Ray. 'Maybe a slightly sexier wardrobe.'

'I meant about the music,' said Willy.

Vincent Ray shrugged. 'The music is fine, but the lyrics sound like a girl wrote them,' he said. He stepped out of the booth. Simon and Willy exchanged a quick glance before Willy walked out after him.

'So . . . I'm thinking we'll start with "Indigo,"' Vincent Ray said to the band. 'Tomorrow.'

'But it's only three,' said Jane.

Vincent Ray ignored her. 'I'll see you then,' he said, without looking at Jane. He left.

'Great first day,' said Willy, clapping loudly. 'Really.' Jane looked at Rich. He shook his head.

The next day, the Breakers arrived around 9:30 a.m. to lay down the basic tracks for 'Indigo.' Simon had them record as a group, but his attention was on Greg. Percussion set the foundation for any track; nailing the drum part was paramount, as it would be virtually impossible to adjust later on. Simon took the Breakers through the song a dozen times with limited improvement from Greg; still, the band had incredible chemistry, and Simon was impressed by their concentration and focus.

When they broke for lunch, Vincent Ray had yet to make an appearance. Simon was the only person left in the studio when Luke Gaffney showed up with his tenor saxophone.

'Hey, Simon,' Luke called into the booth. Simon looked up in surprise.

'Hey, Luke,' he said. 'I think you have the wrong room – the Adelaides are down the hall, in F.'

'I'm here for the Breakers?' said Luke.

'Luke G,' said Vincent Ray, entering the studio. Willy trailed behind him, his face ashen. 'So glad you could make it.'

Luke unpacked his instrument and was warming up in the studio when the Breakers returned from lunch. Jane Quinn took one look at him and walked into the control room.

'What's going on?' she asked. 'Who is this guy?'

'*This guy*,' said Vincent Ray, 'is Luke Gaffney. I brought him in to try to save the bridge.'

'Thanks,' said Jane. 'But I actually play fiddle during the bridge on this one.'

Vincent Ray looked at her through bored, watery eyes. 'Not anymore,' he said.

Jane didn't budge. 'Why?' she asked.

A vein began to throb in Vincent Ray's temple. 'Because I said so,' he said.

Jane was about to respond when Willy cut her off. 'We don't need to decide right now,' he said. 'Why don't Jane and Luke each lay down a version, and we can listen and make the decision later?'

'Fine,' said Jane. 'I'll go first.' She left the box.

'Don't even bother recording this,' said Vincent Ray.

'I'd better,' said Simon. 'Just in case.'

If Simon hadn't already been impressed with Jane Quinn, this would have won him over – in terms of both musicianship and stamina. She took her time preparing the fiddle, even as they all stared at her. She walked over to Rich's guitar and plucked the A string to tune. She lifted the violin to her shoulder and held it there with her chin as she tightened the bow. When she was ready, and only when, she placed the headphones over her ears and nodded to Simon in the booth. She played exquisitely, like a nightingale singing on the wind. When she finished, a mist of rosin dust rose from the violin's bridge. Simon hit the com box.

'Got it,' he said.

Luke Gaffney played his version next. He was as clean and professional as ever, but his instrument wasn't right for the song; it sounded too jazzy, too legato. Luke did three takes and then waved to the control room on his way out. Vincent Ray roused himself.

'Let's get this over with,' he said. He and Willy walked into the studio and turned up the lights.

'Well, this was interesting,' said Vincent Ray. 'I'll see what I can do with the mix when I'm back from London.'

'You're going to London?' said Greg.

'Bulletin needs me.'

'What about us?' said Jane.

'What about you?' said Vincent Ray.

Jane said nothing.

'I'll be back in two weeks,' he continued.

'Two weeks,' said Rich. 'That's almost all of our time.'

Vincent Ray shrugged. 'Can't be helped,' he said. He turned to Willy and shook his hand. 'Tell Jack I say hello.'

87

'Tell Freddy the same,' said Willy almost inaudibly as Vincent Ray cut out the door. They all stood in silence for a moment; then Jane turned to Willy.

'This is not okay,' she said.

'I know,' said Willy.

'You said we would have complete artistic control, and you just let him walk all over us,' she said. 'This is our chance to make something of ourselves, and he's just pissing it away.'

Willy shook his head. 'I don't know what's happening,' he said. 'I've never seen him act like this.'

'I'll tell you what's happening,' said Rich, his voice shaking with anger. 'Jane's a girl, so he's treating us like we're a joke.'

Willy blanched, but Jane nodded. 'Yes,' she said. 'That is exactly it.'

Simon could tell Willy's disbelief was genuine. Willy had never gone into a room like this one and been treated with anything other than automatic deference. His psyche seemed to reject the idea that he had just been dismissed by one of the biggest producers in the business. Simon watched Willy's own narrative start to overwrite what he had just experienced.

'Let's get a drink,' said Willy. 'I'm going to figure this out. I promise.' They waved to Simon as they walked out of the studio, leaving Simon to log the recordings.

A couple hours later, Simon rode the elevator down to the lobby and stepped out onto Forty-second Street. Blue and pink streaked the sky between the buildings as he made his way toward the Astoria-bound Yellow Line. Simon loved sunsets. Maybe he would move to L.A.

The next morning, Jane and Willy were waiting for him in the control room when he arrived.

'Simon,' said Jane, 'what would you say if we tried to get the album done . . . before he gets back?'

Simon raised his eyebrows. 'Recorded and mixed?' he said.

Jane nodded.

Simon considered. It would be a tight turnaround, but the Breakers had been rehearsing all summer, and the takes were relatively clean. Technically speaking, it was doable.

'Sure,' he said.

Jane grinned. 'Thank you,' she said. She walked back into the studio and began to unpack her guitar. Willy stood looking out at the studio, self-assured, noble.

'Are you sure about this?' said Simon. 'Vincent Ray is not going to be happy.'

Willy shrugged. The possibility that he could overstep didn't seem to exist in his mind. He'd pushed to get Jesse Reid through even though folk was dead, and now didn't think it was possible to push too far.

'It's rock and roll,' he said, adjusting his aviators.

Simon wondered if he had any idea what he was in for when Vincent Ray returned and was suddenly reminded that Prometheus had once been a Titan.

11

Alex Redding only took these conveyor-belt jobs to fund his art. Pegasus called him whenever they were getting ready to release a new catalogue, and he would set up backdrops and lighting equipment in one of their conference rooms, board table and chairs stacked to the side. The artists would file through one after another, and he would photograph them like kids at the start of a school year.

These were the records with low production budgets; the big releases had the money for outdoor shoots, elaborate sets, original art. Not these albums. These albums would go to market bearing images of their creators' faces in tight-angle shots; most would sell fewer than five hundred copies. The photographs might not be iconic, but for one day like this, Alex could pocket upward of ten thousand dollars. That would be enough to fund his forthcoming show of black-and-white candids.

Alex had already shot a singer-songwriter duo and an R&B group by the time the Breakers came in to pose. He was actually curious about this one – there was a rumor going around that when Vincent Ray had blown them off for Bulletin, they had gone ahead and produced their entire album without him.

That was only a part of the rumor. The other part was that they were actually good.

Alex watched the band trip into the conference room; they were like puppies, partway between being children and adults. The girl, Jane, stood out immediately; she drew light toward her, dimming her surroundings.

Alex was used to being around models and wasn't often fazed by beautiful women. He wasn't particularly handsome, but he had two main things going for him: he was just shy of six foot five, and he had very blue eyes. That was really all it took, he'd found. There was something about Jane, though, that leveled him.

'Hi there,' he said, startled. Jane looked up at him and smiled, almost as if they knew each other. Willy Lambert came in behind the band and shut the door, the large windows along the conference-room wall making grids in his green aviators.

'Alex, great to see you, man,' he said, shaking Alex's hand. Willy was a real artists' advocate, from what Alex could tell; they'd met the year before, shooting the cover for Jesse Reid's debut, and Alex had rarely seen such an attentive label rep.

'Meet the Breakers,' Willy said. 'Jane, Greg, Kyle, Rich.'

'Hi again,' said Alex. They wore an array of flannel and corduroy except for Jane, who was in a blue peasant dress, hair in two long yellow braids. They stood in a row, fidgeting, like eggs about to hatch; Alex could tell they'd never been professionally photographed before. He smiled.

'This'll be a piece of cake,' he said.

He put *Beggars Banquet* by the Stones on the turntable and turned up the volume until the opening rhythm of 'Sympathy for the Devil' bounced off the tall windows. As Alex began to adjust the lighting equipment, he heard Jane Quinn harmonizing with Mick Jagger under her breath. Alex felt a chill; she definitely had the careless talent of a rock star.

Alex began to position the band – the two brothers, Kyle and Greg, had darker skin and jet-black hair, and needed to be closer to the light source for their features to render properly in the photo. He tried Jane in the middle, and then switched her with sandy-haired Rich.

None of the backdrops felt right. The band looked so homespun, they made the backgrounds – tropical sunset, winter tundra, urban streetscape – appear even more artificial than usual. Alex posed them against pure black and pure white next, which was an improvement, but only just.

'What do you think?' said Willy, standing next to Alex as he hunched over his tripod, adjusting the focal length on his lens. Jane took a step forward.

'Could we try some over there?' she asked, nodding to the dismembered conference table and chairs in the corner. The light in the frame would be almost perfect – Alex would only need to bring over a reflector to take care of the shadows.

'Someone might have already tried it,' said Jane. 'But if not, I think it would be funny for a bunch of hippies to be hanging around all this corporate furniture.' She let out a little tinkle of laughter, and Alex died. He glanced at Willy, who shrugged approvingly.

'Why not,' said Alex. 'I've never shot that.'

Kyle and Rich helped him bring over his tripod and the reflector screen, and the band set to work arranging the furniture into a pyramid. By the time they finished, Jane's hair was full of static.

'Jane, your hair looks nuts,' said Rich. Kyle laughed.

'Here,' said Kyle, reaching over to fix it.

'No, no, no,' said Rich. The two of them began to tuck Jane's hair back into her braids, Greg looking on in concentration. Jane folded her arms.

'Jane,' said Alex. She looked up as the camera snapped.

'Let it out,' said Alex. Jane took out her hair, and the group began to climb all over the furniture as if it were a jungle gym. As they got into a pose reminiscent of *Washington Crossing the Delaware*, the conference-room door flew open, and in walked Vincent Ray.

The faces in front of Alex's lens went blank. Both Kyle and Greg seemed to be fighting the urge to hide under the tables. Rich looked at Jane; her eyes narrowed. Their reaction was nothing to Vincent Ray's; when he saw them mounted on the furniture, his shoulders began to shake. Willy stepped between them, a fox trying to outwit a predator.

'Vincent Ray,' he said. His tone was light, as though he were greeting an old friend and the two of them were in on a joke together. Vincent Ray's expression was lethal. He ignored Willy and spoke directly to Jane.

'You must think you're hot shit,' he said. 'What, ordinary photo shoot not good enough for you?' He nodded to the abandoned backdrops hanging lifeless from the ceiling.

'Relax, man,' said Willy. 'We did the regular portraits, we just had some extra time.'

'This shoot is finished,' said Vincent Ray. 'This album is finished, *man*.'

'What do you mean?' said Jane.

'Alex, pack it in,' said Vincent Ray. Alex nodded, pretending

93

to break down his lenses, while keeping everything intact. Something interesting was happening inside the frame. The boys had begun to creep toward Jane, who stood firm in the center, unyielding. Alex snapped a photo.

'I said shut it down,' said Vincent Ray.

'You don't have the power to cancel our album,' said Jane. 'Our contract's with Pegasus, same as yours.'

'Do you think the board will be impressed by your use of studio resources . . . mixing your album without your producer . . .?' Vincent Ray stepped forward. Just another four feet and his shoulder would be in the shot.

'You fucked off to London and left us alone – do you think that will impress them?' said Jane.

'Someone needs to teach you a lesson,' said Vincent Ray. He took another step forward. Alex tightened his angle. 'You have no idea who you're dealing with. You've ended your career before it's even begun.'

'Now, hang on a second,' said Willy, still trying to affect a note of camaraderie. 'Surely this is just water under the bridge. We're all in this to make a good record. Isn't that what this is about? Breaking boundaries, subverting expectations—'

Vincent Ray rounded on him, teeth bared. 'Having tits doesn't count as subverting expectations, even if Jesse Reid likes them,' he said.

Jane went rigid.

'That is completely uncalled for,' said Willy. 'You need to—'

'I hope for you that Jesse Reid turns out to be as big as people think,' Vincent Ray said. 'Because this is a small industry, and if he's not . . . I'm not even sure your father can save you from this bullshit. And don't think he doesn't know about this.'

Willy reached up to remove his glasses, hands shaking; the glasses fell to the carpet soundlessly. As Willy bent to retrieve them, Vincent Ray raised his foot; Alex heard the lenses crunch.

Jane planted her hands on her hips and stepped forward.

'Jane,' Willy cautioned.

'Get out,' said Jane.

Vincent Ray loomed over her, his shoulder now clearly in Alex's frame, blocking Willy from view. Jane stood in the center, radiating heat, the boys behind her, half protective, half terrified. Not Jane, though. Her eyes were set.

'What did you just say?' said Vincent Ray. He was so irate he could no longer hear the shutter clicking.

'I said get out,' said Jane.

Vincent Ray looked like a contender on the ropes, and for a moment Alex thought he was going to have to step between them. He drew up to his full height. Then Vincent Ray let out a cold laugh.

'You are so fucked,' he said. 'All of you.' He stalked out of the room.

Willy straightened up. 'I'm so sorry,' he said. 'Jane, I—'

His eyes were on the green lens shards now embedded in the carpet. He looked as though the air had been cut from him. He began to drift toward the door after Vincent Ray, like a spent tire rolling down the highway.

'I should get someone to clean that up,' he said, eyes unfocused. 'I should . . . Excuse me a moment.'

He walked swiftly from the room. Jane looked after him, her features in shadow. Kyle, Rich, and Greg sighed and shook their bodies, trying to dispel the tension.

'I thought he was going to murder you,' said Greg, patting Jane on the head.

'I thought Jane was going to murder him,' said Kyle.

'Hope this was your last shoot of the day,' said Rich, in Alex's direction.

Alex was already thinking about how he was going to process the negatives, what kind of filters he'd try, whether there was a way to make Jane's gray eyes show as they had a moment ago, searing and intelligent. This wasn't just going to be a cover, this was a real moment captured on film; this was art.

12

Jane sat on her bed, scraps of paper scattered around her like dried flower petals. They all said some version of the same thing: 'Jesse called.'

Grace's stint as Jesse's full-time caregiver had ended while the Breakers were recording in New York; by the time they returned, Grace's shifts at the Shack had dwindled to biweekly physical-therapy sessions. After returning from one such appointment, Grace found her niece hanging laundry beneath the yellow sycamore in the front yard. She helped Jane unfold a damp sheet, catching her eye.

'Jesse mentioned that you're not returning his calls,' she said as they pinned the fabric to the clothesline. Jane's cheeks colored.

'Is everything all right?' said Grace.

'Everything's fine,' said Jane. 'I just . . . You were right. Better not to get attached.'

Grace studied her face for a moment, then nodded and let the conversation move on to Millie, her new charge, in Perry's Landing.

Jane had arrived home the last week in October chastened; she had thought she was prepared to take on the record industry and found herself utterly outmatched. She didn't regret how she had handled matters with Vincent Ray, exactly; she just wished she had foreseen the repercussions.

She had loved every part of the actual album-making process. The recording sessions had been some of the best hours of her life, and the days and nights she had spent mixing the tracks with Simon had been instructive and exhilarating. She doubted this knowledge would be needed again, though; Jane knew it was unlikely that she would ever get to make another album.

Willy had phoned a few days after their return to let her know that Vincent Ray had trashed *Spring Fling* to the label's executive board, after which Pegasus had reduced their initial print of the album to three hundred copies.

'This number could go up if, say, a popular DJ falls in love and decides to give it some play time,' said Willy.

'But odds of that are low,' said Jane.

'We knew there was some chance of backlash,' said Willy. 'But I've never seen anything like this. Vincent Ray has black-balled the album from most major print publications and the bulk of the countdown programs. We'll still be able to get some support, but it will have to be more grassroots. I'm sorry.'

Kyle, Greg, and Rich took the news in stride.

'Fuck 'em,' said Kyle. 'We made a damn good album, even if no one hears it.'

After that initial dispatch, the silences between Willy's calls began to stretch to days, and then weeks. Jane feared that the Breakers had been tainted to the point where even their most stalwart supporter could no longer afford to be associated with them. Vincent Ray was too powerful. And he had been right: Jane hadn't had any idea what she was doing.

She couldn't bear to face Jesse. It made her cringe to think back on how cocksure she had been; her remarks about how she wouldn't need the label now seemed like the death knell for her album. He had warned her, and she had been brazen and royally fucked her career.

Jesse had once referred to Vincent Ray as a 'visionary producer'; Jane knew better than to hope he'd take her side. And even if he did . . . Jesse was destined for global stardom, and Jane would always be tied to the Island. This was an exit ramp, and Jane had decided to take it.

It hadn't been easy. Jesse had called every day for several weeks after her return. Then, the third week in November, the calls stopped. The first night the phone didn't ring, Jane had stayed up late, staring at his messages. She liked to look at his name. Around midnight, Elsie knocked on her door. She saw the notes on the bed and sat beside Jane, picking one up and tracing the writing with her finger.

After a moment Jane spoke. 'I just think this is easier,' she said.

Elsie gave her a hard look. 'What in your young life made you think love is easy?' she said.

Jane took the note out of Elsie's hand and smoothed it out on her knee. 'Everything's getting tangled,' she said. 'Between the label, and Mom, and Jesse . . . it's starting to feel like a labyrinth.'

'And you're Theseus?'

Jane creased the note in her hands. 'I'm Daedalus,' she said.

Elsie looked at her sadly but said nothing further.

Jane insulated herself within her regular shifts at the Carousel, weekends at the Center, the occasional client at the salon. The faces she saw every day were the faces she had seen her whole life, and by all appearances, it was as though that summer had never happened.

But it had, and no matter how Jane tried to convince herself she was fine, part of her knew she wasn't. The album might have been something. Jesse might have been something. Was she so afraid of losing control that she'd sabotaged both? At night, she lay awake, imagining herself older, puttering around the Center. What would her mother say if she was here?

The Breakers' record went on sale the Friday after Thanksgiving. That morning, the band headed to Beach Tracks. When the Breakers walked in, both owners, Pat and Dana, rushed around from behind the counter, shouting, 'Happy Breakers Day!'

'You have to sign our copies!' said Pat. 'We've already sold three this morning!'

'How many of those were to Elsie?' asked Jane.

'Two!' said Pat, walking back around the counter and turning up 'Run' on the stereo. Jane grinned. It was thrilling to hear their song being played in their hometown music store.

Pat and Dana had propped up the album case at the register. Jane picked it up and held it in her hand. It was an incredible shot: Vincent Ray's blurred shoulder in the foreground, Jane fearsome in the center, the boys milling behind her. The album's title, *Spring Fling*, made it seem like she might be a rebellious student staring down a principal, though the juxtaposition of the blue dress and the pride in her bearing almost suggested a peasant uprising. Jane flipped the album; the reverse side showed Rich and Kyle concentrating on her hair as Greg supervised. It lightened the overall feel, mocking the intensity of the front in good spirit.

'Iconic,' said Dana.

'I want to see it in the stacks,' said Greg, combing through the Rock section for 'The Breakers.'

'There's a lot of love for this one already!' said Dana when Greg lifted out the copy behind their name tab. 'Don't worry, I've got more in the back.'

Jane smiled. She wondered what percent of the three hundred would go to this store. Probably most of them.

That night, the Carousel was packed to the gills with familiar faces in support of the Breakers. Jane felt happy and calm. The album was out, they'd have a party, and then everything would just go on as it always had. She tried not to let this burn her up inside.

'Give it up for our very own Janie Q and the Breakers,' said Al.

As they walked onstage, the house exploded. Jane wore jeans and a white tank top, hair spilling around her shoulders, wrists covered in bangles. She looked out at the crowd and saw Maggie and Elsie standing in the front. Grace had stayed home with Bea. Jane kicked off her shoes.

'Seems only right,' she said into the mic. 'We are home, after all.'

Most of the room was already standing, but after 'Dirty Bastard,' the crowd was on their feet. Jane could even make out Mark Edison nodding along beside the bar.

They played 'No More Demands,' and then 'Don't Fret,' and then 'Indigo.' As the night went on, Jane was reminded of why she loved to make music – not to sell records, but to connect with people. Their songs were so well rehearsed from preparing to record that Jane found herself floating above the room as she played; she looked down halfway through 'Caught' and wondered how she'd gotten there. She felt weightless and free; it was as if she'd been storing up her every emotion, and this performance was her release.

'Run' had a different feel tonight; as she watched Maggie swaying in the crowd, twinkling up at Greg, it struck Jane that over time Rich's words had come to resemble her more than Maggie.

> *'Oh, living in your bubble,*
> *You think that I am fine,*
> *But darling I am trouble,*
> *My code's hard to define,*
> *And I am never going*
> *To put it all on the line,*
> *For you or anyone . . . so,*
> *Run. Run.'*

Jane thought of Jesse, and her voice soared over the guitar, as tender and uncertain as she'd allowed herself to feel since coming back from New York. It was the Breakers' second-to-last number, slow and soulful, and when they finished, Jane found she had tears in her eyes. She laughed as the crowd applauded. Rich cleared his throat, turning inward to tune.

'Jesse's here,' he said quietly.

'What?' said Jane.

Rich nodded toward the back of the room. As the crowd undulated, Jane caught a glimpse of blue. Her stomach contracted, and her body registered Jesse's presence, semi-hidden behind a pillar. She felt as though she'd just been talking about someone standing right behind her. Rich adjusted his capo for 'Spring Fling,' and Jane followed suit.

'You've been a great crowd. This is our last song,' said Jane. As she spoke, the audience oscillated, and her eyes met Jesse's. Her heart skipped a beat and she said, 'It's about having a crush.'

She counted them in, and the call-and-response intro between Kyle and Rich reverberated off the walls. Jane watched Maggie dancing as she sang the first verse; her pretty cousin, who so rarely looked pleased with anything, looked so happy right now. She and Elsie swung together, and the crowd rejoiced around them. As the room swirled, Jane looked into Jesse's eyes and sang,

> *'You make me feel groovy,*
> *Light it up and go,*
> *Light me up and go.'*

Then she looked at the boys, and the four of them ended on a chord.

The din of the room was the best noise Jane had ever heard, and she once again felt herself on the verge of tears.

'Everyone grab a drink!' Al shouted from the bar. Kyle, Rich, and Greg hopped down off the platform, Greg embracing Maggie, Kyle and Rich heading straight for the keg.

Jane placed her guitar on the stage and looked out at Elsie, who winked at her, then went to join the revelers. Jane stepped into the room. All around, hands reached for her; she didn't register what she was saying or to whom, she just had to get to Jesse.

By the time she made it to the back of the bar, he had gone. Jane spun around, her stomach sinking. Had he left? She glanced over at the stairs leading outside. Without thinking, she slipped into the night.

Outside, the moon was high. Jane felt the sweat on her chest and arms prickle in the cold. She stepped onto Main Street and looked around – the town seemed abandoned. Then she saw the red eye of a cigarette glinting beside the hotel railing. Jesse stood before her, a flannel jacket hanging open around his shirt. Without his cast and sling, he looked broad to Jane, repaired.

'Nice show,' he said. Jane took a step toward him. His physicality matched the one etched in her memory – the way he stood, the way he looked at her.

'You came,' she said. Those blue eyes surveyed her, unreadable.

'I did,' he said. 'Grace invited me.'

Jane looked up. 'Grace did?'

Jesse nodded.

'Arm's looking better,' said Jane.

He opened and closed his hand reflexively to show her. 'Good as new,' he said, smiling. As their eyes met, his expression became inscrutable again. Jane didn't know what to say, so she nodded to his cigarette. He considered for a moment, then stuck the cigarette in his mouth, handing her his jacket instead. Jane tried to ignore how good it smelled. Her ears were still ringing from the show.

'How's your album coming along?' she asked.

'It's coming,' he said. 'I head out to L.A. to record in a week or so.' He took a drag on the cigarette. 'They've already started booking a twenty-five-city tour – starting in March.'

Jane looked down to hide her envy. She had left her shoes onstage, and her feet looked blue next to his work boots on the sidewalk.

'Willy told me about what happened with Vincent Ray,' he said. Jane kept her eyes low. After a moment he continued. 'It sounds like you called the shots, as you said you would.' Was that amusement she detected?

'And now my career is over,' said Jane.

'You don't know that,' said Jesse.

Jane laughed.

'You don't,' he said. 'I love what you made. I bought the record this morning and have been listening to it all day – hell, I'll pay you to mix mine.'

Jane smiled a little. 'That's . . . nice to hear,' she said.

Jesse seemed heartened by this. 'I think you guys should open for us,' he continued. 'Our sounds are different enough, and you're amazing with a crowd. I'm sure Willy will say yes if I ask him.'

Jane gaped, torn between awe at his offer and jealousy at his confidence. 'Jesse,' she said, 'it wouldn't be fair, we didn't earn it—'

'Like hell you didn't. You didn't earn this bullshit from Vincent Ray. . . . I still can't believe what he said to you.' Jesse was angry. 'Let me make this right.'

'We'd be in your debt,' said Jane. 'How would I ever make it up to you?'

Jesse swallowed. 'Honestly, I'm just sick of being without you.' He took one last drag, then flicked his cigarette to the curb. The orange speck flared on the ground and went out. His face clouded. 'You disappeared,' he said.

Jane's mouth went dry. 'I'm sorry,' she said, steeling herself. 'I should have called. But, in the end, it's the same. I can only take this so far. After what happened with my mom, I'm . . . limited. No matter how bad I might want you, there are certain things I just can't risk.'

Jesse's hand found hers in the dark. His touch sent a shock up her arm. He took a step toward her.

'I know you're scared,' he said. 'I'm scared, too. But I'm trying to tell you I physically cannot bear to be apart from you.' Jane bit her lip. Jesse took another step closer. His voice was low and urgent when he spoke. 'Did you just say you want me?'

'God, yes,' said Jane. The words were out of her mouth before she could stop them.

As champagne popped and the jukebox switched on downstairs, Jesse pulled her close. His hands found her hips and then her cheeks, tilting her head toward his. Jane felt a swell of anticipation as his eyes searched her face, beautiful blue. A sigh escaped her as his nose brushed her cheek; Jesse whispered her name and brought their lips together, softly, then hungrily.

13

Pegasus Studios

Los Angeles
March 1970

'Are you sure this shirt doesn't make me look like a dad?' said Greg. Inspired by California, he'd purchased a Beach Boys-esque blue-and-white-striped tee to wear on the first day of their tour. He hadn't realized then that there would be a photo shoot.

'It's too late now,' said Kyle.

'You look good,' said Jane. 'For a dad.'

Greg winced. 'Rich?' he said.

Rich glanced at him. 'You look good,' he muttered.

'Can we get some quiet? Please and thank you,' said Archie Lennox, the publicity director for Pegasus Studios. The Breakers shuffled off to the side like they were in a time-out. Jane looked up to find Jesse's eyes on her and felt her cheeks grow warm.

'Jesse,' said Archie. 'Eyes over here.'

Jesse and his band were posed in front of the *Painted Lady* tour bus, a navy-blue coach covered in the orange, yellow, white, and green psychedelic art from the back of Jesse's album. Archie had presented the idea to them as 'just a few quick photos in the studio lot.' That had been almost two hours ago, and no one was happy.

Huck Levi, Jesse's drummer, had been late, so instead of Jesse's group getting priority, they had been forced to stand around and watch the Breakers awkwardly pose in front of the bus. The Breakers had been nervous and compensated by goofing around; this had done little to ingratiate them to Jesse's band, their new bus-mates. The longer the shoot continued, the more exposed Jane felt in front of arguably the best studio musicians in the world.

When Huck finally showed, Archie shooed the Breakers away from the bus and began to position Jesse's bandmates around him. Huck shook Jesse's hand and then attached himself to the side of the bus for support, still hungover at three in the afternoon. Jesse had bunked with Huck in Laurel Canyon during the sessions for *Painted Lady,* and it sounded like Huck's bedroom had a revolving door. This made sense when Jane saw him: she knew from Jesse that his father had been a grocer in Forest Hills and his mother had been a Thai beauty queen, and the combination had given Huck one of the best faces Jane had ever seen.

'You doing okay?' Jane heard Loretta Mays say to Jesse, who was deep in his own thoughts. Jesse nodded, and Loretta adjusted the sleeve of her striped cotton dress, tossing her brown curls over her shoulder. Jane was a bit starstruck by Loretta, who played the piano in Jesse's group and was an accomplished songwriter in her own right. She was only a few years older than Jesse, but her raspy voice and recent remarriage made her seem much more sophisticated to Jane. Jane and Loretta were the only two women on the tour, and Jane desperately wanted to be her friend.

'He's fine,' said Benny Vogelsang, jostling Jesse's arm. 'Look at that smile.' Jesse continued to brood.

Benny was Jesse's Rich: his staunch ally and backup guitarist. They had met at preparatory school, and Benny had been the person who had insisted Jesse pursue music after getting out of McLean. He would often shadow Jesse on the melody, picking up exactly where he left off if Jesse needed to pause in order to sing.

'Duke, look alive,' said Archie, scowling over the photographer's shoulder.

Duke Maguire shuffled back into the frame, nodding courteously to Benny. Duke was a bit older, a studio bassist, and an industry professional with three hundred albums and several national tours under his belt. He kept to himself and didn't seem to want a close relationship with anyone else in the band. For him, this tour was strictly business.

These five – Loretta on keys, Jesse on vocals, Duke on bass, Benny on guitar, and Huck on drums – had been Jesse's chief collaborators on *Painted Lady,* his second studio album, which had gone on sale two weeks prior.

The album's first single – 'Strangest Thing,' backed by 'Morning Star' – was already climbing the charts. In anticipation of tour sales, Pegasus had pressed 150,000 copies. Thanks to Willy, Pegasus had also reissued five thousand copies of 'Spring Fling' as a single backed by 'Spark.' Jesse's sales were rising, and everyone on the tour felt they were on the verge of a hit.

'All right,' said Archie. 'Do we dare try a group shot?'

As the Breakers timidly stepped into the photo, the bus door winced open and out stepped Willy. He had a brand-new pair of yellow-lensed aviators and had regained most of his swagger. There was nothing like having a single careening toward the top ten to put the bounce back in an A&R man's step.

'Well, isn't this a picture,' he said, walking over to Archie.

For the sake of the photo, the two bands gathered and smiled as if they were actually friends. But once the picture had been taken, Jesse's group filed onto the bus without a word. Kyle, ever the most sociable member of the Breakers, was the only one who followed.

Jane and Rich hung back as Greg went to find a pay phone. His initial excitement about the tour had quickly given way to apprehension about abandoning Maggie and Bea. They'd all been paid a small sum upon the completion of their album; both Greg and Jane had left theirs with the Quinns, but it wasn't the same as being there. Greg hated the idea of being without his girls; leaving them behind made him feel uncomfortably like his own father.

In an uncharacteristically committal gesture, Maggie had promised to join the Breakers for the final, East Coast leg of the tour, but that wouldn't be until June. Until then, it would be pay phones.

Archie Lennox walked over to Rich and Jane, checking items off on a clipboard.

'Not our most efficient shoot, but it's done,' he said.

'What are these photos for?' asked Jane. Archie's smile did not reach his eyes.

'You know, the works,' he said, waving the question away with his pen. 'Don't you worry, we're gonna make you a star.'

Jane glanced at Rich.

'That's a good question,' said Rich. 'I've been wondering the same thing.'

Archie looked up from his clipboard. 'Promo and merch. We'll have posters and flyers with these images on them ready to go at all of your venues,' he said. 'For some of the bigger stadiums, we'll also have banners. And then these'll be on tee shirts, pins, and frameables for sale.'

Even as Archie answered her question, he directed the response to Rich. Jane began to edge back toward the bus. She had always felt like she was the one looking out for her band-mates, but she now found herself looking to them to set the tone in her interactions with other men. She had hoped that making their album had been an isolated experience, like a strange experiment in an underground lab.

It turned out, though, that the lab had been more or less representative of the whole institution. Everyone in music was male – from the booking agents, sound directors, and lighting technicians to the record execs, journalists, and photographers. Outside the protection of Bayleen Island and her tribe of Quinns, Jane had been disturbed to discover that many men initially reacted to her with condescension, skepticism, or dismissiveness. She stepped onto the bus without Archie's realizing she'd left the conversation.

'Jane,' Jesse called after her. She looked back at him, standing with Willy. 'Save me a seat,' he said. Jane gave him a small smile.

As she climbed the bus's stairs, she greeted Pete, their bearded driver. Jesse's band had situated themselves in the front few rows; they nodded to her as she passed, but none of them tried to engage. Jane made her way toward Kyle in the back, but paused momentarily by Loretta.

'Hey,' said Jane. 'I like your shirt.' It was the first remark that came into her head.

Loretta squinted at Jane as though trying to decide whether she was unoriginal or just plain dumb. 'Okay,' said Loretta. She looked back out the window toward Jesse.

Jane blushed and continued to the back.

Kyle patted her shoulder. 'I'm sure that line would have worked on Greg,' he said.

Jane settled into the seat in front of him and watched Willy and Jesse shake hands with Archie. There was no question that Jesse was the center of it all. Gentle, mild-mannered Jesse, who never raised his voice or gave the impression of conceit, was the person that everyone wanted a piece of. And Jane was the person Jesse seemed to need.

Given her clash with Vincent Ray, Jane knew that Jesse's feelings for her were the only reason she and her group had made it on this tour; so did everyone else. This was part of why Jane had insisted the two of them keep a low profile in public. She feared that if the world knew her as Jesse's love interest before she'd ever opened her mouth on a national stage, that was all she'd ever be.

The tour's itinerary began with a soft opening: two weeks to work out the kinks in smaller venues across the Pacific Northwest. Their first 'official' tour show would follow in San Francisco.

Jane watched Rich staring out toward the highway. He looked small to her in a way he never had before. As Greg returned from the pay phone, Rich stubbed out his cigarette, and the two of them climbed onto the bus, followed by Jesse. Jesse gave high fives to his band and stopped for a moment to confer with Loretta before settling into the seat next to Jane. He kept his eyes ahead, but Jane felt a jolt as his knee lightly brushed against hers.

Willy, the last one on, did a quick head count before giving Pete the thumbs-up. The air brake wheezed, the headlights switched on, and the bus pulled out onto the Sunset Strip. Jane stared out the window. She had never been on the West Coast before and still couldn't fathom its unfamiliarity: the buildings, the shrubbery, the hugeness.

She felt Jesse's hand casually slide between her left thigh and the seat, heat radiating off his chest as he looked out the window over her shoulder. As they pulled onto the 101, the whole bus was quiet; they didn't realize, but it was because Jesse was quiet. If he'd been talking, they all would have started talking, too.

14

The Breakers' tour set was four songs – 'Dirty Bastard,' 'Spring Fling,' 'Indigo,' and 'Spark' – their most pump-up, crowd-pleasing numbers. The band was in peak condition: they knew their songs backward and forward and had an uncommon level of comfort with each other. More than anything, though, they wanted to prove themselves. Now, their first night, playing the Carlson Theater at Bellevue College, they were as restless as runners awaiting the starting bell.

'Let's just be excellent,' Jane said to them as they huddled together.

And they were. The stadium came alive at the sound of Jane's voice and Rich's guitar.

Jane and Jesse had not warmed up together, so, that first time she came offstage, exhilarated and radiant, she was startled to find him drawn and gaunt, like a man walking toward a firing squad. Jesse normally lit up when he saw her, but this time he just raised his eyebrows and turned back to Loretta and Benny.

'Great show,' said Willy, handing Jane a cup of water. 'You guys killed it out there.'

'Is Jesse okay?' asked Jane, watching the back of his neck.

'Sure,' said Willy. It sounded like he might continue, and Jane waited. He cleared his throat and spoke in a low voice. 'You just nailed it, right?' he said.

Jane nodded.

'Which is great for you, as the opener. The expectation for you is that you'll be okay. If you're not, doesn't matter – people will just go grab a beer. If you're good, then they're happy. But if you're amazing, like you were tonight, you have the possibility of walking out of here with thousands of new fans. The only way from here is up.' He made a launching movement with his hand as if it were a plane taking off.

'For Jesse, though,' said Willy, lowering his voice even further, 'the expectation *is* amazing. He's not going to convert anyone to a believer – if they weren't already a believer, they wouldn't have bought a ticket with his name on it.' He glanced over at Jesse in the huddle with his group. 'If *he's* not amazing, they'll ask for their money back,' said Willy. 'It's a lot to carry a show. You're not allowed to have an off night.'

Jane and Willy watched Benny give Jesse a pat on the back. Jesse glanced back at Jane and gave her a quick smile before walking onstage, his face flooded by light. The crowd erupted, and Jane felt a wave of awe. She vowed to herself that someday she would be the one whose name was on the ticket.

That night, as the bus drove to Seattle, Jesse snoozed on Jane's shoulder. Willy stopped by their row.

'The merch vendor at the theater said we sold out of *Spring Fling*,' he said, giving Jane a wink. 'I'm going to ask Sales to run a revised projection. I think we might have under-printed.'

Jane couldn't help but smile at the thought of this information's reaching Vincent Ray.

The Breakers nailed their shows again at the University of Washington and Seattle University. Jesse's sets were steadily improving, and his fans – particularly the college girls, who came out in droves to scream his name – had no idea that the band was still tightening up their act. They didn't notice if the bass was a beat late on the key changes in 'Chapel on a Hill,' or that Jesse had stumbled over the lyrics on the second verse of 'Painted Lady.' But Jesse and the band did. These kinds of adjustments were a natural part of the process, and none of them had expected any different; it was why they had scheduled the two weeks of college-town shows to begin with.

What Jesse's band hadn't expected was for the Breakers to rock out of the gate. Talented as they were, a professional ensemble couldn't match the chemistry among a group of kids who had played together their whole lives. Some of them were gracious about it – Jesse was more excited for the Breakers' sets than he was for his own, and Huck gave each member of the Breakers a high five whenever they came off the stage. Others were not.

'It's like they've never seen a blonde before,' Loretta commented dryly after the Breakers had aced their third show in a row.

That night, Pete drove the bus to a roadside motel just across the border between Washington and Oregon. Jane and Jesse always took separate accommodations, but Willy went out of his way to make sure they were next door to each other. Jesse said good night to his band, and Jane said good night to hers, and the two of them retired to their rooms.

Moments later, Jane heard a knock on the adjoining door. When she opened it, Jesse walked through holding a toothbrush, a tee shirt, and underwear, as if it were a sleepover. These were thrown on the bed as Jane reached for him. Jesse's fingers threaded through her hair and drew her lips to his. After a whole day of stolen glances, Jane felt weak with the need to touch him.

Jesse pulled off his shirt and led her into the sparse bathroom. Jane took off her clothes and turned on the shower as Jesse unwrapped an unbranded bar of soap from its shiny white paper.

'Only the best for Pegasus.' Jane laughed and pulled him in with her. Jesse made quick work of the soap, covering Jane in a lather, his hands inciting riots on her skin wherever they touched her. Jane took the soap from him and washed his shoulders, his hips, his rear. The bar clattered to the drain as he pulled her to him, catching her tongue in his mouth, a low growl in his throat. Jane could feel him hard against her stomach as he slipped a finger inside her.

They kissed until their skin was smooth, and as the soap washed down the drain, Jesse turned Jane around, Jane on her tiptoes, and entered her. With one arm around her waist and the other resting on her pelvic bone, he moved their hips together, water cascading down off their backs.

'Fuck,' said Jane, arching her back in response to the intensity of the sensation. His arms were strong, and she gave in to the pleasure of it, leaning on him fully for support as she came.

'Come on, baby,' he whispered in her ear. She stayed there for a moment, melting in the heat, as he thrust into her with measured control. Jane could tell he was getting close and pulled away just as he was about to finish. He chased her onto the bed and pinned her down, looking into her eyes as he entered her again. Jane reveled in his weight, his breath ragged in her ear.

His hands found hers and held them both over her head, pleasure silently rocking both of them.

'Fuck, Jane,' he whispered in her ear, his hand squeezing her hip as he came. Jane nuzzled his cheek with her nose. They lay like that for a moment, listening to each other's breath. Then Jesse rolled off her and kissed her on the forehead. He went and turned off the shower, then lay back down without a stitch of clothing. His hand swept up her spine, pausing at the base of her neck to trace her tattoo, the Quinn family crest.

'You all have this,' he said.

Jane nodded. 'Sun, moon, water,' she said.

'That's all you need,' he said. 'I wish it could just stay like this. Once we're in the cities, it's . . . different.'

'What do you mean?' said Jane.

Jesse shrugged. 'It's all planned out, every minute accounted for. It's like being back in the Zoo.' His body tensed; Jane reached out and touched his cheek. Jesse smiled and took her hand and kissed it. He reached over and turned out the light, wrapping her snugly in his arms, and both of them drifted off for a while.

Headlights passed through the panel blinds like ghosts on the ceiling, rushing by in swishes and whirs. Jane awoke and turned on her back, heart galloping, as the still frames of her nightmare dissolved into the room: lilac dress, front hall, mirror, lipstick. She took a breath; the air felt thin in her lungs. She called to mind the moonlit beach, but the footprints appeared too fast, keeping time with her heart's fluttering.

Of everyone she knew, only her mother had walked this road. Jane wished that she could talk to her again. She searched herself for any thread connecting them: Jane could picture Charlotte in a room not unlike this, with a hummingbird trapped inside her chest. Was this how she had felt, to do as she'd done?

Jane slipped out of bed and threw on Jesse's tee shirt, grabbing her lighter and a pack of Pall Malls she'd stolen out of Elsie's bag. She wedged one of her shoes in the door, stepped into the outdoor corridor, and lit a cigarette. Jane looked out past the highway to the darkness beyond: this was Oregon, a mysterious land she had never conceived of visiting. She knew this was a part of her country but had no knowledge of her fellow countrymen who lived here. The moon was full, but Jane could barely find the Big Dipper, which shone in a different place than it did in Massachusetts. Americans lived under different stars.

The door opened, and Jesse emerged, wearing only his jeans. Just the sight of him made Jane want to go again. He replaced the shoe in the door and took the cigarette from her, inhaling. 'Same dream?' he said.

Jane nodded.

He handed the cigarette back to her but didn't let go when she tried to take it. Jane smiled at him and stepped closer.

'Have you tried writing it down?' he said.

Jane shook her head. 'That won't work for me,' she said. Everything around them was tinted by the hard yellow of the highway lights, but Jesse's eyes, as always, were cool and blue.

'Why not give it a shot?' he said.

Jane shrugged. 'I just don't like writing.'

Jesse shifted his weight. 'That strikes me as odd,' he said. 'Because you can write. I mean – 'Spark' is a good song, maybe the most lyrically advanced on your album.'

'"Spark" was a one-off,' said Jane.

119

Jesse raised one eyebrow at her. 'Why would that be? Your mom wrote – it's in your blood.'

'Well, I'm not her,' said Jane, chilled to remember how disembodied she'd felt after writing 'Spark.'

'Maybe so,' said Jesse. 'But I for one would like to see what you can do.'

She took the last puff and stubbed the end against the banister. They stood together in silence as a few cars whooshed by.

'We're far from the Island,' said Jesse. Jane looked up at him. He took her hand and pulled her into a hug. 'Come back in,' he said.

Jane let him lead her inside. He unpeeled the covers from her side of the bed, and she slid in. He switched off the lamp and began to rub her back. In a soft, gentle voice he sang:

> *'Let the light go,*
> *Let it fade into the sea.*
> *The sun belongs to the horizon,*
> *And you belong to me.'*

Jane got very still. 'That's pretty,' she said quietly.

'It's yours,' said Jesse.

'Mine?' said Jane.

'I mean, I wrote it for you,' he said. He cleared his throat. 'Listen, Jane. A lot can . . . go wrong. But whatever happens, between us, whatever . . . happens . . . that song will always be for you.'

For a moment, Jane was quiet. Then she said, 'Is there more?' She smiled in the dark.

15

Willy had been touring every year since he'd turned twenty-two, and if there was one thing he'd learned, it was that success split people apart and failure brought them together. The Breakers wanted so badly to impress Jesse's band that they were repelling them. Willy wasn't worried. Sooner or later, something would go so wrong that they'd have no choice but to bond.

It happened in Portland. Partway through the Breakers' set at Portland State University's Lincoln Hall, the speaker system went on the fritz. During the first verse of 'Indigo,' Jane's mic began to feed back; hundreds of people covered their ears in agony as a metallic shriek rang through the auditorium like a fire alarm. Willy saw Jane turn to Rich.

'What do we do?' she said. His sound and Kyle's were still working properly, and the two of them strummed to cover the air. The house speakers that had been projecting Jane's and Greg's amps had been fried.

'"Don't Fret,"' said Rich. 'Kyle, you're up.'

They hadn't rehearsed 'Don't Fret' in weeks, but Kyle was a showman. He took center stage, and he and Rich began to jam. The two of them could throw a phrase back and forth longer than a Little League pitcher could practice his fastball, but the song depended on its percussion section. Jane had known this before Willy – as Greg continued to play, albeit mutedly, Jane walked upstage to Loretta's piano and opened the lid. Willy watched as she lowered herself to the keys, as though bowing in prayer.

'Can we get the sound up on the keys?' Willy called to the tech hand. Jane began to vamp as Kyle passed the melody to Rich. One by one, Jesse's bandmates crept into the wings to watch the Breakers; first Jesse, then Huck, then Benny, then Loretta, then Duke. The Breakers played for just under ten minutes, the same amount of time left in their set, ending with a show-stopping solo from Kyle. The crowd thundered when they finished.

'What just happened?' Greg exclaimed as they ran off.

'Holy shit,' said Rich, clutching his heart.

'Those triplets – total smoke,' said Jane, giving Kyle a high five.

'What about you, piano tamer?' said Kyle, closing his hands around hers and shaking her arms. They stopped abruptly when they realized that Jesse's band was watching them. Duke was the first person to speak, bassist to bassist.

'Brother,' he said, embracing Kyle, 'that was music.' Kyle beamed. It was as if the two groups had suddenly realized they spoke the same language; they began to chatter like long-lost relatives. Willy watched Jane grow flustered as Loretta sidled up to her.

'Next time you commandeer my piano, you might want to lay off the damper,' said Loretta. 'I've heard cathedral organs with more chill.'

As Jane opened her mouth to respond, Loretta's eyes softened. 'Still,' she said, 'that wasn't half bad. For a girl.'

She winked at Jane, then turned to Benny.

Loretta had done everything by the book, first as a writer, then as a performer. Willy knew her ultimate goal was an album of her own, and she had been working steadily for years to build up her reputation and ingratiate herself to the label. It must have gutted her to see beautiful twenty-year-old Jane Quinn whirl in, break every rule, and end up with an album and an opening slot on a national tour.

Willy watched Jesse and Jane. Jesse was speaking to Kyle, but his arm kept bumping into Jane as though to reassure himself of her presence. Willy had never seen someone so smitten. Jane liked Jesse fine, but she was in it for the music. This was probably why she appealed to him. Most girls would kill to have the world know Jesse Reid had chosen them, but Jane didn't want anyone to find out.

'Hey,' said Jesse, gathering everyone to him, 'what if we end the show with a big number – everyone together?'

'That's a great idea,' said Willy reflexively.

'What song?' Benny asked. 'We've already gone through the whole album.'

'How about "My Lady"?' said Kyle.

'Or we could do another Breakers song,' Jesse suggested.

'What about "Let the Light Go"?' said Jane. Jesse looked as if she'd just volunteered her Social Security number.

'I don't know that song,' said Huck.

'It's new,' said Jane. 'Jesse wrote it. It's really good.'

'If that's what you want,' said Jesse. He gave her a small smile, but as he turned to grab his guitar, Willy saw a shadow of disappointment pass over his features. Then the two groups began to speak to each other in technical terms, forming a phalanx of phrases like 'watch me on the changes' and 'I'll take the minor second' that left Willy on the outside.

Willy's grandfather Seb had emigrated from Egypt in 1875, along with an Arabian stallion that he ran to victory at the Preakness before continuing west. Once in L.A., he changed his name from Laghmani to Lambert and used the stud fees from the horse to invest in the Volta Laboratory's graphophone technology. He gave his son an American name, Jack, and two obsessions Jack would grow to dominate: horse racing and the music industry. Willy had been raised with one as the default metaphor for the other.

Jesse was a Thoroughbred, pure stock, a sure bet, the kind of performer who would finish first every time. Jane was a wild gelding; Willy had thought at one point he could tame her, but he had been wrong. She would just as soon run head-long into the stands as she would across the finish line. As it happened, though, sometimes a champion horse who was otherwise tame needed a training partner to keep its spirit intact. This was how Willy had positioned the Breakers as Jesse's opening act to his father and the rest of the Pegasus executive board. 'She will make him run further and faster,' Willy had said. Despite protests from Vincent Ray, the room had agreed.

Willy had always been taught that labels sold records, not artists; the public didn't know what they liked, and record companies told them. Willy's loyalty to Jane went against this, and not even he knew how far it would extend. Willy was different from his father in one key regard. Jack Lambert liked horse racing because he loved to win. Willy loved to win, but he also loved to watch the horses run. And Jane could run.

It wasn't attraction, exactly – not that he hadn't thought about it, but Willy preferred mature women (his wife, Rebecca, was seven years his senior). His fascination with Jane went deeper than that – it was existential. Willy and Jane both had an inheritance from the music business: Jane's was a vendetta, Willy's was a kingdom. Willy had once thought he would like to reshape that kingdom, but going up against Vincent Ray last summer had revealed to him that he would sooner die than jeopardize his birthright.

Jane Quinn had no such constraints and had become Willy's avatar for that which he would never allow himself to do or say. If someone like Jane could become a household name without the support of her label, it threatened the establishment's control and power, his very legacy; and yet Willy found that at times what he wanted was for her to level it all to the ground.

It took the sound technicians twenty minutes to fix the speakers; once Jesse started playing, it took him less than twenty seconds to win back the crowd. His band flew through their set with new vibrancy, as though watching the Breakers had given them permission to put on a show. When they finished, they bowed, and the Breakers ran back on to squeals of delight that seemed to amplify, the closer Jane stood to Jesse.

'Thank you,' said Jesse. 'Thanks. We've got one more for you.'

Willy watched from offstage as Jane began to sing the first verse of 'Let the Light Go,' Jesse beside her playing the guitar. The tune was strange and beautiful, halfway between a love song and the blues.

'I'll watch over you,
As long as I am here,
As long as I am near,
You can dream, dream away.'

As the musicians felt their way through the accompaniment, Willy observed a cluster of starry-eyed coeds staring up at Jesse and Jane. Their expressions took Willy back to the winter of 1964, when a cancelled tour had forced him to spend a season gofering for *The Ed Sullivan Show*. This was how the audience had looked up at the Beatles: euphoric, obsessed. The wheels in Willy's head began to turn as he watched these young faces question: were they, or weren't they?

Not knowing the answer had the makings of a mania. It seemed that Jane's desire for privacy had the unwitting potential to spray lighter fluid on the many hearts holding a candle for Jesse; that was enough firepower to launch his star into the stratosphere. As Jane and Jesse bowed together, the screams reached a deafening pitch.

After the show, a freckled girl with auburn hair and glasses was waiting for them in the parking lot, as though on cue. She had a camera strapped around her neck and a notepad poised in her hands, evidently from the college paper.

'Sorry,' said Willy. 'Sorry, Jesse isn't doing interviews.'

'It's okay,' said Jesse, still on a high from the performance.

'I don't know—' said Willy.

'It's fine,' said Jesse. 'Hi, I'm Jesse.'

'I'm Marybeth Kent,' she said, shaking Jesse's hand as if she were interviewing for a job. Willy rolled his eyes and held up his hand, mouthing, 'Five minutes.'

'The fans want to know,' she said, cheeks reddening. 'Are you dating Jane Quinn?'

Jessie laughed and looked up, just as Jane ambled past him toward the bus.

'What do you think, Janie Q – are we dating?'

'Is this how you ask a girl out?' said Jane, without stopping. Marybeth Kent scribbled frantically.

'So . . . the song "Morning Star" – is that about Jane Quinn?' said Marybeth.

'It's a composite of people I've known,' said Jesse.

'But one of them's Jane Quinn,' said Marybeth. '"Morning star, and your guitar" . . . '"I'd follow that golden hair anywhere." Seems pretty clearly to be her.'

Jesse shrugged.

'What attracts you to her?' asked Marybeth.

'Okay, that's enough,' said Willy. 'Thanks for coming tonight.' And, with that, he steered Marybeth back toward campus. She kept looking over her shoulder to catch a final glimpse of Jesse.

That night, the bus was as merry as a tavern. For the first time, the groups sat mixed together, chatting and laughing. Jesse seemed peaceful. Jane was alert.

On Sunday, the *Painted Lady* bus headed back down the coast to San Francisco, the radio tuned to Casey Kasem's new program, *American Top 40*. The group had their first surprise at number thirty-eight, when 'Spring Fling' came on the air. As the opening notes of the intro twanged, Jane's eyes widened. The whole bus began to shout.

'Listen to that,' said Jesse, beaming.

'"*Strong, yeah, you bring me along,*"' they all sang together. When the Breakers' song finished, a new tension settled on the bus. If 'Spring Fling' – which hadn't been remotely close to a chart the week before – was number thirty-eight, then where would 'Strangest Thing' be? The lower the countdown went, the quieter the bus became.

Jesse sat beside Jane, looking at his shoes. Willy began to make a list of the calls he would need to make if the song was in the top ten. They were twenty miles outside of the city when the final countdown began. The Golden Gate Bridge drifted into view just as 'Huguenot' by Bulletin finished at number five.

'And now, for this week's number-four spot, we've got . . . 'Strangest Thing' by Jesse Reid.'

Startled voices exclaimed all around Willy. Jane grinned at Jesse, and Pete the bus driver turned up the volume as 'Strangest Thing' began to play.

While the group rejoiced, Willy sank into thought.

'What is it?' Kyle asked him.

Willy rubbed his chin. 'I've been in this business for ten years, and it doesn't matter how good a song is,' he said. 'You don't jump nine spots in a week because you played a few college campuses. Something else must have happened.'

The answer presented itself an hour later, when the bus parked right in front of a dispenser for *Snitch Magazine*.

There they were in print: Jesse watching Jane stride onto the bus, Jane looking back at Jesse over her shoulder. The headline read: THE GIRL IN THE SONGS: IS JANE QUINN JESSE REID'S "MORNING STAR"?

It seemed that Marybeth Kent hadn't been a college reporter after all.

16

In San Francisco, they played at Stern Grove to a lawn check-ered with sweaters and jackets dug out for a sudden cold spell.

'This is not how I pictured California,' said Kyle, breathing into his fingers to warm them up. The crowd was mellow to the point of somnolence – when Jane told them to make some noise, they clapped as though they were at a golf tournament.

'Tough crew,' she said to Rich between 'Indigo' and 'Spark.'

'They're all stoned,' said Rich, inhaling the pungent aroma wafting toward them, a mix of weed, smog, and that legendary fog. Jesse had been right – the cities were different.

By the time they reached L.A., *Tiger Beat* and *Flip* had picked up the lead that Jane and Jesse might be an item, and the audience at the L.A. Memorial Coliseum was a hive of conjecture. Would the surprise number they'd read about in *Snitch* be repeated? Would they get a chance to see Jane and Jesse together for themselves?

When Jane walked onstage, she experienced a frenzy unlike anything she had previously encountered. The crowd was large, fashionable, and hip, but it wasn't until halfway through their first number that she realized the real difference. As she belted out the chorus to 'Dirty Bastard,' Jane heard the audience singing along – they knew the Breakers' songs. Hearing their lyrics ripple through the stadium made Jane's heart leap – even though she understood that most of them had only heard them because she was allegedly dating Jesse.

'It feels like cheating,' said Jane to Greg as they stood in the wings, watching Jesse shyly smile to the crowd from his seat onstage.

Greg shrugged. 'Is it cheating any more than your being beautiful?' he asked. 'Than him being rich?'

Jane loved to watch Jesse perform. The tension he held in his shoulders before going onstage melted away as he stepped under the lights, guitar cradled in his hands. Jane was like a supernova, all sparkle and energy; Jesse was like a black hole, a well of gravity that drew legions toward him. He often sang looking down, or with his eyes closed, which had a hypnotic effect: the crowd watched him as though afraid of waking a sleepwalker.

After his dream of a set, Jesse invited the Breakers back onstage to sing 'Let the Light Go,' and the audience lost their minds. Jesse got to his feet and looked at Jane, and to the crowd it appeared she had woken him up, all the more exaggerated by his change in posture. Willy had strongly encouraged them to do the encore for the fans. Jane was aware of being scrutinized, but only distantly; when she and Jesse sang together, she forgot about everything else.

They bowed together and walked offstage, careful not to touch. The minute Jesse stepped out of the lights, his face went blank as a slate. Willy handed him a cup of water and told him what a good job he'd done, and Jane waited a few minutes before speaking to him; she'd learned that his initial reaction to coming down off a performance was catatonia.

'I envy you,' he told her that night in her hotel room. 'You love it.'

The next morning, Willy sought them in the hotel's restaurant to deliver some news. '*Rolling Stone* is sending Curtis Wilks to write a feature on you,' he told Jesse. 'He's going to be with us for the rest of the L.A. shows. We need to show him a good time.'

Jesse had just cut a bite of omelet, and replaced his fork on his plate.

'The whole visit will be on the record,' said Willy. 'So – if you don't want him to know about you two, I'd suggest laying extra low until we get to Vegas.'

'For the record,' said Jesse, 'I don't care who knows about us.'

'For the record,' said Jane, picking up his fork and eating the omelet, 'I do.'

When they arrived for their show that evening, Curtis Wilks was waiting backstage. He was about thirty-five, with thick brown hair and a handlebar mustache – a teddy bear with a press badge. But if Mark Edison had taught Jane anything, it was that the press wasn't cuddly.

'Jane' – Willy motioned her over – 'come meet Curtis.'

Jane smiled and offered him her hand. 'I'm the singer in the Breakers,' she said. 'We open the show.'

'I know who you are,' said Curtis, grinning as he gave Jane's hand a hardy shake. 'I was there last summer at the Folk Fest. *Spring Fling* is a hell of a debut. And you're a hell of a singer.'

A moment later, Willy swooped in to take Curtis Wilks back to Jesse, leaving Jane to round up her band. The Breakers tuned and went into their trailer to await their call. Greg and Rich turned on a baseball game, and Kyle had just asked Jane to play cards when Jesse knocked on the door.

'Curtis is still backstage with Willy,' he said. 'Can I steal you for a sec?'

He led her behind the trailer. A magenta horizon glimmered behind the stadium, already humming with voices.

'What's up?' Jane asked.

Jesse looked as if he was about to say something, then he took a step forward and wrapped his arms around her middle. Jane grasped his shoulders, surprised, and held him like that for a minute. *Rolling Stone* was big. The biggest of the big. They both knew that. When this article came out, things would be different. It was hard to say how yet, but they both could sense it; one way of being was ending, and another was beginning. Jesse drew himself up and pulled her to him, burying his face in her hair.

That night, Jesse played like Orpheus aboard the *Argo*, his performance powerful and entrancing. After, both bands escorted Curtis Wilks to their bus, and Pete drove them to Beverly Hills for a party hosted by Willy's brother and the founder of Counting Sheep Records, Danny Lambert.

'Hideous,' said Willy under his breath as they pulled into an elaborate stone courtyard reminiscent of a Venetian piazza.

The interior looked like a cross between a beach house and a vampire's lair – palm trees mixed with red velvet, crystal light fixtures illuminating coral floors. Danny was an older, ritzier version of Willy. He waited in the octagonal entryway, hair slicked back, teeth glinting.

'There they are,' he said, homing in on Jesse and Curtis Wilks. Willy rolled his eyes and tagged along behind. Clearly, this article had become a family affair – although it wasn't clear whose idea that had been.

'Come on,' said Loretta, taking Jane's arm. Jesse's band led the Breakers into a palatial ballroom, then scattered toward other people they knew.

Jane felt as though she'd stepped onto a film set. A cocktail waitress wearing fishnet stockings and a bow tie brought them drinks on a silver tray. The Breakers stood awkwardly, sipping their drinks, beside a two-story window overlooking an elaborate poolscape. Jane scanned the glittering crowd for Jesse; she had no idea where he'd gone.

'Please, tell me the rumors aren't true,' a low Kentish voice growled behind them.

'Holy sh—' Kyle lost his voice as they spun around to find themselves in the presence of Hannibal Fang, the legendary bass player from the British invasion band Fair Play. Hannibal Fang flashed his trademark wolfish grin and took one of Jane's hands in two of his, both laden with rings.

'Jane Quinn, light of my life, fire of my loins,' he said. 'I will die an even earlier death if you are dating Jesse Reid. Go on, lovey, say it isn't so, and let's elope.'

'Okay, Janie Q,' said Kyle, 'you heard the man.'

'Janie Q,' said Hannibal Fang. 'Love that.'

'This is Kyle, Greg, and Rich,' said Jane. His eccentricity made her strangely comfortable. It was as if she were serving a flirtatious customer back at the Carousel, only instead of a bar separating them, it was a break in reality.

'Charmed, lads,' said Hannibal Fang. 'Adore your record – the absolute tops. So – what do you say, Jane, should we get out of here and get to know each other Biblically?'

'We can't leave yet; this party's barely started,' said Jane.

'What d'you mean?' said Hannibal Fang. 'People are rolling all over the place.'

'I don't know,' said Jane. 'No one's jumped fully clothed into the pool yet.'

'Tut-tut,' said Hannibal Fang. 'One doesn't just jump "fully clothed into the pool," love; these things must be done with style and finesse. Come, I'll show you.'

He led all four of them upstairs, and they all took a bump of coke from his personal stash, which he wore around his neck in a hollowed-out tiger fang.

They'd all experimented a bit on Bayleen Island, but drugs were expensive, an extravagance reserved for the week of the Folk Fest. L.A. was different. Here, pills and powders and joints were as common as breath mints.

'Just let me know when your throat starts burning – I always have more,' he said.

Then they did another line and flew back into the party, with Hannibal Fang as their guide. They danced past a top-forty band playing live in the solarium, linking arms with exotic dancers painted to resemble garden flowers. They giggled as Hannibal Fang introduced them to a regiment of industry brass who were as giddy and wanton as the Breakers themselves.

Then they moved out to the pool, a luxuriant utopia modeled after the lagoon in Bora-Bora. Just as Kyle and Greg began to compete over who could drink more from the dolphin ice-luge, Jane saw Willy emerge onto the patio looking exasperated.

'So tacky,' he said, shooing aside a woman whose exposed breasts had been painted like daisies.

Jesse and Curtis Wilks followed a moment later, laughing

at something Danny Lambert was saying. Jesse's eyes found Jane's and lingered on her a little longer than they should have.

'Right,' said Hannibal Fang. 'It's time.' He grabbed Jane's hand and pulled her into the pool.

Jane sank into the warm water and felt splashes around her as Kyle, Rich, and Greg followed.

They weren't the only ones – before long, half the party was in the pool, including several of the dancers. Colors swirled on the surface, a liquescent oil painting.

'Seriously, though,' Hannibal Fang growled in Jane's ear. 'Is it that he can sing?'

'Who says it's anything?' said Jane.

'Oh, Jane, you celestial minx,' he said, and the two of them floated on their backs, watching planes pass over the city.

It was 3:00 a.m. when Jane drew herself from the water. She looked around for Jesse and spied Curtis Wilks passed out on one of the lawn chairs, torches burning on either side of him. Hannibal Fang was sprawled below the ice sculpture, straddled by a dancer painted like a rose, who was feeding him individual grapes from a golden horn.

Jane felt a hand close around her wrist and looked up to see Jesse. Without a word, he pulled her into Danny Lambert's bath house and nailed her on top of a stack of foam pool-toys. It was an act of possession, his fingers digging into the flesh of her thighs. Jane closed her eyes, reduced to chlorine and plastic and alcohol and his cock drilling into her as they both tried to restrain themselves. After, they slipped out of the pool house one after the other, returning to opposite sides of the party before Curtis Wilks regained consciousness.

17

The next day, they were all hurting.

'I used to think rock stars did a lot of coke because it was glamorous,' said Rich. 'Now it just seems like a logical decision. I honestly don't know how I would have made it through last night without some kind of assistance.'

That night, Jesse and the Breakers both played killer sets, then went to Willy's house to 'relax' after the show, which meant a Malibu-style reprise of the previous evening. Willy's beachfront house might have been smaller than his brother's mansion, but it was no less aspirational.

Willy showed them into a geometric wood-paneled entryway vibrating with disco beats and a fresh crop of music-industry scensters. Jesse looked fairly at ease. He nodded to Curtis Wilks, and the two of them grabbed beers and headed out onto a large veranda overlooking the ocean.

A woman approached wearing a teal minidress, whom Willy introduced as his wife, Rebecca. Her cat-eye makeup, tanned physique, and no-nonsense demeanor made Jane think of Cleopatra.

'You're Jane!' said Rebecca, embracing her. Rebecca smelled like candied moonbeams.

'Here,' she said quietly, handing Jane a tablet and a glass of water. 'Vitamin C. Gotta keep your immune system strong. I don't know how you guys do these weeks.' Jane decided that, if things didn't work out with Jesse, she would devote her life to Rebecca.

The Breakers grabbed drinks and headed onto the dance floor, already bumping in Willy's living room, as guests continued to filter in. Every time the door opened, Kyle's head whipped around.

'Hannibal Fang isn't coming,' said Rich.

'I just miss him,' said Kyle.

'I miss the ice luge,' said Greg.

'Everyone having fun?' said Willy, sidling up to them as though sensing the comparison with his brother.

'Yes,' said Jane, patting him on the shoulder and taking the drink from his hand. 'How's it going, do you think?' She nodded toward the deck, where Jesse was deep in conversation with Curtis Wilks.

'Well,' said Willy, lowering his voice, 'Curtis reckons we have a shot at next issue's cover.'

'*The next* issue?' asked Jane. 'As in, out next week? How is that possible?'

Willy shrugged. 'Apparently, he's been pitching this article since last summer. Just wants to supplement the copy with a bit about the tour and some recent photos. It sounds like they're holding the slot for him, pending fact-check.'

Jane let out a low whistle.

As the clock struck midnight, the door opened to reveal a resplendent Black woman wrapped in shimmering pink from her lemon-blonde bouffant to her strappy silver sandals. It was impossible not to look at her – she exuded such infectious warmth. Jane felt a jolt; she knew this woman, had seen her face on album covers, had heard stories of her friendship with her mother for years.

'Is that . . .' said Rich. Jane nodded.

'Lacey Dormon,' she said.

Everything else grew dim as Jane watched the crowd part so that Lacey could embrace Loretta. Loretta made a joke, and Lacey's rich laughter rang around the room; the noise level of the assembly rose in response. It was clear that the party didn't really start until Lacey arrived.

'Lacey,' said Willy, calling her over. Jane felt her face flush. For weeks, Jane had craved a conversation with her mother about music, and now she was about to meet one of the few people who had known her as a composer. Would Lacey even remember Charlotte? If she did, *how* would she remember her? Jane recalled her own last memory of her mother and shivered.

Lacey appeared beside Jane like a rose-tinted vision. As she looked at Jane's face, her eyes grew round with surprise, then soft with nostalgia.

'You're Jane Quinn,' she said in a low, unmistakable voice. 'You look exactly like Charlotte – I feel as if I'm seeing her double.' Jane was speechless.

Kyle swooped in. 'Jane gets that a lot,' he said. 'I'm Kyle.'

Willy introduced the boys, then took them to get another round of drinks, leaving Jane alone with Lacey.

'Congratulations on your album, sweetie,' said Lacey, touching Jane on the shoulder as if she were a beloved niece. 'It's so good. You really have Charlotte's talent with melody.' Jane looked at Lacey in awe. Jane could go months without ever hearing anyone say her mother's name, years without anyone's acknowledging what she had accomplished. Lacey Dormon had just done both in under two minutes.

'I'm so glad to meet you,' was all she could say.

'Me, too, hon,' said Lacey. 'Ah, if your mom were here! How is she doing?'

Jane felt the blood drain from her face.

Lacey's eyes fixed on hers. 'She's okay, isn't she?' Lacey asked softly.

Jane lowered her gaze. 'I don't know,' she said. 'She ran out over ten years ago.'

Lacey's hand drifted to her sternum. 'Ran out,' she repeated, transfixed by light from a star that had long since gone dark. Her eyes gleamed with sadness; Jane felt numb.

'You poor thing,' Lacey murmured. 'I can't believe that. I really can't. Charlie – Charlotte. Her songs were the start of it all for me. I owe her everything.'

They stood together quietly. Jane couldn't think of what to say. Then Loretta stepped between them, holding a drink for Lacey.

'I see you've met our Jane,' she said. Jane watched Lacey accept the drink, but as Loretta began to inch toward another group, Lacey hung back.

'There's more for us to say,' she said. 'Another time, just the two of us.' She reached into her pink shoulder bag and pulled out a card.

'Please,' she said, closing Jane's hand around the paper. 'Promise you'll call me the next time you're in town. We'll have a proper chat about Charlotte and everything else.'

'I promise,' said Jane.

Lacey beamed at her. 'You really do look just like her, it's uncanny. I would have known it was you anywhere,' she said, and floated back into the crowd as Jesse and Curtis came in from the balcony.

'Well, that was . . . unexpected,' said Greg, appearing at Jane's elbow. Jane could tell he'd been keeping an eye on her the whole time, and suddenly she felt small and shaky: homesick. She was also growing tired of being apart from Jesse; that much she could fix.

'Come on,' she said to the boys. They meandered over to Curtis and Jesse, who looked surprised to see them.

'Having fun?' said Curtis Wilks.

'Always,' said Jane, as Benny and Huck joined them.

'Here's the real party,' said Benny, clinking bottles with Jesse.

'I was thinking,' said Huck. 'It might be a good night for some stargazing.' He produced a sheet of colorful blotter paper from inside his vest with a mischievous grin.

They headed onto Willy's roof, and everyone took a tab, including Curtis Wilks. As they lay on their backs, discussing the war in Vietnam and the price of tomatoes, the stars began to walk in animal patterns through a moonless sky. Jesse's hand found Jane's in the dark, and the two fell asleep like that, with Kyle's head on Jane's stomach, and Greg spooning Rich.

In the morning, the bands waved goodbye to Curtis Wilks, and boarded the *Painted Lady* bus to Las Vegas. When they reached Caesar's Palace, Jane and Jesse surrendered the pretense of going into different rooms. They lay collapsed on Jane's bed for the next fifteen hours.

The following day, a new issue of *Rolling Stone* hit the stands, featuring a psychedelic portrait of Jesse's face and the headline 'The New Rock, Mellow and Blue.'

18

Vietnam rages on, but rock and roll has screamed itself out, leaving a new wave of songwriters no choice but to dive headlong into the mellow. These days, the soulful tunes coming out of Laurel Canyon are often more blues than rock, a phoenix of nuance and subtlety rising from the ashes of burned guitars and shredded vocal cords. If one man embodies this rebirth, it's the soft-spoken 21-year-old Jesse Reid, whose Heathcliffian demeanor belies a talent so undeniable he may lead an entire generation of guitarists to learn Travis picking.

Thus began the eight-page *Rolling Stone* cover story, 'A Day in the Life of Jesse Reid.' The article was well written and informative, but in the end what people remembered most was the iconic photo of Jesse that appeared on the seventh page of the layout. Amidst ephemera of the Coliseum, a magenta sunset, and lovestruck girls, there was a single shot of Jesse seated in a folding chair, gazing at something outside the frame. The bright-blue color of his eyes had been captured in the image, and he looked thoroughly absorbed, as though he was restraining himself. The caption read 'Reid watching Jane Quinn tune her guitar backstage at the Coliseum.'

The text itself sidestepped the subject of Jesse's love life, but it didn't matter; the fans picked up the scent on the photo like a pack of wolves. Overnight, the questions of 'Who is Jane Quinn?' and 'Are they together?' became of national importance, and this reverberated all the way up the charts. In week seventeen of its life, 'Spring Fling' entered America's top ten.

This was nothing compared with the reaction to *Painted Lady*. After the article was published, there was no turning back. 'Strangest Thing' took up weekly residence in the number-one slot, with 'Morning Star' as number four, and 'Sylvie Smiles' hanging on at twelve; *Painted Lady* was the number-one album in America for twenty weeks running, catapulting their tour into a maelstrom of mass hysteria and media coverage.

Jane had begun to get some interview requests. To Willy's dismay, she rejected them all.

'Jane, these are great hits,' said Willy as Jane loaded her guitar into the bus's undercarriage.

'*Tiger Beat? Teen?*' said Jane. 'Pass.'

He gave her a look.

'The record's selling – isn't it?' she said.

'Because of you and Jesse,' said Willy, in exasperation. 'You should be taking advantage of every opportunity you can to branch out on your own.'

'Have you ever read those magazines?' said Jane. 'All they're going to ask about is Jesse.'

'You just need to be on a cover or two – talk about how you do your hair, or that your favorite nail polish is Natural Wonder.'

'I am in a rock-and-roll band,' said Jane. 'I don't want to talk about how my favorite nail polish is Natural Wonder.'

Willy shook his head.

Fans and paparazzi delayed their Vegas departure for two hours, swarming the bus with flashing cameras and painted signs, chanting lyrics in the air. Most of them were there for Jesse, but not all of them: more than one sign read 'Breakers for Life' and 'What Would Jane Do?,' riffing off a line from the 'Indigo' chorus: 'What would I do if you were violet and not blue?'

A line of girls linked arms in front of the bus as Pete leaned on the horn.

'Goddamn it,' said Willy, a 'Jane + Jesse Forever' sign bobbing in his aviators.

After, the tour switched to a generic black bus that would be harder to track. Even so, Jane didn't comprehend how big they were becoming until Utah, where the churlish man pumping gas giddily insisted on Jesse's autograph. It took ten minutes to get inside to buy cigarettes.

'You must be Jane,' said the cashier. 'If things don't work out with Jesse, just come on back here to old Rex.'

Jesse's expression darkened. 'The lady said she'd like a box of Pall Malls,' he said, sending a chill through the room.

Jesse had become like a polar bear, watching his privacy evaporate around him like a rapidly melting iceberg. Part of building a legend was being a legend, and each town had its own press corps, its own local personalities, its own joints that needed to be visited, anointed with song, adorned with photos of the bands and the proprietor. To capitalize on a success like *Painted Lady,* the tour had to create the sense that, if the band was in town, there was a chance that they *might* show up where you were. This meant the tour group had to be 'on' from dusk until dawn.

After a show, sometimes the musicians would change clothes, sometimes they wouldn't; then they'd get on the bus and consume whatever was around – speed, blow, dexies, black beauties and white lines – until they were grinding in the aisle, radio dials turned up high. They'd arrive where they weren't expected and dance on the tables and feed quarters into the jukebox and give the fans a night to talk about for the rest of their lives. Then they would drive back to the hotel and collapse.

Jane and Jesse's time alone together had been reduced to episodes of empty sleep. There was nothing left for sex, or even dreaming – they'd pass out with their clothes on, his nose tucked into the crook of her neck, both of them sour with sweat and booze. They'd awake the next morning, fumes in their mouths, yellow and purple in places they didn't remember bruising. They were being slowly peeled by their own exhaustion; each day began a little later, a little more raw.

In Aragonite, Utah, Jane awoke to find her skin crawling. She forced herself into the shower, humming as she scrubbed the grime from her limbs. She emerged in a towel to find Jesse awake and taciturn.

'Morning,' she said, smiling at him. He stared at her with hollow eyes.

'Would you mind keeping it down when I'm trying to sleep?' he said. The coldness in his voice made Jane's body smart with shame.

After that, Jane began to notice that she was increasingly getting on his nerves.

'Bet you guys have great pickles,' she joked to their server in Salt Lake City. Jesse looked right through her, his lips a thin line.

As they boarded the bus to Denver, Jane paused in the aisle to select her seat.

'Big decision,' said Jesse, behind her. 'Don't fuck it up.'

Jane looked up at him in surprise. His eyes were blank, two blue disks. Jane slid into the nearest seat. Jesse kept walking to the rear of the bus and stretched out across the back row.

'He's just exhausted,' said Rich, when Jane asked if he'd noticed a change between them. Jane wasn't convinced; Jesse's annoyance felt personal. He was getting bored with her.

The night of their first show in Denver, woolly clouds gathered around Fillmore Auditorium. Jane stood backstage with Jesse and Willy. 'I hope this rain won't affect the crowds,' she said.

Jesse blinked at her, then turned away to talk to Benny instead. As Willy offered his assurances on the weather, it struck Jane that they were probably going to break up soon.

During Jesse's set, Jane watched the sea of pretty faces swimming before him; why wouldn't he want to dive in?

The after-party was at a cavernous downtown bar; Jane resigned herself to her drink; all around, bright eyes tracked Jesse like bats in a cave. After they returned to the hotel together, Jane lay awake, silently listing the ways this was expected and for the best. The next morning, Jesse came out of the shower to find her stripping their bed.

'You don't need to do that,' he said. 'It's a hotel.' Jane looked at her hands as though waking from a trance.

'I don't know what I'm doing,' she said. They eyed each other. Jesse took a step toward her, head hung. This was it. He was going to tell her it was over. Jane braced herself.

Then he grabbed her. As their bodies collided, Jane's panic dissolved into primal instinct. His towel fell to the floor and Jane pulled him down on top of her. He didn't remove her underwear, just shifted them enough to get inside her. Jane had never been so wet. She pulled his hips into her and fucked him until she came. He watched as she finished, then flipped her over and took her from behind. He swore as he climaxed, fingers leaving white marks on her shoulders. After, they lay side by side, staring at the ceiling. Jesse swallowed and cleared his throat. Then he reached for her hand, and she gave it to him.

While in Denver, Huck managed to link up with a weed dealer and procure a half-pounder of hash. After that, Jesse began each morning with a joint. He would toke up at intervals throughout the day, disappearing into his dressing room for a full hour before each show to get high. He never expressly told Jane not to come in during this time, but she never did. After the show, the whole group would switch to uppers for the rest of the night. This new routine rendered Jesse docile, a house cat content to lie around as long as no one asked anything of him.

Jane told herself there was nothing so wrong with this, but a sense of foreboding began to follow her around like a debt collector. When the bus stopped for gas one night outside Goodland, Kansas, Jane left Jesse sleeping on board and dialed Grace from a pay phone. After the usual exchange of information, Jane told her aunt in a few broken sentences that she sensed a shift in Jesse

'It's probably nothing,' said Jane. She watched prairie grass ripple beneath a lavender sky, the crescent moon etched between the clouds like a comma.

'It sounds like he's self-medicating,' said Grace, after a beat. 'Do you know what he's using?'

'Weed, coke-type things, booze, acid occasionally,' said Jane.

'Anything else?' said Grace. Jane took it as a joke.

'Honestly, it's no different from the rest of us,' she said, requesting her aunt's confirmation.

'Jane, listen to me – you need to make sure you're taking care of yourself,' said Grace. 'I know that stuff is fun, but it's not sustainable. Sooner or later, your bodies are going to give out.'

'I know,' said Jane, wishing she could slip into the phone line. 'How's work? How's Millie?'

'Fine,' said Grace. 'She's invited me to come to London with her this fall as companion-nurse.'

'Would the Center let you do that?' Jane couldn't imagine her aunt would actually go.

'We'll see,' said Grace. 'But I want to. Seeing you go out there has been . . . inspiring for me.'

The operator asked Jane to insert a nickel.

'I'm out of change,' said Jane.

'Keep the boys close,' said Grace. 'And be safe.'

As the *Painted Lady* tour entered the Midwest, Jane and Jesse's shared performances of 'Let the Light Go' became their tether. Each night, Jane would sing the words he had written for her, calling him back. Sometimes he heard her, sometimes he did not. After their first show in Kansas, they took a bow and he walked off the stage without another look. The next night, he grabbed hold of her while they were still in the wings and kissed her with so much venom, his teeth left an indent on the inside of her lip. Hours later, watching him dance around like a scarecrow in a country bar, Jane ran her tongue over the mark to prove to herself it had really happened.

19

The night before they drove to Chicago, Jane dreamed of her mother: lilac dress, front hall, mirror, lipstick. She cried until Jesse woke her, gently smoothing the damp hair away from her eyes. Sand, footprints, ocean, moon: she slid into an uneasy sleep.

The next morning, Jane still felt shaken. She wanted to talk to Jesse, but as soon as they got on the bus, he stretched out in the back and went to sleep. It didn't matter – she knew what he'd say:

Have you tried writing it down?

The longer her anxiety persisted, the more desperate she became.

Fuck it.

Jane took a notebook out of her bag. At first, she logged what she'd seen, then what she'd felt, alternating between the two. As she wrote, a scrap of melody spun off the bus's wheels; Jane held it in her mind as though cupping a minnow in her hands. Then, all at once, her anxious thoughts receded, depositing three neat lines on the page.

Flowers painted on the wall,
Tattered paper bouquets fall,
Your laugh echoes down the hall.

Jane sensed someone approach and closed the notebook. Loretta took the seat beside her.

'I have some news,' said Loretta, glowing. 'My album's been green-lit. We start recording as soon as we get back from tour.'

Jane couldn't believe Loretta had sought her out. It occurred to Jane that she was filling in for Jesse.

'Congratulations,' Jane said. 'You'll have to let me buy you a drink tonight.'

Loretta smiled. 'I'd take some pointers,' she said.

This made Jane laugh. 'You don't need my pointers,' said Jane. 'Unless you want to get blackballed. Then I'm your gal.'

Loretta laughed. A blur of farmland streaked by the window in blue, yellow, and green.

'I've heard good things about Chicago,' said Jane.

'They *loved* Jesse on our last tour,' said Loretta. 'How are you finding all that?'

'His fans?' said Jane.

Loretta shrugged. 'And other things,' she said.

As their eyes met, Jane had the sense of being probed. 'I can't complain,' she said. 'They're buying the record – even if it's just because of Jesse.'

Loretta gave her a hard look that reminded Jane so much of Elsie she had to smile.

'That may be how they're hearing of you,' said Loretta. 'But people don't part with their cash unless they actually like something, I don't care how obsessed they are.'

149

This remark surprised Jane. She knew Loretta was feeling generous from her own news, but Jane couldn't help but feel a rush of gratitude. 'I really appreciate that,' she said.

Loretta smiled. 'We girls have to stick together.' She stood, her eyes lingering on Jesse's inert form. 'Speaking of . . . If you ever need to talk about anything, my door is open.' Her eyes were kind as she said it, but Jane felt taken aback. Loretta gave her a quick squeeze on the shoulder and headed back to her seat.

Kyle turned from the row in front of Jane and whispered, 'I think she's really starting to not hate you!' Jane stuck out her tongue at him.

Their first gig in Chicago was an intimate benefit concert at the London House. The fundraiser was for pancreatic-cancer research, and the cheapest ticket available cost a thousand dollars. Jesse had agreed to participate in honor of his mother, but having to think about her was taking its toll. He slept the whole way to Chicago, and headed straight to his own hotel room when they arrived. Once at the venue, he barricaded himself in his dressing room; Jane stood outside the door, wondering if she should try to go in. She let her hand rest on the brass knob as Rich approached.

'Let's tune,' he said. Jane detected a hint of concern in his expression.

'Yes, let's,' she said. She let herself be absorbed back into the pack.

Jesse emerged from his dressing room as the Breakers received their call. He smiled at the group without looking at Jane directly, then continued toward Huck and Benny for a cigarette.

The Breakers took the stage. After so many stadium sets, it

felt disorienting to be so close to the audience. Jane could see every single one of their faces, even those seated at the rear. She could feel her own energy pulsing within the confines of the space, pressed up against all that money.

'Hey, Chicago, great to be here,' she said, checking her strings. She nodded, and Greg counted them in. Once the music started, life offstage retreated into the wings, and it was just Jane, and the lights, and her band, and their songs. When they finished 'Dirty Bastard,' the room broke into applause.

Jane laughed. 'I needed that,' she said into the mic. The crowd laughed, too.

Midway through 'Spring Fling,' Jane noticed a woman glaring at her from the third row. She felt a prickle at the back of her neck as she turned toward Rich for their duet during the bridge. By the end of the number, the woman was still in the same position, a look of loathing hardened on her face like a mask. Jane inched toward Rich as she took them into 'Indigo.'

> *'What would I do if you were violet and not blue?*
> *If I let my colors show, could we both be indigo?'*

Jane didn't look at the woman again until they finished 'Spark,' but as they joined hands for a bow, Jane saw that she still hadn't moved. As Jane turned to leave the stage, her pulse spiked.

'Great set,' said Willy as Jesse and his band entered stage right. Jesse nodded shyly to the crowd, who stood to applaud him.

'This way,' said Willy. He led the Breakers to a reserved table in front of the stage. A server came by with a bottle of Bordeaux, and they all touched glasses as Jesse finished 'Painted Lady.'

151

'This next song is for someone I really care about,' he said.

He glanced over at Jane as he said this, and Jane felt her heart flutter as he went into 'Morning Star.' The music felt like a signal, sonar waves reassuring her that he was there and okay.

Just as Jane's nerves were starting to settle, Greg leaned toward her and whispered, 'I think you have some competition at three o'clock.'

Jane knew whom he was talking about before she even looked. The woman in the third row sat at attention, but her glare had been replaced by a euphoric grin. She was about forty, primly dressed in a purple frock, and appeared to be on her own. She didn't notice that she was drawing covert stares from around the room; she didn't blink as her eyes bored into Jesse.

Jane's heart continued to rampage inside her chest; she finished her glass of wine and helped herself to the rest of the bottle. There was something unsettling about this woman beyond the obvious, something almost familiar.

'Why don't you go ahead and have the rest?' Kyle teased as she replaced the empty bottle on the table. Jane smiled, but she couldn't feel the humor in it. She tried to focus on Jesse, as he played the opening chords of 'Strangest Thing.' But even as Jane admired him, she felt alarmed.

'For this last tune,' said Jesse, 'I'd like to call the Breakers back on the stage. You've been a great crowd.'

The audience had been drinking throughout the performance, and some of their decorum had begun to slip. They whooped and hollered as Jane and the boys made their way back onstage. Jane took her spot next to Jesse, who looked down at her with a soft expression.

'Shall we?' he said.

Jane nodded. She felt her body pulling toward Jesse as he played the intro to 'Let the Light Go'. Jane smiled up at him as she sang, and as he bent forward to share the mic for the chorus, his face broke into a smile as well.

Something hard flew toward Jane. She turned her head away just in time; a crash fractured the song. Jane and Jesse stumbled back; one by one, the others ceased playing until the only sound to be heard was the woman from the third row screaming at the top of her lungs.

'How could you?' she shouted. 'You love me. You love me! Jesse, what are you doing with that slut? That dirty whore? Jesse, we're engaged, Jesse. We're getting married, Jesse. Jesse. Jesse!'

Jane looked down. Red splotches were pooling inside delicate shards; the woman had hurled her wineglass at them. The splatter had stained Jesse's pant legs, his guitar.

The crowd was in an uproar.

The house lights came up, and security guards moved in from the main entrance. They lifted the woman from her seat by her arms as she thrashed, shrieking, 'Jesse, Jesse!'

Willy appeared and ushered the band off as the proprietor of the Winery leapt onstage. 'Let's remember that we're here for a good cause,' he yelled over the crowd stampeding toward the backstage exit.

Jane's vision began to blur. Her heart was beating so fast she felt as if her rib cage might snap. The people around her became bodies, jostling against one another like cattle in a caravan. She felt as if she had been submerged underwater, her limbs weighted down by a great unmovable mass. She struggled for breath, gasping as the mob burst into the alleyway.

As shoulders bumped past her, Jane reached for the side of

the building to steady herself, brick crumbling like sand under her palm. She must have been drugged. Her head spun, and a wave of heat passed over her. She was going to throw up. Her eyes closed, and the grotesque woman leered inside her mind.

'Jane,' she heard Jesse's voice, felt his hand on her back. 'Jane, are you okay?'

'Jesse,' she said. She opened her eyes, and the first thing she saw was the splatter of the wine on his pants. She turned away from him and threw up.

Cold sweat coated her brow. She wiped her mouth and felt him crouch beside her.

'Oh, Jane,' he said again. His hands pulled her hair back around her shoulders. They stayed like that for a minute. Then she put her hand on his knee and pushed herself up. Jesse stood, regarding her with worried eyes.

'I don't . . .' said Jane. 'I don't know why I'm so upset.'

Jesse pushed the hair out of her eyes.

'It's upsetting to see someone go crazy,' said Jesse. 'Trust me, I get it.' He hesitated.

'What?' said Jane.

He cleared his throat. 'In your dreams, isn't your mom always wearing a purple dress?'

Jane stared at him. 'Jesse, there's something I—'

She felt another wave of nausea and leaned against the wall.

'Easy,' said Jesse. Jane waited for the feeling to dispel before attempting to speak again.

'I wrote about her this morning,' said Jane. 'I did what you said. What if—'

'What if your writing somehow conjured her?' he said gently.

It sounded crazy when he said it out loud, but it didn't feel impossible to Jane. Jesse clasped her shoulders to keep her upright.

'This is the panic talking,' he said. 'You'll feel better after it's cleared your system.'

'When will that be?' said Jane.

Jesse shrugged. 'Not long,' he said. 'Let's get you somewhere quiet.'

Jane didn't move. He took her hand. 'Come with me,' he said. 'I've got you.'

Slowly, the two of them walked out of the alley.

20

On Highway 60B, outside of Louisville, the bus began to struggle; Jane could hear Pete cursing from the driver's seat. Willy stood to have a word with him.

'We're going to stop to have the engine looked at,' he announced as Pete pulled the bus into a gas station. The bands perched around the pumps like crows as Pete opened the engine compartment for the mechanic.

'It's a good thing y'all pulled over,' he said in a slow drawl. 'This steering belt's about to go – a few more miles and this wagon woulda been toast.'

'How long will it take you to fix it?' asked Willy.

The mechanic shrugged. 'I gotta get the part,' he said. 'I'll put in for it on our night shipment from the city. Should have y'all back on the road by noon tomorrow.'

'Is there any way to speed this up?' asked Willy. 'We've gotta be in Memphis by tomorrow night.'

The mechanic stared at Willy. Willy swallowed.

'Motel's about a mile up the road. Y'all can leave your luggage on the bus; we lock the garage at night.'

It was about five as they began the walk toward the motel, single file on the side of the road. Jesse carried his guitar, but the rest of them had left their instruments dead-bolted in the garage.

'This is really the sticks,' said Huck. The air was dense with humidity, but the golden light filtering through the underbrush reminded Jane of home.

It took them twenty minutes to reach the 'town,' which consisted of three structures: a motel, a diner, and a windowless warehouse whose sign read *Peggy Ridge Opry House.*

Inside the diner, waitresses in matching blue uniforms whistled along to a country station as they ferried plates of fried steak and grits from the kitchen window. By the time Jane's food was served, the restaurant had filled with locals. The women wore thick eyeshadow, hair implacably sprayed; their men all dressed like Buddy Holly.

'It's like we've gone back in time,' Kyle whispered to Jane.

Jane looked across the table at Jesse. No one seemed to know him here. People were looking, but not in the bashful way they do when peeking at a celebrity; they were openly staring, as if to say, *This is our town, and you're strangers in it.*

Around seven o'clock, the door opened, and a man stepped in. He was about fifty and wore a plaid shirt, black suspenders, and a black cowboy hat with a feather in the brim; Jane realized that this quorum had gathered in anticipation of his arrival. He shook hands with all of the men and kissed most of the women, all of whom greeted him as 'Raymond,' with warmth. Finally, he looked over at Jane, Jesse, and the rest of their crew.

'Well, what have we here?' he said, approaching them. 'Y'all a church group?'

'Musical group,' said Jesse, playing up the South Carolina intonation in his words.

'Well, in'n that nice,' said Raymond. 'Bluegrass music?'

'Blues,' said Jesse. 'Folk.'

'Rock,' said Greg.

'Like the sound of that,' said Raymond. 'Y'all should come on over to the Opry when you're finished. See what we're about.'

With that, he took leave of them and returned to his admirers. At a quarter to eight, everyone besides the out-of-towners stood up and filed across the street. A chorus of cricket song became audible as their waitress placed the bill in front of Willy.

'Well, if that's everything,' she said, 'we're closing.'

It was early June, but the humidity made Jane's hair cling to her neck. They stood at the crosswalk, smoking and listening to the voices float out from inside the Opry.

'Well, I don't know about you,' said Kyle. 'But I'm going in there.'

Jane, Greg, and Rich all began to walk with him.

'Actually,' said Jesse, 'I think I'll turn in for the night – catch up on some sleep. Hope it's grand.'

Jane felt a stab of disappointment.

'I'll come,' said Huck.

'Same,' said Benny. Jesse, Loretta, Duke, and Willy all turned back toward the motel, and the others crossed the street to the warehouse.

The Opry was a community center of sorts. Bingo tables had been pushed up against the walls to accommodate square dancing on the main floor. Jane wasn't surprised to find Raymond atop a raised platform, tearing through a bluegrass tune on his banjo. Beside him, two other men Jane recognized from the diner played acoustic guitar and upright bass.

'Come on, partner,' said Kyle, pulling Jane into the formation.

A cluster of girls near the door giggled; one approached Rich, and her friends followed suit with Greg, Benny, and Huck.

As Jane hooked arms in a grand reel, this room full of strangers didn't feel all that strange to her. In a way, these people were much more like the ones she had grown up with on the Island than any she'd met in her travels – isolated, insular, a collective. They would protect their own.

Kyle loved meeting new people, and when the band took a break around 9:30 p.m., he went right up to Raymond and introduced himself. The next thing Jane knew, the bassist was on the dance floor and Kyle had taken his spot onstage. Kyle had originally learned on an upright, which was why he'd sanded all the frets off his instrument when he switched to an electric. Raymond seemed delighted to find a new musical companion who could keep pace with him.

'Whoever heard a Yankee play like that?' Raymond said. The audience laughed.

Around 10:30 p.m., the doors creaked open, and Willy and Jesse walked in. Jesse looked better than he had in recent weeks, eyes soft, a pleasant, dreamlike expression on his face. Jane felt heartened to see him.

'Look who the cat dragged in,' Benny called, clapping his friend on the shoulder. Rich popped the cap off a beer and handed it to Jesse; he sipped it nonchalantly, but the minute the dance ended, he crossed the room to Jane in a few quick strides.

'You changed your mind,' said Jane.

Those blazing blue eyes smiled down at her. 'May I have a dance?' he asked.

They danced the next number together, and then the next; no one else asked Jane once she started dancing with Jesse. There was freedom in the movement, in being told what to do, in not having to think. The more Jane looked into Jesse's face, the brighter she felt herself shine.

When the dance finished around 11:00 p.m., the crowd applauded, then began to peel away in twos and threes. Raymond came down off the stage, clapping Kyle on the shoulder, eager to meet the rest of his band. Jane, Rich, and Greg shook his hand.

Then Raymond turned to Jesse. 'You the manager?' he asked.

'I'm the boyfriend,' said Jesse. Everyone went along with it, as if for tonight they'd stepped into an alternate universe where Jane was the superstar. They pooled some folding chairs together, and Raymond's guitarist retrieved two cases of beer from the kitchenette.

'My father was a Chickasaw brave, and my mother was the daughter of the Baptist preacher who came to convert him,' said Raymond with a grin. He had toured the world with his banjo, and then wound up back in Peggy Ridge, playing at the Opry each weekend. 'It's my home,' he said.

As the first case was finished and the second opened, Raymond asked them about their home. The Breakers talked about Bayleen Island, about what it was like to grow up there, about how they had played together as children and then become a band.

'So you're the singer,' Raymond said to Jane, who was seated in the chair beside him. Jesse was sprawled out on the floor, his head resting against her thigh. Jane nodded.

'Would you sing something for us?'

At this, Jesse roused himself. 'Would you?' he said. His earnestness moved Jane; the clouds that had been obscuring him with each new city had momentarily parted, and here he was, the same person she had met last summer.

'Sure,' said Jane. She accepted the guitar she was handed and tuned it to her own chords.

'This is something new I've been working on,' she said. Jesse sat up a little at that, and Jane felt her cheeks grow warm. 'It needs another verse, but I'll play you what I have. Maybe you all can help me finish it.' She laughed a small silvery laugh, and then began to play.

Ultimately, she envisioned this song for the piano, but she'd had to put it together on her guitar since that was all she had on the road. She strummed the intro, a progression of dark, biting chords that sizzled with longing.

> *'Flowers painted on the wall,*
> *Tattered paper bouquets fall,*
> *Your laugh echoes down the hall.'*

As she played, she felt her spirit taking solace in this place, sheltered from the bright lights and complexities of the world she had entered on tour. The chorus was a conversation between her and the guitar, in which she sang and the guitar answered back.

> *'I've never known a girl like you,*
> *Dress so faded, eyes so blue,*
> *Lord in heaven, see me through.'*

She played what she had and ended the song with another round of back and forth between the verse and the guitar. The final chords hung in the room like the ghost of a perfume.

'By and by, how time flies.'

She looked up at the men sitting around her and found herself momentarily alone as each of them had his own private reaction.

Raymond was the first to speak. 'Woman, you've got a cathedral inside you.'

Jane bowed her head in thanks.

Greg rose from his seat and cleared his throat, tapping his own chest a couple times. 'I'm gonna head back to the hotel, give Maggie a call,' he said. As he went, Jane caught a mournful look pass behind the veil of Rich's eyes. Was he upset she'd written a song without him?

'I like this part,' said Kyle, taking the guitar from Jane and playing back the bridge. Jane could tell he was already thinking about what the bass would sound like.

Jane looked at Jesse, who was watching her quietly, legs crossed on the floor. As their eyes met, his shone with pride. Jane felt humbled.

Their gathering disbanded just after 1:00 a.m.

'Don't be strangers,' Raymond said, tipping his hat and disappearing down the street with his banjo case.

The group made their way back to the motel by the light of the full moon and turned in.

'Just give me one moment,' said Jesse, slipping into his room. Jane heard the sound of paper shuffling and a hand clamping guitar strings as Jesse replaced his instrument in its case. He reappeared at the door and stood in the frame, separating the blue light of the parking lot from the yellow light of his room.

'Were you writing?' asked Jane.

Jesse hesitated, then nodded. 'It seems you were, too,' he said.

Jane placed her hand on his and kissed him in the moonlight, a chaste kiss of pure affection. He stood for a moment, looking at her, then took her hand and led her inside. They undressed and lay down on top of the sheets.

'This town,' Jesse said, 'it makes me feel like I'm back on the Island.'

Jane nodded, tracing a figure eight on his sternum.

'I bought some land, you know,' he said. 'Up in Caverswall.'

'Did you?' said Jane.

'About a hundred acres,' he said. Jane lifted her head in surprise.

'What?' he said. 'I've got to do something with this cash. Nothing safer than real estate.'

'What do you need with a hundred acres?' Jane asked.

Jesse touched her hair, pushing it away from her eyes. 'To build a cabin where no one can find me,' he said. He shrugged. 'Except you.' He turned toward her, his head resting in his hand.

'You know,' he said, 'not only are you my favorite person, but you're my favorite singer.'

Jane laughed.

'I mean it,' he said. 'That song was . . . Don't get me wrong, I love seeing you rock. I love to see your joy. But not a lot of people can do what you did there.'

'What do you mean?' asked Jane.

Jesse's hand brushed the hair from her face.

'Catharsis,' he said. Jane looked at him for a long moment. Then she kissed him. As he pulled her close, she felt something crush inside her; it had been wafer-thin, a thread, a wishbone, but she knew it would never be whole again.

163

21

The next day, they were back on the road by noon. Jesse sat beside Jane, watching a tapestry of green rush by the window. She could feel the ease slipping away from him with each passing mile, like water from a cracked urn; by the time they arrived in Memphis, he had retreated fully into himself. Jane spent the night watching reruns with Kyle and Rich, and didn't see Jesse until the following morning, when they were all scheduled to appear at the Pegasus offices in the financial district.

The record company's headquarters were in L.A., but three of their most profitable labels – Lovelorn (R&B), Night Rider (Pop), and True Twang (Country) – were Memphis outposts. Lenny Davis, the head of the company, happened to be in town for a week of marketing meetings and wanted to shake hands with Jesse to congratulate him on his success. Jane found herself in his office, staring at her own reflection in a polished oak coffee table; around them, golden records punctuated the walls at intervals like portholes in a battleship.

Lenny Davis entered the room, flanked by two large men. All of them wore gingham shirts, bell-bottoms, and tinted glasses similar to Willy's. Lenny had all the trappings of success:

a big gold watch, a big round gut. He had almost no hair on his head, but tufts spilled out from his plaid shirt, glinting with chains like a conifer decked in tinsel.

'Welcome,' he said. His smile revealed a large gap between his two front teeth.

Jesse, head to toe in denim, looked like a factory worker who had been brought to the foreman's office for a commendation. He held himself like one, too, head bowed, shoulders up around his ears. Willy had to bring him over to shake Lenny's hand, as if he were a shy child being introduced to an ancient relative.

Lenny Davis seemed not to notice, and beamed at Jesse. 'Jesse,' he said. 'Jesse. Welcome.'

They seated themselves on the white plastic furniture atop a red lawn of shag carpet.

'What a year it's been,' he said. 'Our projections are showing that, by the end of this quarter, *Painted Lady* will have sold over a million copies. What do you have to say to that?'

Jesse smiled vaguely – he looked as if he was having a hard time keeping his eyes open. Jane knew that despite Lenny Davis's overtures of warmth, they were being assessed.

'It's been quite a year,' Jesse repeated.

Lenny Davis smiled at him, nodding slowly. Without warning, he turned to Jane. 'And this is Jane Quinn,' he said, looking at her but not speaking to her.

'And the Breakers,' said Jane, indicating Greg, Kyle, and Rich standing around her. 'We're so pleased to meet you.'

'It's been a good year for you, too,' he said. His eyes lingered on her for a moment, then flicked to Jesse, then back to her. Jane wondered if he knew about what had happened with Vincent Ray, and whether that still mattered.

'Good,' said Lenny Davis. 'Good.'

He rose from his chair, and his men followed suit, each placing a hand on the door in anticipation of Lenny's exit.

'I think I will come tonight,' he said to Willy, continuing an earlier conversation. 'Nice to meet you all.' Another gap-toothed grin, and he was out the door.

'I think we really won him over,' said Kyle. Everyone laughed except Jesse, who didn't appear to have heard him.

'Did you sleep okay?' Jane asked Jesse as they rode the mirrored elevator down to the lobby. His reflection made a face, and hers made one back, and then they filed out into the lobby, having never directly looked at each other.

As promised, Maggie met the tour in Memphis, bringing Bea with her by train. That afternoon, the Breakers went to the station to collect them.

'I'm so glad you're here,' said Greg as they embraced. Jane could tell he was choked up.

'You look good,' said Maggie, putting a hand on his shoulder. Jane bounced Bea on her hip. A whistle sounded in the yard, and Bea searched for its origin through her halo of yellow ringlets.

'Choo-choo,' said Jane. 'Choo-choo.' She lifted Bea toward Rich, whose face had gone as pale as the steam rising from the engines.

That afternoon, Greg insisted on taking Bea to the aquarium.

'She's not going to remember it,' Maggie said to Jane as the two of them sipped coffee at the hotel restaurant. 'But I think it's sweet that he wants to take her.'

'He really missed her,' said Jane. 'He missed both of you.

Whenever we'd go out, he'd just stare at the clock the whole time, waiting to call you.'

'We missed him, too,' said Maggie. 'This is a big adventure for us.'

Maggie seemed so much smaller to Jane in the context of her new world. For the first time in Jane's life, she was aware of being more put together than her cousin. This was both empowering and disorienting. Craving Maggie's approval had been a way of life; now Jane found she simply cared less, and this left her unmoored. 'Of course,' Maggie was saying, 'this is nothing compared to what Mom's doing.'

'Is she really going to London?' said Jane.

Maggie nodded disbelievingly. 'Apparently, Mom really is a good nurse,' she said. 'Millie goes overseas every fall to visit with her grandkids and is hiring Mom to go with her as a traveling aid. They leave in September.'

Jane's mind reeled. 'So, what's going to happen with—'

'I guess she worked something out with the Center,' said Maggie. 'Millie's a patient there – I think they're looking at it as some kind of exchange program.'

'I can't believe it,' said Jane. The idea of Grace leaving the Island felt impossible to her.

'I know,' said Maggie. 'I didn't think she would go through with it. But there are a lot of things I didn't think would happen.'

Maggie shook her head. They sipped their coffee in silence.

The Breakers' call that night was for 6:00 p.m. at Minglewood Hall. Jane finished tuning early and went out back for a smoke. There, she found Rich staring morosely into the twilight.

167

'Got a light?' Jane asked.

Rich flipped her his lighter, and Jane offered him a cigarette. He took the box and tapped it against his hand, but didn't open it.

'What's eating you?' asked Jane.

Rich shrugged.

Jane lit up and let the smoke fill her lungs.

'Janie,' said Rich. 'Have you ever . . .' He stopped. He was nervous. He shook his head, turning over the cigarette box in his hands.

'Have I ever what?' said Jane. Rich swallowed.

'Have you ever wanted someone you shouldn't?' he said.

Jane stood perfectly still.

'I kept hoping at some point he would lose interest in her,' said Rich.

Jane looked up at him.

'But he didn't, and now she's here. And even if she weren't, he still wouldn't be interested in me.' He laughed and shook his head.

If I let my colors show.

Jane reached over and took his hand.

'Rich,' she said. 'How long?'

Rich blinked a few times. 'Oh, years,' he said. 'Since high school. I thought I'd get over it. Then I tried to convince myself that there was a chance, holding on to little moments. Like that one night in L.A. he fell asleep with his arm around me? I thought about that for weeks – even as we would be falling asleep a bed over from each other. Pathetic.'

'It's not,' she said.

'It is,' said Rich. 'And now that I see him here with Maggie,

I'm reminded of how pathetic it is. I think they're going to move in together after the tour.'

Jane hadn't thought about what would happen after the tour; the idea that it would ever end came as a shock to her.

'If they do, I'm moving to California,' he said, offering her back the cigarette pack. When she reached for it, he didn't release it right away. 'Don't . . . tell anyone,' he said.

Jane nodded. He let the cigarettes go and went back inside.

Jane's mind was in a fog as she walked backstage. Her initial surprise at hearing Rich's confession had given way to a mental inventory of prolonged glances and signs she now felt she should have seen. *I'm moving to California.* Surely he didn't mean that – what would happen to the Breakers? Jane was hardly aware of where she was going when she heard Willy's voice, low and pleading, around the corner. She slowed her pace.

'It's unfortunate,' Willy was saying. 'But it is what it is. I've tried to talk to him about it, but there's only so much I can say before he shuts me out.'

There was a long pause; then the response came in Lenny Davis's unmistakable rasp. 'I sure hope you know what you're doing. I don't need to explain to you that there's an awful lot riding on this kid – on his image.'

'Today was bad,' Willy said. 'Honestly, he's a pleasant guy; he's usually more engaged. He doesn't like the business stuff, so he may have gone a little overboard.'

'I don't need him to like business – hell, if he did, he'd probably never sell another record. But we can't have people seeing him this strung out – the fans can't see that.'

'They don't,' said Willy. 'Trust me, you'll see – that's why I wanted you to come tonight. I thought it would be reassuring.

When he's up there, he's everything he's supposed to be and more. When he and Jane sing together, the last thing anyone's thinking about is whether he's stoned.'

'She's a cute little piece,' said Lenny. 'That was smart to put them up there together – no one who's fucking her could be seen as anything other than a paragon of health.'

'Jane is very special to all of us,' said Willy, and Jane was gratified to hear a tremor of fury in his voice. 'They genuinely care for each other.'

'Oh yes, of course, of course,' said Lenny. 'Forgot she's one of yours, too. Say – you think they'll get married? Nothing says "stability" like a wedding ring. That would give us some air cover to deal with the smack.'

'Can't say that I know,' said Willy.

'Well, you work on that and we should have no problem,' said Lenny.

'Right,' said Willy.

Jane ducked behind a curtain just as Lenny passed. Had he just said *smack*?

Willy followed a moment later. He wasn't wearing his aviators, and Jane was reminded that he was probably younger than Grace. He wiped his hand over his face, standing not two feet from her hiding place. Then he walked away in the opposite direction from Lenny. Jane waited a beat, then stepped out from behind the curtain, and turned the corner.

They had been standing in front of the door to Jesse's dressing room. Jane felt the overwhelming compulsion to go inside. Her heart began to pound as she reached for the knob. She didn't want to knock, she didn't want to think. The rounded medal pressed into her palm; Jane took hold of it and turned.

The room was dark and musty; there was no light except a single candle, the windows bolted shut. As Jane's eyes adjusted, her brain refused to make sense of what she saw.

She thought of the time she'd come across a hulking mass in the middle of Main Street on her way to Widow's Peak. It had taken her a moment to identify what she had been looking at, because she had only ever heard about it; and then the context clues filtered in – yellow tape, the ambulance, the onlookers. A car had flipped, and this shape she was struggling to identify was the underside of a vehicle.

Her mind now grasped at strands of thought to keep her from comprehending what lay before her. Jesse was sprawled out on the floor, a black cord wrapped around his arm like an asp, his veins pulsing as though he had been bitten. His head rolled back against the radiator.

Jane rushed into the room to check his vitals. He let out a sound like an animal being freed, his expression familiar – the same dreamlike look he wore on the bus, onstage. A dirty spoon lay beside his arm. His hand rested over a syringe, as though he'd just used it to sign his name. Jesse struggled to open his eyes.

'Jane,' he said softly. He looked pained, as if he were hearing a sad story about someone he'd never met. He was too out of it even to try to get up; he could barely keep his eyes open. A wave of revulsion passed through Jane, followed by the urge to kick him away.

'Jane.' Willy had appeared in the doorway, holding a towel and a glass of water. At the sight, Jane's fury redirected like lightning to an airplane.

'What the hell,' she said. She could see Willy calculating the best way to handle her, and she continued before he could speak. 'This is so fucked,' she said, voice shaking with anger. 'He's back here shooting up, and you're performing a beverage service.'

'Jane,' he said, stunned, 'I thought you knew—'

'You pushed us together – fucking great for publicity. I'm just what his image needs, right?' she said, the walls closing in.

'Jane, slow down,' Willy said. 'That's not fair. You two met on your own, I never—'

'You lied to me,' said Jane. She moved to the door; if she didn't get out of this dark, poisonous room, she was going to lose her mind.

'Let's go somewhere quiet and talk about this,' said Willy, putting a hand on her shoulder. Jane slapped him away.

'I'm not going anywhere with you,' she said.

'Just five minutes, that's all I ask,' he said.

'Or what? You'll tell your dad on me?'

'Jane—'

'No,' she said. 'You just do whatever the fuck you want while everyone around you pretends like they're not part of it. I'm done.'

Jane lunged toward the door. Willy blocked it.

'Let me out of here,' Jane shrieked.

'Jane, I can't let you go out there like this,' he said.

Jane hit him again, this time in the chest. Willy was about her height, but he was much stronger; he didn't even flinch at the blow, so she hit him again. And again, and again, until a great, heaving sob welled up inside of her, and she crumpled into his arms like a kite with a broken sail.

22

Island Folk Fest

Saturday, July 25, 1970

From the wing of the Main Stage, Jane listened to the crowd whirring in the meadow. With a dull ache she thought of the last time she'd been here. She hadn't known as she'd sung 'Sweet and Mellow' that everything had been about to begin. Now it was almost over.

It was fun while it lasted.

For three weeks, Jane had refused to examine her breakup with Jesse. All the things she had said and all that she hadn't were trapped in a compartment deep in her mind, straining for release; whenever a snippet managed to escape, she'd shove it back down.

You cannot think this was just fun.

Shove.

Soon, she would be able to shut herself away and process all that had happened; she just had to stay angry for a few more hours. That wouldn't be a problem. She had plenty of ammunition.

Jane watched Morgan Vidal onstage, and her heart sank. Morgan was fashionable and golden, her reddish-brown hair billowing out in feathery wisps. Offstage, in shadow, Jane was reminded of how she'd felt the last time she'd seen Morgan, the night she'd met Jesse: invisible.

'You ready?' said Rich. Jane turned to him and nodded. Greg and Kyle fidgeted a little ways off. Rich was the only person on tour who wasn't nervous to be around Jane right now.

Rich was the only person she was speaking to.

It had happened in Baltimore, a week after Jane's split from Jesse. Willy had called the Breakers into his hotel room to discuss the newly green-lit European leg of the *Painted Lady* tour. Jane had assumed she was being invited.

She stared Willy down as the Breakers seated themselves on stock hotel furniture; they hadn't spoken since Memphis. Jane knew it would be awkward, but she wasn't going to give up a spot on an international tour. To her surprise, Greg spoke first.

'I'm out,' he said. His face reddened, but his jaw was set. 'It's been a hell of a ride, and I wouldn't take a second of it back. But my place is on the Island. Maggie has agreed to move in with me. I feel like I've already missed so much – I don't want to miss any more.'

A buzzing filled Jane's skull. 'Okay,' she said, mouth dry. 'So . . . we need a drummer. There must be someone – a studio hire.'

Willy cleared his throat. 'It's not that simple,' he said, taking Jane's stare in stride. 'It would be one thing to replace one member, but you're looking at replacing two, and at that point it's not even the Breakers anymore.'

'Two?' said Jane. She realized that they had all been speaking without her.

'What is he talking about?' she demanded, turning to Rich, and then to Kyle. Kyle looked even guiltier than Greg.

'Kyle?' said Jane.

He swallowed and looked at Willy.

'Duke's contract is up at the end of this month,' said Willy. 'He's headed back to L.A. to start another gig in two weeks.'

'So?' said Jane, staring at Kyle. She knew what it meant; she just wanted to make him say it.

'Jesse's offered me a spot in his band,' Kyle said, voice breaking. 'And I said okay. Janie, I—'

Jane's eyes flew to Rich; suddenly he was the only person in the room who didn't make her want to scream. This was a once-in-a-lifetime opportunity for Kyle. Under different circumstances, Jane would have been ecstatic for him; right now, though, if he'd been any closer to an open window, she would have pushed him out.

'I didn't realize when I accepted that Greg was out, too,' said Kyle. 'It's just six weeks—'

'Exactly,' said Jane, panic rising in her chest. She couldn't be losing her band. It wasn't possible. She turned back to Greg. 'Can't you give it six more weeks?' Greg's face contorted.

'What?' said Jane. 'What aren't you saying?'

Greg gritted his teeth. 'Lenny Davis offered to buy me out of my contract,' he said. 'I can't afford not to take this. I . . . we all know I was lucky to be here in the first place. I'm just not as . . . I . . . I have to take this. I want to give Maggie a house.'

Jane felt her eyelids droop as she began to understand. Willy hadn't been inviting them on the tour at all – she had failed

175

to perform her function as Jesse's sweetheart, and now Pegasus was edging her out using her own band.

'I can't breathe,' said Jane.

'Jane,' said Willy, 'I know you're hurting, but believe me when I say this is in your best interest. You don't want to be on that tour.'

'Yes, I do,' she said, speaking to him for the first time in a week.

'No, you don't,' said Willy. 'Trust me. You don't want to be here when the media realizes you and Jesse have broken up.'

'They didn't even know we were together,' she said.

Willy gave her a hard look.

'I have a right to go,' said Jane.

'This is bigger than you,' said Willy. 'You're contending with the label, and you don't want to see what they'll do to protect their headliner.'

'I would never do anything to hurt Jesse,' said Jane. Tears began to roll down her cheeks.

'But you could,' said Willy quietly. 'If people start digging into your split, you could.'

Ever since Jane had walked in on Jesse, Willy had been unflappably calm, the picture of an operator. But as he spoke now, he sounded desperate. The person beneath the veneer was breaking through just long enough to send a message. 'Jane, they will feed you to the wolves before they let a speck of dirt touch his name. I don't want that for you.'

Willy cleared his throat. 'Why not get some space and regroup before your next album?' he said.

Jane stared at the floor. A full minute passed before she responded. 'Yes,' she said. 'I think there will be a lot of space between all of you and my next album.'

She had walked out of the room, and hadn't spoken to Willy, Kyle, or Greg in the two weeks since. The Breakers were so practiced that their performances hadn't suffered – it was remarkable what could be accomplished onstage among people who weren't on speaking terms.

After that conversation, the Pegasus machine kicked into full gear. As furious as Jane was with Willy, part of her had begun to suspect that he really had been looking out for her. The speed with which Morgan Vidal had been pegged as Jane's replacement had been astonishing; when the label needed to protect its investment, it could move mountains. Distraction was paramount; before anyone could question where Jane had gone, she would be replaced by someone shiny and new. This performance at the Folk Fest was a handoff of sorts.

It was fun while it lasted.

Jane had no idea how Jesse felt – they hadn't spoken since they'd broken up. But rumors were already circulating around the Folk Fest about him and Morgan.

As she watched her now onstage, Morgan's presence here made more sense to Jane than her own ever had. Morgan came from money on both sides; her grandfathers were Hector Vidal and Edward Riley. Vidal had founded Banreservas, the largest bank in the Dominican Republic, now chaired by Morgan's esteemed father, Victor. Riley had been the president and CEO of CBS before retiring to a ten-bedroom Colonial mansion in Perry's Landing. Jane guessed that Lenny Davis had been happy to sign Morgan, fresh out of Barnard College, for more reasons than one. *She's a natural,* Jane thought as she watched her sing a Judy Collins cover.

Jane heard footsteps and turned to see Willy.

He lit a cigarette and offered it to Jane, who refused it. He inhaled; his aviators were two yellow screens of Morgan singing.

'Jane,' he said, 'before we go, I really want to say—'

'Go to hell,' said Jane.

Willy exhaled. He shook his head and walked away amidst a sprinkle of applause. Jane looked up and saw Mark Edison watching her through the lattice track.

'What do you think about the rumors, Janie Q?' he said.

Jane gave him a look.

'I mean, about the Fest going under?'

The Fest was in dire straits. Attendance had diminished to a record low, and there was talk of shutting it down. Not even Jesse had been enough to draw in the mainlanders this year. Without the crowds, the backers would likely pull out.

As Jane turned away from Mark Edison, she caught Rich's eye. He would go to California now for certain, Jane knew – he wanted to be across the country when Greg moved in with Maggie. Jane looked into his familiar features, the source of comfort and stability during so many rehearsals, so many shows. Dread curdled inside her at the thought of losing their partnership. Rich's lyrics had always made her feel safe expressing herself; how would she do that now?

Jane put the thought from her mind as a wave of applause swept Morgan Vidal off the stage. Up close, she looked flushed and breathless; Jane remembered how she had felt after her first performance in front of a crowd this large, and felt a surge of envy.

'Nice job,' said Kyle, giving Morgan a wave.

'Thanks,' she said. Jane wasn't surprised they were already acquainted, given Kyle's outgoing nature and desire to ease tension; Jane was sure he was going out of his way to be kind to everyone he'd be traveling with in the coming weeks.

'You're Jane Quinn,' Morgan said, brushing past Kyle. To Jane's surprise, Morgan started to stammer. 'I have to tell you, "Spark" got me through this past spring.'

Jane smiled, caught off guard by the flattery. It was satisfying to hear that something she had written so specifically for herself could have relevance for another person – even if that person had come here to replace her.

'It's so great to meet you,' said Morgan.

'It's great to meet you, too,' said Jane, stifling the urge to point out that they had met before. 'Nice show out there.'

'Thanks,' Morgan said. Her shyness seemed to give way to discomfort. 'I also wanted to say – I'm sorry to hear about your grandfather. I wish we could be going together. This is a huge chance for me.'

'My grandfather . . . ?' said Jane. Morgan was looking around.

'Hey, have you seen – Oh, there he is. Hey!'

Morgan's face blossomed into a pearly grin as Loretta and Benny entered the backstage area, followed by Jesse. He looked worn out, but it did nothing to detract from his handsomeness. After this show, he would be on a flight off Bayleen Island; Jane's part in the tour would be over, and they need never speak again.

Jane's eyes landed on Loretta, who gave her a quick wink and cast a skeptical eye over Morgan. Jane felt a tiny tremor of enjoyment; her one consolation in all of this would be imagining Morgan trying to ingratiate herself to Loretta.

Jesse's expression was somber. His eyes swept over Morgan to Jane, and then back to Morgan, who was aggressively waving him over to them.

179

'Hi,' he said, standing between them. Jane felt Greg and Rich shifting behind her.

'Hope I didn't keep you out too late last night,' said Morgan. Jesse looked so uncomfortable that Jane didn't know whether to laugh or scream.

'You know, dinner at the club may very well be the thing that puts me over,' he said, disdain audible in his pronunciation of 'the club.'

Morgan seemed determined to be cheery. 'Well, my parents enjoyed seeing you.'

Jesse nodded. 'I better go warm up,' he said. Jane could tell he was just looking for an excuse to get out of this conversation, but his expression changed as he realized his remark could be interpreted as a reference to dope. 'I just meant "tune,"' he said, looking at Jane.

'I think Jane Quinn knows what "warm up" means,' said Morgan.

Jane smiled politely.

Jesse ran his hand through his hair, and Jane wondered why he wasn't leaving. Then she realized he was hoping Morgan would, so that he could speak with Jane. Morgan wasn't going anywhere.

'You're on in two,' the stage manager said, flashing a hand at Jane and the boys. Jane could feel Jesse growing more desperate as she picked up her guitar. She allowed herself to look him in the eye – something she hadn't done in weeks, for fear of what she'd see and what she'd feel.

It was fun while it lasted.

'I just wanted to say . . .' said Jesse.

You cannot think this was just fun.

His voice broke, and for an instant, Jane felt the urge to pull him back to her, a visceral longing that took her breath away. Then their eye contact was severed as he glanced at Morgan, staring up at him with open adoration. He coughed and muttered, 'Good luck,' to his feet.

Jane slung her guitar over her shoulder, the strap cutting a line across her heart. She took one last look at Jesse and walked onstage without another word.

23

That night, Jane collapsed on her bed and wept great heaving sobs. After some time, Grace came into her room and sat beside her, placing a hand on Jane's back as she cried.

'What if I hadn't gone in that room?' said Jane.

'It wouldn't have changed anything,' said Grace. 'Not really.'

'I'd still be on tour,' said Jane. 'I'd still have my band. I'd still have—'

Hollow notes floated up from the wind chimes on the porch.

'I'm proud of you,' said Grace. 'Not a lot of people have your integrity.'

Safe at home, Jane's breakup with Jesse began to unpack itself in her mind. She could barely remember her performance that night in Memphis. The crowd had roared like an invisible ocean concealed behind a screen of light; as Jane sang, she had the sensation of being crushed by wave after wave and wanting it, wanting oblivion.

She and Jesse had performed 'Let the Light Go' for the last time, standing six inches apart, not looking at each other. After they bowed, Jane put down her guitar in the wing and walked as fast as she could out the stage door.

Jesse followed her into the alley. Jane vibrated with the energy of performance, unable to stand still; Jesse stalked after her slowly. Finally, he caught her by the shoulders. She didn't let him hug her, not exactly, but she stopped moving. Jesse let his hands fall to his sides.

'You did say you don't mind needles,' said Jane.

Jesse flinched. 'This . . . isn't something I'm proud of,' he said. 'I didn't want you to find out.'

'Who else knows?' said Jane.

'The band – my band, at least. Willy. My parents.'

Jane thought back to Dr. Reid's harsh watch over Jesse; to Loretta's concern on the bus. She felt a wave of anger. 'Since when? L.A.?' she asked. 'The *Rolling Stone* cover?'

Jesse let out a long breath. 'The truth is, Jane, I've had this habit on and off since '65. It's why I crashed my bike last summer – I shot up before the Fest and thought I was good to drive. . . .'

Jane felt the color drain from her face. Jesse's crash had been the genesis of her career. This 'habit,' as he called it, was the reason she was here. The thought was unbearable.

'So, last summer, you were using the whole time?' she said.

He shook his head vehemently. 'No,' he said. 'No. Last summer – after I met you – was the first time in a long time I felt whole without it.'

'What happened?' said Jane, bone-tired all of a sudden.

'What always happens,' he said dully. 'It was there, so I used it. It doesn't take any more than that.'

Jane held her forehead in her palm. She searched the sky for a moon that wasn't there. 'Where was it? I never saw—'

Jesse's eyes were empty. 'In my guitar case,' he said.

The air around Jane grew hot. 'Peggy Ridge,' she said. 'You

said you were writing. You lied to me.' Jane felt surprised. Somehow, it had never occurred to her that he might do that.

'I know,' said Jesse. 'I'm so sorry. I . . . I never meant to.'

The words lit up a circuit deep inside her brain; Jane could hear her mother pleading the same excuse to Grace. She felt something inside of her snap.

'I need to know that reality is reality,' she said.

The color drained from Jesse's face. 'I'll quit,' said Jesse.

'You'll quit,' said Jane. Her fury glowed white, illuminating an emerging awareness. Jane had been down this road before: if she didn't exit now, she'd be on this track for miles.

'Yes,' said Jesse. 'I . . . I will leave the tour right now and go back to the Zoo. Honestly, Jane, I will. I'll do anything.'

Jane could picture the two of them walking down the sterile hallway of the Center's secure ward, Jesse in white, Jane in blue. She had vowed to herself that she wouldn't get stuck in that place; had she somehow managed to land in the role of caregiver on this tour?

Now Jane was floating above her body. She heard herself say, 'You probably should, but not on my account.'

'What do you mean?' said Jesse, stricken.

Jane shrugged. 'I mean, it was fun while it lasted, but if it wasn't this, it was going to be something else.'

Jesse's eyes grew round.

'You cannot think this was just fun – not with everything we share,' he said. 'Jane, I love you.'

Jane watched a moth flutter toward the light by the stage door.

'I'm sorry,' said Jane. 'But that's not how I feel.'

Jesse's temper flared. 'I don't believe you,' he said. He stepped toward her.

Jane froze him with a look. 'I told you up front I would only be able to take this so far,' she said. Then, after a moment, 'I do hope you are able to get help.'

'Jane, please, don't . . .' His beautiful face trembled.

Jane felt an errant hope sprout inside her.

'It's over,' she said, before she could give herself the chance to waver. She refused to look or speak to him further.

Each day, when Jane awoke at Gray Gables, it took her a few seconds to remember where she was – then it struck her anew what she had left behind, and her mind would sink into a marinade of the shows she should be singing, the people she should be meeting, the places she should be visiting. At night, she dreamed of her mother, of clicking heels, and closing doors, and blue eyes that would never look at her the same again.

After a week of this, Jane walked down to Beach Tracks in her bathrobe and a pair of sandals.

'Give me the opposite of pop,' she said without removing her sunglasses. Dana led her to the classical section.

Jane began to listen to piano concertos in her room, night and day, trying to draw out the devastation inside of her with music. Her grief had made her feral, and the Quinns gave her a wide berth. As July melted into August, none of them commented when Jane didn't go back to work. They ignored her infrequent showers. They didn't press about what had happened.

By now, Jane had perfected a new routine. Each day, she slept until noon. Then she went out and bought two packs of Pall Malls, which she brought back to her room. From there, she played records and lay on her bed, chain-smoking until she fell asleep.

'Turn it down, the baby needs to nap,' Maggie screamed, banging on the door.

'Sorry, I forgot you still live here,' said Jane, staring at the phonograph across the room.

As promised, Greg had used his buyout money to put down a deposit on a half-Cape cottage for Maggie and the baby in Lightship Bay, inspection pending. Whenever Maggie talked about it, Jane left the room. Greg was the prime reason she was stranded here and not on tour. Jane hated him, and Maggie by extension. She had no interest in hearing about their life and couldn't wait for Maggie to move out.

'Don't blame us for your problems,' Maggie shouted at Jane through her locked bedroom door. 'Greg's not the one who made you break up with Jesse.' Jane turned up the record player.

The moment Greg and Maggie closed on the house, Rich booked a one-way ticket from Boston to Los Angeles. He planned to crash with Duke until he found a place.

'Do you have to go?' asked Jane as they walked to the ferry. Rich felt like her last link to her music, and the thought of his being across the country made her frantic.

'You know I do,' said Rich. 'There's nothing for me here.'

'There's me,' said Jane. 'There's our next album. Rich, how am I supposed to write without you?'

Rich paused, resting his duffel bag on the sea wall. He took her hands in both of his.

'Janie,' he said, 'you don't need me to write. You never did.'

'Yes, I do,' said Jane, tears rising in her throat.

Rich shook his head. 'We both know that's not true,' he said. 'How many songs have you made knowing the words from the start? How many times have you thrown out your own lyrics to make room for mine?'

Jane said nothing to this, her eyes brimming. Sure, she'd written 'Spark,' but that was just one song. Rich squeezed her hands.

'You'll be just fine on your own,' he said.

'But I don't want to be on my own,' said Jane, tears falling down her cheeks.

'Then come with me,' said Rich. Jane didn't want to do this, either; Kyle was planning to move in with Rich when he returned from tour, and the idea of living with him made Jane ill.

'I'll call you when I get there,' he said, and kissed her on the forehead. He heaved his duffel bag onto his shoulder and walked up the gangplank, looking lighter with every step. Jane stood on the pier until the ferry became a speck on the horizon. It was the longest she'd been outside since coming back from tour.

Maggie moved in with Greg later that week.

Jane had forgotten about Grace's trip to London until Grace sat her and Elsie down to discuss coverage at the Center while she was overseas with her current charge, Millie.

'It's all arranged,' said Grace. 'If one of you can check in on Sundays, they'll be fine keeping everything in place until I'm back.'

Elsie nodded.

'Jane?' said Grace.

Jane's mind was in Memphis. 'Sorry, yes,' she said. 'Once a week.'

Grace and Millie were scheduled to leave via ocean liner at the end of August. Elsie and Jane drove Grace to the pier in Lightship Bay to see her off. When Jane saw that Maggie had brought Greg, she refused to get out of the station wagon, burrowing into the passenger's seat. Her unwashed hair clung to the inside of her sunglasses.

'Jane,' said Grace, 'I know it doesn't feel this way, but you're going to get through this. By the time I'm back for Christmas, you will be in a different place.'

'Sure I will,' said Jane. She didn't remember to wish her aunt luck. As she watched Grace walk toward the pier, she noticed that Grace looked about twenty years younger out of her nurse's uniform. Millie pulled up in a taxi, and Grace hugged Elsie goodbye, then Maggie. Jane calculated the current time in Europe; everyone on tour would just be sitting down to dinner.

As Grace helped Millie up the gangplank, Greg wrapped his arm around Maggie and Bea, and together they walked back to his VW Bug. Maggie paused and looked over her shoulder toward Jane, who stared right past her at the ship leaving the harbor.

'Hey,' said Elsie, rapping on the car window. Jane reached over and undid the lock to let her into the driver's seat.

The sun had set by the time they returned to Gray Gables. Jane felt empty. She would no longer come down the stairs in the morning to find her aunt, cousin, and grandmother sitting around the kitchen table. The days of Kyle, Greg, and Rich taking turns wearing the floral apron and serving 'lasagna à la Kyle' had passed. From the driveway, the darkened house looked worn and cold.

'Guess it's just us,' said Elsie.

24

By the first week in September, Jane's nicotine consumption had begun to manifest as a light-yellow stripe between the first and second fingers of her right hand. On her Saturday supply run, Jane found that the magazine rack had turned overnight, its shelves now resplendent with colorful images of Morgan Vidal. Here she was, golden and grinning, on *Tiger Beat*, *Teen*, and *Seventeen*. According to the headlines, Morgan and Jesse were officially an item. Jane found herself contemplating arson.

That night, she put on a dress and went to the Carousel for the first time since she'd arrived home. Al's excitement to see her gave way to mild concern, as she seated herself at the bar and ordered up a line of tequila shots. This way, she wouldn't have to speak again for a while.

'Are you expecting someone else?' he asked.

'No,' said Jane. 'That reminds me; when I finish one, can you just add another to the end?'

Al scowled and headed down to the cellar.

Jane drank, watching her shadow swim in the bright rows of bottles behind the bar. She'd made it through four shots when she noticed Mark Edison a few stools away. He raised a glass.

'*Salut*,' he said. Jane raised a glass but said nothing. They drank. Then he slid toward her.

'Care to comment on Morgan Vidal and Jesse Reid?' he said.

'You'd love that, wouldn't you,' said Jane.

'You know, Janie,' said Mark, 'your fans are wondering where you are. Maybe you'd like to tell them about your go-to watering hole?'

'Fuck off, Mark,' said Jane.

He retreated to his corner like a crustacean backing into its shell, and Jane took her last two shots. When Mark left, around midnight, Jane headed to the bathroom; she didn't realize how drunk she was until she stood. On her way back to the bar, the jukebox began to play 'Jive City' by Fair Play, and suddenly it seemed like the right time to dance. The twinkle lights on the ceiling blurred into neon streaks as Jane moved. She felt good – better than she had in weeks. As hands grasped her hips, she wove through a jungle of faceless bodies, swinging between partners as if they were birch trees.

The next song was 'Sylvie Smiles.' The air around Jane grew warm, only it wasn't the air; Jane herself was aflame. She wrenched herself toward the jukebox – she couldn't make it stop fast enough. She banged on the window with her fists. She grabbed a beer stein off a table and brought it down over the machine. The mug smashed to pieces, but the jukebox continued to play. Jane screamed and reached for a metal napkin-dispenser.

A firm pair of arms wrapped around her middle and pulled her away.

'That's enough,' came Greg's voice. The sound made Jane's rage double. She kicked and screamed as he dragged her into the cool night.

'How dare you,' she slurred; they were inches from where Jesse had asked her to join him on tour.

'How dare I what?' said Greg. 'Stop you from destroying the jukebox? Or stop you from embarrassing yourself?'

'Traitor,' said Jane. She came at him, but at that moment, her stomach ejected its contents onto the pavement.

Jane only had snippets of the rest of the night. She remembered seeing Greg's VW Bug; she remembered pulling down the window to throw up again; she remembered seeing Elsie and Greg talking on the porch. She had no idea how she got upstairs or into her bed.

The next morning, Elsie woke her by yanking back the curtains.

'Today's going to be a big day,' she said.

'Agh,' Jane moaned as the sunlight burned her eyes. Her mouth tasted like death, and her hair was brittle with what she suspected to be green bile.

'Get up,' said Elsie. She stepped over a thicket of dirty laundry and cigarette butts, forcing open Jane's closet and extracting her blue uniform.

'You're going to the Center,' she said. 'I've gone every week, and you have yet to go once.'

'Maybe next week,' said Jane, rolling over in her filth. The idea of facing those silent, sterile halls right now made her intestines lurch.

'Now,' said Elsie. 'Or, so help me, I will throw you out and leave you to the mercy of Maggie and Greg.'

'Fine,' said Jane. She began to root around her room for a towel.

*

EMMA BRODIE

When Jane returned from the Center that evening, she felt like she had been doused in cool water. She stepped out of the station wagon, soft breeze on her skin, and exhaled in relief. An afternoon of scrubbing bedpans and dressing wounds made the worn house look wonderful.

Jane waved to her grandmother through the screen door, then went to lie down on the front lawn. As her eyes adjusted to the dark, stars winked around a crescent moon.

Sometime later, the screen door creaked, and Elsie came out. She lay beside Jane, shoulder to shoulder, their legs stretched out in opposite directions.

Jane kept watching the sky. 'Tell me what Mom used to be like,' she said.

Elsie shifted in the grass beside her. 'She was a night owl. Sometimes, I'd come down and find her working in the living room by the light of the moon. She used to say it was the only time she didn't feel invaded by other people's thoughts – the psychic space was clear.'

'Little did we know,' said Jane.

Elsie snorted. 'How was the Center?' she asked.

Jane pictured the white utility stairwell, a helix of blue uniforms scaling stories.

'The same,' said Jane. 'I'm sorry I left it all on you.'

Elsie squeezed her hand. 'I know this hasn't been an easy time for you. I haven't seen you this upset since you were little. Of course, back then, we couldn't get you to stay *in* your room.'

Jane had regularly run away the first year without Charlotte at home. She took a breath. 'I don't know what I'm doing,' she said. 'I don't know who I am. I used to be a singer in a rock band . . . and now I'm just . . . angry.'

'What are you angry about?' said Elsie.

'Kyle for leaving, Greg for backing out. Pegasus for booting me off the tour. Willy for letting Pegasus get away with it.'

'Not Jesse?' said Elsie.

'It was my decision to end things with Jesse,' said Jane.

'That doesn't mean you're not mad at him,' said Elsie.

Jane shrugged. 'It was just a fling,' she said, ignoring the pang she felt as her mind conjured the blue of Jesse's eyes, his smell, his taste. 'It was nothing.'

'You can still be upset that he lied to you,' said Elsie.

'No, I can't,' said Jane. 'I lied to Jesse plenty.'

Elsie frowned. 'These things aren't black and white,' she said.

'They are to me,' said Jane. 'They are to Grace.'

Elsie sighed. 'Grace and I have different opinions on this subject,' said Elsie. 'But I know she didn't intend for our decisions to keep you from living your life.'

Jane watched a plane dot a line across the heavens.

'They're not,' said Jane. 'I can figure all that out later. Right now, I have bigger problems.'

'Like?' said Elsie.

'Like Willy,' said Jane.

'Oh?' said Elsie.

Jane squirmed. 'Last we spoke, I may have told him to fuck off,' she said.

Elsie laughed. 'No one can accuse you of false flattery,' she said. A sliver of moon shimmered in her eyes.

'He was the one who told me I needed to leave the tour,' said Jane. *And the one I yelled at when I found Jesse shooting up.*

'So you shot the messenger,' said Elsie, as though riffing off Jane's thoughts.

Jane swallowed. 'The more time passes, the more I think he might have been looking out for me,' said Jane, her eyes welling. 'There's so much I still want,' she said. 'And now I'm back here with less than I had when I started. I feel like the world is passing me by, and it's burning me up.'

'You sound like your mother,' said Elsie.

'That's what I'm afraid of,' said Jane. She shuddered. 'I see myself right now and it's like history repeating. Being in a band always made me feel like we were different. But now . . .'

Jane placed a hand on her stomach and spoke slowly to keep her voice from shaking.

'What if I have it, too?' she said. 'Sometimes I get so mad I could just . . .'

Her voice trailed off as a cloud passed in front of the moon. Jane glanced at her grandmother – there were tears in her eyes.

'What do you see?' said Jane.

Elsie cleared her throat. 'I see a young woman with unlimited potential, if she would only trust her instincts.'

Jane's head throbbed. 'That's exactly what I don't want,' she said. 'I watched her go down. I *know* how alike we are. My instincts are her instincts. . . . They're dangerous.'

'Jane, we can't pick and choose who we are,' said Elsie. 'The best chance any of us has is to embrace the whole picture and try to make some sense of it. If you cut yourself off from your mother's bad traits, you will cut yourself off from her good ones as well. You can't tear a light from its darkness.'

As Elsie spoke, Jane thought not of her mother, but of Jesse and his addiction.

'Maybe it's better to have neither,' she said.

'That would be a real shame,' said Elsie. 'Because, in reality, they're all your traits. You're your own person, Jane. You don't need the band to prove it. I think you'll find that sometimes the things we think are protecting us are really holding us back.'

'What do you mean?' said Jane.

Elsie looked at her with gray eyes that mirrored her own. 'I know what the band meant to you, but think of how much energy it took to carry them.'

An image of the shining grand piano at the Shack drifted through Jane's thoughts.

'Don't run from your pain. Put it to work for you,' said Elsie. 'This struggle – to be able to struggle – is a gift your mother never had. The question is, what will you make of it?'

Together, they looked up at the stars and breathed in the night. Jane watched clouds spiral across the glittering canopy until she could no longer tell her grandmother's fingers from her own.

25

The next morning, the front page of *The Island Gazette* confirmed that, after much deliberation, the Festival Committee had voted to disband; for the first time since its inaugural year, the Fest hadn't turned a profit, and – given the increasing costs of production – it didn't make financial sense to continue. As Jane replaced the paper on the kitchen table, she felt the final piece of her old life crumble away.

That day, she went for a swim. She biked out to the clay beach beyond the Fest grounds and waded in up to her knees, watching the seaweed knit lace patterns on the surface. Then she dove, feeling the salt coat her body, feeling the force of the ocean rock her.

Underwater, the only sound she could hear was the hushed rumble of the waves – not the gulls up above, not her own muted screaming. Blood pounded in her ears as she propelled herself to the surface. In her lungs, the air was sharp and clear; Jane watched it lift the gulls from the water. She watched it fill a fleet of distant sails.

On her way home, she purchased a notebook along with her daily cigarettes. She cleared a spot on her bedroom floor, wedged herself between her bed and her closet, and began to write.

The words came slowly at first; then they began to pour. This writing was the work of excavation; she was digging to uncover the wild forces inside her she had once sought to bury. She was digging to find out what they might have to say.

Over several days, she watched her handwriting shift from loops, to jags, to electrocardiograms, to large caps, to tiny scrawl, to first-grade penmanship. She had filled five composition books when she felt a song beginning to simmer. It wasn't the same frenzy she'd experienced when she wrote 'Spark'; it was more like watching a pot come to a boil.

> *There's a devil in Kentucky,*
> *Plays the banjo fast as sin,*
> *Says there's a church inside me,*
> *But he don't know how bad I've been.*
> *Well, if that cathedral's in me,*
> *He's gotta know the truth,*
> *My chorus sings a love song,*
> *And my altar's built to you.*

Jane flipped to a new page and kept writing as the lyrics crested through her. She reached for her guitar and tuned it in a trance. She found the chords with ease and had the song, start to finish, in twenty minutes.

When she sat back on her bed, looking at what she had transcribed, she felt a sense of purpose for the first time in weeks. Jane may have distrusted her psyche, but she had never doubted her taste: she knew this was a good song. What's more, it felt like a connection to the past year, a possible means of return, like coordinates coming through a telegraph wire.

Before she could lose momentum, she grabbed her guitar and her notebook and headed to Beach Tracks. As Jane entered the shop, she waved to Dana; the customer she was helping stared at Jane, a copy of *Painted Lady* tucked under her arm.

Jane turned to Pat behind the register. 'Could I use your sound booth in back?'

'Of course,' said Pat. 'It's nothing state-of-the-art, mind you.'

'Please,' said Jane. 'I'm just looking to make a quick tape. I can pay you for the time.' Pat swatted away the thought.

The room Jane had been referring to was the broom closet where Dana taught guitar lessons, muted by carpeting stapled to the walls. Inside, a bare light bulb illuminated a chair, a microphone, and, a tape recorder.

'Perfect,' said Jane.

She recorded the track in an hour, twice on two separate tapes, and marched straight to the post office, guitar strapped to her back. As the postal worker weighed the package and calculated the shipping, Jane dashed off a note to Willy.

Willy –
I'm sorry I yelled at you for things you didn't do.
 Guess I'm a work in progress –
 Speaking of, let me know how you like this.
 Xx Jane

She addressed the parcel to Linda's attention, and watched the postal worker throw it into a bin.

'Anything else?' he asked. Jane clutched the duplicate tape and shook her head.

The following day, Jane donned the teal-and-pink Widow's Peak uniform she'd consigned to her closet the previous summer. Inside her right pocket she found a spare cigarette and Willy's business card. It seemed like a good omen as she trudged into town.

Maggie was sectioning off a client's hair as Jane entered the salon.

'She's chattering away but not saying any real words,' Maggie was explaining to the woman in her chair, a recently retired Harvard psychologist.

'And you say she's crawling?'

'She's all over the place,' said Maggie, looking up as Jane shut the door.

'That sounds perfectly normal,' said the client. 'Of course, all babies really develop at different rates. As do people.' She smiled at her own joke, and Jane could easily picture her making the same one in a lecture hall full of coeds like those she'd seen on tour.

'So I hear,' said Maggie, eyeing Jane.

Jane had spent the whole walk over thinking about what she would say to Maggie, or, worse, what Maggie would say to her. And yet, as Jane stood before Maggie, her mind returned to the year she lost her mother: all the times Maggie had helped her run away, and all the times Maggie had let her sleep in her bed after she'd been caught. That's when they'd devised their signal.

Outlaws don't ask questions.

Behind the chair, Maggie's hand formed a wayward coyote. Jane responded in kind.

'Grab a broom,' said Maggie.

199

As she began to trim dead ends, Jane swept them away.

That night, Jane accompanied Maggie back to her new home in Lightship Bay. They parked Greg's VW Bug outside a blue-and-green cottage overlooking the water.

'Cute,' said Jane.

'Yup,' said Maggie as Greg came out to greet her. He stopped when he saw Jane.

'Guess I'd better go check on the baby,' said Maggie, leaving Jane and Greg on the porch. They eyed each other warily.

'Thanks for taking me home the other night,' said Jane. 'I'm sorry I . . . I'm just sorry.'

Greg shuffled in place, a hand scrunching the hair on the back of his head. For a second, Jane thought he was going to tell her to go fuck herself. Then he gave her a smile and pulled her into a big bear hug.

'Janie Q,' he said, 'we'll always be family.' He led her inside for dinner.

They hadn't yet acquired a table, so Maggie threw a scarf over an upside-down moving box, and the three of them sat around it cross-legged, Bea crawling over their legs.

'Janie, you'll find that spaghetti à la Greg is an improvement over lasagna à la Kyle,' said Maggie, pouring red wine into an assortment of coffee mugs.

'How is Kyle?' said Jane, sprinkling Parmesan over her pasta.

Greg rifled through a nearby stack of mail and tossed Jane a postcard. She held the deckled edge, flipping the image of a masked gondolier to a short note written in Kyle's scrawl.

Hey Bro –
Great about the house. Venice is amazing – their streets are made
of water!
    Kiss the girls for me.

Jane felt a stab of envy as she replaced the card on the pile.

'They're in Madrid by now,' said Greg. Jane did her best to smile.

As Jane began to tend to her roots on the Island, she could feel the star matter of a new album materializing around her. Enfolded in familiarity, she began to sense that maybe her unconscious didn't have to be a scary thing. Maybe she was growing into this and would be able to do as Elsie said, to channel the good parts of her mother while befriending the bad. She'd take it slow – there was no reason to rush, no reason to let these surges of creativity knock her off kilter.

The night she reconnected with Maggie and Greg, she wrote a song called 'Little Lion' for Bea; when Greg heard the chorus, he bawled.

> *'No matter where you roam,*
> *You'll still find your way home.*
> *No matter where you'll be,*
> *Little lion, you've got me.'*

The following week, she wrote another, called 'New Country,' about her experiences on tour.

Golden city,
Hive above the bay,
Lips are buzzing,
But they've got nothing to say.
Where's a body
Supposed to go to get away,
To find a little peace in this new country?

The more Jane wrote, the more hopeful she became. She couldn't wait to hear from Willy. Sure, she'd been difficult last summer, and the recording process hadn't been ideal. But hadn't he told her the first time they met that she was unlike anything he'd ever encountered? Hadn't *Spring Fling* exceeded the label's wildest expectations? That was what counted, wasn't it? Her new song was good; Willy would agree.

The *Painted Lady* tour should have arrived back the third week in September. Each night, Jane lay awake, wondering if tomorrow would be the day she'd get a call. It seemed impossible that she wouldn't hear something soon.

One by one, the days began to stack up like expired lottery tickets. Jane reasoned that the tour group would need some time to recover from the jet lag – Willy most of all, since he had the farthest to travel, back to L.A. It was possible they hadn't even returned yet. If Jane had been in Europe, she would have stayed a little longer to do some sightseeing.

Then, the last week in September, Jane caught a glimpse of a familiar profile as she helped Mrs. Robson into a dryer chair.

'May I?' Jane asked, gesturing toward the *Island Gazette* in her hand.

'Oh, of course, dear,' said Mrs. Robson. 'Fancy that, the pair of them going to *our* flea market. So great for the Island economy, what with the Fest going under . . .'

Morgan's toothy grin glowed white in newsprint as she held up a Tiffany lamp. The Grange Hall was visible behind her; Jane could make out the top of Elsie's friend Sid's booth at the corner of the frame. Elsie hadn't gone yesterday, because there had been too much to do at the salon; if she had, she would have been there when this photo was taken, would have seen Jesse standing next to Morgan, holding her bag, and looking at her with those unmistakable eyes.

'Are you all right, dear?' said Mrs. Robson.

'Fine,' said Jane, handing back the paper. As she straightened up, she saw her mother staring at her from the mirror at Maggie's station. Jane opened and closed her eyes to confirm that it was her own dismayed reflection.

They were back.

No one had called her.

No one had wanted to.

Jane felt a cavity opening within her, a canyon, a fault line. Then her rage tipped in, like a lit match into sulfur.

26

As Jane left the salon, her ears rang; it was as if she had just shed a skin, revealing a new layer, raw and smarting. In an instant, the balance she had been cultivating around her creativity shattered, energy surging through her body. She had spent the summer suckling on a fantasy. Now that it had been punctured, she could see the facts with brutal clarity.

Willy had received her tape and said nothing. Jane could now see that Willy had no reason to work with her again; she'd made herself a nuisance at every point in the process and had refused to promote her own image despite his urgings. Her success had been totally fueled by Jesse's star power. Now Morgan was in that position and was doing everything Willy had wanted Jane to do.

Only I'm still better, she thought.

Elsie arrived home half an hour later to find Jane browning beef in a skillet. When Jane saw her grandmother enter, she flattened the meat against the pan until it hissed.

'Good evening to you, too,' said Elsie. 'This wouldn't have anything to do with the *Gazette* article on Jesse, would it?' Elsie removed a bottle of dandelion wine from under the counter. Jane shook her head, turning up the stove.

After dinner, she went down to the Carousel and found Mark Edison in his usual corner.

'*American Teen*,' she said.

'What?' said Mark Edison.

'*American Teen*,' said Jane. 'They've invited me to do a "Five Things" piece a few times. If you interview me and pitch it to them, they'll buy it.'

'Why would I want to do that?' said Mark Edison. 'It's not exactly a prestigious byline.' *American Teen* was a weekly gossip rag for high-schoolers that specialized in fashion advice.

'Think of it as a favor,' said Jane.

Mark Edison eyed her. 'Is this a sad attempt at a media coup?'

'It's an olive branch,' said Jane. 'To my label.' She saw no reason to conceal the truth.

He considered her. 'Okay,' he said. 'But . . . when your next album comes out, I get an exclusive.'

Jane laughed. 'I'm flattered,' she said.

Mark Edison squinted. 'Don't be,' he said. 'I'm just thinking of myself.'

Jane bought him a round, and he took out his notepad, and they banged out the interview then and there. Mark left at midnight, but Jane stayed and drank until last call. As she walked home, she thought about her album; it now represented the entirety of her hope. She was adrift on a raft, and these songs, forming around her, were the constellations that would guide her onward.

When Jane fell asleep that night, she had three songs in her pocket, the others floating out of reach like clouds in a nebula. But while she slept, the day's realizations catalyzed inside her mind, speeding up reaction time and synthesizing material. When she awoke, several stars had begun to form where before there had only been phosphorus and vapor.

There were seven among them, new songs clustered together in a dense mass of sound and light. Jane's sense of abandonment had cracked her album wide open, and the tracks she had been gently easing into existence were now bursting forth all at once. She didn't have time to indulge in self-pity or self-doubt. There was peril in this cacophony; if she didn't get this music out of her body, it would devour her. Her urgency gave her focus. As she tried to untangle the melodies from one another, her guitar became inadequate.

'I need a piano,' she said to Elsie that night at dinner.

Her grandmother's eyes glinted. 'I know just the one.'

Sid's shop was at the end of Main Street in Perry's Landing, tucked between the Victoria Inn and a renowned seafood restaurant called The Hook. Sid had decorated both outfits at a steep discount, and as a result, their highbrow clientele filtered into his shop for a good six months of the year. This was the first week of October, and the tourist season was just winding down.

'Jane, what a pleasure,' said Sid, placing his book on a velvet chair, where his cat, Tomas, sat curled on the armrest. He kissed both Jane and Elsie on each cheek.

'Does C.C. happen to be on hand?' said Elsie.

'In fact, she does,' said Sid.

He led Elsie and Jane through the main shop to a rear annex that served as a sunporch and storage room – stacks of paintings leaned against Grecian sculptures, the tendrils of a dismounted chandelier reaching across the floor like a crystal jellyfish. At the center of it all stood a Steinway grand piano overlooking the harbor through a bay window.

'Jane, meet C.C.,' said Sid.

C.C. was the favorite revenge consignment of the couple who owned the Victoria Inn next door. Every other year, one would threaten the other with divorce, and C.C. would end up in Sid's shop.

'She's like the child being sent to the aunt's estate in the country,' said Sid, fondly raising C.C.'s lid and propping it up with the stand.

C.C. was older than Jesse's piano – her keys were slightly yellowed whereas his had been blue-white, and not all of them played perfectly in tune. She had a richness of sound, though, that Jesse's instrument did not. Jane bowed over her keys, then sank her fingers in, watching the notes vibrate off the chandelier's crystal, tiny rainbows dancing on the wall.

Whenever she wasn't working, Jane drove to Perry's Landing and played. With the stays pulled from the annex's velvet curtains, she had the sense of total privacy, even if her playing could be heard throughout the shop.

'It lends the furniture an air of the *bohème*,' said Sid when Jane asked if she was disturbing his customers.

He was being generous, Jane knew. Her playing at times verged on violent as she wrestled with the creative forces inside herself. Sometimes, she played for hours just to find one moment of peace. Other times, she sat in silence and spied on the chef from The Hook taking his cigarette breaks on the pier. The antiques around her became totems of comfort, and she grew irritated whenever Sid would move them. To Jane, they were kindred spirits: not brand-new, perhaps, but still worth something.

207

Jane had difficulty describing her artistic vision to her loved ones. She tried one night on the phone with Rich, who had called to tell her about his new rental cottage in Laurel Canyon.

'I don't want it to be like anything that has ever come out before,' said Jane, watching the moon rise through the screen door.

'How do you mean?' asked Rich.

'Like, if you paint an egg only using white and black, it would look like a cartoon. You have to paint it using all the colors of an egg to really make an egg.'

'Yellow?' asked Rich. 'Janie – I'm not sure I understand what you're saying.'

Jane missed Jesse terribly in these moments. The way this album was forming was beyond her – but she recognized herself in what she had seen of his process. She knew that if he were here he would understand how she was feeling – how powerful, how obsessive, how terrified. She could picture them at the Shack, seated side by side at the piano. Then she'd remember that Jesse was probably there with Morgan, and she'd suppress the thought.

Elsie had been right: by freeing the words inside of her, Jane had been granted access to a deeper kind of music, the core sounds and themes that emanated like a wellspring from the bedrock of her being. As she played and wrote and played and wrote, she had the sense of raising a sunken ship from the ocean's floor.

The first time she saw Jesse's piano, Jane had had the sense of being engulfed by the night sky; that was the first time this music had made its presence known to her. Jane had kept it at bay, fearing its enormity, its shapelessness.

Now she ventured through it, note by note, passage by passage.

She pulled out one song and then another until there was nothing left to exhume, and what had once been unknowable now had a beginning and an end. She wove sails out of melodies and hoisted them with verse.

By the first week in November, Jane had ten record-worthy tracks, and the *American Teen* 'Five Things' piece had hit the stands. The story had been buried deep inside the issue and had no mention on the cover, a single shot in the dark. Two days after it published, Jane received a call.

'Rebecca just showed me the most interesting article,' said Willy. '"Five Things You Didn't Know About Jane Quinn" – number one, Jane's favorite nail polish is Natural Wonder.'

Jane smiled. 'Did you get my tape?' she asked.

Willy exhaled. 'I did,' he said. 'It's a killer track. Guess it turns out you *do* do lyrics.' He didn't sound excited.

'Guess it does,' said Jane, mouth dry. 'And?'

'And . . . I need to have some conversations on this end. The way things went last time . . . I can't make any promises.'

Jane felt her heart sink. 'Aren't I still under contract?'

Willy sighed. 'You were as part of the Breakers, but when the Breakers dissolved, so did the contract,' said Willy.

'Okay, so what about a new one?' she said. 'A solo contract? Isn't that what you wanted all along?'

Willy hesitated. 'If – and this is a big if – I can get the board to sign off, this one will have to be different. I'm not going to be able to offer you much, if anything – basically, enough to cover your travel expenses.'

'Travel expenses?' said Jane.

'Yeah, production consolidated,' he said. 'Everything is in L.A. now.'

209

'Okay,' said Jane. 'Yeah, sure.' This was going to be life, post–Jesse Reid. She had better get used to it.

Willy cleared his throat. 'For what it's worth,' he said, 'I still don't think there's another quite like you.'

27

Willy looked tanned and rested sitting in his blue Mustang convertible at Arrivals. His face broke into a grin as he took in Jane's jeans cutoffs and transparent silk shirt, a stark contrast to the gaggle of uniformed flight attendants marching behind her. The pilot they accompanied almost stumbled over his left flank to get a better look at Jane's chest.

'Didn't anyone ever tell you you're supposed to dress up for a flight?' Willy asked, leaning over the seat to unlock the door on the passenger's side.

'I did,' said Jane.

Willy laughed as she threw her luggage – one of Elsie's more radical carpetbags – into the rear seat and slid in beside him.

Jane had left autumn behind; here, palm trees swayed along the freeway, hinting that summer never had to end. The drive out to Malibu took just under an hour. Willy's house was exactly as Jane remembered; walking in, she had the sense of visiting a venue where she'd once performed.

After a brief visit with Rebecca, Willy led Jane into his office to go over the final details of her contract. His desk looked out across the water like the bow of a ship; Jane marveled that he could concentrate.

'This took some doing,' said Willy, handing her a stiff packet of papers. 'I'm sorry the advance isn't much. Same royalty as the first contract, five options.' Jane looked it over. Willy had been right – this would barely cover her stay in L.A.

Had she been too hasty in turning down Rich's offer to crash with him and Kyle? Jane wasn't sure where she and Kyle stood. As a musician, she had never questioned that he would be the bassist on her album; as a friend, she still felt sore. It couldn't be avoided – she needed her own place.

'I appreciate it,' said Jane. She flipped to the back page of the packet and signed her name.

'I'll get everything confirmed. No producer this time – just you and Simon,' said Willy.

'Great,' said Jane.

Willy nodded, but his brow creased. 'I'm going out of my way to make a plan you can stick to,' he said. 'But, Jane – it's imperative that you stick to it. There's no safety net this time, no . . .'

His voice trailed off, but Jane understood that he meant to say 'Jesse.' Willy sighed.

'I told them you would run a straight race – staked my name on it. Okay?' Jane nodded her understanding, but inside she thought, *For now*.

The following day, Willy arranged for a real-estate agent to show them around Laurel Canyon.

As they followed the realtor's burgundy Chevy up Polk Street, Jane took in bronzed bodies draped on porches, potted cacti hanging from windows, and bare feet walking from door to door. Perhaps the Folk Fest had been reincarnated as a neighborhood in the Hollywood Hills.

212

Jane rented a furnished wood-and-stone cottage ten minutes from the Pegasus lot. It belonged to a couple of music teachers on a six-month sabbatical, and had been lovingly decorated with plants, antique furniture, and books. Great rectangular windows surveying the valley gave Jane the impression of being inside a tree house. The living room housed a large tiger-striped piano, a vase of dried wildflowers mounted on its back like an oxpecker. By the end of the day, Jane had moved in.

To celebrate, Willy treated her to dinner at Chateau Marmont, the legendary hotel overlooking Sunset Boulevard. A hostess led them into a small dining room with red banquettes, the walls decorated with silver serpents that seemed to slither in the candlelight. Once they'd ordered, the discussion turned to Jane's thoughts on production.

'This record is intimate,' said Jane, as salads appeared before them. 'I want the recording to be as private as possible – I don't want anyone coming in or out but us.'

'I've booked you Studio C for the next month,' said Willy, reaching across the polished wooden table with his fork to capture a loose tomato on Jane's plate.

'So . . . it will be ours exclusively?' said Jane.

'Well, no,' said Willy. 'You'll have the studio every day from 10 to 2 p.m. Other times, other musicians will be able to book it.'

Jane frowned. 'I want to be able to record whenever I want,' she said.

'Well, you can use the studio if it's available, but if it's not you'll have to use another one,' said Willy. 'I thought you'd be happy – the piano in Studio C is legendary. Loretta is insisting on using it for her record as well.'

'She's recording . . . now?' said Jane. The Breakers' record had been produced in such a blur, Jane hadn't been cognizant of other artists in the space – and she wouldn't have known any of them anyway. This record would be a different story.

'Yes,' said Willy. 'She's about midway through her sessions, I would say.'

Jane nodded. 'Do you know if anyone . . . else will be recording while I'm here?'

Willy looked uncomfortable. 'At this exact moment, no,' he said.

Jane's eyes bored into him as the server cleared their salad plates.

Willy sighed. 'I'm expecting Jesse sometime in the next month to begin work on his follow-up.'

Jane sat back in her chair and watched the bubbles in her glass float to the surface and evaporate. 'I thought I was getting Kyle and Huck,' she said. 'How's that going to work?'

'Listen, you're both my artists, and I have both of your best interests at heart. You'll be in mixing by the time his sessions start,' said Willy. 'And I'll make sure his studio time isn't the same as yours.' Willy looked uneasy. There was something else.

'What is it?' said Jane. 'If you're afraid to tell me he's with Morgan, don't worry about it. I already know.'

Willy relaxed slightly, though he continued to eye her. 'Have you two spoken?' he asked.

Jane shook her head. '*The Island Gazette* has never been so fascinated by a single subject,' said Jane. Willy laughed.

'He didn't waste any time,' Jane added to see how Willy would respond.

He gave her a look. 'Breakups are never easy,' said Willy.

'Sage, thanks,' said Jane.

'I'm not a go-between, Jane,' said Willy. 'Don't put me in that position.'

'I'm just curious,' said Jane.

Willy rolled his eyes. 'Didn't you break up with him?' he said.

Jane glared. She didn't want to rehash their split. It wasn't that she wasn't over it; she was. She just hadn't quite moved on.

'Why can't he just give it an extra few weeks?' she said, unable to let it go.

'We need his album out ASAP to keep the momentum going,' said Willy.

'Then I'll wait,' said Jane. 'I'll go home and come back.'

'Jane, stop,' said Willy. 'You got your contract. You've been given a second chance. This isn't worth fucking it up.'

Jane said nothing as a server placed their entrées on the table.

'Be happy,' Willy urged her. 'You're here with the best musicians and the best facilities on the planet. I'm sorry that I can't shut down the whole studio for six weeks. But I can't. So – get a tan and make your record. What are you calling it, anyway?'

Jane regarded him; record titles were notoriously tricky, but she had her heart set on this one.

'*Songs in Ursa Major*,' she said.

Willy's eyes lit. 'Yes,' he said.

That night, the full moon shined so bright that Jane couldn't sleep, so she padded into the living room. A pattern of leaves threw shadows across the floorboards, serrated, like paper snowflake cutouts. Jane sat at the piano, bowing over its keys, and played until she tired herself out.

The next day, Willy came by with Huck, who unfurled himself from the passenger seat holding a conga. Jane had been nervous

215

asking one of Jesse's musicians to be on her album, but she didn't want to record with strangers, and Huck was the only drummer she knew besides Greg. He smiled when he saw her, and Jane took a breath.

'Janie Q,' said Huck, embracing her. 'You're in California!'

'I am,' said Jane, patting him on the arm and leading him into the house. 'How've you been?'

'Well enough,' said Huck as she led him and Willy over to the piano. 'Recovered from tour. I have to say I prefer the bus to those little planes. We all missed you.'

Jane felt her cheeks color. 'I think the best thing would be to show you what I have,' she said. Huck nodded.

The album called for piano and guitar, and Jane pivoted between the two from the piano bench. As she played, Huck kept time on his conga. He had detuned the instrument to the point where it sounded like he was beating on his own chest. Jane could feel him respond to her in a way Greg never had. Her guilt admitting this to herself was soon overcome by her excitement at what Huck would bring to the record. When she had finished playing all ten songs, she felt tired, as if she had just spent half an hour crying to a friend. Huck's hands rested on top of his drum. Willy looked at Jane glowingly.

Huck cleared his throat. 'Wow, Jane,' he said. 'That is – I've never heard songs like that.'

Jane regarded him. 'What do you think?' she asked. 'Percussion-wise. What do they need?'

Huck sniffed twice and wiped his eyes. 'Honestly,' he said, 'you have a very strong rhythm to your playing – I never need to look for the heartbeat when I'm listening to you. I think my job will be to support that, to accentuate what is already there.'

Jane smiled.

After Huck and Willy left, her nerves returned. Rich and Kyle were coming over for dinner, and Jane had no idea what to expect. She went to the Country Store to buy a roast and wandered the aisles for an hour. She had just put the pan in the oven when they approached the cottage.

Jane could tell from the way Kyle was bouncing that he was even more apprehensive than she was. She opened the door, and they looked at each other, and he cocked his head to the side.

'Are you still salty about the tour?' asked Kyle.

'Yeah, a little,' said Jane.

'Fair enough,' said Kyle. He took a step closer. 'If it helps, I'm sorry about the way it went down. It was never my intention to leave you behind.'

'I know,' said Jane. 'And if it helps, I probably would have done the same thing.'

'Great,' said Rich. 'You're both dicks.'

Kyle bounded onto the porch and hugged Jane.

'I'm so stoked to be collaborating again,' said Kyle.

Jane and Rich smiled at the industry lingo tripping off his tongue. Kyle rolled his eyes.

'I'm allowed to say "collaborating,"' he said.

Jane sat them down in the exact chairs Willy and Huck had occupied earlier that day and played through the album set. She was so unselfconscious around them, it felt like playing alone. When she finished, she looked up to see their reactions.

'This is going to be amazing, Janie,' said Kyle. He picked up Jane's guitar and began to thumb through one of the riffs she'd played, always eager to jump in. Rich said nothing.

Over dinner, Kyle recapped the tour, which he had spent

mooning over a mysterious beauty called Elena, who had accompanied them from Paris to Venice, then disappeared in Lucerne. 'She took all my money and the last of my Luckies,' said Kyle, with admiration.

He asked Jane for updates on the Island, and she told him about Maggie and Greg's new house. 'I'm hoping to get out there for Thanksgiving,' said Kyle.

Rich began to clear the dishes.

'You'll have to come over to our place for the next one,' said Kyle, wrapping Jane in a hug. 'See you at the studio.' He went out the door.

Rich gave Jane a nod and was about to follow when she caught his arm.

'What's the matter?' she asked.

Rich didn't meet her eyes.

'You don't have anything to say about the album?' she pressed.

Rich rested his arm on the door frame and gave her a grave look.

'Is this sour grapes?' said Jane, taken aback. 'You were the one who told me I should write.'

Rich shook his head. 'Don't get me wrong, Jane,' he said. 'There are aspects of it that are brilliant. But . . . sometimes you sound like you're in agony. It's too much. You should keep some things to yourself.'

Jane felt her mouth drop open. Rich looked as if he might say more. Then he shook his head, tapped once on the door-frame, and stepped out into the night.

Jane gaped after him, feeling as if she had been punched in the gut.

28

When Jane Quinn swept into Studio C, she reminded Simon of a swallowtail butterfly fresh from her chrysalis. The seriousness he'd noted the year before had evolved into a powerful air of vision and focus, leaving only a trace of girlish sparkle, like luminescence on a wing.

Jane invited Simon out of the sound booth and into the studio. He watched her take a seat at the coveted red piano, stretching her hands across the keys. Unlike with the Breakers' album, Jane had not sent material in advance. 'I want your first impression to be from me,' she said.

Simon had been looking forward to working with Jane again and had no doubt that she would deliver on her sophomore album. After he heard the tracks on *Songs in Ursa Major*, he knew that this was going to be bigger than he or anyone had expected.

That night, he walked down Sunset Boulevard, a cigarette dangling from his lips. He thought about his mother's family, taken by the death camps – he would never hear their voices again; he thought of the first boy he'd kissed, ankle deep in river rock; he thought of the first time he'd picked up a saxophone and realized he could make sense of it. A pill-sized cylinder of ash dropped onto his shoes; he still had a cigarette in his mouth.

> *Starless, heartless night above a sea of stone,*
> *A distant dial tone.*

As he entered his apartment, his thoughts returned to Jane Quinn. It was clear to him now that every sound he had recorded in the last year, every note, every chord, had all been the prelude to her arrival in Laurel Canyon. Simon didn't articulate this thought to anyone, but from that moment on, he felt a sacred duty to protect the space around the *Ursa Major* sessions.

The next day, Willy Lambert joined him in the booth.

'Simon,' said Willy, nodding, 'glad to have you on this one.'

'Thanks for bringing me on board,' he said.

'Jane wouldn't have had it any other way,' said Willy. The last year had tempered him. Simon wondered what strings he'd had to pull to get Jane a second contract; it was no secret how much Vincent Ray despised her, and little wonder. Even after Vincent Ray had blacklisted her, the Breakers' album had sold over fifty thousand copies with his own photo on the cover.

Kyle Lightfoot arrived next with Rich Holt. Jane greeted them with the familiarity of a sister, but Simon could sense a distance that hadn't been there before. Rich was still as handsome as ever. Simon had seen him at parties, but had never spoken to him outside of a session. He doubted he ever would. It never hurt to look, though.

Huck Levi arrived last. It made sense to Simon that Jane had parted ways with her old drummer, but he was surprised that she had tapped one of Jesse Reid's musicians. He had heard the rumors about Jane and Jesse dating and knew Jesse would be arriving in L.A. soon.

'Good to see you, bud,' said Huck, cuffing Kyle on the shoulder. Rich and Huck shook hands.

'You guys tuned?' said Jane.

From the way they followed her commands, Simon could tell that each of them had also been initiated into the album – not as musicians preparing to record, but as sentinels preparing for a siege.

Jane had expressed the need for total privacy, and from those first basic tracks, the sessions had been locked. Simon understood why. She was like an artist creating a self-portrait in the nude: each day, she came into the studio and stripped down all of her defenses until her emotions were bare. Then they began to record. Track by track, she inverted all of the raw energy that had made *Spring Fling* such a good pop album into an astonishing surrender.

Simon had worked with Rich, Kyle, and Huck before, but never in this exact combination. As the sessions progressed, *Ursa Major* began to test the limits of their skill. The music itself required an exacting amount of precision, and Jane would not accept less than perfection. She had a strong sense of what she wanted but wasn't always able to articulate it; if anyone else had an idea, she assumed credit for it. She couldn't tolerate less than total control.

Huck had come up under some notoriously difficult producers. Simon doubted whether any of them compared to Jane on the bridge of 'A Shanty.'

'Here,' she said, handing Huck a sheet of music. Huck's eyebrows lifted as he looked it over.

221

'Is there a problem?' asked Jane.

'No problem,' said Huck.

Later, he showed Simon the indiscernible marks Jane had scrawled above the bridge's lyrics.

'What is this?' said Simon.

'It's Jesse's shorthand,' said Huck, shaking his head. 'He must have taught it to her.'

Apparently, the scribbles called for a single sound to play on the downbeat coinciding with the word 'boards.' Jane wanted to emphasize the rhythm – 'Like a wink across a room' – but she couldn't articulate how.

'It's not a click, and it's not a pop, it's somewhere in the middle,' she kept repeating.

Huck assembled a range of hand instruments, from maracas to spoons, and sat on a blanket in the middle of the studio, trying and retrying them, for two sessions.

'What about the cowbell?' Jane said. Huck picked up the cowbell and began to play.

'Not the bell part,' said Jane. 'The handle.'

It took them six hours and forty-two takes until they landed on a güiro: tapped, not stroked.

'Brand New Cassette' was the most like a traditional rock track; Kyle and Rich liked it because the arrangement centered on a basic chord progression the two of them strummed in sync. Jane wanted the last part of the third verse to pop, like a sample excerpted from another song.

'It should be electric,' said Kyle.

'I don't want anything electric on the album,' snapped Jane. The next day:

'I figured it out. The radio section should be electric.'

Kyle gaped at her.

Simon sneaked them into Studio D for an hour while Starlight Drive was on break, and they grabbed the 'sample' in just two takes, using their instruments. Watching Rich and Kyle shred while Huck let loose on the drums was like watching horses that had been locked in a paddock gallop through an open field.

As the sessions wore on, Rich grew increasingly irritable; he just didn't like the album. It wasn't until they began work on 'Wallflower' that Simon allowed himself to speculate why.

> *I stand aside, I watch you go,*
> *I start to cry, nobody's home,*
> *I love you so, but you'll never know.*

The song was about an unnamed female subject. From the descriptors – 'hair of yellow, lips of red,' 'eyes so blue' – Simon suspected it might be Jane herself; it wouldn't be the most narcissistic song he'd encountered. It didn't matter – hearing Jane yearn so viscerally for another woman always put Simon in mind of his tortured eleventh-grade crush on Hank Lipson. As he watched Rich's jaw tense, he sensed that the song might be excruciating for him in the same way.

With the Breakers' old drummer gone, Rich was now the least versatile musician in the ensemble, a carpenter who had mastered the tools in his box and had no interest in branching out. After weeks of working around this, Jane became intransigent over the chorus for 'A Thousand Lines':

> *Oh, you run through me like fountain dye.*
> *Parchment dried with pigment stains.*

'It needs to be delicate,' she insisted. Rich's face reddened. They had been going over the same riff for close to an hour; Kyle and Huck sat nearby, pretending not to be there.

'How about this,' said Rich. He played the notes exactly as he had before. Kyle and Huck wilted.

'No,' said Jane. 'I want it to sound like wind chimes weaving in and out of the bass.'

'I don't know if I can do what you're saying,' said Rich.

'Or you just don't want to,' said Jane.

'You're right,' said Rich. 'I don't.'

Rich put his guitar down and walked out. Jane stared at the place on the floor where he had been standing. She had been so fixated on what she wanted, Simon didn't think she had noticed that Rich was upset until he left.

Willy roused himself from the booth and came into the studio. 'Should I go?' he said.

Jane shook her head and walked out after Rich; from the window in the sound booth, Simon could see Jane catch up to Rich in the hall.

'Guess it's one thing to say you think someone should do their own thing and another to watch them actually do it,' said Jane.

Rich rounded on her. 'I told you, that's not what this is about.'

'Then what is it about? You've hated this record from the start,' she said.

'I don't hate the record,' said Rich. 'I hate how it's made you. You're acting like Mussolini.'

'I just want it to be good,' said Jane. 'You're supposed to have my back. I need you to believe in what I'm doing. I need you to at least try. I need—'

'I think we both know who you need, and it isn't me,' said Rich. 'I'm sorry – I just can't play like him. You know that, Jane.'

Jane slumped against the wall. Rich walked over and stood beside her.

'I don't hate the record,' he said. 'Sometimes it just makes me . . . ashamed.'

'Of me?'

Rich shook his head. 'Of myself,' he said. 'Of the things I've never been able to say.'

Jane's expression softened.

'And if I'm being perfectly honest, yes, it does suck a bit to see how fucking good at this you are.' Rich sighed. 'But I always have your back.'

Jane took his hand.

After that, Jane made an effort to lighten her touch. Privately, though, Simon didn't think any of them would have walked, no matter how difficult she became. Even when they didn't have to be there, Huck, Rich, and Kyle would sit in the booth with Simon, keeping vigil, as Jane crossed into another realm, retrieving melodies, and transporting them back to earth.

In these moments, it was as though her spirit expanded to fill the whole room, stretching beyond the limits of her own consciousness. And yet, if you were to speak to Jane between takes, she was as lucid and focused as she had been standing over Huck with the güiro. The part of her that was creating the album and the part of her that was producing it coexisted within her like two sides of the same coin, spinning endlessly around and around but never meeting.

29

Halfway through the sessions for 'A Thousand Lines,' Jane stepped into the hall for a cigarette and saw Loretta charging toward Studio C, the rest of her team following like a troop of cavalry. They slowed when they saw Jane, a silvery spirit shrouded in smoke.

'I'm right behind you,' said Loretta as her engineer, producer, and bass player filed past them.

'Should've known you'd be the broad hogging my piano,' said Loretta. Her tone was arch, but her eyes were warm.

'You must be almost finished,' said Jane.

'Indeed,' said Loretta. 'Just grabbing a couple extra takes for the mixing. How's yours going?'

'It's coming along,' said Jane. She offered Loretta a cigarette, which she accepted.

'Who's on your crew?' asked Loretta.

'Simon Spector. Huck, Kyle, and Rich.'

Loretta's eyebrows jumped as Jane said Rich's name. 'Which of these things is not like the other?' she said.

Jane flicked ash onto the carpet. 'We're making it work,' she said, although she wondered if that was true.

Loretta gave her a hard look, then exhaled slowly. 'You

didn't strike me as the kind of person who wanted to settle,' she said.

Now they were talking about Jesse.

'I have a lot of respect for how you handled things back in Memphis,' said Loretta. 'But it was a real loss, not having you on the rest of the tour.'

Jane's face broke into an involuntary smile. 'Morgan seems . . . talented,' she said.

Loretta rolled her eyes. 'Just ask her,' she said.

Jane laughed.

'You *seem* like you're taking everything in stride,' said Loretta, scanning her.

'What do you mean?' said Jane.

'They're here,' said Loretta.

'In L.A.?' said Jane. Loretta nodded, cocking her head toward Studio A.

'In the building. Jesse started his sessions yesterday.' Adrenaline shot through Jane's body; she became acutely aware of the hum of the lights, the stale air, the grainy walls.

'I can put a feeler out about a guitar player,' Loretta said. 'Strictly on the QT.'

'That's okay,' said Jane. 'But thank you. And thank you for what you said.'

Loretta nodded. 'Well, better get in there while I can,' she said. 'You could always consider using Studio B. . . .'

Jane gave Loretta a small smile, and Loretta disappeared into Studio C.

Jane stared down the hall toward Studio A, which suddenly loomed like the forbidden wing of a fairy tale castle. Surely Jesse couldn't be so close to her at that exact moment; Willy had promised that he would not schedule them in the studio at the same time. Jane lit another cigarette and inhaled.

It would be so easy to find out, to take the twenty steps to Studio A and open the door. Jane tried to deny it, but, faced with the tangible possibility of seeing Jesse, the idea thrilled her. She knew going in would be courting drama, so she made a deal with herself to stand in the hall and finish her smoke; if Jesse came out before, then so be it. One uneventful cigarette later, she left.

That night, Jane didn't want to be alone. She phoned Kyle and Rich, and let it ring twenty times before hanging up. She tried Willy and left him a message on his answering machine: 'Hey, Willy, it's Janie. I was wondering if you and Rebecca are free tonight. I know it's last-minute. Actually, never mind, you're definitely busy. Sorry, I'm . . . tired. I'll see you tomorrow.'

Jane found a bottle of whiskey in the freezer and poured herself a glass. She wandered into the living room. Her landlords had a floor-to-ceiling library, including an alphabetized vinyl section; Jane's eye was drawn to a Doris Day album, *I'll See You in My Dreams*. The album beside it was Lacey Dormon's *Greatest Hits*. Jane took another sip of whiskey. She still had Lacey's card.

'Jane, sweetheart, you've been on my mind,' said Lacey's unmistakable voice in the receiver. 'Why don't you come on over? We've just got a couple of friends here.'

Lacey and her husband, Darryl, lived a ten-minute walk up the mountain from Jane in a large ranch house covered in bougainvillea. Colorful figures leaned against the porch, guitar chords floating on the breeze; 'a couple of friends' meant a small party. As though sensing her presence, Lacey emerged from the house in a frothy pink robe.

'So glad you called, Jane,' she said. 'Tea? Something stronger? My mom always used to make hot toddies on nights like this.'

'That sounds great,' said Jane. She had the sense of being transported into a strange dream in which Gray Gables had been recast as a variety show – Lacey's home had a similar shabby charm, only hers was filled with young, talented artists instead of Quinns.

'I'm telling you, man,' a beautiful tanned boy was telling a waifish girl in a purple dress, 'Matala is where it's at. Just you, and the ocean, and the caves, and the stars.'

Lacey guided Jane past them into her kitchen. Jane hadn't had someone make her a tea since she had left Bayleen Island, and she felt a twinge of homesickness.

'I've been in California fifteen years, and I still think it's funny they consider this fall,' said Lacey, easing herself into a chair as the kettle began to heat. 'This would be May in Alabama.'

'This would be June on the Island,' said Jane.

'How is the Island?' asked Lacey. Jane watched a wave of nostalgia ripple across her features. 'Is Elsie still at Gray Gables? Jeanie? Zelly? Louise?'

Jane smiled at how well Lacey knew her family; Elsie's sisters used to stay at Gray Gables for long stretches when Jane had been younger and Elsie's mother, Jeanie, had still lived there.

'Once Jeanie relocated to New Orleans, Zelly went down to Peru and shacked up with a peyote farmer. Last we heard from Louise, she was in Newfoundland.'

Lacey laughed. 'That sounds about right,' she said. 'Is that place the Carousel still around?'

'Oh yeah,' said Jane. 'The Carousel will outlive us all.'

Lacey laughed. 'Your mom and I used to have so much fun there,' she said. Her expression saddened. 'I've thought about her so much since our last conversation – I still can't believe I didn't know.'

They sat in silence for a moment, each alone with their memories of Charlotte.

'What was she like when you knew her?' asked Jane presently.

'So smart,' said Lacey. 'She could size someone up in a minute. Funny, too – such a mouth on her. I remember the first time I met her at the Fest – I told her I couldn't believe she had a toddler, and she looks at me and goes, "Do you have any idea how hard I worked for these stretch marks?" I knew right then I had to be her friend.'

The kettle sang, and Lacey stood to prepare their drinks.

'You know, your mother was the first person to take me seriously.'

Jane watched as she sliced a lemon in half without placing it down on the counter, squeezing the wedges into tin mugs.

'A black girl with an acoustic . . . wasn't very common on the folk circuit in the 1950s. I used to sing show tunes at the Fest, and people would just stare. Then, one night – the second or third year – your mother takes me aside and says, "I'm sick of this." And I say, "Don't you think I am?" And she says, "You say you are, then you keep picking songs that hide your voice."'

Lacey set a mug on the table before Jane, whiskey, honey, and lemon wafting into the room. Jane touched the rim – it was too hot to pick up.

'I was so mad,' said Lacey. 'Who was this little blonde thing to tell me about *my* voice? She had no idea what it was like for me up there. But, deep down, part of me knew she had a point. The next day, I found her at your grandmother's house and said, "If you know so much, show me a song that's right for my voice." And that's how she came to write me "You Don't Know."'

'I love that song,' said Jane. '"*Yeah, you don't know, and it's a crying shame / Because life's a riddle and love's a game.*"'

'I do, too,' said Lacey. 'It was such a breakthrough for me – after *that* was released, I moved out here, and the rest is history. I always meant to come back east for the Fest – she and I would always talk about it – but it just kept not happening, and then . . .'

Lacey spoke as though in a trance. 'The Fest was so much smaller in the beginning. In those early years, the crowd was just a couple hundred, just kids getting away from their parents on a family vacation. After the labels took over, it really blew up, but those first years, it really was just a bunch of local folksingers. I can picture her up on that stage – hair up in a French twist, playing "Lilac Waltz" on her ukulele. She had a really sweet voice – such a pretty sound.'

'She used to sing it all the time,' said Jane.

'She loved that song,' said Lacey. 'Until what happened with Tommy Patton.' She shook her head in disgust. 'I've never forgiven myself.'

'What do you mean?' said Jane.

Lacey's eyes creased with sadness. 'She called me for help when that song went on the radio,' said Lacey softly. 'I . . . I turned her away. I had just been green-lit to host my show, and she wanted to fly to L.A. and call him out on the air.'

Lacey shook her head. 'I was just starting out, and the show was meant to be beautiful people, singing tunes and feeling

231

groovy. I wanted to help her, but I knew my producers would never allow it. She told me I was a sellout and hung up. That was the last time we ever spoke.'

Lacey's eyes became glassy. 'The problem was, she had no proof she had written the song,' she said. 'It would have been her word against Tommy's. And I don't need to tell you how big he was in those days. But I wonder . . . if I'd let her . . . would things have turned out differently?'

'The only way things would have turned out differently is if Tommy Patton didn't steal her song,' said Jane.

Lacey looked far into the distance. 'She always had such fire in her,' she said. 'All piss and vinegar. Not the type to run from a fight – certainly not the type to run out on her family.' She shook her head

Jane sat frozen, wondering whether Charlotte would want her to say more, feeling somehow sure she would. She took a sip from her mug and held the liquid on her tongue until the whiskey had lost its taste.

She stayed at Lacey's house until the moon had risen so high she could see her own shadow. The air had a slight chill as she walked back to her cottage – an easterly wind, a portent from home.

That night, Jane dreamed of a long, sterile hallway. She stood at one end, wearing her blue Center uniform; she could see Jesse at the other end, dressed in formal attire. Heart racing, Jane began to run toward him; he didn't seem to notice and turned as he came to the end of the corridor. When Jane reached the end of the hall, she turned to follow and ran straight into a glass wall. As she got to her feet, she could see Jesse on the other side – and Lacey, and Elsie, and Maggie, and Grace. All of them wore blue Center uniforms. Jane looked down; she was wearing a formal purple dress. She felt her hair; it was up in a French twist. She called for them as they spoke to one another, pointing at her, as though she were a specimen in a cage.

When Jane awoke, she had a phone message from Willy: 'Jane, sorry I missed you, and sorry you're not feeling your best. It's been a hell of a few weeks, and I know you're putting everything you've got into this record. I've been thinking – wouldn't it be great to do a show here? Just something casual, to get you in front of a room. It can be so isolating recording, and I think this could be just the thing. Call me back.'

30

The Troubadour was a stucco fortress at the very end of West Hollywood. Inside, Gothic lanterns cast a ruby glow over wooden pews; the air was thick with sugar and pine; as Jane descended the stairs to the stage, she couldn't have pictured a more magical space to perform.

'Hi, everybody,' she said, seating herself at the piano. She wore a long green peasant dress, her hair loose around her shoulders.

The crowd was pressed right against the stage; beards and beaded necklaces swayed before her, as silhouettes drifted in the balcony like deities obscured by the stage lights. Tonight, she would be soloing on her old Breakers repertoire; this would be her first time performing without her band. She caught a glimpse of Rich and Kyle standing by the bar and felt a pang.

'I'm so glad to be here with you all. L.A. is such a special place.' She let out a tinkle of laughter that rang around the room like a chime. The piano at the Troubadour was a great black Steinway; as she bent over the keys to play her opening chords, Jane felt like a mermaid swimming up to the body of a whale.

She began her set with 'Indigo,' her left hand taking the place of Kyle and her right the place of Rich. She wanted to raise people's energy, and this up-tempo number had always been a crowd pleaser. From there she moved to 'Spark,' and felt the room vibrate as she sang:

> *'Shock comes quick, a wave in the dark,*
> *This will make it better, this little spark.'*

Willy had been right – this was what she needed. Jane felt like a crocus breaking through the winter frost. The more she connected with the crowd, the stronger she became; she hadn't realized how long she had been without sunlight.

She alternated between fast and slow, guitar and piano, until she had worked the crowd into a lather. As she finished 'Sweet Maiden Mine,' she felt a rush of affection for the audience. She wanted to play them something new. The song was right there – she had been playing it for weeks and knew that she could nail it.

Jane placed her guitar on the floor and turned back to the piano.

'See what you think of this,' she said, letting her fingers rest upon the keys. You could have heard a pin drop as Jane began to play the intro to 'Ursa Major.'

> *'Starless night, I am a stranger,*
> *I sail the black and white,*
> *By the key of Ursa Major,*
> *Sending songs to points of light.'*

The song was composed in four parts that unfolded in geometric tessellations, beginning with rectangles and ending in stars. The opening chords were plodding and linear, like piano keys themselves, the tone of Jane's voice skimming the overtones like bird wings on water.

> *'This one pours, and this one sighs.*
> *This one needs a lullaby,*
> *This one just got too damn high.'*

As Jane sang, she found her lyrics narrating the lives around her; the ingenue by the bar, the hippie at her feet, the record exec in the balcony. They no longer appeared to her as archetypes but as fellow travelers, adrift in this land of fallen angels.

With a key change, Jane plunged them into the heart of the song. Vaunted root chords rose in a dome of sound, shimmering with arpeggios spun from her right hand.

> *'Now's the time to be alive, they say,*
> *Their tones as sharp as knives,*
> *When, hidden in your crescent,*
> *You're just trying to survive.'*

Here was the center of longing: not sadness, but wonder at life's fragility. As the bass chords dropped into the refrain, Jane could no longer feel any separation between herself and the crowd; her own fear floated like a blue flame above her head, and all around her, she could see identical blue flames flickering like heartbeats, craving breath, craving release.

> *'Starless, heartless night above a sea of stone,*
> *A distant dial tone.'*

She gathered herself and let her fingers lap the keys, a final wave pushing her to shore.

'Please don't leave me alone.'

When she finished, the final notes hovered in the air. Jane had never heard a pause go on for so long after a song. She smiled and broke the spell; the sudden crash of applause was deafening.

As the cheers died down, Jane glimpsed Willy descending the staircase to her left joined by several men. Jane knew he had invited his brother Danny, and wondered if perhaps their other brother, Freddy, was in town from London.

She closed out the set with three more songs: taking the energy of the room back up with 'Caught,' keeping it level with 'No More Demands,' and then finishing with an acoustic version of 'Spring Fling.' As she bowed, she could see Rich and Kyle clapping and whistling in the back.

Jane climbed the stairs to her dressing room, a small loft partitioned off by a curtain. When she caught sight of her reflection in the vanity, she couldn't believe how much more herself she looked than she had before the show. There came a knock on the door frame, and Willy pushed in without awaiting her reply.

'Hey,' said Jane as she opened her guitar case. 'I'll be down in a sec.'

'Actually, I think we should probably get going,' said Willy. His tone made Jane look up.

'Wait, you mean leave?' she said. 'Rich and Kyle are waiting – I thought your brother—'

'Just trust me,' said Willy, bending down to help her place her guitar into its carrier. 'My car's in back—' Willy glanced over his shoulder.

At that moment, Danny Lambert swept in, followed by Vincent Ray and a silver-haired man Jane recognized instantly as Tommy Patton. Jane felt viscous from her set, and these apparitions slipped off her brain like Jell-O from a plastic mold. Maggie had been right, she thought – holding on to one's signature look did have an aging effect. Willy's hand closed around Jane's arm, helping her to her feet.

'Janie, great show,' said Danny Lambert, kissing her on both cheeks, oblivious to their ashen color. Not so with Vincent Ray; his watery eyes looked glutted with the pleasure of seeing Jane so uncomfortable.

'Vincent and I were scheduled to have dinner tonight,' said Danny, following Jane's gaze. 'When I told him you were performing, he insisted on coming to see you instead.'

'Yes, we go way back,' said Vincent Ray, reaching for Jane. His fingers fastened around her shoulder like a wiry clamp.

'I hope you don't mind, I brought my friend Tommy,' added Vincent Ray. 'He's always had a great eye for new talent.'

He knew. How? The gears of Jane's mind seemed to be stuck. Jane turned to Tommy Patton, trying to shake off Vincent Ray.

'Nice show,' Tommy said, offering his hand to Jane; his grip felt weak and slippery.

'Tommy Patton,' said Jane.

'That's right,' said Danny encouragingly.

'I don't usually come out to shows, but Vincent Ray convinced me to make an exception,' said Tommy. 'You've got a swell act, kid.'

His eyes glinted at her, and Jane felt a wave of revulsion. Her many imaginings of this moment had never involved her being cornered like a doe in a briar. She searched her brain for the scripts she had written should she ever confront the man who had ruined her mother's life, and discovered, impossibly, that all she had were empty scrolls.

As her eyes swam into focus, they fixed on a purple scar that streaked Tommy's jawline like a handprint reaching out from beneath his collar.

'Don't mind the scar,' said Tommy. 'It's a souvenir from *my* days as a troubadour. How long are you in town for?' he asked.

All Jane's life, people had commented on the uncanny resemblance between her and her mother. If Tommy Patton could see it, he was a very good actor.

'Just two more weeks,' said Willy, when Jane didn't respond. 'We're actually heading out right now – got a double session in the morning, so early to bed.'

'Nice try,' said Vincent Ray. 'We're all going out for a drink – I know Jane wouldn't want to miss the chance to hear about Tommy's beginnings, being such a fan.'

'Aw, that's sweet, doll,' said Tommy Patton, looking at Jane as if she had been speaking. In that moment, Jane felt a certainty break loose inside her. She had so many unanswered questions about her mother, but she had never once second guessed Charlotte's grief over 'Lilac Waltz.' Now, as Tommy Patton flashed her an artless grin, doubt began to roll around inside her like a pinball. Charlotte's mental state had been deteriorating toward the end – was it possible she'd made the whole thing up?

Danny Lambert stood in the door; he had already tired of this exchange and kept glancing down the stairs, as though hoping someone better might come along. Jane wondered what it would take to run past him. Just then, his face lit in satisfaction.

'Jesse Reid is here,' he said. 'I see him at the bar. Hey! Jesse!'

Jane felt as though she had been knocked out of her body into another dimension. This had to be a nightmare. She couldn't be facing Jesse now, not in front of Vincent Ray, not in front of Tommy fucking Patton. Willy knew. As Vincent Ray and Tommy Patton pivoted toward the stairs, Willy placed his keys in Jane's hand and nodded to the fire escape.

'Go,' he said. 'I'll be right there.'

As the men formed a wall on the landing, Jane slipped behind them out the exit, a rusted cage of stairs that deposited her in a small parking lot behind the theater. She didn't look back until she was in the passenger seat of Willy's blue Mustang. She jammed the key into the ignition, crouching beside the dashboard until the convertible roof had enveloped her.

31

Jane didn't speak again until Willy had parked outside her cottage.

'How did he know?' she asked. Willy switched off the motor. For a moment, the only sound was the jangle of his key chains.

'After the cover shoot last year,' said Willy, 'I went out after Vincent Ray to try to smooth things over. Up until that point, I'd known him to be a pretty reasonable guy, and I thought I could salvage things if I just explained why his attitude with your album was particularly painful. So I told him what happened with your mom. Honestly, I'm shocked he even remembered; he was so irate, I didn't think he was hearing a word I said.'

Willy crossed his arms and stretched his legs, as though trying to propel himself through the roof. 'I underestimated the whole situation,' he said. 'Using his image on the album was a mistake.'

'I love that cover,' said Jane. 'So did the fans.'

Willy shook his head. 'Exactly,' he said. 'Vincent Ray prides himself on being an enforcer; to him, every copy of *Spring Fling* that sells is a personal affront. It's blown this whole thing way out of proportion. I'm so sorry, Jane. I never imagined he would do something like this.'

'It does seem like a lot of effort to put down a nobody,' said Jane.

'You're not a nobody,' said Willy. 'That's why he's doing this. No matter what he says or how he tries to fuck with you, you have something he cannot control, and it infuriates him.'

'What's that?' said Jane.

'Your music,' said Willy. 'As long as you have an instrument in your hands, you're trouble.'

Jane slumped back in her seat. The streetlamp highlighted the ridged contours of her cottage. Soon California would be a memory to her.

'Jesse came,' said Jane.

Willy adjusted his wedding ring. 'I told him not to,' said Willy. 'Curiosity must have gotten the better of him.'

'Curiosity,' Jane repeated.

Willy nodded. 'Jane, I know tonight was unsettling, but if there's anything you should take away from it, it's that *Ursa Major* is going to be huge,' he said. 'You were magnificent.'

Jane stood in the driveway, holding on to her guitar case as his taillights retreated down the hill. She felt sore then, as though a blade had been extracted from her chest after running her through.

She knew Willy would never intentionally hurt her, but he had. Willy knew it, too; after their recording sessions wrapped the following Tuesday, he all but absented himself from the mixing.

This was just as well; Jane had left what little barrier remained between her spirit and the outside world backstage at the Troubadour and was content to be alone with Simon. He was

242

skilled and patient and safe; he wanted nothing from Jane personally, and everything from her musically.

'The vocals here are too harsh – they're overwhelming the guitar,' he said.

'Should we overdub?' said Jane.

Simon shook his head. 'Let's run it through the equalizer first; if we de-ess the consonants, that will help the sibilance.'

Each day, they convened in the control booth, a pair of surgeons ready to operate. Jane was the specialist called in to consult while Simon performed a procedure on one of her blood relatives. This was how, one by one, they mastered the tracks and put them in order.

The album opened with 'New Country,' a restless song recalling Jane's first days on tour. The track had a strong engine, an insistent rhythm that showcased Huck's earthy conga, Kyle's creative bass line, and Rich's strummy style.

'Little Lion' followed, a deceptively simple lullaby with an arrangement as spare as Bea's crib. The first verse was just Jane on guitar, and the subsequent verses pulled in Huck's maracas and Kyle for the bridge.

'Wallflower' came next, the song Jane had first played at Peggy Ridge. For the album, she had transposed it onto the piano, her voice trembling over anthemic A-minor chords, singing, 'Car pulls up, a screen door slams, / Clicking heels, a beige sedan, / Inside is another man.'

The tracks were lilting and jagged, like half of a heart-shaped necklace.

'*Last Call*' was an up-tempo drinking song, with a braying instrumental and a chorus perfect for radio play: 'We'll have a ball until last call, / And then we're splitting town.' Kyle and Rich strummed an interwoven line that called to mind Celtic dances. It was the most percussive song on the album, with Huck on the bongos.

'Ursa Major' was the last track on the first side. Jane had insisted it be recorded all in one take; she and Simon had locked themselves in the studio, modulating the amplifier levels between renditions until they captured it on the twenty-seventh try. After, they shared a cigarette in the hall.

'This one reminds me of the thread Ariadne gave Theseus,' said Simon. Jane looked up, surprised to hear him refer to the myth she'd once cited to Jesse; she was indeed following a cord out of the darkness.

'How does it go?' said Simon. 'No love without pain.'

'No love without sacrifice,' said Jane.

The reverse side of the album began with 'A Shanty,' a play on a nautical work song, chanting, 'I know the truth, you can't stop being you / No matter whether blue, this storm's just passing through.' The track was a palate cleanser featuring elements of a traditional shanty mixed with pop accents from Huck and Kyle.

This transitioned into the blues-rock tones of 'Brand New Cassette,' a highway ballad that burned like a cigarette on a parched throat. Simon took care placing the 'sample' section into the master, as though transplanting a vital organ.

'No Two Alike' followed, an unapologetically nostalgic song with bass, keyboard, and guitar painting a rose-colored tableau around a melody that harked back to children's nursery rhymes. The song's real power came from the bridge: 'Be a man, find a job, learn to pay your dues, / They say you have your father's stride, but can you fill his shoes?'

Next came 'A Thousand Lines,' an up-tempo song with an accompaniment as finely wrought as a flower crown. Every time Jane and Simon thought they had it, they'd replay the track and Rich's guitar would poke out like a sprig of pine.

The album closed with 'Light's On,' the third track featuring only piano and vocals. Simon showed his skill balancing the coda, in which Jane's melody line dropped into a dissonant harmony between the keys. The song was equal parts dexterity and disenchantment.

Jane and Simon mixed and remixed 'A Thousand Lines' every way they could conceive; they put a low-pass filter on Rich's track, chorused it, ran it through a distortion, brought down the reverb, overdrove it. No matter how they tried to dress it up, his playing just didn't have the agility necessary for the song. In desperation, Jane tried rerecording the line herself, and even that was like trying to thread a needle with a piece of twine.

Defeated, Jane and Simon sat beside the console and surveyed their tape reels like two raccoons who had just looted a studio trash can.

'We could cut the song,' Jane said, finally. Simon swallowed.

'There is one other thing we could try.' He opened a drawer in a nearby filing cabinet and pulled out an unmarked tape Jane had never seen before. Carefully, Simon removed Rich's track, replacing it with this new one. He rewound the masters and hit 'play.'

Jane's entire body began to vibrate as she heard the unmistakable timbre of Jesse's guitar slide seamlessly into the song. She listened, heart pounding as his fingers intuited her express wishes.

245

'How?' asked Jane when the track had finished playing.

'Don't know,' said Simon. 'I found this sitting at the control station a few weeks ago – just a couple of tracks. I asked Willy about it, and he said to put them away. But, Jane, if we're at the point of cutting the song – it's worth considering.'

Jane cleared her throat. 'What other songs did he record?'

Jesse had also left tracks for 'New Country' and 'A Shanty,' both up-tempo numbers, the least fraught on the album. As she listened to him play, she felt warmth rush into her body. He had heard her lyrics, must have liked them if he'd wanted to contribute to the songs.

'What do you think?' said Simon. He seemed uneasy, and Jane knew why. If they used the tracks, they risked hurting Rich; if they didn't, they risked hurting the album.

Jane exhaled. 'Use them,' she said.

'Which ones?' said Simon.

'All,' said Jane.

Simon looked relieved, like he was glad she had been the one to say it.

Together, they worked to strip Rich's tracks from 'A Thousand Lines,' 'A Shanty,' and 'New Country' and introduce Jesse's. It was after 11:00 p.m. when they left the studio.

'I think you made a good call today,' said Simon, locking the door behind them. He hesitated. 'What are you going to say to Rich?'

Jane fished in her pocket for her cigarettes. 'I'll tell him how grateful I am to him, and that, in the end, it just wasn't right. I think he'll understand,' she said.

Simon nodded but didn't move.

'You know,' said Jane, 'it wouldn't hurt if you wanted to take him out to dinner, just to smooth things over. I have a feeling you two might be working together again.'

A ghost of a smile flashed across Simon's face. 'Maybe I will,' he said. He looked boyish to Jane as she watched him walk down the hall toward the exit by Studio D. She lit a cigarette.

After a moment, Jane let her legs carry her up the ramp and around the corner to Studio A. The light above the door was off; the studio was not currently in use. Jane let herself in.

Studio A looked almost identical to Studio C. Jane stood in the booth, staring at the tape mounted in the controller, smoking her cigarette. She hit 'play.'

A basic track began to spool for 'Let the Light Go.'

It had been months since Jane had listened to Jesse's voice, and yet she could still recall every other time she'd heard him sing it, from their motel room in Washington State to Minglewood Hall in Memphis.

Jane rewound the basic and hit 'play.' She lit another cigarette as she listened. She rewound the tape and played it again.

32

On Christmas Eve morning, Jane and Elsie drove to the pier to pick up Grace. They waited in the station wagon as the ocean liner pulled into port, carols jingling on the radio.

'There she is,' said Elsie.

Grace waved to them from the ramp, a flurry dusting her coat like confectioners' sugar.

Grace wasn't the only Christmas arrival; according to that morning's *Island Gazette*, Jesse and Morgan had flown in to spend the holiday with their families. Elsie used the article to cover the kitchen table as she, Grace, and Jane cooked dinner; soon, the photo spread of Morgan and Jesse holding hands at the airport was covered in a mound of potato peels.

Morgan's first single, 'Broken Door,' had dropped the first week in December, the same week Jane had returned to the Island. Since then, there had been a barrage of media about Morgan and Jesse. Unlike Jane, Morgan had given several interviews specifically about their romance, covering how they'd met on the Island as kids and how, in many ways, their love seemed to be predestined. The local coverage was even more saccharine than the national media's.

Jane felt like a ghost watching someone else move into her

house as, week over week, 'Broken Door' rode the same wave of Jesse fanaticism that had taken 'Spring Fling' into the top ten. She had never wanted to be known as Jesse's girlfriend, but as Morgan eclipsed her, she began to fear for the first time that, without him, she might not be known at all.

Jane's only consolation were the ten final tracks up in her room, which Rich and Kyle had delivered upon their return earlier that week in the form of a test pressing. Willy had wanted to wait until after the holidays to schedule her cover shoot, at which point the release date for *Ursa Major* would be confirmed. Jane guessed the record would go on sale at the end of January; until then, her life would be on hold.

That night, everyone gathered at Gray Gables for a feast. Rich and Kyle came over early to help, and Jane felt as if her life had been rewound. When Greg arrived with Maggie and Bea, Jane could sense Rich guarding himself, but without some of the old heaviness. Come to think of it, Jane hadn't seen Rich this good in a while. He had been relieved when Jane told him about Jesse's tracks, and he and Kyle both had studio gigs lined up for the new year. Jane refrained from asking Kyle how Jesse's sessions had gone.

Elsie served a Christmas goose, crisply roasted alongside heaping platters of butternut squash, mashed potatoes, green beans, and zucchini bread. They toasted and ate and drank until all that remained were plates streaked with plum sauce and gravy. After supper, Grace handed out party poppers from London; they cracked the canisters and traded the paper crowns inside for their favorite colors.

'So, this is what *Nate* is into,' said Maggie as Grace donned an orange tiara. Grace blushed. Nate was the live-in tutor for Millie's grandchildren, whom Grace had started dating in London.

'Mags, give me the blue one,' said Greg, taking the crown off Maggie's head. As Maggie swatted at his hand, Grace inclined toward Jane.

'You know,' she said, 'I never would have gone if it weren't for you. Seeing you go on tour, take your fate in your hands – you inspired me.'

She gave Jane's arm a squeeze, then crossed the room to check on Bea. Jane recalled Grace's parting words – 'By the time I'm back for Christmas, you will be in a different place.' Jane hadn't believed her at the time, but Grace had been right. Her life wasn't perfect, but she had made an album she was truly proud of – and that was something.

'Come on,' said Greg, pulling Jane from her chair. 'Let's make some music.' Rich was already playing 'Jingle Bells' on his guitar as Greg prodded Jane into the living room.

By the time the party fizzled, Bea had fallen asleep on the couch, and Jane felt as though she could never look at another goose. She couldn't remember the last time she'd laughed so much.

'Merry Christmas,' said Grace, wrapping her arm around Jane and giving her a squeeze. Greg silently waved to Jane, not wanting to wake Bea as Maggie carried her outside. Jane watched from the porch as the four of them walked to Greg's beat-up VW Bug, and thought no family had ever looked so perfect. Kyle and Rich stayed to help with the dishes, then drove off, leaving Jane and Elsie to snuff out the candles.

'And to all a good night,' said Elsie as they headed upstairs.

Jane awoke some hours later to an urgent rapping sound on the front door. She saw Elsie's light go on across the hall and heard her creak down the stairs. For a moment, all was quiet.

'Janie, you better come down,' Elsie called. Jane roused herself; she was wearing an overlarge tee shirt for Bongo's Whale Watching Tours and tube socks. She threw a blanket around her shoulders and followed her grandmother downstairs.

'What is it?' she mumbled. Elsie was peering through the peephole in the door.

'It's Jesse,' said Elsie.

Jane thought she had misheard. 'Jesse?' she said.

'Should we see what he wants?' said Elsie.

Jane swallowed.

'Or not – he'll get the hint,' said Elsie.

'See what he wants,' said Jane.

Elsie undid the latch, and there he was. His hair was longer than Jane remembered it, and he had grown a mustache; he wore no jacket, shoulders scrunched up by his ears.

'It's a bit late,' said Elsie. Jane stepped down so she was on the landing. When Jesse saw her, he couldn't take his eyes from her face.

'May I come in?' he said. 'I sincerely apologize for the hour.'

Jane nodded once, and Elsie undid the latch on the screen to let him pass. She bolted the door once he was inside.

'I'm going back to bed,' she said.

Elsie hesitated as she passed Jane on the landing but said nothing further. Jane's heart was pounding so hard she felt faint. Here was Jesse Reid, standing in her hallway. How strange it was, how much like a dream. She took a step toward him.

'What are you doing here?' she said, her mouth dry. Jesse ran a hand through his hair.

'I was at home,' he said. He took a step toward her. 'Having

251

Christmas.' He shook his head. 'But the more I sat there, the more I thought, *This isn't my home.*'

He took another step. 'This is my home,' he said, looking around the hall. 'You are my home.'

Jane couldn't breathe.

'I knew being here wasn't possible. But the more I thought about it, the more it began to seem like all I would need to do was get in a car and drive over. And so I did.'

He was edging closer, as though she were a wild creature he was trying not to frighten. Jane stayed perfectly still.

'Please, don't send me away,' he said. She looked into his eyes, and he brushed the hair from her shoulder. The familiar gesture caught both of them by surprise, and neither knew how to react.

Then Jesse pulled her to him, holding her to his chest. Jane could hear his heart beating, and she began to sob. She cried and cried until there were no more tears and all that was left was the sensation of his fingers combing through her hair.

She led him upstairs and shut the door to her room behind them. In the morning, there would be questions, but none of that mattered right now. Jane, whose existence had been drifting further and further into the ether, snapped back into her body. She felt desire, but more than that she felt relief; relief to finally, for a moment, admit how much she still wanted him.

Jane didn't have words for this, but she heard music in her ears as he began to kiss her. She felt, as they undressed, that she was being allowed passage into a sacred space she never thought she'd find again. Here, she had access to this person, but also the person he allowed her to be, someone decent and shining who was capable of hope.

Jesse's thumbs traced her cheekbones, and he pulled her into another kiss; he smelled so good, and tasted so like himself, that the months of his absence evaporated into memory. Jane took off his shirt and pulled him down into the bed with her, and gasped as she felt him hard through the cool fabric of his jeans.

He took off his pants so only his briefs remained and yanked the nightshirt off her so all she was wearing were the tube socks. His hands traced the outline of her shape as though reassuring himself it really was her. Satisfied, his fingers spread across her lower back and he pulled her against him, a small moan escaping his lips.

'We have to be quiet,' Jane whispered. He nodded, fixing her in his indelible blue gaze.

Then he began to kiss her again, and she lost herself, panting into the crook of his neck, waves cresting and breaking between her legs. He pulled himself deeper inside of her, moving over her, his hands gripping her hips until he shuddered. He stayed on top of her for a moment, forehead pressed against hers. Then he rolled her onto her side, enfolding her in his arms as their hearts slowed, and their breaths grew shallow. Together, they slipped into sleep.

Jane dreamed that it was morning. Had he already gone? She left her room and walked downstairs. It was night now as she approached the hall mirror. There, she saw her reflection, hair swept up in a French twist, a lilac-colored dress wrapped around her figure. Jane looked down and saw that she was holding a tube of lipstick. She uncapped it and twisted out the color. She looked up and dropped the tube. Her reflection still wore the lilac-colored dress, but her face had changed; she was now the woman from Chicago, grimacing in blind adoration.

Jane's eyes flew open. It was still night. She looked over: Jesse was still there. She still had time.

33

Jane awoke again in the gray light of dawn. They had shifted positions in the night; Jesse's nose was tucked into the crook of her neck, his limbs sprawled across her body. She smelled his hair and felt the lovely weight of his head beside hers.

Jesse stirred, and Jane felt consciousness encroaching. His hands seemed to wake first, reaching for her hair. He opened his eyes and looked around the room; satisfied, he gathered her in his arms, holding her hand on his chest.

'Is that your test pressing?' he said, nodding toward the phonograph where Jane had placed the package from Pegasus. Jane nodded.

'Did you ever find the tracks I left you?' he said.

Jane nodded again. 'What prompted you to do that?' she asked.

Jesse held her hand up in both of his, tracing the lines on her palm with his thumbs. 'After we split up, I tried to convince myself it was for the best. Morgan liked me, and people seemed to think we would be good together, so I figured, *What the hell.*

'Willy wouldn't tell me anything about you. It drove me insane – I had no idea what you were up to, who you were with. I had no idea when I got to L.A. that you were there, recording.

'Then I saw you were performing at the Troubadour. I confronted Willy, and he told me you were wrapping up your album and were all but on a plane back east. He told me it would just complicate things if I went, but I had to see you.

'I promised myself I would stay out of sight – but then I heard "Ursa Major," and . . . I wanted so badly to talk to you about it. By the time I went backstage, the only people left were Vincent Ray and Tommy fucking Patton.'

The tone of his voice darkened. 'I assume one brought the other.'

'Yes.'

'Unbelievable,' he said.

Jane silently agreed. At the time, having Jesse show up had seemed like a curse; now hearing him acknowledge it without her having to explain felt like a blessing.

'After that, I didn't know what to do with myself,' he said. 'I couldn't bear to go home to Morgan, and I didn't know where you were, so I went to the studio.

'When I got to Studio C, "A Thousand Lines" was in the deck. . . . It didn't seem like it had a guitar part, so I thought I'd give it a try. "A Shanty" and "New Country" seemed like fair game as well. The rest were just . . . perfect. I always knew you could write, Jane.'

He grinned, then his face clouded. 'I thought maybe you'd reach out when you found the tracks.'

'My engineer didn't show them to me until we were on the verge of pulling "A Thousand Lines" from the record,' said Jane. 'Your track saved the song.'

'So . . . you're using it?' said Jesse.

Jane nodded, holding on to his hand. She knew it was her turn to speak. She wished that it weren't.

'That night at the Troubadour . . .' she began. She could feel herself approaching the edge of a cliff. She knew she would need to jump off if she ever wanted to reach the next place, but it was dark and dangerous, and she didn't know how she would land. So she stood at the edge, stalling.

'I haven't felt the same since that night – since seeing Tommy Patton,' she said. 'I look like my mom – unusually so. And he didn't seem to know me at all.'

'From what you said, they only met briefly,' said Jesse. 'I doubt your mom was the only person Tommy Patton took advantage of whose face he forgot.'

Jane took a breath. 'What if he didn't take advantage of her?' said Jane. 'What if she was lying? Her claim to "Lilac Waltz" is a part of who I am – but seeing him be so totally unaware really made me wonder . . . what if it didn't happen that way?'

Jesse considered. 'People heard her perform the song, right?' he said. 'What reason do you have to doubt her?'

This was it – the moment Jane would have to leap. She opened her mouth to respond.

Be careful what you tell him.

As Jesse squeezed her hand, Jane noticed a yellow-and-blue bruise on the inside of his elbow. She reached over and touched it. Jesse lowered his arm out of view.

'Does Morgan know about that?' said Jane.

Jesse exhaled. 'Yes,' he said.

Jane felt herself backing away from the cliffside. 'And?' she said.

'She doesn't like it, but she knows I'm trying,' said Jesse. He gripped Jane's hand. 'Jane, there's something I have to tell you.'

His tone made her look up.

'I'm supposed to propose to her today,' said Jesse, his eyes on her face.

Jane felt as though she'd fallen through ice. 'Why would that be worth mentioning?' she said, dropping his hand.

'Sorry, I know,' he said.

Jane's mind spun. So – Lenny Davis was finally getting his respectable wedding. This was the reason Willy hadn't scheduled the release for *Ursa Major*. He had known that this proposal was coming, and had realized, as Jane did, that the tidal wave of publicity it would generate would blow every other album out of the water for months. By delaying her release, he'd been throwing her to dry land.

'Are you going to do it?' said Jane.

'I don't know,' said Jesse. He took a breath. 'I just keep thinking, what if it was us – you and me? How much better it would be.'

What if it was? All that media coverage would be Jane's. She would be back in the spotlight – but now she'd be the other woman. Jane looked over at the test pressing, her own verses running through her head, recast as the ballads of a homewrecker. 'My love light's on, / And I've got nothing left to lose.' Jane shuddered. This record had the potential to actually matter, and the gossip rags would carve it into headlines. Her credibility as a musician would be ruined.

But she'd have Jesse. The thought stopped her heart.

But for how long? And what would happen to her music if they broke up? Jane had barely pulled herself back from the brink of oblivion this time; if they split up again, the label would bury her. She had a vision of herself straightening the magazines in the Center's rec room: Jesse, Loretta, and Morgan on the covers of *Time, Rolling Stone*, and *Life*. She could not let that happen.

'I'm never getting married,' said Jane.

'We wouldn't have to get married,' said Jesse quickly. 'I just want you by my side.'

'I can't,' said Jane. 'If I do, everything I've worked for will be cheapened. I'll be a punch line in a *Rolling Stone* diagram of women you dated.'

'But that will all subside,' said Jesse. 'I'm talking about our lives – are you saying a record is more important than that?'

'This record is everything to me,' said Jane. 'I wouldn't expect you to understand.'

'What's that supposed to mean?'

'You're ambivalent about what you have – I'm not,' said Jane.

Jesse regarded her. 'Be my partner in this,' he said. 'It's meaningless to me without you.'

'I'm sorry, but I can't,' said Jane. 'There's too much at stake.'

Jesse was incredulous. 'Can't you see that this is also what's best for your record?' he said.

'I need to be judged on my own merit,' said Jane. 'I don't want to depend on reflected glory.'

Jesse groaned. 'All glory is reflected glory,' he said. 'You can't will the world to be different than it is. This idea you have of some pure appreciation that transcends money and sex and power . . . it's not real. What's real is that I want to take care of you.'

Jane's temper flared. 'That's not real,' she said. 'You can't even take care of yourself.'

Jesse looked as if he'd been slapped. For a moment, he sat, stunned. Then he grabbed her face and kissed her. Jane was caught off guard and kissed him back. She gasped, and he pulled her in to him. When she drew away, both of them were breathless.

'You love me, Jane,' he said.

'You don't know me as well as you think,' said Jane, still dazed from the kiss.

'I know your songs,' he said. '"A Thousand Lines," "Brand New Cassette," "Ursa Major" . . . they're about us.'

Jane gave him a strange look. 'I wouldn't presume to think you understand "Ursa Major,"' she said.

Jesse wasn't having it.

'"Evenings turning to a spoon, / Wish that you would come down soon" – that's about me.'

'It's not about what you think,' said Jane.

His eyes searched her, and she stared into their brilliant color, feeling the space between them pulse. Jesse reached for her again, bringing her close, but this time Jane held herself an inch from his face. His brow furrowed; his eyes went to her lips and he bent toward her. Jane was still.

'Jane, please,' he said.

Jane bit her lip. It would be so easy to kiss him, to take him back to bed. Her muscles coiled in anticipation of his weight, of his limbs stretching around hers, the roughness of his cheek against her neck, his voice low in her ear.

'No,' she said.

It took Jesse a moment to respond, as though he couldn't find the will. Then he released her. He closed and opened his hands.

'Fine,' he said.

He rose from the bed and dressed as the first rays of sunlight crept in through the curtains. Jane felt numb; within minutes, he would be gone. Jesse ran his hands through his hair and looked at her, his expression blank; his beauty made everything he touched seem important.

259

Jane sat up, and they watched each other for a moment, not speaking. 'Do you even want to get married?' she said.

A cold front was closing over Jesse's features; his eyes had turned to ice. The polite tone in his voice didn't slip, but Jane was returned to her worst days with him on tour. 'Don't much care one way or another,' said Jesse. 'I liked the idea of being with the person who means the most to me. But since I'm told that's not possible, guess it doesn't matter much what I do. So long, Jane.'

She listened as his boots clomped down the stairs, heard the screen door creak and close, then the larger wooden door.

Only then did she follow. Jane stood in the hall, the white light of morning revealing the cracks in the wallpaper.

Flowers painted on the wall,
Tattered paper bouquets fall.

She regarded her reflection in the mirror. After some time, she heard Elsie on the stairs behind her.

'Did Jesse go?' said Elsie. Jane nodded; this question from her grandmother felt like her only proof that he had actually been there.

Elsie stepped off the landing into the hall and stood behind Jane. She held Jane's shoulders and met her eyes in the mirror.

Jane lowered her gaze.

'Don't tell Grace,' she said.

34

Alex Redding had never been to Bayleen Island before, but he'd always wanted to photograph it. Even as he stepped from the plane, he could see the difference in the April light, soft with salt.

Jane Quinn stepped out of a beat-up woody station wagon beside the overgrown runway and waved. Alex beamed at her, and the two embraced. He had always had a thing for Jane and couldn't wait to shoot her again; she looked perfect here, with her flyaway yellow hair, calico dress, and leather boots. They got in the car, and she turned onto a forest road.

'How long will you be here?' she asked. They cruised beneath a cover of budding boughs, colors popping inside a woodland kaleidoscope.

'As long as it takes,' said Alex. 'Pegasus is paying. I don't have another job until next week.'

Jane flipped on the radio; 'Under Stars' by Jesse Reid was playing.

> *'Imagine, a life with you,*
> *Makes me complete*
> *Imagine, a dance hall*
> *Rip your stockings, move your feet.'*

Alex rolled his eyes and switched the station.

Trying to avoid 'Under Stars' was like trying to skirt an epidemic; it was the only song on every channel, every jukebox, every cassette player. The only other records that got any play time were those closest to the oubreak's source: Morgan Vidal's, of course. And Loretta Mays; Jesse Reid had featured her song 'Safe Passage' on his album, and now her debut, *Hourglass*, was charting.

Production had been halted on most of Pegasus's winter catalogue so it wouldn't be cannibalized by the monster success of *Under Stars* and Morgan Vidal's self-titled debut; there was no point in competing until these two mega-hits ebbed. Alex knew Jane's new album had been tabled until June.

He had heard rumors that Jane and Jesse had dated while on tour last year, but she didn't seem fazed by the song, and had begun asking him questions about his process.

'What determines the emotion in the photo?' she asked.

'A combination of things,' said Alex. 'The subject. The light. The angle. How I'm seeing it.'

'When you shot the Breakers' cover, what were you seeing?' said Jane. Alex considered, summoning the image in his mind.

'I saw a girl standing up to a bully,' he said.

Jane tilted her head. 'So the photo really is your perspective,' she said.

'More or less,' said Alex.

They drove past a sign that read 'Fishing Village, 2 miles.' The terrain thinned into beach shrubbery until the road spat them onto the long pier. Boats bobbed in the harbor, moored beside stacks of green and yellow lobster crates. Beyond a handful of shops, a rock jetty stretched half a mile into the ocean.

Jane parked and led Alex out onto the jetty so they could look back at the village. She squatted and motioned for him to follow. He bent so that they were at eye level, and she pointed to a spray of cottages nestled into the marshy bay.

'You see?' she said. 'Those seven lights?' Alex squinted – from this angle, the cottage lights looked like the Big Dipper. This worked, given what he knew of Jane's album, which was its title.

'I like it,' he said. 'So – you want to be in the foreground?'

'Yes,' she said. 'I want it to be close up and dark.'

'That'll be groovy,' said Alex. Jane looked at him. Even crouched beside her, he was twice her size.

'What do you see right now, when you look at me?' she asked.

Alex regarded her pretty gray eyes, her sharp cheekbones, her bewitching lips. 'I see a woman who knows what she wants,' he said.

Jane considered. Then she stood, and he followed her back to the car.

She took him to the Regent's Cove Hotel, where he checked in, and the two of them headed to the hotel restaurant for dinner. Everywhere Jane went, people spoke to her on a first-name basis – not as a celebrity, but as a native daughter. After dinner, she took Alex down to the pub in the hotel's basement.

A bespectacled man drinking at the bar nodded to her as they passed his corner. 'Jane,' he said. Jane nodded back.

She sat Alex down at the other end of the bar and bought him a drink. Alex felt relaxed and excited; he could feel the chemistry crackling between them. As they talked about her album, he knew it was only a matter of time.

'The budget's considerably higher for your new album cover,' Alex observed as another round of drinks appeared.

'A consolation prize from Willy for the five-month delay,' said Jane.

'You must be flattered on some level,' said Alex. 'They wouldn't have delayed it if they didn't think it would succeed.'

Jane considered him and took a sip of her drink. 'Your eyes are really blue,' she said. Alex smiled at her and placed a hand on her knee.

He knew Jane would be fun in bed, but he hadn't anticipated how bad she needed to fuck. They only just made it to the room before she was undoing his belt. Alex barely registered that she hadn't been wearing underwear as she lifted her skirt and started riding him. She was blind with desire; she didn't care what he was thinking, she just wanted to be on his dick. . . . It was all Alex could do to remember the teams in the NBA. She swore as she finished, and he grabbed her ass, pumping her over him, until she moaned. He pulled off her dress and let out a growl; Jane had great tits, these little cones that bounced gently every time he thrust into her. He tugged on her left nipple with his teeth as he fucked her and both of them came.

After, she slid off him and reached into her bag for a cigarette.

'You have no idea how long I've wanted to do that,' he said.

Jane glanced at him as though she was about to tell him exactly how long, then thought better of it. It struck Alex that there had been more affection in that look than there had been in their sex.

The next morning, breakfast arrived on a silver tray with the morning paper.

'*The Island Gazette* sure loves Jesse Reid and Morgan Vidal,' said Alex as he skimmed a front-page article about how the couple's new construction projects – an 'up-Island' mansion and a trendy nightclub – were employing nearly 10 percent of the Island's workforce.

Jane took a drag from her cigarette, pulling on a hotel bathrobe that matched the drapes.

'It's been a real roller coaster,' she said, flicking ash into a glass dish. 'First we loved them because they were planning a big Island wedding. Then we hated them because they eloped in New York. Now we love them again because of the club. We're a fickle people.'

Alex tried to decipher Jane's past with Jesse from these remarks; from the way she talked about his notorious marriage, their affair couldn't have been very serious. She seemed almost bored.

'I'll be ready for some new music,' Alex said. 'If I have to hear "Under Stars" one more time . . .'

Jane exhaled a puff of smoke and shot him a wink.

That day, Jane drove Alex around the Island, showing him the mansions that had once belonged to the whaling tycoons, the private beaches, the clay cliffs. As the sun lowered in the sky, they arrived back at the fishing village, and once again Jane took him out onto the jetty.

'What do you see now?' she said. 'When you look at me.' Alex considered. He had the impression that he was a lens she was trying to calibrate.

'I see a complicated woman with many layers,' he said. They left the jetty without taking a single photo.

They picked up lobster rolls from one of the fish stands in the village and ate watching an orange sun sink into the water.

'Would you like to hear the songs?' Jane asked. 'From *Ursa Major*.'

Alex looked up. 'Sure,' he said.

He thought she might play him a tape in the car, but they drove back to Regent's Cove in silence. Jane parked outside a green storefront with a sign that read 'Widow's Peak,' and let them in with a set of keys from her pocket.

'This is my grandmother's shop,' she explained, locking the door behind them. She led Alex to a storage room at the rear of the salon and walked over to a guitar case leaning on a stack of crates.

'This is where my band used to practice,' said Jane.

They sat on facing crates, and Jane tuned the guitar from a note inside her head. As she handled the instrument, a focus set over her features that gave her the look of an enchantress.

Alex had never been in love, or he'd been in love a hundred times, depending on how you viewed it; he had known women for whom feeling attractive involved feeling impressive. He suspected that's what this would be and didn't expect to be moved by it.

Then she began to play.

The more Jane sang, the more Alex realized that she wasn't showing him herself so much as she was guiding him to a secret place, each song leading him further down a darkened tunnel.

> '*Oh, the moon is new tonight, little lion,*
> *Nowhere to be seen, peaceful and serene,*
> *Have a dream and sleep, little lion,*
> *Have yourself a dream.*'

Alex found himself drifting through time. His older sister, Kathleen, had left when he was nine; he recalled the empty feeling he'd had visiting her room, as unchanging as a shrine.

> *'Wooden poles and telephone wires,*
> *Clotheslines running through the plains,*
> *You were right, I am a liar,*
> *And I will never love again.'*

Occasionally, Alex would catch a glimpse of Jane in the tunnel ahead and be struck by her youth and her sadness. But with each progressive song, he felt himself sink further and further into himself. He had been to war. He had held men as they died. It wasn't something he thought about if he could help it. But he thought about it now.

> *'Maybe you'll remember me after I'm gone.*
> *If this is all right, then why does it feel wrong?'*

Alex didn't realize when Jane stopped playing, and didn't know how long she had been looking at him when he did. He looked at her then, too, and thought that, in fact, her breakup with Jesse Reid had devastated her, she just didn't know it. Jane placed the guitar back in its case. As she did, Alex rose to his feet. A younger part of himself surfaced, one that wanted to console her.

He bent down to kiss her and felt her retreat behind the same hunger she'd shown the night before. Her hands slid down Alex's chest, resting on his belt; in thirty more seconds, they'd be fucking. Alex pulled back, holding her hands.

'Let's go back to my room,' he said. He didn't say it was because he wanted to hold her afterward.

Jane slept in fits that night; Alex didn't sleep at all. He lay awake, watching the pale moonlight move across her features, wondering, not for the first time, how much good love had been laid to waste by poor timing.

The next day, when they drove to the fishing village, Alex felt like a flounder splayed open by a fillet knife. As he and Jane walked from the station wagon onto the jetty, storm clouds gathered above, giving the light a blue tint.

Jane reached her spot and stopped. 'How do I look to you today?' she said.

Alex felt so tired he said the first thing that came into his mind. 'Honestly, I just wish I could fuck the sadness out of you.'

Jane was still. 'Okay,' she said.

Alex wasn't sure he'd heard her. 'Okay?' he said.

'Okay,' she said. 'You should take the photo now.'

Alex climbed down the far side of the jetty so that his lens would be angled up at both Jane and the cottage formation. As he zoomed in on her face, cheekbones precipitous as a granite quarry, he thought to himself that no one would see *Songs in Ursa Major* coming.

35

Rolling Stone

July 8, 1971

Mark Edison

Siren's Song: On Jane Quinn and
Songs in Ursa Major

The first thing to know about Jane Quinn is that she doesn't give a fuck.

The notoriously private songstress is more likely to be found smoking in the corner of her local watering hole than bumping elbows with the industry's elite. Which she can pull off, because Jane Quinn has *it,* that ineffable quality recognized in prom queens the world over (and, no, I'm not just talking about her cascading sunshine-colored hair); Quinn has an innate knowledge of hip that most of us couldn't hope to emulate – but we know it when we see it.

I first met Quinn performing on the festival circuit with her rock band, the Breakers, and it was clear even then that she was a star on the rise; everybody loved to be around her, from the audience, to her bandmates, to her tour companions, to Jesse Reid, her rumored paramour. What the high-energy pop of the Breakers obscured is that Quinn is a musical virtuoso. Luckily, bands break up.

With her solo debut, *Songs in Ursa Major* (referred to throughout this piece as *Ursa Major*), newly released from Pegasus Records on June 22, Quinn demonstrates that her compelling stage presence and exotic looks have been a prelude to her true gifts: unfettered originality and breath-taking musicality.

The album's ten tracks are more blues than rock and roll, although the same musical hooks that made *Spring Fling* a hit are still present in *Ursa Major* (sometimes with several per song). Not all of the tracks on *Ursa Major* subscribe to a traditional pop structure, but, no matter how complex the songs, there is never a moment's doubt that Jane Quinn is in control.

Stripped of the electric sound that made *Spring Fling* an overnight sensation, the centerpiece of *Ursa Major* is Quinn's vocal talent, from her acrobatic soprano to her sonorous chest voice. While her performance is breathtaking, it's her ability as a composer that puts Quinn in the same class as Dylan, McCartney, and Simon. The play between melody and verse on *Ursa Major* marries poetry with a variety of styles that make this album nothing shy of a feast.

The first time you hear *Ursa Major,* you won't be thinking about Jane Quinn at all, because you'll suddenly be swept back to your first love and the shattering disappointments most of us encounter as a result. It's not until after several listens that you will find yourself wondering about the album's creator and the stories that must have compelled these songs.

Quinn's music is strongly influenced by her upbringing in a seafaring community; the youngest of a locally known matriarchal clan, Quinn has ancestors who were reputed to have been sea witches during the Whaling Era. Quinn's lyrics are as populated by waterways and starry nights as her history, and tracks like 'Little Lion,' 'Last Call,' and 'A Shanty' have the sea etched in their bones.

Another great influence on Quinn's life and work was the Island Folk Fest (1955–1970), where Quinn's own mother performed before her disappearance in 1959. Ten years after that, Quinn would be discovered by star-maker Willy Lambert after the Breakers were thrust into the spotlight as last-minute replacements for an injured Jesse Reid. From there, Lambert signed Quinn and her band to Pegasus's roster, and the rest is history.

In some ways a series of letters, in other ways a narrative from innocence to disillusionment, *Songs in Ursa Major* packs all the earmarks of a classic into thirty-six minutes that might just change your life.

The title track is one of the record's true feats; the listening experience is one of leaving the party of radio single 'Last Call' and stepping into a darkened sky. 'Ursa Major' opens with a self-portrait, a sailor navigating the 'black and white,' referring to both the night sky and piano keys. In Quinn's hands, the constellations Ursa Major and Minor become, 'Starry signs themselves reflecting like mirrors in a bar; all those tinted bottles, all those tinted scars.'

With this, Quinn unmasks the song's central metaphor, a

271

comparison between the Ursa Major constellation and the cycle of addiction; here, the 'cub' (or 'Ursa') of midday is the bearish behavior that precipitates 'evenings turning to a spoon,' a reference to the Big Dipper and, one assumes, heroin. The song's operatic climax reflects the ecstatic agony on the album's cover, quietly receding into Quinn's final entreaty, 'Please don't leave me alone.'

The real secret ingredient of the album, though, is its ninth track, 'A Thousand Lines'; here Quinn transcends the genre of sad-girl-heartbreak and gives us something heretofore a stranger to pop: the ugly truth, recalling, 'How pretty a pair we always made, even liars go in twos.' No matter how bleak the verse, the chorus admits, 'I could write a thousand lines, and you would still be on my brain.'

Quinn is joined on this album by bassist Kyle Lightfoot and guitarist Rich Holt, two of her bandmates from the Breakers. Lightfoot's seamless transition to an acoustic bass from his better-known work on the fretless electric gives the album a dynamic foundation, while Holt's fervent style contributes to the restless anxiety driving the record. *Painted Lady* vet Huck Levi's percussion is the essence of subtlety, and it's not until the third or fourth listen that you really begin to hear the complexity of his choices, and how they both ground and propel the record.

Jesse Reid also has guitar credits on three tracks: 'New Country,' 'A Shanty,' and 'A Thousand Lines,' although those hoping to gain insight into Quinn's alleged affair with Reid will have better luck analyzing the album's ultimate track, 'Light's On': 'I can't promise you tomorrow, couldn't promise you today. You'll be on a billboard, and I'll be on my way.'

Ursa Major is not without its defects. 'Wallflower,' though well sung, feels incomplete, like a duet with only one part recorded. At times, Quinn verges on pretentious; the liner notes reveal some questionable Emily Dickinson–esque capitalizations, the worst perpetrator being the title track's 'Now's the time to be alive, they say, their tones as sharp as knives, when, hidden in your Crescent, you're just trying to survive.' Of course, it's still a gorgeous musical phrase. Occasionally, Quinn's vocal acrobatics distract, and there are several instances where she stretches the bounds of what can be considered a rational number of syllables to a line.

These minor trifles pale in comparison to the impact *Songs in Ursa Major* is sure to have. The album distinguishes itself from other pop like a crucible in a room full of teacups: within *Ursa Major*, Quinn's soaring hopes transfigure into dark despair, then back into resilience, with a vibrancy unmatched by her more mellow contemporaries. When asked how she reconciles these contrasting elements, Jane Quinn takes a drag of her cigarette and says, 'When I'm sad, it's usually because I was happy first.'

36

'You're on in five,' a production assistant told Jane. She smiled, her face stiff with makeup.

'One last question,' said Archie Lennox, publicity director for Pegasus Records, as he flagged down the PA.

After the *Rolling Stone* feature published, Archie had succeeded in booking Jane her first late-night television spot, on *Tremain Tonight*. Jane had been shocked when the show offered to fly her out to L.A. for the live broadcast; even as she awaited her cue, she couldn't believe she was going through with it.

On set, Nick Tremain stood from behind the desk where he had just read his monologue and walked over to a pair of facing armchairs. Another PA handed him a stack of flash cards emblazoned with the *Tremain Tonight* logo – the questions he'd be asking Jane. Jane groaned.

'You hanging in there?' said Willy, standing astride two giant power cords.

'Why can't I just tour?' said Jane. She'd booked a few 'local' gigs herself, but getting to and from Bayleen Island cost more than she made on the shows. It was all a very far cry from the *Painted Lady* bus. Willy shrugged.

'Get a few of these TV spots under your belt, sell some records, and maybe you can.'

'I'm not even playing on camera,' said Jane.

'There's more than one way to sell a record. Today, you're selling yourself.'

Jane grimaced. 'I connect through my music,' she said. 'If I can't bond with the crowd, what's the point of even going out there?'

'It's your first solo album, Jane,' said Willy. 'Any little bit helps.'

'Jesse toured on his first album,' she said.

'That was different,' said Willy.

'Meaning, the label liked him,' said Jane. She paused. 'Is Vincent Ray trying to sabotage me?'

Willy shook his head. 'You don't have the name recognition yet to justify the expense of a tour.'

Jane rolled her eyes.

'Try to be happy,' said Willy. 'Most people would kill for this exposure.'

'I should be playing,' said Jane.

'I agree,' said Willy. 'But that's not what the producers requested. They want you.'

Archie cued Jane to go on before she could respond.

Jane stepped out from behind a battery of hot cameras and technicians into a bright, mid-century living-room set. Nick Tremain had been polished within an inch of his life; his jovial expressions, beloved from sofas across America, looked cartoonish in person. He stood and kissed Jane on the cheek as if they were old friends, keeping his own face closer to the camera.

'From the *Rolling Stone* piece, I thought you'd be an Amazon – but look at you, you're just a little slip of a thing!'

'Uh, thanks,' said Jane. She glanced over at Willy, who gave her an encouraging look. Archie motioned for her to smile.

'You've got some pretty catchy songs on your new record, *Songs in Ursa Major*. Is it true you wrote those all yourself?' Nick motioned her toward a chair, and they both sat.

'Yes,' said Jane. She could feel Archie, off camera, urging her to be genial. 'I like writing songs.'

'And you're very good at it,' said Nick, as though complimenting a child on her crayon art. He flipped his cards to the next question.

'These songs are extremely personal,' he said. 'How did you come up with them?'

'Observations,' said Jane. 'Things that have happened to me and people I know.'

'Anyone in particular?' said Nick. 'I heard a rumor that some of these are about Jesse Reid.'

Archie had coached her on what to say if this came up – the party line was that all the folks at Pegasus were friends, and they all influenced one another. This idea was as much a part of the product as the records: if you liked one Pegasus artist, they became a gateway to the others.

'My songs . . .' Jane started. She looked around the studio, past the lights, and her eyes landed on a girl in the audience. She was about twelve and was watching Jane with a concentration Jane recognized because it was how she had once watched Maggie – to learn how to be. Jane felt a surge of protectiveness; she didn't like the idea that she was showing this girl how to suffer invasive questions. She cleared her throat.

'What are my songs about for you?' she said to Nick.

Nick looked surprised. 'Me?' he said. 'Oh, I don't profess to be an expert.'

'Everyone's an expert on their own taste,' said Jane. 'Which is your favorite song on the album?'

'Oh, I liked all of them,' he said. That meant he hadn't listened to any of them.

Jane's eyes narrowed. On the opposite side of the set sat Nick's in-house jazz band, awaiting their next segment. One of them had a guitar.

'Why don't I play you one, and then we can discuss it?' said Jane.

The audience thought it was planned, and burst into applause as she crossed the set, the cameras panning after her.

'Yes, why not?' said Nick, with a winning smile.

Jane didn't look back to see Willy's and Archie's reactions. The guitar player handed Jane his instrument, and, before anyone could stop her, she began playing 'Brand New Cassette,' mainly because it had traditional tuning, so she wouldn't have to pause to adjust the strings.

> 'Yellow neon rest-stop sign,
> Humming in the cool night air,
> French fries, coffee, diner fare,
> Now I know you won't be mine,
> Now I know that I did care.'

She sang to the cameraman, the sound technician, the mom from Chicago, that little girl. By the second verse, the bass player and drummer had joined in. While the cameras were on

Jane, a runner rushed to tell Nick Tremain the title of the song. When Jane finished, he stood.

'Ladies and gentlemen, Jane Quinn playing "Brand New Cassette."' The audience went wild.

When they broke for commercial, Nick Tremain made a beeline for Archie. 'You need to keep your talent on a fucking leash, asshole,' he said, and stormed off to his dressing room.

'Nice work, Jane,' said Archie sarcastically, walking after Nick and his producer.

Jane, still glowing from the audience's warm reception, looked at Willy. He gave her a warning look. 'You're playing with fire,' he said.

Despite this initial reaction, the segment generated so much buzz that soon Archie was fielding requests from *The Tonight Show*, *The Mike Douglas Show*, *The Phil Donahue Show*, and *The Des O'Connor Show*, to name a few. Jane accepted the requests on the condition that she could play on the air. She couldn't stop the men who interviewed her from treating her like a child, but once she played, they couldn't come between her and her fans.

'Now, all of these songs are from your new album, *Songs in Ursa Major*, is that right?' said Don Drischol, host of *Variety Nightly*.

Jane had just finished playing 'Last Call' and took a seat in the chair across from him. 'That's right,' she said.

'Tell us what it was like to actually record the album,' said Don. 'Bet you'd never seen so many buttons before.' He chuckled at his own joke.

'I actually had, on my band's album,' she said lightly. Archie had coached her to refer to *Spring Fling* as her 'band's album' rather than her 'first album,' to keep viewers thinking they were just discovering her for the first time.

'And you don't work with a producer, is that correct?' said Don.

'If you can have Simon Spector on your record, you don't need a producer,' said Jane. She'd meant the remark to be a compliment to Simon, but she could see from the way Willy blanched off camera that he thought she was taking a jab at Vincent Ray.

'And the instrumentalists?'

'Kyle Lightfoot, my bassist, and Rich Holt, my guitarist – they were both in my band, the Breakers.' A sprinkle of applause for the Breakers. 'And my friend Huck Levi – he did percussion on the album.'

'You met Huck on the *Painted Lady* tour, is that right?' said Don.

'Yes,' said Jane.

'Is that also where you met Jesse Reid? He helped you out on a few songs as well.'

'I met Jesse on Bayleen Island, where I grew up,' said Jane. 'He was nice enough to lend me a few guitar tracks.'

'It must have been quite a moment there at the Pegasus lot – you, Jesse, and Loretta Mays, recording all at the same time – must have been like a reunion of the tour.'

'The only thing missing was the bus,' said Jane.

'What do you think of Jesse's whirlwind romance with Morgan Vidal?' asked Don.

'Seems very romantic,' said Jane.

'A little birdie told me that some of the more heartbreaking songs on *Ursa Major* are about Jesse,' said Don. Jane could barely see the whites of his eyes behind his mascara as he leaned in for the kill. 'You two used to date, didn't you?'

Jane leaned forward, on the verge of making a confession. 'Don,' she said.

'Yes?' said Don, mirroring her posture until he was almost squatting.

Jane held his gaze. 'How could I date Jesse when I'm in love with you?'

The audience roared with laughter.

As Jane walked off, she caught Willy's eye.

'Any word on the sales numbers?' she asked.

'Keep this up and you'll get your tour,' said Willy, handing her a cup of water.

'Keep this up?' said Jane, taking a sip. 'I thought this was the last one?'

'The last one on the West Coast,' said Willy. 'Archie's booked you a whole lineup in New York – you pick back up in three weeks.'

'And then I'll get my tour?'

'Aren't you at all curious to see if you'll chart?' said Willy.

Jane shrugged. She squinted past the lights, into the audience. When they saw her looking, a flock of teenage girls stood and flapped their 'What Would Jane Do?' signs to ensure they had Jane's attention. She grinned and waved – the girls exchanged looks and squealed.

Let Jesse keep the charts – all she needed were her fans.

37

The week Jane returned to Bayleen Island, her single 'Last Call' reached number eight in the *Billboard* Hot 100, knocking Loretta back to number nine, and Morgan out of the top ten. Jesse was unaffected at number one.

That Sunday, a courier delivered a silver envelope to Gray Gables. Instead of a return address, a barn silo had been etched into the flap. Inside, a thick black card stamped in silver foil invited Jane to the grand opening of Silo, Morgan and Jesse's nightclub. Jane wondered if her name had been mistakenly added to a list. Willy informed her otherwise. 'It's all hands on deck,' he said. 'This event has the full backing of the label, and it's going to be heavily photographed. You need to be there.'

'I can't,' said Jane.

Willy grunted. 'Look, I know it's not ideal, but you need to make an appearance. I'll drive you there myself, and I'll be with you the whole time. This isn't a discussion, I'll see you in two weeks.' He hung up before she could argue.

Jane found a shimmering blue gown in Perry's Landing that imbued her hair with a silvery sheen. As she stood waiting for Willy in the front hall, Grace and Elsie admired her.

'Marvelous,' said Elsie. She gave Jane a wink and disappeared into the kitchen. Grace stood behind Jane, eyes misty.

'I'm so proud of you,' said Grace. 'You've handled this whole thing with Jesse so beautifully; now you can go in there and hold your head high.'

A car horn outside informed Jane that Willy had arrived. Grace walked her to the door, holding the screen so she could pass through. Willy hopped out to let Jane in the passenger's side.

'Looking good,' said Willy as he pulled out of the driveway. Grace waved from the porch.

'I know this is a drag for you,' said Willy. 'And I really appreciate you going.'

'Anything for Pegasus,' said Jane.

Willy nodded, a gleam in his eye. 'Well, that's just it,' he said. 'You've been killing it with your media, and sales have picked up nicely, and it hasn't gone unnoticed by the board that you've been . . . cooperative.'

'What are you saying?' said Jane.

'I'm saying,' said Willy, 'that we've been green-lit for a five-city tour of New England, all expenses paid.'

'Is that New York?' said Jane.

'It's Burlington, Nashua, Portland, and two others . . . I forget. I was going to wait to tell you until everything was a hundred percent confirmed, but since you've been such a sport about tonight, I figured why not give you something to look forward to. Are you excited?'

'Should I be?' said Jane.

'I think so,' said Willy. 'You've been asking me about a tour for three months, and now you're getting one.'

'Does five smaller cities really qualify as a tour?' said Jane.

Willy rolled his eyes. 'It's a start,' he said.

As they turned down a dark gravel drive, the silhouette of Silo loomed into view. They pulled into a grand circular driveway full of cars dropping guests in front of two behemoth barn doors. Jane watched glittering figures approach the entrance beneath an arbor of wisteria and fairy lights, crushed seashells beneath their feet.

At the front of the line, parking attendants swarmed like ants around Willy's car. One opened the door for Jane as another took Willy's keys and handed him a parking stub.

Jane felt a pang of nervousness as she turned toward the entrance. Willy seemed to sense this and offered her his arm. She gave him a small smile, and the two of them walked inside.

Silo felt both comfortable and fancy – a living room designed by rock stars. A plain wooden stage at the back recalled Jane to Peggy Ridge, although this rig boasted state-of-the-art sound and lighting. Upstairs, a spacious balcony looked down on the stage, dance floor, and an enormous wagon-wheel chandelier. Full bars had been carved into all available walls.

Jane saw Jesse immediately, standing at the base of the stage, engrossed in conversation with a man wearing a ten-gallon hat. She felt a thrill at his presence and the familiar pull toward him. Willy guided her to a ring of reserved cabaret tables at the edge of the dance floor, and a server approached to take their orders. Jane could see Willy taking stock of the people he'd need to glad-hand in his periphery. When their drinks arrived, he gulped his down.

'I should do a round,' he said. 'Are you okay here?' Jane nodded, and he joined the throng.

283

Her heart began to pound as she took in the room – not even the parties she had attended in L.A. had been this star-studded. So – this was what it looked like to have Pegasus's support.

'Janie Q,' came an unmistakable Kentish accent behind her. Jane turned around as Hannibal Fang swaggered up to her table. Relief flooded her body.

'Light of my life, fire of my loins,' he said, taking Willy's seat beside her. 'I was hoping you'd be here tonight. Been devouring *Ursa Major*. It makes me . . . feel things.'

'Good things, I hope,' she said.

'For you, always,' he said. 'Take it from me, you're a shoo-in for a Grammy.'

'Really,' said Jane.

'Best New Artist, easy,' he said with a wolfish grin. 'So – is tonight our night?'

'It very well might be,' said Jane. Hannibal lifted a roguish eyebrow and flagged down their server. Around them, cameras flashed like lightning bugs.

Jane felt someone watching her and looked up to find Jesse's eyes, as bright as two blue flames, across the room. She felt her stomach clench, but at that moment, Morgan walked onstage, and the room broke into applause. She wore a blue-and-orange-striped jumpsuit, her feathery hair an auburn halo in the spotlights. Hannibal rolled his eyes as Jesse joined Morgan onstage.

'Thank you all so much for being here,' said Jesse into the mic. Morgan stood confidently beside him, exuding energy and sensuality. The rings she wore on her fingers glittered like coins in the stage lights whenever she moved.

'This is our home,' she said into the mic, her voice giddy. 'So it's your home, too. Welcome!' She kicked off her shoes, and Jesse looked down at her adoringly. Jane's body tensed.

'What do you think, Mrs. Reid?' he said. 'You want to sing these people a song?'

'Why, yes, I do,' she said. Her eyes lit up as she looked at him, her cheeks glowing rosy. The tension between them made the room hum. Jane sipped her drink.

Jesse struck up the intro to 'Broken Door,' and the crowd went under. The difference between a good performer and a great one, thought Jane, was that a good performer made you feel like you were two feet away from the stage, and a great one made you forget you were there at all; Morgan and Jesse were both great. Their presence was magnetic. It was like watching professional tennis players serve up hit after hit; 'Sylvie Smiles' into 'Sweet and Mellow' into 'Painted Lady' into 'Under Stars' into 'Strangest Thing.' After 'My Lady,' Hannibal leaned toward Jane. 'If this is what they're like onstage, wonder what they're like off. . . .'

Jane motioned to their server and ordered another drink – this one a double. She knew what Hannibal meant; it was like watching a game of strip poker being played, in which each song teased at another layer of their private life. By the time they sang their duet, 'Summer Nights,' it felt as if they were a hair's breadth from grabbing each other onstage.

As Jane looked around the room, it struck her that none of this was real. There was no love, no real connection; just other sharks in the business, trying to solidify their positions in the food chain. Jane felt a wave of disgust; she and her fans existed outside of all this.

The crowd rose to their feet as Loretta joined them onstage. She took a seat behind the piano, and Jesse counted her in on 'Safe Passage,' with Morgan harmonizing on the chorus.

> *'When darkness falls upon you,*
> *And the cold begins to bite,*
> *Just reach for my hand, dear,*
> *And we'll walk back to the light.'*

Loretta had written the song in response to 'Strangest Thing,' and you could hear it in the lyrics of the second verse. The three of them were so good that, for a moment, Jane forgot her jealousy and just watched. As they bowed together, Jesse leaned in to the mic.

'Yes, Loretta is a very special part of our family,' he said. 'She'll be joining us on our upcoming *Under Stars* tour – we're aiming to hit all fifty states, so it really will be stars and stripes forever.'

The crowd laughed, and Loretta left the stage. Jane lifted her glass to her lips and took a cube of ice in her mouth. The cold burned her tongue, but she held it there until it began to melt.

She had always thought less of Loretta for doing things by the book; and yet one of them would be headlining a national tour while the other fought for scraps. Jane looked around the room again and entertained a terrifying thought: what if it didn't matter how many people out there liked you if the people in this room did not?

All glory is reflected.

Jane had always believed that her talent would carry her. But what if Jesse had been right and that wasn't real? What if talent didn't matter if certain people wouldn't allow it to?

All around her, faces swam into sharp relief, one more calculating than the next. Jane's eyes landed on Willy. Willy had a good heart, but she could never be sure how far he'd be willing to strain his corporate ties.

Only one person here had always seen Jane at the level she saw herself, had advocated for her whenever he could, had believed in her talent when she hadn't, had wanted to take care of her.

And she had sent him away for a five-city tour.

'Okay, we got one more for you,' said Morgan, breathless, as Jesse checked his tuning. He played a few notes, and the room went still. He seemed to be waiting for this moment – expecting it, even – he was making them wait. He played a few unrelated chords, to make them wait some more. Then he began to play the introduction to a song as familiar to Jane as one of her own.

> *'Let the light go,*
> *Let it fade into the sea.*
> *The sun belongs to the horizon,*
> *And you belong to me.'*

Jesse himself sang the part that had once belonged to Jane, and Morgan joined him on the chorus. Morgan's voice was like a mist, and Jesse's was like a light; the way her tone surrounded his was spellbinding. Jane couldn't breathe.

As Jesse turned to Morgan, Jane sat rigid, tears smarting in her eyes. She hadn't known until this moment how much she had been counting on the fact that Jesse still loved her.

'I'll watch over you,
As long as I am here,
As long as I am near,
You can dream, dream away.'

The crowd stood before they'd even finished the song. Jane stood as well. So did Hannibal.

'I could use a cigarette,' he said. 'You?' Jane nodded and followed him out of the club.

Outside, the night was humid and fragrant; Jane could feel the air conditioning melting off her skin as she took a drag from one of Hannibal's Newports.

'You know,' he said, twisting his cigarette in his mouth with his thumb and index finger, 'I could bring my Rolls-Royce round, and the two of us could just drive off into the night.'

Jane didn't need to consider. 'Sure,' she said.

Hannibal looked delighted, though not surprised. 'Excellent,' he said, reaching into his pocket for his parking stub. 'Now, who do I give this to?' All of the parking attendants had disappeared; as polished as the club appeared, it was still opening night. 'Don't move,' said Hannibal. He began to walk in the direction of the parking lot.

As Jane placed the cigarette between her lips, the front door of the club opened behind her. Amidst a gale of laughter, a low voice remarked, 'I just need to check on something – I won't be long.' Jane looked up to see Jesse before her. Without speaking, he touched her arm and led her away from the club.

Once they were out of view, Jesse slowed his pace; Jane could feel the heat of performance radiating off him. His hand was still on her arm; he didn't seem capable of removing it, nor did she want him to. Slowly, he brought her in front of him; Jane stepped back and felt the trunk of a tree against her back. He looked at her and leaned forward as though about to kiss her.

'Why did you come here?' he demanded.

Jane blinked, struggling to find her voice.

'This was supposed to be a happy night,' he said. 'You had no right to come.'

'You invited me,' said Jane.

He opened his mouth and closed it. 'I . . .' His voice trailed off. 'The label must have.'

'Morgan's something else,' said Jane, unable to help herself.

'Careful,' he said.

'She sang our song pretty well,' said Jane.

'My song,' he said.

Jane shook her head. 'You told me that song would always be for me,' said Jane. 'I guess that was a lie.'

Jesse stepped toward her, his arms pinning her against the tree. His face was inches from hers.

'You are in no position to call me a liar,' he whispered.

Jane felt unnerved. 'Calm down,' she said.

His fingers brushed against the shoulder of her dress. Jane's breath caught in her throat.

His expression softened. 'I remember the first day you came to the Shack,' he said. 'It was so that Grace could be with Maggie. I remember thinking, *This girl is good as gold*.' A shadow fell across his features. 'I really believed that,' he said. 'No one lies like you, Janie Q.'

He lowered his arms. Despite the warm air, Jane felt a chill sweep through her.

Be careful what you tell him.

'What are you talking about?' said Jane. All she wanted was to say that she had made a mistake and instead the conversation was barreling in a direction she could not bear.

'"When, hidden in your Crescent, / You're just trying to survive",' he said. 'I always thought there was something strange about that phrase. "Crescent" with a capital "C." It's just so obvious, isn't it?'

'Jesse, what on earth—' she said. Jesse watched her reproachfully.

'Don't do that,' he said.

Jane's breath caught as she met his eyes, understanding implicit in their very color and shape. Sometimes, when Jesse looked at her, it actually felt as if he knew. Like she didn't need to tell him, because he could somehow intuit it. But as resentment steeled his features, Jane had to own that this recognition had only ever existed in her head.

You were right, I am a liar.

'Jesse, I wanted to tell you,' she said.

Jesse's stare was ice. 'Well, you didn't,' he said. 'You told me she disappeared, that you didn't know where she was or if she was alive or dead. What utter bullshit. She's been at the Center this whole time – you see her every week. I know, Jane. I asked my father to check.'

Shame cracked through Jane like an electric current.

'You lied to me about the only thing that mattered,' he said.

'It wasn't like that,' said Jane. 'It wasn't my place—'

'Yes, it was,' said Jesse. 'You let me believe that we shared something sacred. I can never forgive you for that.'

'What are you saying?' said Jane.

'This,' said Jesse, taking her face in his hands, his cigarette a hair's width from her ear.

'Thank you,' he said. 'This whole time, I thought it was my fault that we got lost. I thought it was my addiction, my weakness, my lying that fucked it all up. But now I know – you are even more fucked up than me. So – thank you. Now I might actually have a shot at enjoying my life.'

He released her. Jane felt her knees quaver as he backed into the light.

And I will never love again.

'I better get back to my wife,' said Jesse.

His steps retreated up the path, and Jane felt a nauseating cold overtake her.

Be careful what you tell him.

Jane couldn't go back to Gray Gables; she couldn't bear to face Grace.

She became aware of the immensity of the night bearing down on her. She didn't want to wait for Willy. She didn't want to go with Hannibal. She kicked off her shoes and felt the Island, alive beneath her feet.

She began to run.

38

Jane reached Middle Road by dawn and began to walk south into Caverswall. The morning fog lingered as she found herself at the base of another long driveway, this one paved with precision. She stopped outside the guard booth.

'Wild night?' asked Lewis, nodding to Jane's dress. He raised the gate to let her pass, and Jane walked up the drive, carrying her shoes in her hand, as though trying not to wake the house after sneaking out past curfew.

She followed the flagstone path around the main building to the staff entrance, passing a sign directing visitors to locations around the facility: parking, recreation lawn, long-term housing, secure units. At the top of the sign, the words CEDAR CRESCENT HOSPITAL AND REHABILITATION CENTER had been gilded over embossed type.

'Who hit you with a pretty stick?' said Monika from behind the desk. Everything about the Center was clean and bright, from the halls, to the rooms, to the staff check-in area.

'You're here early,' said Jane.

'Can't argue with time and a half,' said Monika.

Jane signed into the log, ducked into the locker room, and took a uniform from Grace's locker, pulling it on over her dress.

She exchanged her stilettos for Grace's spare tennis shoes and pulled her hair up into a knot. Jane went back into the office and picked up the phone on Monika's desk.

'I actually don't have you scheduled today,' said Monika as Jane replaced the receiver.

'I'm not,' said Jane. 'I just figured I'd check in.'

'No problem,' said Monika. She rose, a ring of keys as thick as a fist jangling against her hip.

Jane followed Monika up the back stairs, weaving in and out of other, identical blue uniforms. They climbed past the intensive-care patients on the second floor, and the teen and elderly wards on the third floor, to the adult ward on the fourth floor.

The hallways in movies about mental hospitals always flickered and shook with muffled screams; the halls at the Center were quiet and white as a fresh fall of snow. Monika chatted about the new bike she was saving to buy her daughter as she led Jane down the hall to Room 431. Monika peered through the door viewer and smiled, shaking her head.

'We're up, all right,' she said. 'Today's going to be a big day.' Monika rapped on the door.

'Hey, Charlie,' she said. 'You have a visitor.'

'Come in, come in,' a soft voice crept into the hall.

'Jane,' she said. 'Darling.'

Charlie rose slowly from her vanity table to greet Jane. She was two years younger than Grace, but looked ten years older, with sallow skin and stringy hair – vestiges of a long line of medications. She wore a starched white jumpsuit, but her elegant carriage suggested couture.

'Call if you need anything,' said Monika, nodding to the red call button inside the door.

293

'Maybe some cocktails?' said Charlie. Alcohol was prohibited at the Center, but that didn't matter, because Charlie didn't know that's where she lived.

'I'll see what I can do,' said Monika, and with that she left.

'My darling girl,' said Charlie, kissing Jane on each cheek. 'Did you get the message about tonight's party?'

Jane found a seat on Charlie's bed.

Charlie resumed her position before the vanity and examined her face. She picked up an imaginary compact and began applying powder. 'Today is going to be a big day,' she said. 'And we need to be ready. Doris will be by in about an hour to pick us up.'

'Right,' said Jane. 'How is Doris?'

'Dramatic as ever,' said Charlie, rolling her eyes. 'She's in an uproar because Bob invited me to this party before he invited her, and I told her my name is just first in his address book, but would she listen? Of course, she would not. And that was just the start of it.' As Charlie spoke, she 'applied powder' to her face in a continuous brushing motion. Jane sank into the pillow on the bed and watched – round and round and round.

'So I told her,' Charlie was saying, '"If that's how you feel, you need to tell Bob. What am I supposed to do about it?"' She turned to Jane and looked her in the face, disbelievingly.

Jane shook her head. 'No idea,' she said. Charlie was like a jukebox; with occasional input, she could play all night.

'Well, what do you think she did?' said Charlie, turning back to her own reflection. 'She went right to Lucy and told her the whole thing!'

Charlie lived in a world mainly populated by stars of the silver screen from her own childhood: Doris Day, Bob Hope,

Lucille Ball. Her primary psychiatrist, Dr. Chase, had once explained it to Jane: 'She believes this is where she belongs. Since her break, she can no longer tolerate a world in which she is not a star – and anything that threatens that world risks extreme volatility.'

In the beginning, Jane would never have been allowed in the room alone with Charlie; back in those days, the slightest glance could provoke an outburst. Years of dedicated care had rendered her more or less docile. It had been over two years since her last physical episode; despite this, she still wasn't allowed to keep anything that could be weaponized in her possession – be it a plastic cosmetic case or a metal spoon.

'Will you see who it is?' Charlie said, nodding toward the door. No one had knocked, and Jane hesitated a moment too long before reacting.

'Oh, never mind,' said Charlie, getting flustered. 'It's just Doris. I can't deal with her right now, I'm too busy.'

'Okay,' said Jane.

'Delusions' and 'hallucinations' were the clinical terms for what Charlie experienced. So far, no medication had been able to keep them at bay for long. Doris and Bob were both imaginary figures who spoke to Charlie in real time; Lucy was Charlie's favorite nurse, whose name was actually Mary, but who bore a striking resemblance to Lucille Ball.

Charlie's world was fairly consistent; her existence organized itself in dramatic episodes, same as a television show, mostly centered around a string of imagined parties. As long as you obeyed the rules, it wasn't a bad place to be. The rules were simple: let Charlie talk, and don't ever point out that none of this is real.

There was a knock on the door.

'I thought I told you to tell Doris to go away,' said Charlie. The door pushed open a crack, and Mary entered, carrying a tray containing two plastic cups: one with water and one with pills.

'Hey, Jane,' said Mary. 'Hey, Charlie.'

'Lucille,' said Charlie, standing and kissing Mary on both cheeks. 'Speak of the devil.'

'Looking glam,' said Mary, distractedly. 'Is it Sinatra's party tonight?'

'That was last week,' said Charlie, irritated. Jane sat quietly on the bed. The more stimulation Charlie had, the harder it was for her to integrate people into her world. Any more than two visitors, and she began to grow agitated and lose track of who was who.

'This isn't a good time right now, Lucille,' said Charlie. She had taken out an imaginary tube of lipstick and was in the process of applying it, bringing her pinched fingers close to her lips, then ripping them away as though she had been burned. She pretended to adjust the length of the tube, then tried again. The pills sat untouched on the vanity.

'The least you could have done was wear a dress,' Charlie scolded Mary. 'I told you tonight was a big deal. You're never going to find a man looking like that.'

'You're right,' Mary said.

Charlie rounded on her. 'Don't humor me,' she said, her blue eyes glaring at Mary. 'I can tell. I think you should go!'

Mary nodded. 'I just need you to take these, then I'll be gone.'

Charlie rolled her eyes and complied. Mary gathered up the

cups and turned to Jane. 'Your ride is here,' she said in a low voice.

Jane nodded, and Mary left. Jane watched Charlie pantomime spraying herself with perfume, then roused herself and stood from the bed.

'I'm going to head out, too,' she said. Standing behind Charlie, Jane could see the crest tattoo on her neck. It had bled some into her pallid skin, but there it was: sun, moon, water.

'Jane, dear, will I be seeing you at the party?'

Sometimes when Charlie asked her questions like this, Jane's mind translated them into more normal comments, like, 'Will I see you soon?'

'Probably not,' said Jane. 'Mom — I came here because . . . I'm going away for a while.' Charlie laughed uncomfortably.

'Don't call me that, dear, I don't like it.' She began to re-adjust the phantom lipstick tube.

As Jane watched her motions, slow and precise, she could almost convince herself it was real.

'Anything else?' said Charlie. 'Doris should be along any moment.'

Jane shook her head and excused herself without further exchange.

On the stairs down, Jane passed several day nurses, who greeted her by name. She replaced the uniform in Grace's locker, leaving everything except the tennis shoes. She signed out at the desk and walked into the parking lot. Greg's VW Bug was idling in a handicap spot. As Jane approached, Maggie unlocked the door and let her in.

'I need you to drive me to the boat,' said Jane. She formed their sign with her hand.

Maggie looked her up and down, taking in the dress, the bun, the shoes. Then she signaled back.

'You'll need cash,' said Maggie.

Outlaws don't ask questions.

39

Jane stood in line, waiting to hand her ticket to the Lufthansa desk agent. She wore one of Greg's flannel shirts over her blue dress, and carried a carpetbag full of Maggie's clothing. A large pair of plastic shades covered her eyes. When the agent read her name, he did a double take. 'Sixteen F,' he said, in a thick German accent.

As the plane taxied out onto the runway, Jane felt self-recriminations closing in on her like an angry swarm of hornets. If the plane would just take off, maybe she could outrun them.

* * *

It had happened when she was nine, just as she told Jesse. Just as she told Jesse, her mother had gone out one night and never returned. Just as she told Jesse, it had all been because of 'Lilac Waltz.'

Here's what she hadn't told Jesse. Ever since Charlie had heard that song, 'Lilac Waltz,' on the radio, she had suffered terrible mood swings; she'd be up one minute, down the next – dancing around because the mail had been delivered, crying and screaming because all of it was junk. Charlie would tell anyone who would listen that she had written 'Lilac Waltz,' whether at home or at the grocery store checkout.

It wasn't until they received a cease-and-desist letter from Tommy Patton's record company, Elektra, that the Quinns realized Charlie had been sending him hate mail. Jane remembered hiding in Maggie's room while their mothers screamed at each other.

'What are you hoping to gain from this?' Grace cried.

'"Girl" rhymes with "pearl,"' Charlie shrieked. 'GIRL RHYMES WITH PEARL.'

After the fight, everything had been quiet for a few months, and it seemed like Charlie had snapped out of it. Her mood swings lessened, and she regained her sense of continuity and focus.

Then the National Academy of Recording Arts and Sciences announced they would be joining the Fest as co-sponsors, throwing in a headline performance by Tommy Patton to seal the deal. Grace and Elsie braced themselves for another fight, but Charlie took it in stride.

'I just won't go that night,' she said, easy as a dream.

True to her word, the night of the Fest, Charlie made plans to go out on a date instead. Jane could still remember how she'd looked, in a faded lilac dress, standing by the door, her hair pulled up into a French twist.

Her suitor had been a Texan named Bill who drove up to the house in a beige Cadillac, a toothpick in his mouth. He honked three times to prompt Charlie to come out.

'Charming,' said Elsie.

'Don't wait up,' said Charlie. The last image Jane had of her mother at Gray Gables was of Charlie checking her lipstick in the hallway mirror before walking out the front door.

*   *   *

Jane's plane touched down in Frankfurt seven hours later. She surveyed the departures board and walked over to the desk at Olympic Air.

'One ticket to Greece,' she said.

'Very good, miss. I can seat you on the eleven-fourteen to Athens,' said the ticketing agent. 'One way?'

'Yes,' said Jane.

*   *   *

The way Grace described it, an alarm had gone off inside her around 8:00 p.m., an hour before Tommy Patton was slated to perform. Grace wanted to believe her sister, but as she sat watching *The Honeymooners* with Jane and Maggie, her heart began to flutter. She wandered into Charlie's room to gather herself and found a second cease-and-desist letter on her bed, and hundreds of identical letters underneath, written over and over again in Charlie's hand:

'I'm gonna kill you for what you did, Tommy Patton.'

Elsie stayed home with Maggie and Jane, and Grace drove to the Fest. She parked the station wagon in a field above the Main Stage and stood on the hillside overlooking the crowd just as Tommy Patton made his entrance. In the twilight, the audience swayed, an indistinguishable mass. Even if Charlie was there, there was no reason Grace should have found her.

But she did. Because Charlie was standing right in front of the stage, her golden twist of hair illuminated by the spotlights. The people nearest her had begun to stare as she grinned up at Tommy Patton with a plastered expression on her face, like a mask. Grace's stomach turned.

She pushed her way into the throng just as the introduction to 'Lilac Waltz' began to play. As Grace threaded through the crowd, her feet crunched over cigarette stubs where a lawn should have been. She reached her sister just as Tommy Patton began the second verse of the song.

> *'I count to three and suddenly*
> *The moon hangs low,*
> *White as a pearl.'*

Charlie held up a liquor bottle, gripping the neck as though about to take a swig. As Charlie turned her face to the side, Grace saw a cigarette clenched between her crimson lips. Wings fluttered in her hand: a piece of fabric inside the bottle's neck.

Charlie touched the cigarette to the fabric, and hurled the bottle at Tommy Patton as he sang:

> *'I'm the guy in your arms.'*

'Charlie, no!' Grace screamed, her voice ringing out over the crowd.

The bottle hit the stage and exploded in a wreath of flame at Tommy Patton's feet.

As chaos broke out, Charlie lunged towards the stage. Grace's hand closed around her sister's wrist like a manacle.

'Let go of me,' Charlie hissed, snapping her jaws at Grace.

Tommy Patton's shirt was on fire, and he was screaming. He wasn't the only one – all around him, victims jumped off the stage like cinders raining from a volcano.

* * *

Jane reached Athens five hours after purchasing her plane ticket. She had gone so far that she could no longer read the signs, written in an unfamiliar alphabet.

'I want to go to Crete,' she said to a man sitting beneath a large logo she would later learn read 'Hellenic Airlines.' The agent printed her a ticket.

'This take you to Heraklion,' he said. Jane took the ticket.

* * *

'Could this night have been any more beautiful?' Charlie said gaily as Grace dragged her back toward the parking lot. 'I'm so happy I had the chance to perform with such fine musicians. Do you think they'll invite me back next year?'

'What are you saying?' Grace screamed. 'What happened to your date?'

'My date?' said Charlie blankly.

'The man who brought you here?' said Grace.

'That wasn't a date,' said Charlie, disgusted. 'That was just a random fan I met in town who offered to give me a ride to my performance. He came all the way from Texas just to see me!'

'Do you know what you have done?' said Grace.

303

'I am the greatest songwriter of my generation, and not you or anyone else can take that away from me,' said Charlie, seething with anger. Without knowing what she was doing, Grace slapped her. Charlie growled, baring her teeth.

'You're going to pay for that,' she said. 'Do you have any idea who I am?'

'Do you?' shouted Grace, as Charlie grabbed for her throat. The sisters rolled over on the ground, each trying to subdue the other, until Grace's hand found an empty can.

She called Elsie from a pay phone up the road as Charlie lay unconscious in the back seat of their car.

'Thank God you're safe,' said Elsie when she heard Grace's voice. 'It's all over the wireless – what happened?'

Grace glanced at the oncoming traffic.

'It was Charlie,' she said. 'She's totally lost it. I don't know if – I don't know if it's safe to bring her home.' There was a pause on the other end of the line, and Grace could hear the laugh track echoing from the television.

A gray Crown Victoria pulled into view.

'Was she seen?' asked Elsie.

The car slowed beside Grace. A siren flashed.

Grace swallowed. 'Yes,' she said.

* * *

Jane found her way to the bus station in Heraklion by following a group of American hippies out of the airport and up the road.

'Where is this bus going?' she asked, as they queued to buy tickets from a woman sitting inside a stucco shed.

304

'Matala,' said a young man with long hair. An overheard remark from Laurel Canyon floated to the top of Jane's mind like a wish:

Matala is where it's at. Just you, and the ocean, and the caves, and the stars.

Jane turned to walk toward the end of the line.

'Hey, you're Jane Quinn,' said the young man, eyeing her.

'Who's that?' said Jane.

* * *

Dr. Chase testified at a preliminary hearing that Charlie Quinn was unfit to stand trial because she had had a psychotic break, and the judge ordered that she be held at a treatment facility until such time as she could be declared competent.

'You have the option to commit her to a private institution,' said the judge. 'Otherwise, she will become a ward of the state.'

There was only one place on Bayleen Island that fit that description. The Center was a stately private hospital where leading clinicians were paid exorbitant sums to care for the rich's undesirables. When Grace drove through the gate for the first time, she had no idea that this place was to become a daily fixture in her life. Her only thought was that she would do whatever it took to keep her sister on the Island.

After the hearing, the Island community closed ranks around the Quinns: They were an old Island family and a crucial thread in the local tapestry. Plus, it was in everyone's best interest that the matter be hushed so as not to scare away the Festival's backers; the whole Island would suffer if they lost the Fest. Without mentioning Charlie's name, *The Island Gazette* reported that the police had closed the arson case and created a special task force in conjunction with the Festival Committee to ensure that 'such an incident will never recur.' Soon everyone had moved on.

Everyone but the Quinns.

After months of testing, Dr. Chase sat Grace and Elsie down and explained that Charlie had something called schizophrenia, a condition that usually calcified around adolescence but could lie dormant for years, until triggered.

'Her delusions are powerful,' Dr. Chase told them. 'I can't say in good faith I know when I'll be able to release her. She requires round-the-clock supervision; otherwise, she will be a danger to herself and others. But there are some options.'

Jesse had been right the first time he'd heard 'Spark': it was about electroshock therapy. Charlie had begun receiving treatments shortly after being committed. The sessions left her listless, dull, and confused. The Center had also tried her on several antipsychotic drugs, each with side effects worse than the one before.

That first year, Jane ran away to the Center at least once a week, taking the bus up-Island, and begging the staff to let her in to see her mother; in those days, Charlie was being kept in an isolated, secure unit. After about a year, she was granted visiting privileges on Sundays.

Around this time, the Quinns found they had another problem to contend with: money.

'What about a barter?' said Grace to Dr. Chase. 'Labor in exchange for her care?'

Grace had left her job at Widow's Peak and started at the Center as a laundress. Over the years, she worked her way up, earning her full nurse's certification by the time Jane had started high school, and her APTA by the time Jane had graduated. Jane had begun working as soon as she became eligible. Only Grace's long-term-care gigs generated take-home pay; otherwise, the Quinns subsisted on Elsie's income. All of Grace's, and later Jane's, hours at the Center went to offset the costs of Charlie's treatment.

The Quinns began to refer to Charlie as 'Charlotte' outside the home, to draw a line between what had been and what now was. If anyone asked what had become of her, the Quinns told them she had disappeared. This had long been a source of tension between Elsie and Grace.

'We shouldn't be lying,' said Elsie. 'Mental illness is nothing to be ashamed of. By telling people she's missing, we're perpetuating the stigma.'

'The stigma exists,' said Grace. 'We're not going to be the ones to change that. At least, this way, when Charlie gets out, she'll stand a chance of having a normal life.'

This fight resurfaced every so often, but in the end Elsie always deferred to Grace, because Grace had sacrificed so much to help Charlie.

But Charlie couldn't be helped. It had been over ten years since she'd been committed, and all the doctors had managed to do was render her harmless. Still, the Quinns had never shared her whereabouts. They weren't compelled by a hope that she would return, exactly – more an unwillingness to admit that she wouldn't. They had found refuge from their loss in the imaginations of others: as long as someone still wondered about Charlie, she might hypothetically be anywhere. Jane sometimes suspected that Greg knew the truth; if he did, he'd never voiced it to her. Their secret existed undisturbed beneath a veneer of lies.

'One night, she went out and never came back. We never heard from her again. She could be anywhere. She could be dead.'

Jane could recite these lines as automatically as the Pledge of Allegiance. They were her pledge of allegiance to her own family.

* * *

As Jane stepped off the bus, a memory washed over her: golden afternoon light, a library carrel, a tatty volume. Charlie's eyes were glassy; she wasn't reading, she was reciting.

'What is it about, this story?' said Jane abruptly.

Her mother sat up. 'Oh, I don't know, Janie,' she said. 'I like the monster.'

Jane shook her head. 'That's not it.'

Her mother considered. 'All right,' she said. 'It tells the truth about the truth. You can distort it, bury it, halve it – but it never fully goes away. I guess I find that comforting.'

Jane felt perplexed. 'But why?' she said. 'Theseus, Daedalus, the Minotaur – none of it's real.'

Charlie wetted her lips, and Jane felt a sense of unease she couldn't yet name. When she blinked, her mother had softened.

'Reality isn't always reality, Janie,' she said kindly. 'Sometimes stories are truer than life.'

As Jane walked into the blue evening, she thought her mother had been right.

The truth never fully went away.

People did that.

As Jane walked into the village, she reasoned she just needed to go away for a while.

40

Matala was a small town on Crete's south shore, nestled between seashell cliffs and Messara Bay, whose aqua waters boasted temperatures warm even for the Mediterranean. The village contained a handful of buildings scattered around the beach – two restaurants, a grocer, a baker, and a few picked-over tourist shops. The town's main attraction was a set of ancient man-made caves currently occupied by a group of American expats.

Jane spent her first night in the caves, sleeping with her carpetbag grasped in her arms. She awoke covered in small white crabs, and shook them off as several nude Californians watched, too stoned to find it funny. That day, Jane took a modest room in the boarding house beside the Delphini Restaurant. The caves would be fine for a few days, but she intended to stay in Matala much longer than that.

From there, Jane set about casting off her old life. She eschewed television, radio, even clocks; her only point of reference was the Delphini Restaurant. If the restaurant's fishing boat was still out, it was too early to get up; if several dozen squid had been strung up to dry, it was time for Jane to follow suit.

Each day, she walked down to the beach, took off her clothes, and baked herself under the sun. If she sweat through her towel, she crouched in the water just long enough to soothe her parched skin. Then she marched back to her baking post and stretched out like a squid on the line. It was amazing how she could exhaust herself, lying there doing nothing. When the sun went down, she ate a quick meal at the Delphini, then passed out to the jovial sounds below her window. She dreamed of nothing, and that was how she wanted it.

The technological hub of Matala was the grocer, who had a television, a phone, and the only refrigerator in town. This was where Jane first telephoned Gray Gables; Elsie picked up.

'I'm in Greece,' said Jane.

Elsie sighed. 'What happened?' she said.

'Total freak-out,' said Jane.

'Oh dear,' said Elsie.

'How are things there?' said Jane.

'Busy,' said Elsie. 'Grace has been worried. It's been very annoying, Jane.'

'I'm sorry,' said Jane.

'Should I see if she's around?' said Elsie.

'No,' said Jane. She could picture Grace picking up her ten-year-old self from the side of the road and felt ashamed at her own cowardice.

'It's the least you could do,' said Elsie.

'I can't,' said Jane. Once Grace found out that Jesse knew their secret, she would never look at Jane the same way again; in leaving Jesse a trail of breadcrumbs, Jane had broken the one rule she'd been expected to follow in exchange for a lifetime of sacrifice, kindness, and generosity: don't tell anyone about

Charlie. Facing up to this would also mean thinking about Jesse. Jane felt a sudden compulsion to go sun-baking.

Elsie sighed. 'I'm glad you're all right,' she said.

Elsie took down the address and telephone number for the grocery store, and in the weeks that followed, she and Jane struck up a correspondence. Jane sent postcards, and Elsie responded with newsy dispatches: Bea's vocabulary had expanded to include 'lightning' and 'dragon'; Grace would be accompanying her charge, Millie, on another European sojourn, this time to Italy; Charlie was going to titrate up to a higher dosage of chlorpromazine.

Jane was savoring one of these missives over dinner when a gust of wind blew one of the chefs out of the kitchen brandishing a flaming pan. He looked wild, with broad, tanned shoulders and large hands flecked with thin white scars. His hair was sun-streaked, mounted at the crown of his head in a knot, auburn stubble shading the hard angle of his jaw. There was a merry light in his eyes that made him instantly likable. As Jane watched him flip a sautéed fish onto the plate of one of the patrons, she couldn't help but be intrigued.

He paused by her table on his way back to the kitchen, wielding his skillet like a tennis racket.

'Question on the menu?' he asked in a transatlantic brogue.

Jane shook her head. 'Just compliments,' she said.

He shot her a sideways glance. 'Have you ever had Matalan eel?' The way he said it made her laugh. Jane couldn't remember the last time she'd done that.

'No,' said Jane.

'Well, let's see if you like eel, Jane Quinn, and then we can see about being friends.'

311

Over a glass of Minoan wine, he introduced himself as Roger Kavendish, hailing from Saskatoon, via London. He had made it through a year at Le Cordon Bleu before dropping out to cook his way across the world's most beautiful locations.

'And you came here to get away from *it all*,' he supplied for her. It wasn't a question, and Jane didn't argue. She enjoyed the way Roger spoke, as if there were no better place to be than this now empty restaurant, sharing a bottle of wine beneath the stars.

'So – you like the eel,' he said.

Jane didn't want to be around anyone right now, but this person didn't bother her. 'I like the eel,' she said.

His eyes twinkled at that. Jane felt a pleasurable jolt behind her navel.

'Well, well,' he said.

Roger knew a little bit about everything and gave freely of his knowledge. As the two of them explored the caves and beaches of Matala, Jane received the names of the local flora and fauna, in addition to some basic Greek, which up to this point she had somehow managed without.

'It's a bit brazen to leave home without knowing how to ask for the bathroom, even for you,' said Roger, nudging her with his bicep. Jane resisted the urge to brush her hand over it.

Roger's merriness masked a keen intuition. This made being around him easy; he was a deft conversationalist, always ready with a change of subject. He never asked invasive questions.

He also proved a talented chef, and over the next several weeks, Jane ate like a queen. Scallops one night, calamari the next, fresh sea bass, wild tuna. She knew that Roger was seducing her with food, and she didn't mind. As a chef, he had an intrinsic sense of timing, and Jane suspected that he was waiting until the opportune moment. One night, just as she had begun to wonder if she'd misinterpreted his attention, Roger invited her out for a swim.

Under cover of darkness, he grasped Jane's hand under the water, pulling her to him. His lips met hers in a rush of skin and salt. At last, Jane's hands grasped his shoulders and arms, tingly in the briny sea. He growled into her neck as she wrapped her legs around his hips, pulling him into her. Even buoyed to their waists by the water, she could tell he was stronger than Jesse, and she let the sense of being carried lift her out of her head. Her fingers threaded through his hair as he thrust, their sighs rippling on the warm and weightless water. When they finished, they lay back in the gentle waves, and the two of them drifted together, holding hands, like a pair of otters.

As Jane went to bed that night, she felt as though she were still floating.

Roger needed a large amount of personal space; the idea of spending every night in the same bed, much less a bed at all, didn't fit his self-image. No two weeks with Roger ever looked alike; just when Jane thought he might be domesticating, he would take to the caves. Sometimes Jane joined him, sometimes she did not. Despite his allergy to routine, an overarching consistency developed between them, as if they were planets in orbit; Jane knew Roger was there, even if she couldn't see him. As weeks turned into months, her hair grew white with the sun, her skin brown, her feet black with beach tar.

By October, the tourists began to thin out, but the water and air remained warm, and Jane had no intention of going back. She still hadn't spoken to a single person aside from Elsie and Roger. She hadn't sung or played since her departure; there was no guitar in Matala, no piano. *Ursa Major* seemed like a dream to her now, another person's creation. She had no idea how many weeks it had been on sale or how it was doing.

Hearing how she had disappointed Willy was another conversation Jane wished to postpone indefinitely. If he even took her call. Jane had no doubt that bailing on her East Coast media and tour, small as it was, had incinerated any future she might have had with Pegasus.

But, here, none of that mattered.

Here, her only concerns were the weather and her appetites. All she had to think about was what she was going to eat for dinner and whether it might rain.

Mid-October, Jane went to the grocer to pick up some fruit and received a phone message containing a long string of numbers. It was a European line, and Jane dialed it from the grocer's phone, wondering who it could be.

'This is Jane Quinn,' she said. Grace's voice came through.

'I'm so glad you called me back.'

'Where are you?' said Jane, stomach flipping.

'That's just it,' said Grace. 'We've decided to take a little boat trip from Sicily, and I'm coming to Crete. We should be there in ten days – may I come see you?'

'If you want to,' said Jane.

'I do,' said Grace.

They arranged the details, and Jane hung up, feeling stunned. She watched the grocer count out change for the local postman, listened to the hum of the prized refrigerator blend with the local radio station; suddenly all of this felt precarious, as though a gust of wind might blow it away.

41

Jane shuffled in place as Grace's bus pulled into Matala. Jane had put on her best outfit for the occasion – a beige tunic from one of the local tourist shops. Her hair was braided all the way down her back, and her feet were bare. Jane took a breath; she didn't know what to expect. Then Grace stepped off the bus, holding hands with a bookish-looking man in his early forties.

Jane grinned. 'You must be Nate,' she said; she'd never met a boyfriend of Grace's before.

'You must be Jane,' said Nate, clasping her hand. Grace beamed.

Jane brought them to the Delphini Restaurant, and everyone was introduced over a fresh bronzini and a bottle of housemade white wine.

'Nothing beats Cornwall,' Roger was saying to Nate. 'Spent a summer there working at the Spotted Goose.'

'I was a server there in my uni days,' said Nate, lighting up. 'Don't mind if I never see another stargazy pie.'

Roger shivered at the thought.

'Though there's nothing compares to Cornish Yarg,' said Nate.

'That's the queen's cheese right there,' agreed Roger.

After lunch, Roger took Nate to explore the caves, leaving Grace and Jane to catch up at the café.

'He's very affable,' said Grace.

Jane nodded, her nerves returning. They watched two gulls working in tandem to pry open a mollusk shell on the beach.

'You seem . . . easy,' said Grace.

Jane looked out at the gentle sea. 'I like it here,' she said. 'Everything's so . . . simple.'

She lit a cigarette and turned toward Grace, prepared to face her disapproval. But when she looked at her aunt, all she saw was tenderness. Suddenly Jane felt close to tears. 'I'm sorry,' she said. 'I shouldn't have left the way I did. I – I've fucked up.'

Grace got very still. Jane's cheeks burned. Then she spoke the words she'd been avoiding for months.

'Jesse knows about Mom,' she said. 'And it's my fault. Grace, I am so, so sorry.'

Grace looked at Jane with a blank expression. 'I was afraid it might be something like this.'

Jane trembled. This was it, the moment when Grace finally realized that Jane had never been worthy of her kindness.

'I remember when you were little,' said Grace. 'You were always so ashamed when we'd catch you running away; you'd avoid my eyes for days. Maybe that's why you never once saw how happy we were to get you back.'

Jane hung her head. 'I've let you down,' she said.

'That's not what I'm saying,' said Grace. 'I'm saying this doesn't matter. Not in comparison to your well-being.'

'Grace, come on,' said Jane.

'Janie, it's okay,' said Grace.

'Of course it's not,' said Jane, a lump rising in her throat.

'You know it's not. You're the one who told me not to trust Jesse.'

Grace winced. 'That was unfair of me,' she said.

This startled Jane. 'No, it wasn't,' she said. 'You were just trying to protect Mom. All I had to do was keep my mouth shut, and now I've ruined everything.'

Grace gave her a wistful look. 'Janie, there's nothing to ruin,' she said.

Jane stared in disbelief. Grace must not be understanding. Jesse knew. She, Jane, had obliterated their entire way of life – years of secrecy, laid to waste. Her heart throbbed as she struggled to articulate this. 'Jesse knows about Mom,' she repeated. 'About Mom!'

'I understand,' said Grace. 'I'm telling you it's okay.'

'But it's not,' said Jane. 'It can't be. Otherwise—'

Otherwise, I lied to Jesse for nothing.

Tears began to roll down Jane's cheeks. Grace placed her hand over Jane's.

'I'm the one who's sorry, Jane. When everything happened with your mom, we had no idea what we were doing. We were just reacting. Those early days were a nightmare – the highs and lows of treatment after treatment almost broke us. Keeping the whole thing a secret made it feel somehow manageable. It was the one thing we could control.'

Grace withdrew her hand, placing her head in her palm.

'I never meant for it to go on for so long – I just kept waiting for it to feel all right that she wasn't coming back. But it never did. Then, one day, I woke up, and ten years had gone by. Oh, Jane – I think, in delaying my own grief, I've brutally extended yours. I am so sorry.' Tears welled in Grace's eyes.

317

It was too much to take in. Jane felt dizzy in the face of her aunt's candor. She snuffed out her cigarette and reached for Grace's arm. 'It's not like that,' she said. 'The Center is just a fact of my life. And because of you, it's been manageable. I wasn't even aware of concealing it most of the time. At least until . . .'

'Jesse,' said Grace.

Jane nodded. 'I can't understand it,' she said. 'There was just something about him from the moment I met him. When he asked me about Mom, I told him what I always tell everyone, but I just remember thinking, *He would actually get it.*' Grace peered at her.

'Well, of course,' said Grace. 'Who better to understand than another Center patient?'

Jane had never considered this. She lit a new cigarette.

'Being around him, I started to become aware of the burden. Only I wasn't really aware – I just heard this music.'

'*Ursa Major,*' said Grace.

Jane nodded, sprinkling ash onto the sand. 'It wasn't meant to be for him,' she said. 'Most people on the Island don't even know the Center's full name. You'd have to have a connection to the place, and even then you'd have to . . .'

'Have a connection to you?' said Grace.

Tears continued to run down Jane's cheeks as she sucked on the end of her cigarette.

'I've royally fucked that up,' said Jane, exhaling into the sky.

'Jane,' said Grace.

Jane shook her head. 'I have,' she said. 'I have. I didn't understand what was happening with us when it was happening. He tried to tell me, but I wouldn't hear him. I had convinced myself that once I achieved a certain level of success the rest of my life would make sense, and I couldn't bear to part with that idea, so I told myself I didn't love Jesse, and let him go instead.'

She took another drag of the cigarette, her hands shaking so much it took her a few extra seconds to bring the end to her lips.

'I made him believe we had shared grief,' said Jane. 'And now he cannot forgive me.'

'Give it time. I'm sure, when he cools down, he'll understand,' said Grace. 'Lord knows, Jesse's not perfect.'

Jane felt a dull ache in her throat. 'It doesn't matter,' she said. 'He's married to someone else.' She took a drag on her cigarette. 'I was so blind. All I could think about was shining.'

Grace considered. 'You were on a crusade,' she said. 'There was no place for Jesse in that.'

'How do you mean?' said Jane.

The way Grace tilted her head reminded Jane of Maggie.

'Ever since you signed with a label, music has been a sort of quest for you,' said Grace. 'I think part of you saw it as redemption, a way to correct what happened to Charlie – like your success would fix everything that had gone wrong for her.'

Jane sat back in her chair, her cigarette dangling between her fingers. 'It gave purpose to everything I did,' she said softly.

An image of Silo swam into Jane's mind – Loretta, Jesse, and Morgan glowing bright onstage, surrounded by the industry executives who had selected them to be there. 'Or it used to,' she said. 'After Silo . . . I realized that kind of success might not be in the cards for me. And once I started to question that, everything else began to unravel as well.'

For a moment they watched the gulls floating on the water.

'So – what now?' said Grace.

Jane wiped the tears from her face. 'Now nothing,' said Jane. 'Now I live here.'

Grace crossed her arms. 'What about your music?'

Jane tossed her cigarette into the sand. 'My heart's not in it anymore,' she said.

Grace frowned. 'So, if you can't be Jesse, you're not even going to try.'

'I was deluded to try in the first place,' said Jane. 'Every time I got lucky, I thought it was because I was destined for greatness. Now I see that it was all a fluke – none of what happened was meant to happen for me.'

'Jane, how can you say that?' said Grace.

Jane shrugged. 'It's okay. It's been freeing to just own it.'

Grace watched her. 'You never know,' she said. Then, after a moment, 'I don't think the mystery of your disappearance has been altogether bad for publicity.'

Jane laughed.

'I'm serious,' said Grace.

She had brought a folder of newspaper and magazine clippings, all praising *Ursa Major* for its artistry and speculating as to where Jane had gone. Most of the clips were from that summer, but the guessing had continued longer than Jane would have thought. Theories ranged from fleeing a love triangle with Morgan and Jesse, to a slew of possible high-profile elopements, to a vow of silence in a Tibetan monastery.

'I'm actually a little sad I didn't think of this,' said Jane.

They spent the afternoon swimming in the clear water and catching up on Grace's trip. Around 6:00 p.m., Roger dropped Nate back with Jane and Grace at the beach so that he could start his shift at the Delphini Restaurant. Nate looked a bit shaken up by the caves.

'People are just . . . living in there,' he said. 'In the buff!'

'It's a lot,' said Jane. Animosity had been mounting between the locals and the tourists as the caves reached higher and higher levels of putrefaction.

'I can offer you a bottle of local wine as consolation,' said Jane.

'That would be acceptable,' said Nate.

They ate a sumptuous dinner back at the Delphini Restaurant. Roger was in full form, whirling in and out of the kitchen with flaming pans and skewers of vegetables, as curved and colorful as rainbows. After the supper plates were cleared, a few local musicians struck up a tune, and everyone began to dance. They spun and jumped together under the stars until the restaurant's owner, Demetrios, shut off the lights. Nate and Grace took Jane's room in the boardinghouse, and Jane slept under the sky with Roger.

In the morning, Jane felt wistful as she brought Grace and Nate back to the bus.

'You know, Janie,' said Grace, 'there's room if you want to come back with us. We could get you as far as the Continent, no trouble.'

Jane smiled. 'Thank you for coming,' she said.

'Thank you for letting me,' said Grace. 'I'll see you when you get back.'

'Right,' said Jane. She watched the bus vanish into a trail of black exhaust.

Jane still had no intention of going back.

42

By November, the bartender at the Delphini had decamped to the mainland; Roger put in a good word with Demetrios, and Jane took over as barkeep. She already ate most of her meals at the restaurant for free, and tending bar brought in just enough to offset the cost of her room. As far as Jane was concerned, she could go on like this forever.

One night, their limbs entwined on her cot, Jane felt Roger clutch her shoulder.

'What is it?' she said. A chorus of voices swam into earshot.

'I think it's finally happening,' he said.

Jane opened her eyes. Colored lights danced on her window-panes. Roger was right: the villagers had succeeded in their appeals to the local police, who had dispatched several units to kick the hippies out of the caves in the middle of the night.

'Holy shit,' said Jane.

Outside, hundreds of tanned bodies were making their way into town without a scrap of clothing. They skipped and laughed, waving flashlights and torches past a gauntlet of amused policemen. Jane and Roger exchanged looks, then went downstairs to get a better view.

A local camera crew had set up in the courtyard of the

Delphini. The anchor kept trying to get the cameraman to focus on her as his lens bounced after the nude parade. She rolled her eyes and scolded him, then caught sight of Jane and Roger, perched in the doorway.

'Is crazy, yes?' she said.

'I have never seen so many Matalan eels,' said Roger.

Jane watched the bodies process. As the camera's lens bobbed toward a chain of skipping men, she felt a chill roll in over the water.

After the caves were evacuated, the spaces between orders at the Delphini began to stretch longer and longer. One night not long after, Roger and Jane sat alone, watching the moon rise over the restaurant's courtyard. Roger raised his glass to her.

'What are we toasting?' said Jane.

'Rabat,' said Roger, giving the 'R' a nice long roll.

Jane nodded. 'Where's that?' she said.

'Morocco,' he said, once again rolling the 'r.'

'When?' asked Jane.

'A week,' he said. 'Maybe two. I don't like to stay in one place longer than six months. You should come, Jane. It will be warm for the winter.'

In truth, Jane wanted to go home, but she couldn't afford to. She had bought her flight over using her *Ursa Major* money, and had spent the next several months chipping away at that pile without adding to it. She had a small cushion, but not enough for a transatlantic flight.

'I'll just stay put until the next season,' she told Elsie the next day over the phone. 'Once the tourists come back, my income will triple.'

'Won't you be lonely there without Roger?' said Elsie.

Jane took a drag on her cigarette. She could afford to go with Roger, but only just. She had an unformed idea of Morocco and felt ambivalent about moving there; the biggest draws would be Roger and improving her proximity to the Atlantic Ocean. The trip there would clean out what little cash she had, and would mean working for her return ticket from scratch.

'I'll be fine,' she said.

The next morning, Roger went out on the fishing boat to retrieve the day's catch, and Jane stayed behind to keep an eye on the restaurant. Without the tourists, the beach looked small; the water's aqua hue had begun to dull under the cloud cover of winter.

From behind the bar, Jane noticed two men walking toward the restaurant from town. As she watched them approach, she began to list ways she knew of making money. *Tend bar, wash laundry, cut hair, administer injections, change diapers.*

The men were from the Continent. This was obvious from a distance by the paleness of their skin and the quality of their clothes. *Sew a hem, type a letter, wait a table, shuck an oyster.*

The closer they got, the more familiar they seemed. Jane wondered if she had been getting too much sun. Both of them had this walk, this hairstyle, this swagger she knew incredibly well. *Paint nails, change sheets, bake bread, write songs.*

She used to write songs.

The thought occurred to her as she slipped into a hallucination. In this vision, Willy was walking into the Delphini Restaurant, red aviators glowing over his eyes like traffic reflectors, his grin spread from ear to ear. Also, there were two of him.

'Of all the gin joints,' said the Willy-shaped mirage.

Jane blinked a few times. 'Willy?' she said.

Willy took off his glasses. Jane looked at his companion.

'Jane, this is my brother Freddy,' said Willy. 'Of Ear Wool Records.'

'Pleased to meet you,' said Freddy, stepping forward and shaking Jane's hand. Facts sounded in the recesses of Jane's memory – Freddy was Willy's middle brother, the one living in London who produced punk albums. It struck Jane as strange, the way Willy had introduced him, as if they were bumping into each other at a cocktail party.

'You're in Matala,' said Jane.

'Heard you were in town and figured we'd stop by,' said Willy, seating himself on a stool.

'How did you even know I was here?' she said.

Before he could respond, Roger appeared, arms laden with wriggling nets.

'Jane, these squid really wanted to live, I had to be very callous,' he said, dropping the nets on the sand. He began to string up squid on the line.

'Roger,' said Jane, waving him over.

Roger looked from Willy to Freddy. 'Hello, hello,' he said. 'You must be here to take Jane back to civilization.'

Willy and Freddy exchanged looks. 'That's the idea,' said Willy, glancing at Jane.

'I'm not going back,' said Jane. It was the truth – she didn't have the money, but she wasn't going to say that to Willy.

'Jane, these men came a long way,' said Roger, eyes twinkling. 'Let's all have some lunch.'

Jane could tell that Willy and Freddy were skeptical of Roger, but once they'd tasted his fresh pan-seared scallops, they were ready to take him back instead of Jane.

325

'Magnificent,' said Freddy. 'Have you thought about opening a restaurant in London?'

'Once or twice,' said Roger, winking at Jane.

'Seriously,' said Freddy. 'I've never tasted scallops like that.'

Roger grinned. 'It's not hard, mate,' he said. 'Here, I'll show you.'

Roger and Freddy stacked the lunch plates, and the two of them went into the kitchen for a cooking lesson. Willy looked at Jane.

'Care to show me around?' he said.

They walked along the beach. Jane could see sand grains embedding in his penny loafers. She tried to remember the last time she'd worn shoes.

'I don't understand what's happening,' she said. 'Aren't you supposed to be touring all fifty states for *Under Stars*?'

Willy laughed, shoving his hands into his pockets. 'Elsie called me,' he said.

Jane looked up in surprise.

'She says that you need help getting home, but that you'll never ask for it.'

Jane lit a cigarette.

'Freddy lives in London, so when I told him I was coming over, he offered to come with me,' said Willy. 'I can't believe you came out here on your own.'

He waited for her to speak. Jane dug her toes into the sand.

'Gran had no right to do that,' she said. 'I'm perfectly fine here. Roger and I have a good thing going, and this has been exactly what I need. I can go anytime I like.' Even in her own ears, her voice sounded false.

Willy took off his glasses. 'Can you?' he said.

Jane had forgotten how shrewd his stare could be. 'Yes,' she said.

Willy raised his eyebrows. 'I know what I paid you for your last record,' he said. 'I know what airfare costs . . . and if you have the money to get back home, then Roger is a Hapsburg prince.'

'You never know with Roger,' said Jane.

Willy held up his hands in surrender, and they continued their walk down the beach.

That night, Roger and Freddy served grilled sea bass, and the four of them put away their weights in Minoan wine. A warm afternoon had put the remaining local clientele in a celebratory mood, and over the course of the evening, the courtyard filled with so many merrymakers, it almost felt like the high season.

The postman struck up a familiar tune on his dulcimer, and couples began to dance. Jane felt a twinge of amusement, watching the Lambert brothers try to determine if the instrument might have any commercial appeal.

Suddenly Jane found herself short of breath. She walked to the edge of the courtyard, looking across the darkened sea.

Starless night, I am a stranger.

She heard shoes crunching on sand and looked up to see Willy standing beside her.

'Let me take you back,' he said.

Jane stared over the water. 'There's nothing for me there,' she said. 'I'm shocked as it is that Pegasus would pay for you to come here.'

Willy looked uncomfortable. 'They didn't,' he said after a moment. Jane's cheeks grew hot.

'Shit. Right,' said Jane. 'So, that's it, then? They've cut ties?'
Willy sighed.

'It's not that simple, but things aren't looking good,' said
Willy.

Then it sank in.

'You paid to come here yourself?' said Jane. 'You're offering
to pay my way back? Willy, that's too much. I can't put you
out like that.'

'You should,' said Willy, clearing his throat. 'Honestly, you
should. I feel partially responsible that you're here in the first
place.'

Jane opened her mouth to protest, and he held up his hand.

'You told me up front last summer that you didn't want to
go to Silo, and I wouldn't listen,' he said. 'I . . . I don't believe
you would be here now if you hadn't been made to do that,
and it's my fault you were. I told you when we met that I was
in it for my artists, and that's who I want to be – not another
Lambert who pushes the company line at any cost.'

Jane looked at her feet, cracked and dry.

'I don't deserve this,' she said. 'You were just trying to get
me to promote myself. All you ever did was try to make me
famous, and all I ever did was act like I knew better. I . . . I
honestly don't know why you're here.'

Willy gave her a vexed look. 'I wasn't going to leave Jane
Quinn in a cave,' he said. Jane shook her head. 'Jane Quinn is
persona non grata,' said Jane.

Willy sighed. 'Yes, she is,' he said. 'And I'm her rep.'

As they made their way back to the party, Jane caught Roger's
eye. She could tell from his expression that he already knew
what she had to tell him. He led her onto the dance floor and

held her close, grasping the back of her shirt. Jane looked into his twinkling eyes and smiled.

'Of course,' he said, 'if things don't work out, I'll expect you in Rabat.'

43

Most of the media began to assemble outside the Felt Forum at 5:00 p.m.; Marybeth Kent of *Snitch Magazine* arrived at 4:00 p.m., with her photographer Trevor in tow.

'We're getting the edge on *Esquire*,' she muttered to Trevor, as the two of them flashed their passes to Security and stepped onto the red carpet.

By the time the rest of the press arrived, Marybeth and Trevor had already claimed the best spot, a raised platform ten feet before the theater's entrance.

Across Eighth Avenue, fans whooped behind metal barricades. They emitted a collective swell of excitement as a limousine arrived. The car deposited a silver-haired record executive at the base of the red carpet, along with several glittering attendants.

'How do I look?' Marybeth asked Trevor. She wore a long sequined dress, her red hair loose around her shoulders, turquoise cat-eyes peeking out behind tortoiseshell-rimmed spectacles. Trevor, who was wearing red suspenders and a matching bow tie, gave her a thumbs-up.

They just needed to look glamorous enough to blend in.

From her perch atop the red carpet, Marybeth felt more like a hunter than a socialite. These evenings had a rhythm that reminded her of animal migration patterns; by observing the birds, one could anticipate the arrival of the big game.

Here was Lacey Dormon, shimmering up the stairs in irides-cent pink.

'Lacey, any predictions for tonight?' Marybeth asked.

'I'm just here to support my friends,' said Lacey. She sailed into the theater. Marybeth was surprised by the number of stars turning up – even last year, half the recipients hadn't been there to claim their awards. The studios were trying to make the show more of an event, like the Oscars; they must have been leaning on their talent to attend.

Moments later, a limousine slid up to the curb and out stepped Loretta Mays. As the car pulled away, the fans across the street caught sight of her and let out a roar.

Loretta had been nominated for seven Grammys that night, including the Big Four: Record of the Year for 'Safe Passage,' Album of the Year for *Hourglass,* Song of the Year for 'Safe Passage,' and Best New Artist. She had also been nominated for Best Album Cover, Best Album Notes, and Best Engineered Recording, Non-Classical. She glowed as she made her way up the carpet. Tonight was her night, and everyone knew it.

Marybeth, however, was more interested in the pair trailing up the carpet after her: Kyle Lightfoot and Rich Holt. They walked with a slight man in glasses – probably another studio musician. Marybeth didn't care about their current gigs; her thoughts were on the Breakers. If anyone could confirm the rumors of Jane Quinn's attendance, it would be her former bandmates. Marybeth caught them with a smile as they came up the stairs.

'Quite a night,' she said. 'You must be thrilled.'

'We're happy to be here,' said Kyle.

'Off the record,' said Marybeth, leaning in, 'any idea if Jane Quinn is going to show?'

'Jane's hard to predict,' said Kyle.

Hannibal Fang, Best Record nominee for 'Hunger Pains,' stepped onto the landing, and Kyle and Rich took the opportunity to excuse themselves.

Jane Quinn hadn't been seen since the opening of Silo the previous summer, an evening so well documented it had given *Snitch* fodder for months. *Songs in Ursa Major* had been strong out of the gate, and Jane's first single, 'Last Call,' had gotten a ton of radio play over the summer, although not as much in recent months. Speculation about Jane's disappearance had kept the coverage going long after Pegasus had stopped promoting the album.

Although critics had acknowledged *Songs in Ursa Major* as an artistic feat, it hadn't been nominated for a single award. As a journalist, Marybeth knew that this kind of pageantry was always political, but as a fan, she felt that Jane had been robbed.

She wasn't alone. Legions of young women who felt that *Ursa Major* had spoken for them were outraged by the snub; some had gathered across Eighth Avenue, holding signs that read 'Justice for Jane' and 'What Would Jane Do?' Marybeth herself had listened to 'A Thousand Lines' on repeat after being dumped by her long-term boyfriend for being 'too much' and owned a 'No Pain, No Jane' tee shirt.

A week before the Grammys, an anonymous source from inside Pegasus had leaked that Jane Quinn was rehearsing at their studios to perform at the event. Marybeth suspected this was a publicity gambit; it was exactly the kind of intrigue that made at-home viewers tune in. But it had worked; tonight, the question of whether Jane Quinn would return clung to the air like static.

Screams across the street rocketed to a fever pitch: Jesse Reid and Morgan Vidal had arrived. If there was one couple Marybeth – or anyone in her industry – had devoted more column inches to than any other, it was Jesse and Morgan. Their marriage had so much star power it seemed to have been engineered by the record gods themselves. Ever since they started dating, they had been untouchable – in terms of both record sales and publicity.

At least, until now. As Marybeth watched them saunter up the red carpet, her muckraking instincts began to tingle. Marybeth's true talent, if one could call it that, was that she was not enamored of celebrities. This gave her the ability to see them for what they were: people. And, just like all people, they gave themselves away in small interactions; the difference was that most onlookers were too blinded by their halos to notice.

In Marybeth's experience, you could tell whether a couple was having marital issues on the red carpet same as if they were seated beside you at a restaurant. Tonight, her senses told her that the honeymoon period between Jesse and Morgan was drawing to a close.

Jesse looked over the whole business. He smiled as he made his way toward the theater, but there was a mean edge in the curve of his face. He stayed in line with Morgan like an animal on a leash, not really walking with her, or with anyone. His cover of Loretta's song 'Safe Passage' had been nominated for the Grammy for Best Record.

Morgan looked radiant in a nude slip dress that accentuated her long limbs, but Marybeth could see the panic behind her smile. Her eyes kept glancing at Jesse as though checking to make sure he was still switched on. She had been nominated for a Grammy as well, for Best New Artist.

'Who are you wearing?' asked Marybeth in a chipper voice as they passed, Trevor snapping away beside her. As Morgan gave a hushed answer about how her 'dear friend Giorgio' had designed her outfit, Marybeth watched how Jesse tuned her out. She felt a pang of pity for Morgan as she recalled the way Jesse had looked at Jane Quinn just two years prior.

Jesse's eyes, startling blue, turned to Marybeth then, and she had the sensation of being recognized. It occurred to her that this was what had made him a mega-star: less than two seconds of eye contact had the power to make you feel as if you had somehow been singled out.

Jesse and Morgan entered the theater half an hour before the show was set to begin.

'Get what you need?' said Trevor.

'Definitely,' said Marybeth.

Three limos waited at the base of the carpet to drop their cargo. A gaggle of backup singers exited the first, a country duo the second.

'Want to start packing it in?' said Trevor. Marybeth shook her head, watching the last limo pull up to the curb and open its door.

Something was about to happen, Marybeth was certain of it. It took her a moment to realize why: the crowd across the street had gone quiet. Someone they didn't recognize had gotten out of the car, and they didn't know how to react.

A statuesque figure stood at the foot of the carpet, as though she had just stepped down off a cloud. She wore an elegant black shift; silver necklaces dangled from her neck like strands of moon. A veil of yellow hair sloped over her shoulders and down her back. As the car drove away, she waited, taking in the carpet, the stairs, the theater entrance. Then, as though realizing where she was, she turned and looked at the hordes of people watching her.

'It's Jane!' shouted a girl holding a 'What Would Jane Do?' sign. Cheers shook the barricades.

'Are you getting this?' Marybeth said to Trevor, who clicked away in response.

Willy Lambert joined Jane at the base of the carpet and led her toward the theater. She held his arm, blinking in the cameras' flashing lights. As Jane climbed the steps, Marybeth felt stunned. This person looked like Jane Quinn, but her confidence had been replaced by timidity. Then, as Jane stepped onto the landing, her gray eyes lit on Marybeth and she smiled. For the first time in her life, Marybeth experienced what it felt like to be starstruck.

'I know you,' said Jane. 'You're from *Snitch*.' No celebrity had ever recognized Marybeth before.

'I remember you posed as a college student at Portland State,' said Jane.

'Yeah, sorry about that,' said Marybeth.

Jane shrugged. 'Sometimes our jobs require us not to be ourselves,' she said.

This is why I love you, Marybeth wanted to say.

But before she could find the words, Willy had placed a hand on Jane's back, guiding her forward. Jane turned toward the entrance, head bowed, like a priestess about to perform a sacrificial rite. The doors opened, and Jane stepped into the incandescent light.

44

Jane and Willy had been stonewalled from the moment they'd tried to engage Pegasus on Jane's next album. It appeared that Pegasus was opting to run down the clock on her contract.

Willy thought there was a small chance they'd come around. The label hadn't released a second single, but 'Last Call' still got radio play. As she waited, Jane diligently compiled a few tracks inspired by her travels and took up a regular slot performing at the Carousel. It wasn't much, but it was enough to keep her going as the weeks ticked by.

At the end of February, she finally received the call.

'Jane,' said Willy's voice on the other end. 'Something . . . unexpected has come up.'

'What?' said Jane, bracing herself.

'You've been invited to perform at the Grammys,' said Willy.

Jane wasn't sure she'd heard him correctly. 'To perform?' said Jane. 'But . . . I haven't been nominated for anything.'

'I'm as surprised as you are,' said Willy. 'Maybe they think it will help drum up publicity.'

'Award shows are so tacky,' said Jane. The Grammys had been around for ten years or so, and Jane thought of them as an uptight snooze fest.

Willy cleared his throat. 'Tacky as in *Of course I'll do it*, right?' said Willy.

'Yes,' said Jane. 'Of course.'

Jane arrived in New York the week before the show, feeling cautiously optimistic. Pegasus had put her up at the Plaza, and she floated behind the porter on the way to her room. When he stood aside, her heart sank.

'I didn't even know they had rooms this small,' said Willy, looking embarrassed. Jane imagined that his reaction was an indicator of the size of Morgan and Jesse's penthouse suite.

'I'm just grateful to be here,' she said.

The next morning, Willy escorted her to the Pegasus offices for rehearsal. It had flurried the night before, and as they walked west along Central Park they had to avoid yellow and black snow crusted with soot and animal urine. A line of horse-drawn carriages jingled in place; the animals' costumes had been equipped with blinders to keep them from panicking in traffic. Jane felt a wave of nausea as she looked at their heavy, blood-shot eyes.

'This city is disgusting,' said Willy.

When they stepped into the glass-and-marble reception area of Pegasus, Jane couldn't tell if the pair of icy secretaries seated at the front desk were the same set from her first visit. As she looked at them up close, she realized that they weren't all that alike and were probably her own age.

'Ms. Quinn, Mr. Lambert,' said the one on the left. 'We're expecting you. Please, come with me. May I get you some water?'

'We're just going to the old studios,' said Willy.

The secretary frowned. 'Sorry, but that's not what I have here,' she said. 'I'm to bring you to Metropolis A upon arrival.'

337

'Okay,' said Willy. 'We have a rehearsal in ten minutes, so this better be quick.'

'I'm sure it will be,' said the secretary. 'Please, this way.' Willy and Jane exchanged looks.

They followed her to a sunny marble hallway, lined by large glass offices overlooking the city. They were shown into a large conference room with floor-to-ceiling windows on two sides. The other two walls were studded with golden records, the same as the corporate offices in Memphis. Jane blinked.

It appeared that a board meeting was under way. Lenny Davis sat at the head of a polished conference table, his muscle positioned on the wall behind him. The other seats were occupied by men Jane didn't know. Jane wondered if the secretary had made a mistake. She glanced at Willy as Lenny Davis spoke.

'Come in, Jane, Willy.' He gestured to the seat on his left. As Jane took it, she realized she was sitting directly across from Vincent Ray. He stared right through her.

This wasn't a board meeting; it was an ambush.

Jane had the impulse to turn and run as she heard the secretary close the door.

'So good of you to join us,' said Davis. His tone was light, but Jane caught the same calculating look in his eye she'd seen in Memphis. Her skin crawled as she remembered how he'd called her a 'cute little piece' backstage at Minglewood Hall.

'What's going on?' said Willy. His eyes had fixed on a man seated directly to Lenny's left. He wore a tailored cashmere suit and looked like an older version of Willy's brother Danny.

'Dad,' said Willy.

'Will,' said Jack Lambert. He glanced at Jane but didn't greet her. 'Have a seat.'

Jane said nothing as she took in the ring of blank faces around her; she could feel them silently multiplying the years before she aged out of her looks by the number of dollars she might fetch.

'Jane, this is the board of Pegasus,' said Davis. 'I know you know Vincent Ray.' Vincent Ray stared at Jane, and she nodded in response.

'This is just a friendly chat,' said Davis. 'We wanted to hear from Jane what she has in mind for the Grammys.'

'All of you?' said Willy, placing his sunglasses in his shirt pocket. Jane looked up: Willy never would have adopted that tone two years prior. Two more years of hits had made him bold, and his father's presence was making him defiant.

'We just want to make sure we're all on the same page,' said Lenny Davis.

'Okay,' said Jane. 'Well, first, thank you for the opportunity.'

Lenny Davis smiled, but the warmth didn't reach his eyes.

'The producer had mentioned "Last Call," since that was the single on my record. But I'm open to other suggestions.'

Lenny Davis nodded, then turned to Vincent Ray.

'We're thinking "Spring Fling,"' said Vincent Ray.

Jane raised her eyebrows. 'The Breakers song?'

'It's still your best-selling single,' said Vincent. 'We'll use this performance to publicly transition you back to the kind of thing you'll be recording from now on.'

'Hang on a sec,' said Willy. 'I've spent months trying to get even the slightest response on Jane's option and hit nothing but red tape. Now you're talking about it as if it's happening?'

'After the disappointment of *Songs in Ursa Major*, we had been planning to terminate Jane's contract,' said Lenny Davis.

'But then Vincent Ray made the case for exercising Jane's option as an opportunity to cross-sell the Breakers' album.'

This had to be a joke – the idea that Vincent Ray was advocating for *Spring Fling* was absurd. Jane looked at Willy; as she did, she noticed a familiar office-scape behind him.

With a start, Jane realized that this was the same conference room where they'd shot the cover for *Spring Fling*. Her stomach sank. This was still about that cover, only now Vincent Ray would be reclaiming it as a symbol of his power. Having Jane perform 'Spring Fling' at the Grammys would send a message to the rest of the industry that he always got the last word.

'It's clear from the relative success of *Spring Fling* and *Ursa Major* that in your hands, Jane has wandered away from her base,' said Vincent Ray. Willy looked as though he'd been slapped.

'Now, hang on,' said Willy. '"Last Call" started out higher than "Spring Fling." The only reason it hasn't done as well is because this label stopped promoting it.'

'The board agrees that there is an opportunity here if we realign Jane with her image,' said Vincent Ray. 'We're going to use the Grammys as a moment to relaunch her and make it clear that this is what she's going to be doing from now on: fun, beachy pop. No more experimentation.'

'My band hasn't played in a year,' said Jane.

'Oh, you misunderstand. This will be a solo performance,' said Vincent Ray.

Jane cringed at the idea of playing an acoustic version of 'Spring Fling' to an audience of Morgan, Loretta, and Jesse. She said nothing.

'This is lunacy – Jane's base loved *Ursa Major*. You must have seen the "WWJD" shirts,' said Willy, appealing to the larger room.

'Teen girls are like sheep,' said Lenny Davis. 'They like whatever we tell them to like. To get the men, Jane needs to go back to pop.'

Jane had heard enough. 'I'm all set,' she said.

'You're all set?' said Lenny Davis.

'Yeah, I just won't perform,' said Jane.

Vincent Ray sneered. 'You don't have a choice,' he said. 'The publicity clause in your contract requires you to fulfill any promotion we deem necessary. I suggest you take this opportunity to show your gratitude for the leniency you were given last summer.'

Willy was nearing his breaking point. 'So – let's say Jane performs at the Grammys, and "realigns" with her "image,"' he said. 'Then what?'

'Then Vincent Ray has generously offered to produce her next album, a true follow-up to *Spring Fling*,' said Lenny Davis.

Jane suddenly found herself wishing the label had decided to drop her. 'I don't want a producer,' she said.

'You ungrateful child,' said Jack Lambert.

The color drained from Willy's face.

'It's not a question of what you want,' said Lenny Davis. 'You're under contract. If we order up your option, you are obligated to deliver it.'

'I don't write songs like "Spring Fling,"' said Jane.

'Then we'll hire a professional. She's not getting this,' said Lenny Davis, looking to Vincent Ray for assistance. 'Can you try?'

Vincent Ray turned to Jane and spoke slowly. 'You sing what we want you to sing,' he said.

341

'What?' said Jane.

'Still too vague? How about: We own you. Well, the parts of you that matter. Your backlist, your front list, your image, your time. Everything you've made and everything you are belongs to us.'

They owned *Ursa Major*.

Willy's knuckles grew white as his fists clenched. 'You can't talk to her that way,' he said.

Jack Lambert fixed his son with a forbidding stare. 'If you'd been doing your job, he wouldn't have to.'

'This doesn't need to be unpleasant,' said Lenny Davis. 'We've invested in Jane and aren't inclined to waste an asset. If she shows that she can be a good girl and do what she's asked, there's no reason we can't work together.'

'And if she doesn't?' said Willy.

Lenny Davis and Vincent Ray exchanged looks. 'Then we take her next four albums and stick them in a vault with *Ursa Major*,' said Vincent Ray.

Jane took a breath.

Jesse had told her it would come to this; she'd felt so much outrage then, such fire to prove him wrong, to leave her mark on the world. She could picture the light in the Shack, Jesse reclined as she transcribed the notes for his songs. She couldn't wait to be the one with her name on a record; she had thought it would solve everything. Such foolishness – now she would give up every record she'd ever sold to get back the hope she'd felt in that moment.

'Okay,' said Jane.

Willy's head whipped toward her.

'There's a good girl,' said Lenny Davis.

'Okay?' said Willy. 'It's not okay. *Ursa Major* was critically acclaimed.'

'Will,' said Jack Lambert.

'No,' said Willy. 'This is ridiculous. I won't—'

'Willy,' said Jane. 'It's okay.'

For a moment the room was silent. Then Vincent Ray spoke.

'Guess we were all in for a surprise today,' he said. 'Wouldn't have expected Jane to be the rational one, and you to be running your mouth off, Lambert.'

Jane and Willy rose to their feet and backed out of the room as though at gunpoint. Once in the hall, Willy let out a deep sigh, bending forward from the hips.

'I'm so sick of my father's shit,' he said, running a hand over his face. 'It just doesn't add up. To get the whole board involved must mean . . .' He shook his head and turned to Jane. 'And since when are you a *good girl*?'

'Since I'm tired,' said Jane.

'You're tired?' said Willy.

Jane shrugged. 'I'm tired of fighting fights I can't win,' said Jane. 'You heard him. They own *Ursa Major*.' She shook her head. 'Maybe this is just as good as it gets.'

'It's not, Jane,' said Willy. 'I don't want you to give up. You should go somewhere else, somewhere that appreciates you.'

Jane laughed. 'After three or four more albums like *Spring Fling*? What's the point? At the top of every record company is a board of directors just like that one – and those people are always going to see me as arm candy for Jesse Reid, not his equal. Maybe it's better just to embrace it.'

'Jane, I don't want to hear this – not from you,' said Willy.

Jane patted his arm. 'You're a good man, Willy,' she said. 'It's just a dumb award show – maybe people won't watch. I told you, they're tacky.'

Willy looked torn between saying more and remaining silent. After a moment, he nodded. 'Come on, let's get you to rehearsal,' he said, taking his aviators from his pocket.

After production had relocated to L.A., Pegasus had begun renting out the old recording studios as practice rooms. The chambers had been stripped of all the rugs and textiles, leaving harsh concrete walls. Under the hum of fluorescent lights, Jane transposed 'Spring Fling' onto the piano so it wouldn't seem as threadbare without the Breakers.

> *Oh,*
> *We should be a movie,*
> *We should be a show.*

Over the course of the week, Jane had flashes of her recording sessions with Rich, Kyle, and Greg in this very studio. But, to her surprise, she found herself thinking most of *Ursa Major*. Jane would not have thought it possible to feel nostalgia for a time in her life when she had felt such misery; then again, she had not yet realized that there was something beyond misery.

The numbness that filled her now was worse than any of the pain she had suffered in making *Ursa Major*. At least then, she had felt alive.

> *Oh,*
> *You make me feel groovy,*
> *Light it up and go.*

As Jane's limousine pulled up outside the Grammys, she felt as empty and pointless as the lyrics to 'Spring Fling.' Maybe this was what she should be singing after all.

45

Jane's seat was at the very back of the auditorium. Willy deposited her in the empty chair beside Kyle, Rich, and Simon, and headed to the front to sit with the nominees.

'Looking good, Janie Q,' said Kyle.

'You ready?' said Rich.

Jane shrugged as the lights went down. The audience was larger than she had anticipated. They glittered in their seats like jewels in a velvet case as Andy Williams took center stage beneath a sculpted ribbon of electric lights. Applause rippled through the theater as he began his opening monologue, cameras circling like vultures.

Over the next hour, Jane watched as *Hourglass* by Loretta Mays took awards for Best Album Cover, Best Album Notes, and Best Engineered Recording, Non-Classical. They cheered as Huck won Best Pop Instrumental Performance on 'Safe Passage.' The room vibrated as Jesse claimed Best Record for the same song, his tall frame sauntering onstage to accept.

About halfway through the show, a production assistant appeared at Jane's side to escort her backstage. Jane followed him through a series of industrial corridors that landed her behind the stage-right performing platform. Willy was already there.

'How you doing?' he said.

Jane's reflection looked small in his blue aviators.

'It's just three minutes,' she said.

The two of them peered out at the glistening crowd.

'It's time,' said the production assistant. Jane followed him into the wing. She could see Andy Williams smiling back and forth between the audience and a CBS camera.

The stage manager held up a hand to Andy, counting down from five. Andy gestured to the wing.

'Please welcome to the stage Jane Quinn, singing "Spring Fling."'

A murmur ran through the auditorium as Jane stepped in front of the cameras.

Rich and Kyle sat up in their chairs. Even from the back of the house, they could see Jane more clearly than the other performers. It had something to do with the light; Jane glowed.

From stage, Jane could feel time shifting around her, at once pressing on and slowing down. She could see Kyle and Rich, if she squinted; she could make out Lacey Dormon, glimmering in pink, Huck to her left. Several rows near the front had been cordoned off for the NARAS academy; Jane could see Lenny Davis's chains glinting and the shine of Vincent Ray's teeth. She could also see the other nominees, front and center: Loretta and her husband; Hannibal Fang and a Croatian supermodel; Morgan, and Jesse.

Jane's breath caught in her chest; this was the closest she had been to Jesse in almost a year. He sat two rows back, slumped in his chair, gazing at the back of the head in front of him. To Jane, he looked like the worn horses outside of Central Park with blinders on their eyes.

She turned to the piano, which was covered in lights. Her fingers rested on the keys. It was just three minutes, just one number. What had Jesse once said to her? *'Spring Fling' is a perfectly respectable song.*

She looked up and saw Willy standing in the wings. They'd come a long way from the Island Folk Fest in 1969. New York, Greece, L.A. What had he told her that night in Laurel Canyon?

As long as you have an instrument in your hands, you're trouble.

In the back of the auditorium, Rich and Kyle exchanged glances.

'What?' said Simon.

'She's not . . .' Kyle genuflected the way Jane did before playing.

From stage, Jane could see Vincent Ray waiting for her to sink her fingers into the keys and seal his victory. This would be a crowning moment for him, and everyone here would recognize it.

The thought made Jane's stomach turn; but what could she do? The label held all the cards – her future albums, *Ursa Major*. She glanced back at Jesse; even their most prized stallion was being turned into glue. He flickered before her, this beautiful boy on the verge of going out.

Then Jesse looked at her.

You run through me like fountain dye . . .
Starry signs themselves reflecting . . .
No matter where you roam . . .

Jane bent over the keys and closed her eyes. A tempest started up inside the piano.

'That's not "Spring Fling,"' said Rich.

Simon raised his eyebrows as he recognized the third track from *Songs in Ursa Major*.

'It's "Wallflower."'

As Jane played the introduction to the song, she felt a force rising in her body, a galloping in her heart. The label might hold the cards, but she had these three minutes. She had this instrument. They were humble means of resistance, a handful of matchsticks against the winter frost; and yet Jane knew that to relinquish them would mean losing more than she could allow.

You and me, she thought, summoning the notes at her fingertips. She began to sing.

> *'Flowers painted on the wall,*
> *Tattered paper bouquets fall,*
> *Your laugh echoes down the hall.'*

As the cameras panned around, Jane drew breath and continued. She played with tenderness, every note aching. Hannibal Fang's face broke into a grin in the front row.

The only image Jane would be aligning with tonight was her own.

> *'I've never known a girl like you,*
> *Dress so faded, eyes so blue,*
> *Lord in heaven see me through.'*

As she finished the chorus, she was returned to a festival meadow, a crowd of thousands. She felt what she had felt then,

349

courage born of defiance. *Show me what you've got.* She urged the piano on, gathering momentum across octaves like wind over waves.

'Piano tamer,' whispered Kyle.

As Jane's fingers continued to play the accompaniment, she lifted her chin, looking out across the top of the piano into the distance. She let the vocal cue pass, picking up the melody to 'Wallflower' with her right hand. Then she began to sing a different song entirely.

Because, just like Jane, this song had a secret.

> *'I count to three and suddenly*
> *The moon hangs low,*
> *White as a pearl.'*

Jane had written 'Wallflower' as a counterpoint to 'Lilac Waltz'; heard together, the melodies traveled around each other like vines on a trellis. 'Wallflower' told Jane's side of the story she was never supposed to tell. Tears rolled down her face as she sang.

> *'I'm the girl, in your arms,*
> *The air is filled with melody,*
> *And you still think so well of me.'*

For so long, Jane had sought to avenge her mother. But that burden had never been hers to bear, not really. Now it was time to let it go. Jane felt the piano keys, hard and tangible beneath her fingers, and released the last lines of Charlie's part into the room.

'Darling, it was not meant to be
After the lilac waltz.'

The silvery quality of her voice made the haunting tune shimmer against the rich backdrop of the piano, and Jane piloted both with exacting precision. She breathed and let the piano carry her back into the 'Wallflower' chorus.

'I've never known a girl like you.'

The sight of Charlie turning to leave Gray Gables in her lilac-colored dress was the still frame that had haunted Jane's dreams and defined her life. Now she laid it down before a hall of mercenaries, gamblers, players, and Jesse.

'Car pulls up, a screen door slams,
Clicking heels, a beige sedan,
Inside is another man.'

There he sat, not twenty feet away, separated by a gulf of hurt and longing and confusion and regret. And yet, in this moment, Jane held one last match. She found his eyes and sent the final verse into the space between them like a lantern signaling from a distant cliff.

'I stand aside, I watch you go,
I start to cry, nobody's home,
I love you so, and now you know.'

Her gaze lingered on his face as long as she dared; then she turned back to the piano for the final chorus. As the song drew to a close, she inhaled and let her fingers meander through the upper register of the keyboard, weaving strains of 'Lilac Waltz' into the descant.

'By and by, how time flies.'

As the song finished, Jane closed her eyes and bowed to the piano.

For a moment, all was still.

The room exploded with applause. Jane opened her eyes. For a split second, she saw a rainbow of color swirling over the audience.

Then Loretta Mays, the most decorated musician of the year, stood before her. Her face was radiant as she clapped for Jane.

'Bravo,' she said.

The rows behind followed suit. Jane saw a flash of pink as Lacey got to her feet. She could hear Kyle and Rich shouting from the back. Hannibal Fang let out a whoop, and Morgan clapped politely. Jesse stood with the others but did not lift his eyes to the stage.

As Jane rose from the bench, her eyes landed on the record executives. Lenny Davis looked grim. Vincent Ray was ready to teach her another lesson. Let him try; Jane had yet to learn something she didn't want to know.

Andy Williams hurried back onstage, and the cameras swooped around him. For a moment, Jane was left in shadow; then Andy beckoned her into the light.

'Well, that was unexpected, wasn't it?' he said. 'Guess that's rock and roll!'

Jane took a small bow and slipped into the wings as the crowd continued to cheer.

Offstage, her whole body pulsed. She looked back toward Jesse; his face was turned up to Andy now, laughing at a quip.

Willy stepped forward, shaking his head. 'Were you planning that?' he said, handing Jane a glass of water.

Jane shook her head.

He beamed at her. 'That's the Jane I know,' he said.

'Getting us fucked,' said Jane.

'Oh, so hard,' said Willy.

46

The next day, Jane stepped off the ferry and into a four-way embrace with Maggie, Elsie, and Grace. As they walked arm in arm back to the station wagon, they passed a crowd of local high-school girls holding 'What Would Jane Do?' signs.

'Jane, we love you!'

'You're my idol!'

'Jane, will you go to prom with my brother?'

'Aw, you finally got invited,' said Maggie.

That night, the Quinns sat on the porch of Gray Gables, nestled amidst an array of candles and wool blankets. Elsie cracked open a bottle of lilac wine, and all four of them sprawled on the steps, drinking and looking up at the stars.

'Gran knew,' said Maggie. 'You sat down at that piano and she goes, "They're not getting 'Spring Fling.'"'

'You had this look you had as a baby when we'd try to feed you vegetable mash,' said Elsie.

'Still disgusting,' said Jane.

'What happened?' said Grace.

'I couldn't go through with it,' said Jane as an image of Jesse zipped through her mind.

'Interesting,' said Elsie. She winked. 'There's good medicine in sticking it to the man.'

Jane laughed. 'You may have to remind me of that when the man is burying my next album in a place the sun don't shine,' she said.

'It truly was an amazing performance,' said Grace.

Elsie nodded. 'You don't get that from me,' she said.

'I think we know where she gets it from,' said Maggie.

The next day, Jane and Grace drove up to the Center. They watched from the sunporch as Charlie finished her calisthenics class on the recreation lawn.

'Who is she winking at?' said Jane.

'Paparazzi,' said Grace.

After the class concluded, Jane and Grace joined her for a visit on the patio.

'Jane!' said Charlie excitedly. 'You're back! How was your trip? Where were you again?'

Jane never knew how much her mother would remember from their previous conversations; in this moment, Charlie struck her as almost normal.

'New York,' said Jane.

'How exciting,' said Charlie. 'What were you doing in New York? You'll have to forgive me, I've been so busy here, I've lost track.'

Jane looked at Grace. 'I was at the Grammys,' she said. She wasn't even sure if her mother would know what they were – the award show hadn't been around long when Charlie had been committed.

'You were?' said Charlie, her eyes getting large. 'That's so strange. I was, too! We must have just missed each other.'

'How funny,' said Jane automatically.

'I didn't see you,' said Charlie. 'Did you see me? I was wearing a black dress and silver chains! And I went onstage, and I played the piano so beautifully. I was supposed to play someone else's song, and they were so surprised when I played "Lilac Waltz" instead.' She snickered at her own trickiness.

Jane and Grace exchanged looks.

'Well?' said Charlie. 'Did you see me?'

'Yes,' said Jane. 'I did.'

'And?' said Charlie. 'Wasn't I good?'

'The best,' said Jane.

'Do you know, Jane, I wrote that song,' she said.

'Yes, I know,' said Jane.

Charlie smiled, and for a moment she looked like her old self. Then another patient crossed the patio, waving to Charlie; his caretaker followed behind, carrying two badminton rackets.

'That's Tony Trabert,' said Charlie, waving back. 'He's already won the U.S. Open – twice!'

Half an hour later, Mary came out to give Charlie her medication, and Grace and Jane bade her farewell. The moments following a visit with Charlie were always silent. Grace put a hand on Jane's shoulder, and the two of them walked back into the main house. As they passed through the recreation room, Jane paused beside a large Zenith television set.

'They must have had it on in here,' she said.

'Sounds like, in her way, she thought you were good,' said Grace.

It was twilight as they walked back into the parking lot. Jane offered Grace a cigarette, and they stood together, smoking and watching the gulls glide above the trees.

'Do you think she actually wrote "Lilac Waltz"?' said Jane, after a moment.

Grace shrugged. 'Does it matter?' she said.

Jane regarded her aunt with surprise. 'If it hadn't been for that song, she wouldn't be in here.'

Grace gave her a strange look. 'I don't actually know if that's true,' she said. 'After seeing Charlie like this for so many years, I think things would have shaken out this way no matter what.'

'What do you mean?' said Jane.

Grace exhaled. 'Something was always going to trigger her symptoms,' said Grace. 'She was always going to end up in the Center. I was always going to fight to keep her here. Song or no song, there was no scenario that didn't end with this.'

Jane took a drag on her cigarette and watched the birds soar into the darkening sky.

Jane knew there would be fallout from the Grammys, and she waited to hear from Willy as she settled back into Island life. Weeks passed, long enough for several monthly periodicals to print articles demanding a second single from *Ursa Major*.

It was May when the phone rang.

'Jane, it just so happens I'm on the Island,' said Willy.

'No one *just so happens* to be on the Island,' said Jane.

'Well, I am,' said Willy. 'Lunch at the Regent's Cove Hotel in an hour.'

'Okay,' said Jane. 'But Pegasus is buying.'

Willy chuckled and hung up.

The air was warm and sweet with blossoms; Jane threw on a sundress and walked into town.

She knew that Willy must be coming from Jesse and Morgan's

house and tried to put the thought from her mind. She hadn't heard from Jesse after the Grammys, nor had she expected to. She had hoped that the experience would give her more closure. Elsie and Grace continued to tell her to give it time, but Jane doubted there would ever be a time when she didn't think of Jesse.

A hostess showed Jane to Willy's table. He smiled up at her, the harbor reflected in his blue aviators. After they placed their orders, the server returned with champagne.

'What's this?' said Jane.

'We're celebrating,' said Willy.

'You're going to be a father,' said Jane.

'In a manner of speaking,' he said. He lifted a glass, and Jane mirrored him.

'To freedom,' he said.

'To . . . freedom,' said Jane. They sipped.

Willy leaned forward. 'Pegasus is about to file for bankruptcy,' he said, a grin spreading across his face.

'You're joking,' said Jane.

Willy shook his head. 'I knew something was up that day they cornered us,' he said. 'There's no way the whole board would weigh in on a creative matter like that if the company weren't in serious straits.

'Turns out, the Breakers' album was one of the few that actually profited in the past few years, because the production budget and advance were so low. They were trying to produce a few more hits to appease the shareholders without causing a stir.'

Willy gulped from his flute.

'As if that ever works,' he said. '*Snitch* is about to print an exposé on the whole thing. After the Grammys, this reporter

– apparently a big fan of yours – started digging into why you were going to sing "Spring Fling" in the first place, and, lo and behold, it turns out the company is completely insolvent. They're liquidating everything by the end of the quarter.'

'So . . . what does that mean?' said Jane.

Willy grinned. 'It means your contract is null and void,' he said. 'You're free to go anywhere you choose. Which brings me to the second part of this announcement: Black Sheep Records.'

'Oh?' said Jane.

'What do you think?' said Willy. 'Too on the nose?'

'I like it,' said Jane. 'So . . . you're starting a label? At which studio?'

'My own studio,' said Willy. 'I have enough saved up, and with you – hopefully – and Jesse and a few others, we should be turning a profit in a couple years.'

'That's amazing,' said Jane. She and Jesse would still be under the same label; the idea was comforting.

'I don't think you realize how amazing it is,' said Willy. 'Jane, they're going to have to sell off their backlist. You're going to be able to buy back the rights to *Ursa Major.*'

'Willy, I don't have that kind of money,' said Jane.

'You will,' said Willy. 'And until then, I do.'

Jane sat back in her chair.

'To freedom,' she said.

47

Malinda King glimmered onstage, scatting up a storm with her band, The Lost Cause, as the dance floor churned beneath indigo lights. Morgan watched from the balcony as the boy she'd been observing finally pulled his girl into a corner.

She and Jesse had wanted the locals to feel welcome at Silo, and these two were definitely local. The girl wore a peasant blouse and jeans, the boy a starched-collar shirt. Morgan had the sense that she was watching a big night out for two unglamorous people.

Yet she couldn't take her eyes off them.

Over several songs, the girl had blossomed under the boy's gaze. Morgan couldn't imagine his thoughts had been anything profound or poetic, but it didn't matter – the two of them were the lead characters in a film tonight, and the way the boy was looking at the girl was making her feel beautiful. Every time they touched, they held on a little longer, until, at last, the boy pulled the girl to him and kissed her.

Morgan watched them retreat into shadow. She lit a cigarette.

She and Jesse had wanted to make the kind of place where people would brag about who they'd seen perform, or what they'd done in the bathrooms; Silo had been constructed like a labyrinth full of dark corners, nooks, and crannies for this express purpose.

Morgan had loved the idea of Jesse pulling her into such a spot, of stealing away from their hosting duties for illicit moments of passion. In her fantasy, she would catch him staring, and she'd smile, and the two of them would slip away to the nearest closet.

Morgan exhaled a jet of smoke through her nose. She had begun to suspect that that kind of passion wasn't going to be a part of her life anymore. She was still young, barely twenty-four, but when she compared herself with the kids she'd just seen making out, she felt ancient.

She and Jesse had had some of that in the beginning, but as time went on, it had become clear that Jesse was already in a relationship, and that Morgan would always be the other woman.

On the outside, Morgan looked like she had it all – the looks, the career, the marriage. But the truth was that she lived her life in snatches, grabbing handfuls of attention between Jesse's injections. Morgan had loved him from a distance for years, and when it turned out up close he had problems, she had felt uniquely suited to take them on.

Her own father had been talented but distant. Morgan had honed all the necessary skills to live with a great man over a childhood spent waiting for just the right moment to ask for affection, knowing that if she timed her appeals wrong the penalty would be coldness and derision.

Her analyst sometimes used words like 'enabling' and 'enmeshment,' but to Morgan, it felt as though she had a special skill set that had found a home. When she had learned of

Jesse's proclivities, she accepted them in stride. Lots of people had issues; that was no reason to write off someone who was otherwise a catch. When Jesse told her that he didn't want to be this way forever, she believed him.

Time for Morgan now played out in a series of 'maybe when's: Maybe when he finishes his album he'll realize he needs to stop. Maybe when we get married he won't want it anymore. Maybe when the club is open. Maybe when he wins a Grammy.

Each of these benchmarks fueled her hope; but as each one passed without any sign of change, it became harder and harder to justify her belief. The 'maybe when's began to darken. Maybe when I leave for a week and don't tell him where I'm going. Maybe when I leave forever.

The Lost Cause began to play the introduction for 'Sea Runner,' an up-tempo number that usually ran nine minutes. It was nearly 1:00 a.m.; most of the VIPs had gone on to other parties by now. Part of why Morgan had wanted to open a club on the Island rather than in New York was that last call here was at 2:00 a.m. This left her time to hang out with the performers after their shows. Morgan loved every bit of running a musical venue, from sound check to set striking.

As with most things, Jesse had liked the idea of the club more than he had liked the actual club. The two of them usually made an appearance around 11:00 p.m.; the possibility of getting to see them was a huge draw, and they both understood this as part of their investment. But these walk-throughs had become compulsory and contained little joy for either of them; at the first chance he got, Jesse snuck away to shoot up.

Morgan could picture him now, lying in the office behind the stage, sprawled on their green leather sofa with a rubber tourniquet tied around his arm. The first few times Morgan had seen him this way, she had been so repulsed that she wasn't sure if she could go through with it.

But then he'd come out of it and look at her with those eyes, and she'd fall deeper in love, feeling like it was her chosen task to bring him through this, believing him when he told her how ashamed he felt and how much he wanted to stop.

It was a long way from passionately fucking in the bathroom, which is what she felt that local couple must be doing by now.

Morgan inhaled the final puff from her cigarette, the tip flitting like a red tetra in the blue light of the room, and gloried in the sound of Malinda King's voice scrambling over the hills and dales of 'Sea Runner.'

As Morgan exhaled, she coughed, surprised by the amount of smoke in her lungs. Her eyes teared. She stubbed out her cigarette on the balcony railing.

People all around her had begun to cough. Morgan peered through the dim light onto the floor below. Silo had a smoke machine that they sometimes used to make the room feel full as the crowd thinned. Morgan walked over to the intercom and called downstairs to the bar. Her floor manager, Dennis, picked up.

'Hey,' she said, 'do we have the smoke machine on?'

Before he could answer, the mic squealed onstage as Malinda King's powerful lungs began to hack. The band continued to play, waiting for her to recover. Then her drummer ejected himself from behind his set, looking wildly off to stage right.

'Fire!' he yelled.

Morgan's whole body went rigid.

'Get the lights on,' she said. 'Call the fire department.' She hung up the phone and raced down the stairs from the balcony.

The crowd was drunk and uncomprehending. All around Morgan, people twitched their heads this way and that, like rodents confused by their own shadows.

Morgan was halfway across the dance floor when the lights came on. The rafters and balcony had filled with black smoke, thick plumes billowing into the room like tentacles.

At the sight, pupils dilated and dreamers woke. The band rushed past Morgan, leading the charge toward the front exit.

Without the music, a crackling sound became audible, then a ripping; the backdrop curtain burst into flame, crimson holes gaping like mouths between the folds.

'You need to leave,' said Dennis, grabbing Morgan's arm.

'I think Jesse's back there,' she said, shaking him off. The crowd around her shrieked as Morgan sped backstage, Dennis on her heels.

The door to the office had been locked. Morgan's hands shook as she flipped keys around a ring, willing the correct one to rise to the top.

'Here,' said Dennis. He shoved his key in the lock and used his shirt to grab the doorknob.

Black smoke gushed out and Morgan rushed in, almost tripping over two massive feet.

Jesse had passed out on the floor. Something wasn't right; even when he was out of it, he usually responded with a noise or a small movement. Morgan and Dennis sat him up, and a foamy substance plopped out of his mouth, his neck snapping back like a ragdoll's.

'Is he—'

Dennis shook his head – Jesse was alive.

The room had almost completely filled with smoke – falling onto the floor might just have saved Jesse life.

They crouched as low to the ground as possible and dragged Jesse out of the office. Panic rose in Morgan's chest; his skin felt like rubber, his bones like lead.

'He needs a hospital,' said Dennis. But a hospital wasn't an option. People couldn't see Jesse Reid like this – he'd be charged with possession then excoriated by the press.

They had talked about what to do if it ever came to this. A name flashed through Morgan's mind.

'Let's get him out the back door,' she said.

48

Grace and Jane had passed out in front of an *I Love Lucy* marathon, covered in chocolate wrappers. By the time the phone awoke them, the television station had signed off. As Grace moved to answer, her figure cut through vibrating neon strips.

'Hello?' she said. The clock over the sink read 2:05 a.m. 'This is Grace.'

Jane sat up and switched off the TV. She heard her aunt gasp.

'Of course I remember Jesse,' she said. Jane felt the oxygen drain out of the room. All signs of sleep evaporated off Grace as she listened to the person on the other end of the phone.

'You should take him to the hospital,' said Grace.

A pause.

'I understand,' she said.

Another pause.

'Yes,' she said. 'Yes. What is the address?' She took a pencil from the tin beside the phone and wrote down the response.

'I can be there in twenty-five minutes. Keep him on his side.' She hung up the phone. For a moment she was still. Then she looked at Jane.

'That was Morgan Vidal. Jesse's overdosed,' she said.

Jane's heart began to pound. Grace was already moving toward the door. She grabbed her emergency bag from the hall.

'Come, Jane, I need you,' said Grace, taking the keys off the hook by the light switch. Jane was at her side in three steps.

'Let me drive,' said Jane.

As they tore up-Island, Grace filled her in.

'There's been a fire up at Silo,' she said. 'The main roads are all blocked.'

Gray Gables was ten minutes closer to the Shack than Bayleen Island Emergency Services anyway, but with the traffic, they could potentially beat an ambulance by twenty minutes.

'Every second matters right now,' said Grace.

Jane blew past a red light as Grace reached into her bag to make preparations.

'What's going to happen?' said Jane, glancing over as Grace pulled medicine into a syringe and flicked the end.

'Naloxone might be able to halt the overdose, temporarily,' said Grace. 'It doesn't last as long as heroin, so even if it works I'll have to keep administering it. It sounds like he might have taken something else – we'll have to pump his stomach.'

Jane swallowed. She had assisted with the procedure several times over her years at the Center; her role was minimal, but the idea of having to watch Jesse go through it made her quail.

'Is he going to be okay?' she said.

'I don't know, Jane. I don't know when he injected himself or how much he used or what. Don't know if he was burned.'

Jane kept her eyes on the road. She knew that Jesse and Morgan's compound was adjacent to Silo, but she did not know where they had concealed the entrance. As they neared the club, car horns crowed inside a gridlock inching away from the blaze; Jane could see a red-and-blue haze in the distance, thick as pastel smudge.

'Hang a left by Holmes Farm,' Grace instructed.

Jane's adrenaline surged as they switched off the main road away from the jam. Their headlights seared through the dark, tires jostling over the unpaved drive. It looked as if the property was as secluded as Jesse had hoped.

A light blinked through the trees like a spirit guiding them forward. As Jane pulled into a clearing, a lantern came into relief at the foot of a hulking, dark edifice.

A door opened, and Morgan Vidal stepped into the light.

'Here we go,' said Grace.

Jane slowed, and Grace sprang from the car, sprinting after Morgan.

Jane parked and removed a cooler full of emergency medical supplies from the trunk.

As Jane's eyes adjusted, she took in the house. It was a chimera. Conflicting styles of architecture – from large barn doors to a medieval-looking spire – had been jigsawed together in a way that heightened Jane's sense of having fallen into a fairy-tale nightmare.

The kitchen was part Tuscan villa, part country cupboard. As Jane entered, she heard the sound of Morgan's voice in a room beyond. She passed under a lattice of polished copper pots and into a darkened hall. Heart rioting, she followed a light down the corridor into a palatial living room.

Jesse was on the floor, spread out on a bedsheet. He looked skeletal and wan, and so still Jane felt her lungs contract. This person with so much music in him lay before her mute and broken; Jane steeled herself. Until they had finished their work, she had to think of him as an instrument in need of repair, and nothing more.

'Jane,' said Morgan. 'What are you doing here?'

'Jane's trained to perform gastric suction – I brought her to assist me,' said Grace, kneeling beside Jesse, pulling on rubber gloves.

Morgan looked like she might argue; then Grace held up a naloxone syringe and flicked the end.

She lifted Jesse's arm and checked for a working vein.

'Jane, scissors,' she said. Jane reached in Grace's bag and extracted a pair of shears.

'What are you doing?' said Morgan.

Grace cut open the leg of Jesse's jeans. Jane looked away as Grace inserted the needle into his thigh.

A moment passed, then two; then Jesse's eyelids began to flutter. Jane placed the cooler near his feet and put on a pair of rubber gloves.

'Let's get him up,' said Grace. The man standing with Morgan bent forward and helped support Jesse in a seated position. Morgan rushed forward with a chintz ottoman to prop him up.

'Jesse, sweetie, stay with me,' said Grace. She motioned to Jane, who handed her a bottle of anesthetic spray. Grace pried open Jesse's mouth, and he made a noise that sounded like a child's cry. Jane began to lubricate the suction tube.

'What was your name?'

'Dennis.'

'Hold him steady,' said Grace.

She administered the spray and handed it back to Jane, who gave her the tube in exchange.

369

'Jesse, sweetie, I'm going to need you to swallow.'

Morgan watched in silent agony behind the ottoman. Jane caught her eye.

'Do you have a bucket?' she said. 'Or a pot?'

Morgan nodded and left the room.

'Open, Jesse,' said Grace. 'There you go, sweetie. I know, I know.'

Jane turned away and began filling hundred-milliliter plastic syringes with saline solution. Behind her, she could hear Jesse's legs thrashing against the floor as Grace forced the tube down his throat, inch by inch. Jane shuddered. At least he was moving.

'I know, sweetie,' said Grace. 'I know.'

Morgan returned and set a copper lobster pot beside Jane – clearly a wedding gift. She stood there watching Jesse, unable to move. Jane remembered the first time she'd seen her mother sedated and felt a wave of pity. It was easier for her to focus on Morgan right now than on Jesse.

'Almost there,' said Grace. 'Jane.'

Morgan stumbled back as Jane handed her aunt a stethoscope and an empty syringe. Grace attached the syringe to the tube and sent a puff of air into Jesse's stomach; she listened with the stethoscope for the sound.

'I'm in,' she said. She unhooked the empty syringe, and Jane handed her one filled with saline. Slowly, Grace injected the liquid into Jesse's stomach to expel its toxic contents. When she pulled the plunger back out, the barrel filled with a disconcerting yellow fluid.

Grace detached the syringe and Jane handed her another, ejecting the stomach contents into the copper pot with a metallic splash. She refilled the syringe with saline.

They worked in this rhythm until the syringe barrel refilled with the clear liquid they'd been pumping into Jesse's stomach.

'Jane,' said Grace. Jane handed Grace a saline bag. Jesse whimpered.

'Easy there, sweetie,' said Grace.

Dennis and Grace hoisted Jesse onto the couch, and Grace inserted an IV portal into his thigh. Jane handed her a metal stand, and they secured the bag.

As Jane and Grace stood back, Morgan crouched beside Jesse and began to murmur in his ear.

Grace placed a hand on Jane's shoulder. Jane couldn't take her eyes from Jesse's face. They weren't out of danger yet; it wasn't clear that the naloxone had worked, and now Jesse had been completely dehydrated, which presented a new set of problems. Jane just wanted to see him open his eyes. Unfortunately, their fluttering seemed to be slowing.

'Grace,' said Morgan nervously.

'I see him,' said Grace. 'Thank you, Jane. Why don't you get this stuff outside?'

Jane began to pack up the refuse into a bio-waste bag as Grace reached into her supplies and drew out a second syringe of naloxone. Jane heard her aunt snap on a fresh pair of rubber gloves as she left the room.

Jane sat alone in the station wagon, listening to the crickets through the car window.

She closed her eyes and thought about the sad, beautiful boy who had once told her he loved her. There had been a brief moment when she might have been mistress of this place; she'd spent so long regretting that she hadn't been.

She could picture how different it would have looked if the

two of them had made it together, how much happier, how much more cohesive.

You can't tear a light from its darkness.

Jane lit a cigarette with shaky hands.

The one thing she could not picture was a scenario in which Jesse was clean. No matter how she shifted the details in her head, he was always an addict.

Jane exhaled.

She heard a knock on the window. Jane looked up and saw Morgan outside.

'Can I come in?' she said.

'Please,' said Jane. Morgan lowered herself into the passenger's seat. Jane took in her frizzled hair and bloodshot eyes; even in this condition, Morgan still looked glamorous. Jane offered her a cigarette, which she accepted.

'I wanted to thank you,' she said.

Jane handed her the lighter. 'Please, don't,' she said.

Morgan lit up. 'Your aunt is amazing,' she said after a moment. Her graceful fingers closed around her famously simple wedding band, sliding it up to her knuckle and back.

'I used to hear stories about her, when Jesse and I were first together,' she said. 'He'd always talk about the Quinns over in Regent's Cove. I remember, when we started building this place, he'd say, "I want our house to feel like the Quinns' house."' Then, one day, I put together that the Quinns of Regent's Cove were the same as Jane Quinn, and the stories stopped.

'Do you remember the first time we met?' asked Morgan. 'The first time we actually met, at the Shack?' Jane nodded, surprised that Morgan did.

'I remember thinking, *Holy shit, she is beautiful, and he is going to fall in love with her.* I don't think he ever stopped loving you. Not completely.' Jane tensed. Morgan went on.

'I don't think I realized how serious it was until the Silo opening,' she said. 'We've never performed that way, before or since. I'm sure it was because you were in the crowd. I told myself not to be threatened by it – you'd had your chance, and you let him go.'

Morgan shook her head. 'I felt so superior. Even when things started to get bad, I'd think: At least I'm not Jane Quinn. At least I didn't miss out on *Jesse Reid.* As if sticking around for this is some kind of honor.'

Tears glistened in her eyes as she spoke. 'I'm so tired, Jane. Two years of marriage, and I feel like I'm middle-aged. I worry all the time that something like this will happen. And now it finally has, and I almost feel . . . relieved. What if he isn't okay and my first reaction was relief?'

'Jesse's going to be okay,' said Jane. *He has to be.*

'Until when?' said Morgan. 'The next overdose? This isn't what I want. I don't want this to be my life.'

Jane sat with Morgan as she wept. She didn't know what to say. For the first time in a long time, she didn't think she would want this to be her life, either.

49

Jane awoke to Grace tapping on the car window. Morgan had gone, and daylight filtered down through the trees in white shafts. Grace's shirt was covered in patches of varying hues, and her eyes were swollen, but as she slid into the passenger's seat her expression was calm.

'He's stable,' said Grace. 'I've called Betty to relieve me.'

Jane saw that another car had joined them in the driveway. She didn't start the engine; she wanted to go in and see for herself.

'It's time to go, Jane,' said Grace. 'He's going to be okay.'

As they drove back to Regent's Cove, Grace theorized that Jesse had shot up just as the fire was beginning. His survival came down to factors no one could have predicted or controlled.

'He is so lucky,' said Grace. 'I don't think I've ever met a luckier man.'

Silo had not been so fortunate. As Jane and Grace walked into the kitchen, they found Elsie looking at a photo of the club, smoldering in ruins on the front page of *The Island Gazette*.

The fire department suspected it had been started by a cigarette that hadn't been properly extinguished; they had arrived

374

on the scene in less than ten minutes, but the roof had already caught fire. By the time they managed to contain the blaze, the structure had caved in.

This had been the last straw for Morgan. When Grace arrived at the compound for Jesse's follow-up, she had walked in on Morgan imploring Jesse to check himself into a facility. Jesse had outright refused.

'You need managed care,' Morgan said desperately. 'I – I can't handle this. I won't.'

She proceeded to call Dr. Reid, who drove over to collect his son. Grace helped Jesse into the passenger's seat of his father's BMW, holding his IV bag like a child who had won a goldfish at a country fair.

'You'll . . . come?' Dr. Reid said to Grace through the car window. Grace nodded and followed them back to the Shack. A few hours later, Morgan flew to New York.

That night, Jane came downstairs to find Elsie and Grace speaking in hushed tones on the porch. Fireflies wove among uncut lilac branches. Jane paused in the hall, listening unseen at the door.

'Dr. Reid has been giving him methadone to lessen the withdrawal symptoms, but he really needs to be in treatment,' said Grace. 'Once the depression sets in, there will be nothing to stop him from turning back. Or worse.'

'He must be scared,' said Elsie. 'Maybe too scared to accept how serious this is? Is there someone he trusts who can ease him into it?'

'His father cares, but he's too heavy-handed,' said Grace

'What about a friend?' said Elsie.

Grace tutted. 'Show-business people are such phonies. Plus,

people don't show up for mental illness – they don't want to see it.'

Elsie considered. 'What got him through a few summers ago? He was in worse physical condition then.'

'I think it was Jane,' said Grace. 'I still think, for him, it's Jane. When he came to yesterday morning and he saw me, he said her name and started to cry.'

Jane held her breath.

'I feel for the boy,' said Elsie. 'But Jane's just getting over him. This isn't her responsibility.'

'I know,' said Grace. 'I know. I just feel . . . Mom, he might not live.' Jane realized that Grace was crying.

Elsie put an arm around her. 'Grace,' she said, 'it's not your responsibility, either.'

Jane had never seen Grace cry or let Elsie mother her. As she backed away from the porch, Jane found herself staring at her own reflection in the hall mirror. Jesse was truly in danger.

Jane lay awake that night thinking about what would happen if she showed up at the Shack. It had been two years since they'd broken up. So much had changed – but in that moment, she felt as if nothing had. She remembered Jesse's words from Christmas Eve.

The more I thought about it, the more it began to seem like all I would need to do was get in a car and drive over. And so I did.

The next morning, Jane ate breakfast, got in the car to go to Maggie's, and drove to the Shack instead. She had no plan, just the conviction that she had to do this. The way felt natural and familiar; how often had she taken this drive in her mind?

She checked in at the security gate, and when she pulled up to the house, Dr. Reid came out to greet her.

'Jane,' he said, with a warmth that surprised her. The imposing figure she remembered from years before had been replaced by an old man terrified for his son. It struck Jane that this had always been the case, and she just hadn't been able to see it.

Dr. Reid led Jane through the living room to the back porch, overlooking the lawn. Through the French doors, Jane could see Jesse seated in a wicker chair.

'Jesse,' said Dr. Reid, 'you have a visitor.'

As Jane stepped onto the porch, Jesse sat up a little. His eyes met hers, then darted away.

'I'll leave you two,' said Dr. Reid. He disappeared back into the house.

Jesse looked emaciated; large violet circles shadowed his eyes, and his arms were discolored with bruises. He was no longer on the IV, Jane noticed. A cigarette rested in his hand.

'Can I have one of those?' Jane asked. Jesse didn't move, and Jane began to wonder whether this had been a mistake. Then he nudged the cigarette box and matches toward her.

'I suppose it's the least I can do,' he said. He glanced up. 'Thank you,' he said.

'It's good to see you,' said Jane after a beat.

Jesse looked away.

Jane lit a cigarette and inhaled. It was a hazy day, and the air was close. The porch seemed to be holding the sunlight like a broiler – she could see a sheen of sweat on the ridge of Jesse's brow.

'Can you walk?' she asked. He looked at her, then gazed across the yard. He nodded.

'Won't you—' He pushed down on the arms of the chair to

raise himself, and Jane supported him as he stood. She helped him down the stairs, and he continued to hold on to her as they traversed the lawn. He smelled like ethanol, but also like himself. Wordlessly, they headed to a little woodland path that Jane recalled from summers before.

Beneath the leafy canopy, Jesse seemed to breathe easier. They walked together, listening to the forest, following alongside a trickling stream until they came to a footbridge. There they stopped so Jesse could rest against the railing. He let go of Jane's arm and lit another cigarette, and the two of them stood, wordlessly passing it back and forth. Finally, Jesse spoke.

'Why are you here?' he said.

Jane swallowed. 'I wanted to make sure you were okay,' she said.

Jesse eyed her with suspicion. 'You're here to try to get me to commit myself,' he said. 'Is someone putting you up to this? Is my father?'

Jane said nothing.

Jesse let out a groan of frustration. 'You may recall that I haven't exactly had banner experiences with institutions,' he said, his expression closing like a drawbridge.

Jane reacted on instinct. 'You may recall, I know better than most what they're like,' she said.

Jesse's eyebrows shot up. He waited for her to continue.

'I – I hope you know it wasn't personal,' said Jane. 'I wasn't out to deceive you.'

Jesse looked at the bruises on his arm. 'You probably thought I deserved it,' he said.

'I never thought that,' said Jane. 'I . . . I wanted to tell you.'

'Really.'

'Yes,' said Jane. 'The night you asked me to tour with you, I was going to.'

Jesse eyed her.

'So . . . what happened?' he said.

Jane stared at him. 'You kissed me,' she said.

Jesse's eyes involuntarily flicked to her mouth. He looked away. 'You had other opportunities after that,' he said.

'And I made other attempts,' said Jane.

His eyes bored into her. 'Like when?' he said.

Jane took a breath. It had all happened so long ago, she wondered if he'd even remember.

'Chicago,' she said. 'There was that woman at the Winery.'

'Who threw the wineglass at the stage?' said Jesse.

Jane nodded. 'The night of my mom's break, she threw a bottle onstage at the Folk Fest. At Tommy Patton.'

Jesse's eyes flickered in recognition. 'I remember, in the alley, you started to tell me something,' he said.

'I wanted to tell you about Charlie,' said Jane. 'I . . . had been wanting to tell you for weeks, but I lost my nerve.'

Jesse watched her, his expression unreadable.

'Then there was Christmas,' she said. Despite himself, Jesse's eyes shone in recognition.

'That's why you were so shaken when Tommy Patton didn't recognize you,' said Jesse. 'You were afraid "Lilac Waltz" had been a delusion.'

Jane nodded. 'I came so close that night, closer than I ever had before,' she said. 'But when you've been living with a secret for so long . . . the words don't always come.'

'They did in "Ursa Major,"' he said.

Jane tucked a strand of hair behind her ear. 'Yes,' she said.

'"Evenings turning to a spoon,"' said Jesse. 'I was so convinced that was about me.'

'It was,' said Jane. 'I just didn't realize it at the time.'

Jesse's eyes widened.

'There was a lot I had hidden from myself,' said Jane. 'I had so much to face that I couldn't bear to look at head-on, and so it just . . . came out sideways, through my music.

'I . . . I thought I was writing "Ursa Major" about Charlie. It wasn't until later that I began to see what the song was really about,' she said.

Jesse watched her intently.

'"Starry signs themselves reflecting" . . . that's not me and Charlie,' she said. 'It's you and Charlie. Part of why I feel this connection to you is because . . . because you're like her. I mean, you're both original, talented—' Jesse's expression darkened. '—Unstable.'

Jane frowned. 'You inspired me,' she said.

Jesse took a shallow breath.

'I just wasn't available,' said Jane. 'It's taken me years and distance to understand how tied I was to Charlie and her crazy universe. It was sad, but it was safe – safe in that, no matter how hard I tried to fix it, I could always predict the outcome.

'You were different,' said Jane. 'You were dangerous.'

Jesse laughed. 'How was I dangerous?' he said.

Jane took a breath. 'You were dangerous because, with you, I could really hope,' she said. 'And when I saw what you were doing to yourself, I had this vision of myself just waiting for years on that hope, and . . . I had to get out.'

For a moment, Jane thought she had angered him. Then he lowered his eyes.

'You were right,' he said. 'You would have been waiting.'

A gust of wind rustled the trees.

'Ever since my mom died, I've struggled with the fact that I'm here and she's not,' he said. 'I wish you could have known her, Jane. Her light, her goodness . . . it's never made sense to me that she died and I lived.' He rubbed his jaw. 'When I met you, you just shined,' he said. 'I wanted to take care of you . . . like I hadn't been able to take care of her.'

He smiled faintly. 'You weren't having it, though,' he said. 'That's the thing with you. You're the one person who never seemed to want anything from me.'

He frowned. 'I've done things I'm not proud of. I never should have married Morgan. Part of me wanted to believe we could make a go of it, but deep down I knew better. I just did it because the label said I should and because you wouldn't have me.'

Jane blushed.

'That night at Silo,' he said, 'I was so angry. I was angry that you'd lied, but deep down I was just angry you'd said no. I wanted to make you feel regret. Playing that song with Morgan was cruel. And the things I said after . . .' He shook his head. 'Even then, all I could think for the rest of the night was, *Did she leave with Hannibal Fang?*'

He cleared his throat.

'It was only after you disappeared that I began to realize how unfair I'd been,' he said. 'I had put you on a pedestal no one could live up to.'

Jane's cheeks burned. 'And now you know I'm just another person,' she said.

Jesse's brow creased. 'No,' he said. 'You will never be just another person to me.'

381

For a moment, the breeze stopped.

'I thought, for a while, I was over it,' he said. 'Then I heard you sing "Wallflower," and I . . . I'm just a fool for you. I thought, *I have to stay away, or I don't have half a prayer of being a husband.*'

Jane's mouth went dry. 'When I sang that, I'd really been struggling,' she said. 'Everything you had said about the label had come to pass. I felt so defeated, I couldn't see a way out.'

Jesse looked at her with those brilliant blue eyes, and it rushed back to Jane how beautiful she found him – at once startling and familiar.

'I was actually going to play "Spring Fling" that night. But then I saw you, and I just felt . . .' She touched her hand to her stomach.

'What?' he said.

Jane swallowed. 'Glad,' she said. 'You've always made me glad.'

Jesse took a step toward her.

Jane took a breath. 'You looked at me, and I just thought, *Fuck it.*'

Jane looked into his face. The sunlight shifted, and for a moment Jesse looked restored to her, strong and young.

'I've missed you so much,' she said.

'Oh, Jane,' he said. His fingers closed around hers.

He bent so their foreheads touched. As they stood together, Jane shut her eyes and allowed herself to steal into a world where this could just be it. They'd be together, and because of that, nothing else would matter.

They stayed like that, until a breeze stirred. When Jane reopened her eyes, she saw that the sun had moved again, and Jesse had begun to sweat. Fear prickled through her.

Jesse wasn't well.

Cold chains of dread snaked through her chest, pulling, pulling.

Please don't leave me alone.

Jane began to weep.

Jesse wrapped her in his arms, and let her tears soak into his shirt.

'I don't want you to die,' she said. Blood rushed into her ears, filling them with shapeless sound.

As her tears subsided, the whispering of the leaves returned to her. She took a step back. Jesse studied the tracks of her tears, then reached up and wiped them away. He took her hand.

'It's not getting clean that worries me,' he said. 'It's what comes after, when it's just me, trapped in my own brain, every day, for the rest of my life.'

Jane's heart began to pound. He was lowering the drawbridge.

'You don't know what it will be like,' said Jane. 'You don't know. For all we know, you could live to be an old man who looks back on his life in wonder.'

He shook his head.

'I don't think I'll live that long,' said Jesse.

Jane flinched.

'I'm just being honest,' he said. 'Every day I wake up will be a day that I have to face this. There isn't one day that won't be a struggle. Why should I even try?'

Jane remembered a night she had lain beneath the stars, terrified of facing herself. She gripped Jesse's hand. 'Because,' she said, 'you can. Because being able to struggle is a gift.'

Jane could feel the energy of the island thrumming around them, the salt in the air, the taper of the land. There was music in the wind, simple chords waiting to be spun into harmonies. She looked into Jesse's eyes and knew he could hear them, too.

They passed a long moment, listening together to the songs in the trees. Then, carefully, they left the footbridge and made their way back to the house.

When Grace arrived at the Center that evening, the staff room was abuzz; earlier that day, Jesse Reid had checked himself in for treatment.

50

The Island Gazette

August 1, 2022

Jen Edison

This Sunday marked the ribbon-cutting ceremony for Silo Park and Wildlife Refuge. Attendees included park beneficiary Trent Mayhew, as well as members of the town council of Caverswall, and a host of Island figures with personal connections to the legend of Silo.

Much of the original structure has been cleared away in the course of the park's long and often delayed construction, but the development team was able to salvage a few artifacts.

A knowing eye might recognize the planter in the center of the Meditation Garden as the wagon-wheel chandelier, now filled in with colorful perennials. The wisteria arbor leading to the herb garden originally led from the driveway to the club's entrance. And the children's sandbox is nestled in the footprint of what was once the stage.

The ceremony was held in front of *The Spirit of Song,* a

cast-iron sculpture by local artist Lou Stanger depicting a G clef; around the base, one can read the names of every star who attended the club in its blazing year of life, some of whom were present at the ceremony.

Notably absent was former owner, Morgan Vidal. 'It's too emotional,' said the seventy-four-year-old, now based in New York. 'I'm happy for other people to enjoy the property, but I need to leave the past in the past.'

Vidal followed up her high-profile marriage to Jesse Reid with an even more storied union to Fair Play front man Hannibal Fang. After another decade of platinum hits, Vidal retired to spend more time with her family and has found a successful second career authoring the *Rocker Billie* children's book series.

Attendants included EGOT winner Loretta Mays, subject of this past year's biopic *Safe Passage*. Mays and fellow attendant Jesse Reid just posted dates for an intimate-venue *Safe Passage* tour – details can be found at IslandGazette.org.

Beach Track owners Rich Holt and Simon Spector attended with other former members of cult favorite the Breakers, Kyle and Greg Lightfoot, and Jane Quinn. 'We never pass up the opportunity for a reunion,' said Greg Lightfoot, seventy-four, who, along with his partner, Maggie Quinn, and their three daughters, has been instrumental in founding Folk Friends, the not-for-profit that has overseen the production of the Island Folk Fest since its reinstatement in 2009.

'This club is so important to our cultural history,' said film director Ashley Kramer, sixty-two, who attended with her husband, Kyle Lightfoot. The two met while Lightfoot was penning the score for Kramer's 1987 dystopian blockbuster *Black Sand* and flew in especially for the event.

Local residents Jane Quinn and Jesse Reid both spoke at the dedication.

Quinn's recording career spanned the 1970s and 1980s. Her fourth studio album, *Glitter and Grime,* took home Grammys for Best Album and Best Record in 1974. Although *Glitter and Grime* saw more success in its day, *Songs in Ursa Major* is widely acknowledged as Quinn's masterpiece. In the year 2000, *The New York Times* named it one of twenty-five albums that represented 'turning points and pinnacles in twentieth-century popular music,' and the record has since outsold *Glitter and Grime,* and is now certified triple platinum.

After hanging up her recording mic, Quinn paired up with soul legend Lacey Dormon and piloted the female-centric production company *Vit & Vim*, which defined the girl-power pop revolution of the late 1990s. After Dormon's death in 2006, Quinn retired to the Island. Here, she continues her work as an advocate for Mind Matters, the mental-health advocacy group founded by her grandmother Lila Charlotte (Elsie) and aunt Grace Quinn in the late 1970s.

'This is a special place,' said seventy-three-year-old Quinn during the dedication. 'It will always remind me of the women who raised me, and I'm thrilled to be able to share it with my own girls.' The famously unwed songstress attended the ceremony with her own daughters, Lila and Suzie, and her granddaughter, Caro.

Jesse Reid spoke last and performed the ribbon cutting as one of the park's former owners.

A fellow Mind Matters advocate, Reid paid tribute to the

Island's own Cedar Crescent Hospital and Rehabilitation Center, which he called his 'port in a storm' throughout his decade-long struggle with addiction, one that cost him his first marriage, to Vidal (1971–1972), and his second, to entertainment attorney Vita Spruce (1979–1981).

Reid did eventually find sobriety and lasting love with the Island's own Shelby Green, a meditation coach he met on an up-Island yoga retreat in 1987. Together, they had four children, two of whom, Alison and Kate, attended the ceremony. Green passed in 2010 after a long battle with ALS, through which Reid never left her side.

Despite the ups and downs of his personal life, Reid has never released an album that has sold fewer than one million copies. His latest effort, *Lone Pine: A Jesse Reid Christmas,* is due out from Black Sheep Omnimedia later this year.

In his dedication, Reid cited the support of his friends, mentioning Quinn and Mays by name, and thanking his former A & R man, Willy Lambert, whose taste and foresight saw Black Sheep thrive through both the CD and streaming revolutions, before his death in 2012.

'How fraught it all was in the beginning,' said Reid, seventy-six. 'Now all I see is joy. This kind of thing is important – there are so few left who can remember that time anymore.'

A time of myth, a time of beauty, a time of rock and roll.

After the ceremony, Reid joined Quinn for a quiet chat in the shade. Even decades later, it's clear they cherish each other. You wouldn't think to look at them now, she with her cane, he with his cap, that they once walked among us as gods.

Acknowledgments

This book has an extended family large and loving enough to fill a stadium. But there are a few rock stars to whom I must give top billing and some serious fan service.

Thank you to my inimitable agent and friend, Susan Golomb, for making this process so fun and for getting Janie Q on the Main Stage, in more ways than one. Thanks also to Mariah Stovall, Sarah Fornshell, Jessica Berger, and the wonderful team at Writers House – I'm lucky to have you in my corner!

Thank you to Jenny Jackson, my cosmic editor and friend – your deft, instructive feedback helped me do things I didn't know how to do and gave this story such stardust. I have loved every minute of making this book together.

Thank you to my team at Knopf, including Reagan Arthur, Maya Mavjee, Maris Dyer, Erinn Hartman, Demetris Papadimitropoulos, Emily Murphy, Morgan Fenton, Peggy Samedi, Lydia Buechler, Anne Zaroff-Evans, Maria Carella, Kathy Hourigan, Kelly Blair, and Dan Novack. You are excellent.

Thank you to my U.K. editor, the lovely Charlotte Brabbin, her team at Harper U.K., and to all of my international publishers, with so much gratitude.

Thank you to Sylvie Rabineau, Anastasia Alen, and the team at

WME for taking the *Ursa Major* show on the road, and with such style and finesse.

Thank you to Anna Pitoniak, Johanna Gustavvson, and Emma Parry for your insights and encouragement.

Thank you to my beloved mentors, Carita Gardiner, Margie Friedman, Lindley Boegehold, and Sherry Moore, for so much wisdom and humor about writing, being a woman in media, creative integrity, and human nature.

Thank you to my longtime hero, Mandy Moore, whose 2004 album, *Coverage*, first introduced me to Joni Mitchell.

Thank you to Caroline Hill, piano tamer, for letting me tag along to so many sessions.

Let's have a round for the Mental Notes, for teaching me what it's like to be in a band. Especially Phoebe Quin, Tom Murphy, and Kevin Uy. Thank you to Eric Brodie, for being the Jane to my Rich, and for taking me to most of the *Painted Lady* tour locations.

Thank you to the Brodie, Casey, and Garcia clans for so much love and support.

Thank you to Mom, Dad, Clara, and Ben: birds fly to the stars, I guess, and you have always been my guiding lights. Dad, thank you for introducing me to *Sweet Baby James* and for taking me seriously. Clara, thank you for being a most trusted first reader and outlaw. Mom, your voice and teachings had such a fundamental impact on this story; thank you for sharing your magic with me. Ben, your virtuosity is the stuff of folklore; thank you for making the songs in this book come to life with your music.

Thank you most of all to my sweet, mellow, and brilliant husband, Kevin – for making me so happy and for giving me so many good ideas for free. I think I mentioned this a couple Septembers ago, but you crown and anchor me.